Devil of the Pines

James Kaine

For Pete, Pete & Chris

Friends. Brothers. Legends

Author's Note

Thank you for picking up this copy of *Devil of the Pines*, the second book in my American Horrors series.

If you're interested, there will be an entire afterword talking about the origins of the Jersey Devil legend and how I developed it into the story you're about to read. That said, there is one thing I want to get out of the way up front:

I'm New Jersey born and raised and for those of you like me who "don't pump our gas, we pump our fists" (not sure if that's still a thing), I understand Leeds Point is not as big as I make it out to be in this story. It's an unincorporated community part of the larger Galloway Township. My family even used to have a house in town, and I loved spending my summers there enjoying everything from the Smithville Village to the community center pool. It is truly one of my favorite parts of the state.

But this being a work of fiction, I have to take creative liberties here and there, so I hope you'll forgive me for expanding Leeds Point into something bigger for the greater benefit of the story I'm about to tell you.

With that out of the way, let's meet the Devil of the Pines . . .

Prologue

Leeds Point, New Jersey

August 1735

"We will arrive soon, m'lady."

"Thank you, kind sir," Delphia said as she smiled politely at the driver through the slat in the front of the carriage. She clutched the bag in her lap tightly, transferring her nervousness to the pigskin parcel as she attempted to hide it in her facial expression. It was not the driver that was the source of her trepidation. He had kind eyes and a gentle tone. The anxiety was born of something else. Something that worsened the closer they drew to their destination.

The oppressive heat suffocated the summer air, even at this late hour. Delphia felt as if she were roasting inside the coach, her small hand fan providing little relief. The windows on either side of the compartment offered a look at the towering pines lining the path, standing like sentinels in the darkness. A thin fog crept along the ground, threatening to rise and obscure the visibility in front of them. It appeared to thicken the closer they approached, the ominous surroundings only exacerbating Delphia's unease. A flash of lightning in the distance illuminated the sky briefly. The young woman braced herself for the accompanying crack of thunder, but it never came, leaving her tensed in anticipation.

"Soundless lightning," the carriage driver said, as if sensing his passenger's anxiety. "It is rare, but it tends to happen, especially during the hottest months."

"It is a bit . . . unsettling," Delphia acknowledged, "anticipating such a noise that never comes."

"Indeed. But my mother once told me it was harmless. Lacking sound just means it is further away. So, we are in no danger of being struck by a stray bolt, m'lady."

Delphia smiled at the driver's insistence on using that salutation, even if she was not entirely comfortable with it. "There is no need for such formalities, sir. I am a simple midwife, not a woman of noble birth."

"Well, *m'lady*," the driver said, emphasizing the term of address, "you provide a noble service and that makes you of noble status in my mind. But far be it from me to make you ill at ease, so how should I address you, missus?"

"Miss," she corrected. "McNeal. Delphia McNeal."

"Pleasure to make your acquaintance, Miss McNeal."

"Delphia is fine, sir."

"Then it is a sincere pleasure to make your acquaintance, Delphia," the driver revised. "And certainly no need for such formality in my regard. My name is Samuel."

"Samuel," Delphia repeated, liking the way the man's name rolled off her tongue. "And your family name?"

Before Samuel could answer, another bolt of lightning streaked through the sky, much closer this time, now accompanied by a roaring crash of thunder that shook the carriage's interior, eliciting a yelp from its passenger.

The horses whinnied in fear at the abrupt sound and Delphia felt the carriage swerve toward the edge of the path, threatening to teeter off the dirt road and into the rough grass lining the edge of the woods. Through the slat, she could see Samuel maneuvering as he deftly yanked at the reins, getting the skittish animals under control. Once they were back on the path and moving steadily forward, Samuel turned back to view his passenger through the opening.

"Apologies, m'lad—Delphia. Alas, this is not an ideal night for travel. Fortunately, we are nearing our destination." Delphia, still shaken, offered Samuel a tight-lipped smile and an acknowledging dip of her chin. "I assure you I will get you there safely," he added to assuage her fear.

Driver and passenger fell into an uneasy silence as they continued their journey, the clacking of hooves and the spinning of wheels the only sounds breaking the silence. Occasionally, a roll of thunder would build, but mercifully, none matured to a level that would upset the horses.

After fifteen minutes, Delphia could make out a

soft glow in the distance. Looking up, she saw a faint plume of smoke ascending over the trees, mingling with darkened clouds obscuring the night sky, dulling the moonlight.

Delphia knew it was from the fireplace. She had been to the Leeds cabin on numerous occasions over the last three years, having aided with Jane Leeds's last birth as well as visiting several times during her current pregnancy, which had been challenging almost from the first moment.

It is not surprising, Delphia thought. Mother Leeds had birthed a dozen children, making the impending delivery her thirteenth. That was a tremendous strain on a woman, especially one of her advanced age. Delphia would have thought Jane was beyond her childbearing years had she not seen the pregnancy's progression with her own eyes.

The baby was not due for three more weeks, but the Leeds family had sent word earlier in the day informing the midwives that labor had begun. Mrs. Hannigan was able to leave posthaste, but Delphia had been tending to another expectant mother when the messenger arrived.

She had protested at first, knowing Mrs. Hannigan could facilitate the delivery on her own, she being the most senior and, therefore, the most practiced midwife in their group. But she was told Japhet Leeds wanted more than one present due to his wife's health and he had explicitly requested Delphia by name.

Of course he did, Delphia thought, struggling to suppress the accompanying sneer.

For reasons unknown to the young woman, Japhet and Jane Leeds had been relegated to live out their days at a small cabin deep in the woods surrounding Leeds Point, the area that had become known to locals as the Pine Barrens. It was especially perplexing given that Japhet was the brother of Daniel Leeds, the town's founder. Why the younger sibling would be cast into the Barrens whilst the elder lived in a luxurious estate on the edge of town was beyond her comprehension.

"Here we are," Samuel declared, breaking through Delphia's pondering.

She peered through the slat and saw the cabin looming ahead, the glow she had previously seen born from the oil lamps resting in front of the windows on the inside. Her chest tightened and a lump formed in her throat as the small domicile loomed larger the closer the carriage drew to it. There was an energy about that place, a malevolence cloaked by the forest.

"Are you okay?" Samuel asked. He must have sensed something was wrong.

Delphia nodded, becoming aware that she was shaking. Given the humidity, she could not use the temperature as an explanation.

"I am," she replied, hoping it was more convincing than it sounded. "It has been a taxing journey, and I am still a bit shaken from the thunder strike."

"Oh! I am terribly sorry, m'lady," Samuel apologized, forgetting to forego the formality. "I assure you, we were not in true peril."

His reaction made Delphia feel guilty. The excuse was intended to mask the actual source of her anxiety, not to burden the poor young man with blame. For her part, she hesitated, trying to find words of reassurance.

"Oh, no, sir, pardon me, Samuel," she assured. "It was purely the result of the weather. You handled the horses marvelously. I would have been in greater danger in the hands of a less skilled man."

With the driver again at a loss for words, searching for a reply, Delphia realized how flirtatious she must have sounded. She was surprised, however, that it did not make her feel embarrassed.

In fact, a small smile cracked her lips, a momentary respite from her apprehension. When Samuel turned to spare a look at his passenger, she could see his cheeks were flushed red thanks to the glimmer of the carriage light affixed to its front exterior.

He struggled to find words, his mouth opening briefly before closing soundlessly. Tongue-tied, he could do little more than offer an awkward smile before hurriedly turning away, missing Delphia's own widening grin.

"We have arrived," Samuel announced, a slight crack in his voice.

The declaration snatched the pleasantry from Delphia's countenance. A chill ran through her body as the coach came to a stop. The horses sighed practically in unison, the tension and exertion from the ride eased. The young woman sat frozen, as if her derriere were glued to the bench, while Samuel rose from the box seat and climbed down to the side of the carriage. When the door creaked open, washing the cab with a fresh burst of summer air, Delphia jumped slightly, despite expecting it.

"Delphia?" She heard Samuel ask. She turned to face the young man who was standing in front of the door, his hand out, offering assistance. His face wore a look of concern. "Are you all right?"

As if on cue, another thunderous blast rattled the sky, eliciting a yelp and a jerk from Delphia. It also broke her anxious freeze. Thinking quickly, she forced a laugh and nodded as she accepted Samuel's hand. The look on his face told her he was unconvinced by her performance, but he did not press the matter.

Samuel aided Delphia's descent but did not let go of her hand once she stepped off the carriage block and onto the ground. She did not pull away as she met his eyes, the sincerity within them captivating. A silence hung between them, charging the air as both searched for what to say next.

Finally, it was Samuel who spoke, "Would you like me to wait for you?"

Yes! Delphia's mind screamed. *Do not leave me here with . . . him.*

But the shaky words she voiced were contrary to her thoughts, "Thank you, Samuel, but I will journey back to town with Mrs. Hannigan in a few days. They will likely need us to stay and assist post-birth." She unconsciously gave his hand a slight squeeze before releasing it. "Perhaps our paths will cross again."

"I certainly hope so, m'lady."

There was intentionality behind the address this time, and Delphia, rather than correcting him, offered a warm smile. A smile that faded when the cabin door creaked open behind her.

"You are late," a gruff, cold voice observed.

Delphia swallowed hard and turned to see Japhet Leeds standing in the doorway, his width filling the entry's frame. As if on cue, the first drop of rain fell from the sky, landing on her left hand. She hurried to the door, her body fighting her mind's desire to run back to the carriage and have Samuel take her away. Vocation be damned.

"I am sorry, Mr. Leeds," Delphia said sheepishly, keeping her head down to avoid the rotund man's granite gaze.

Japhet did not step aside, denying the midwife entry for the moment.

"The child's arrival is imminent."

"I came as soon as I was summoned, Mr. Leeds. It sounds as if the labor is progressing quickly."

"And painfully," Japhet added in a flat voice devoid of concern. As if his wife's pain were merely an inconvenience for him.

"I will join Mrs. Hannigan immediately," she said, looking up and seeing Japhet's pockmarked face, his heavy jowls causing him to resemble a bulldog as much as a man. His mouth, curled up in a sneer, revealed a sampling of his jagged, yellowed teeth—the same shade as his formerly white shirt now soaked with sweat and stained with remnants of more than one meal.

"See that you do," he stated bluntly, his hot, foul breath wafting over her. Delphia was amazed she managed not to gag. Mercifully, he stepped aside, allowing her access to the interior. She spared one last glance in Samuel's direction. He nodded and watched until Japhet slammed the door behind them.

Once inside, Delphia found herself in the single main room centered on a large fireplace that doubled as the cooking area and the source of the family's warmth. It carried the acrid stench of a now-extinguished fire—surely used to prepare supper but put out as it would only exacerbate the stifling summer heat. Above the mantel, hooks suspended iron cookware, including several pans, a spider skillet, and a Dutch oven.

Delphia had been to the Leeds cabin before—though she would have preferred never to have visited—and it always amazed her how the interior seemed impossibly large, yet somehow cramped.

The walls were constructed with rough-hewn logs chinked with a mixture of clay and moss to provide insulation. Handwoven rush mats blanketed the packed earth of the home's floor.

Furniture was sparse, comprising a trestle table with bench seating on either side. A single chair set at the head, no doubt reserved for Japhet in his position as head of the household.

Wooden pegs were driven into the walls for hanging clothes or various tools and a simple chest rested against the wall opposite the table. Rope beds set with straw mattresses and woolen blankets lined much of the remaining wall space. The multiple beds were necessary to accommodate the dozen Leeds children.

With the fireplace inactive, the oil lamps in the windows and a host of tallow candles provided limited illumination.

In the scant glow, Delphia could make out many of those dozen faces, ranging from toddlers to adolescents. The Leeds offspring wore varying expressions—confusion, anxiety, and hunger among them. Food was likely in short supply and adding a thirteenth mouth to feed, not to mention the parents, would undoubtedly be a challenge.

The sickly sweet aroma of onion permeated the air. Delphia knew the scent was not born of the bulbous vegetable, but from the perspiration seeping from the pores of the huddled family members. It was a pungent odor that stung the midwife's nostrils.

"Get a move on, girl," Japhet ordered in a booming voice.

Delphia did not answer, nor did she look back, only hastened to the door on the opposite side of the room. As she got closer, two distinct sounds grew in volume. The first was the patter of rain that intensified as it slapped against the oiled paper covering the windows. The second was a pained woman's moan emanating from the other side of the door. Although muffled, it was distinct.

When she opened the door to the bedroom, the moan turned to an ear-piercing shriek of agony. The unexpected greeting caused Delphia to jump, almost dropping her bag.

Jane Leeds lay on the bed in the center of the room. The woman's scream diminished to soft cries as she writhed, crumpling the sheet bunched around her legs.

A woman in her mid-forties, harsh wilderness living had taken its toll on Jane. Her full, round face was etched with deep nasolabial folds and her eyes, narrowed in anguish, displayed the harsh lines of crow's feet. Her dark hair, speckled with patches of gray, was free of the tight bun she typically wore it in, strands against her sweat-soaked forehead.

The onion smell was still present in the small bedroom, but not as strong as it was on the other side. It also competed with other odors, namely the metallic scent of blood and a fishy tinge, potentially infection.

Delphia again had to stifle a gasp when she saw the blood soaked into the sheets and staining the bottom half of the gown gathered around Jane's hips, but she kept her composure. Though she had seen more than a few arduous labors, she could not recall ever seeing one with this much bleeding.

"Miss McNeal!" Margaret Hannigan shouted. "We need to move quickly!" The elder midwife was Jane Leeds's senior by a decade and Delphia's by three. Her tall, wispy frame hunched over the bed, pressing a vinegar water-soaked rag to her patient's forehead. Mrs. Hannigan's face betrayed concern as she locked eyes with Delphia. A small table sat next to the bed lined with the senior midwife's tools of last resort—scissors, linen thread, a small pot of goose grease, and a bottle of laudanum reserved for the most desperate of cases. They were not normal birthing instruments. They were needed for an emergency surgical extraction. Behind them sat a basin of vinegar water.

Jane screamed again as her pain crescendoed, causing her to lurch off the bed. Delphia rushed over to help Mrs. Hannigan restrain her. As Jane fell back onto the bed, the older woman whispered to her colleague, "The babe is breech."

This time, Delphia could not hold her gasp. An abnormal presentation such as that could easily result in death for both the child and the mother. Given the amount of bleeding Mother Leeds was experiencing, the situation appeared headed for that tragic outcome.

"Hold her," Mrs. Hannigan instructed as she made her way to the foot of the bed.

"Yes, ma'am," Delphia responded as she pushed down on Jane's shoulders, readying herself to block any further effort by Mrs. Leeds to propel herself off the bed.

Once in position, Mrs. Hannigan said, "Jane, I need you to listen to me carefully. The child is turned wrong."

"Gahh!" Jane screamed, a mix of anguish and aggravation. She gave a half-hearted attempt to rise, but Delphia held her down.

"I am going to attempt to right it. I fear the surgical option will endanger you both." She glanced up at Delphia while continuing to address Jane, "I need you to remain as still as possible."

Mother Leeds cried out again through the pain, the utterance indistinguishable as affirmative or negative. Delphia increased pressure on the woman's shoulders to keep her down. As Mrs. Hannigan reached in to begin the manipulation, Jane screamed again. This time her words were clear, even through the rain that had turned torrential outside as a burst of thunder detonated in the sky over the Leeds home.

"Damn this wretched being inside of me! Damn the

oaf who put it there and damn this whole contemptible town! If God wishes to abandon his children, then this child shall not be one of his! Let this child be a devil!"

Jane Leeds did not live to hear her thirteenth child cry for the first time. The last words she ever uttered formed the curse she bestowed upon it. Mrs. Hannigan had been successful in turning the child and the weary mother had delivered it within minutes of the correction, then took her final breath as she did. While the birth had been traumatic, the child appeared unharmed in the process. It let out a healthy cry, announcing its arrival into the world.

Margaret Hannigan washed her hands in the basin next to the instruments that had gone unused, the blood sluicing off in the warm vinegar water. Delphia held the infant in her arms, a cherubic baby boy who wailed with hunger, unable to feed from his deceased mother.

"We'll need some pap," the younger midwife announced. "This little one hungers."

"Yes," Mrs. Hannigan agreed. "We will send for a wet nurse at first light, but the pap will suffice for now. Go get the flour and see if there is any milk to mix it with."

"Yes, ma'am," she agreed as Mrs. Hannigan toweled off her hands. Once they were dry, Delphia moved to pass the infant to her.

"And please send Mr. Leeds in. We have the unfortunate responsibility to inform him his wife has passed away."

Delphia felt her stomach tighten. In the chaos that had ensued since her arrival, she had almost forgotten about the boorish man of the house. It terrified her to think of his reaction when learning of his wife's death. Would he blame them? If so, would he seek retribution?

"Delphia!" Mrs. Hannigan snapped, breaking her from her thoughts. "Do as I say."

Delphia nodded, but before she could complete the handoff, the door flung open and Japhet Leeds again filled the frame. His eyes bulged at the sight of his wife, bloody and lifeless on the bed, the color draining from her already pallid skin. The baby's cries intensified at his father's arrival as he slammed the door behind him.

"What in the hell happened here?" Japhet asked through gritted teeth, prying his gaze away from the body and glaring at the midwives. "You let her die?"

"Mr. Leeds," Mrs. Hannigan started, "there was nothing—"

"Shut your damned mouth, woman!" Japhet bellowed. "You let my wife die and now what? I am supposed to care for thirteen children on my own?"

"I am sure there are resources," Delphia said before considering how her response may be received. "Perhaps your brother—"

Japhet cut her off as he did Mrs. Hannigan, only

it was not with his words but the back of his hand, showing no concern that the young midwife was holding his youngest child. Delphia felt the sting of her cheek and tasted copper on her tongue, a wet dot forming where she had bitten her lip. She squeezed her eyes shut, trying to trap the tears that pooled, but the action only trapped the salty secretion, stinging the orbs. She gripped the infant tight, but the oaf ripped him from her arms, regarding the child with disdain.

"You hardly seem worth all this trouble, you little runt. Only minutes old and you are already a blight on this family."

The baby's cries grew to a feverish pitch driven by overwhelming hunger and worsened by the malicious presence of his father. Delphia could hardly recall a time when she heard an infant howl in such a manner. But as the sound continued to increase in pitch and volume, she knew she had never heard a sound like that before. And when the noises turned to something else, her disbelief morphed into terror.

The wails became deep. At first, she thought it may have injured its throat from crying so loudly, then they twisted into a growl, a sound not even an animal would make. It sounded *demonic*. That's when the Leeds baby's eyes snapped open wide, revealing glowing red orbs devoid of pupils. The guttural rumble intensified as it unhinged its jaw, impossibly revealing rows of tiny, razor-sharp teeth.

Japhet yelped and dropped the babe, which landed headfirst on the ground below, cutting off the inhuman sounds as it fell still.

"What in God's name was that abomination?" he asked.

Delphia instinctively moved to check on the motionless child, but Mrs. Hannigan grabbed her arm to keep her upright. When the younger midwife looked at her, she shook her head to confirm that she should not attempt to touch it.

"I have never seen anything like that," Mrs. Hannigan said. "It was as if she bore a demon."

"A demon?" Japhet asked incredulously. "That is preposterous."

As if seeking to dispel the notion, a low growl came from below the bed as the three witnesses looked down in unison to see the child struggling to its feet. It had doubled in size since it fell and as it stood, it continued to grow larger.

Its red eyes blazed with hatred as it looked upon its father while its nose extended into a snout. Hair sprouted from its body and its fingers twisted into gnarled, sharpened claws. The thing's kneecaps inverted and the flesh tore away from its feet, cloven hooves taking their place. The beast growled louder as it finished standing upright, its head now resembling that of a horse, save for the jagged fangs protruding from its mouth. Outstretching its arms, the monster released another deafening roar as the flesh underneath the fur lining its shoulder blades tore open, revealing two giant, leathery, bat-like wings that spanned nearly the entire room once they fully unfurled.

Delphia screamed as what was a human infant only moments before had become a monstrous beast, the likes of which she had not imagined in her worst nightmares, standing between the midwives and its father.

Mrs. Hannigan again grabbed Delphia's arm, pulling her back as the duo pressed against the wall, giving them as much distance as possible from the creature. They screamed again as it reared back its right arm before driving it forward and punching it through Japhet Leeds's chest. Blood poured from the massive wound as the man's cries choked off into a gurgle when more spurted from his mouth. Its claw embedded in its human father, it lifted him off the ground and brought him in close to its maw. Much like Japhet had done to Delphia a short time earlier, the beast's hot breath washed over the dying man's face. Another bestial howl preceded the monster clamping its jaws on Japhet's skull, sending him to be with his wife.

With its father dead, the beast pulled its claw from the man's abdomen with a squelching sound. Its back heaved and its wings fluttered as it snorted, a sound not unlike Samuel's horses. Delphia mouthed a silent prayer that it would not turn, and it stood in that state long enough to make her believe it may be answered.

It was not.

Samuel hurried through the pounding rain, moving as fast as his lungs and the muddy ground would allow him.

The carriage had gotten stuck in said mud about a mile away from the Leeds home. He tried his damndest to get it out but had neither the tools nor the manpower needed to extract it. He thought about taking shelter in the cab, but the storm appeared to be getting worse and he could already see leaks forming on the roof of the interior. With no other choice, he cut the horses loose, letting them find cover among the trees while he sought shelter himself. The cabin where he had left his passenger was the best option.

He was soaked through and starting to shiver despite the humidity. He would be lucky not to catch pneumonia at this rate. Samuel was not sure exactly how much distance he had covered, but he figured he was close.

Mercifully, a clearing came into view ahead and a soft glow beyond told him he was near. As he picked up his speed, he heard a sound that froze him in place. It sounded like something heavy flapping in the air above him, like an enormous bird.

What in God's name? he thought.

The carriage driver pressed against a tree and looked upward, doing his best to see through the leaves that formed a canopy above. He could not see anything and, just as he thought it was his mind playing tricks on him, an enormous shadow bolted across the sky. Samuel could not discern what it was, nor did he care to. He pushed away from his cover and ran as fast as he could toward the cabin.

His chest burned and his lungs struggled to keep up with his rapid, labored breathing as he pushed himself to his physical limits escaping whatever it was that hunted him from the sky. He could no longer hear it and he dare not look back, but he felt as if that massive form was bearing down on him, ready to strike at any moment. When he reached the cabin, he did not bother with formality as he burst through the door, closing it quickly behind him.

As he got his bearings, he looked at what lay before him and again froze in place. Whatever he feared from above could not compare to the sheer horror of the scene he viewed. He searched and searched until he finally found his voice.

When he did, his terrified screams echoed into the night.

Chapter 1

Leeds Point, New Jersey

April 2005

"You are so full of shit!"

Patrick Shourds rolled his eyes so hard that he thought he might actually see his brain.

"I am not!" Brandon Murphy defended. "That is totally a true story!"

The two thirteen-year-olds had taken a detour through the Pine Barrens as they typically did on their way home from school during the warmer months. It was the end of April, and as usual, the month started out cold and wet, but last week it was like a switch flipped as the temperatures rocketed from the low fifties to the high seventies. The afternoon sun shone brightly overhead, its rays peeking through the healthy needles of giant pines, lighting up patches of grass as the Earth rotated.

Patrick and Brandon were at that odd, transitional age. Both were very much in the advanced stages of puberty, although it manifested in different ways.

Patrick had grown five inches since August and had thinned out considerably. Brandon was not so fortunate. He had grown maybe an inch and still had a husky build that he would unconvincingly chalk up to "baby fat" rather than his affinity for pizza rolls. Not only that, but while Patrick would have to fight off the occasional pimple, Brandon's forehead was a road map of blazing red pustules. And of course both were experiencing hostile takeovers by raging hormones, but whereas Brandon's computer should probably be in quarantine because of viruses from no-no sites, Patrick was often blissfully unaware of the sidelong glances his female classmates were starting to send his way.

Despite nature's insistence on slingshotting the teens toward adulthood, they still kept a measure of childhood spirit. While some boys in their class put all their focus on sports and a newfound interest in girls, Patrick and Brandon still reveled in their love of comic books and *Star Wars*. The most recent film, *Revenge of the Sith*, had just come out last weekend, and the duo had already seen it twice. Lots of the older kids said the prequels sucked, but Patrick and Brandon knew that people would come to appreciate them eventually. They just hoped—now that George Lucas had finished the backstory—they'd see Luke, Han, and Leia reunited in a sequel someday!

It was this love of the fantastical, combined with their hesitance to eschew imaginary play, that compelled them to take the wooded route home. Sure, some days they'd talk about how hard it was being Giants fans living in South Jersey surrounded by Eagles diehards, or discuss their mutual crush on Jessica Zimmerman, even though neither believed the other had a shot. But there were other days when they'd find the right-sized sticks and become Jedi and Sith, recreating those iconic lightsaber duels far from the judgy eyes of their classmates.

They just weren't ready to give up being kids yet.

"You really believe all that Jersey Devil stuff?" Patrick asked.

Brandon shrugged and stepped carefully onto the row of stones embedded in the ground, all that remained of what had once been the foundation of a house. The only other identifiable feature was the stacked bricks of a chimney crumbled to probably a third of its original size.

"I'm just telling you what Tyler told me," Brandon said as he outstretched his arms to mimic wings, carefully balancing himself while navigating the foundation.

Patrick and his best friend had come across the remnants of the long-forgotten house many times. They would take turns spinning tales of what the place used to be, claiming it was everything from the cabin in *The Evil Dead* to the meeting house for a supernatural biker gang.

This time was different, though. When Brandon recounted the story of a miserable woman cursing her thirteenth child to become a devil, he was sticking to his guns that it was true.

Maybe it was. Everyone in the area knew about the Jersey Devil. It was the state's most famous urban legend. Every state had one. Patrick recalled something he'd seen on Snopes about a playground in Alabama where the ghosts of children supposedly came out at night to play on the swings. That would make a great movie! But Jersey's flying monster was so much cooler! Their hockey team was even named after it, and they'd won the Stanley Cup just two years ago!

So, sure, Brandon's story was as *plausible* as any. But Patrick wasn't going to let him know that. Bro code was to bust balls and that's exactly what he was going to do.

"How do you know Tyler wasn't messing with you?"

"He's my older brother," Brandon replied. "He wouldn't do that."

Patrick cocked a brow. "You sure about that?"

Brandon flashed a knowing smile before answering, his reply deliberate, "Absolutely."

Patrick returned the smile as he reached down and grabbed two sticks large enough to serve the purpose he had in mind. He spoke again, this time with a sad attempt at a British accent, "Only a Sith deals in absolutes," then tossed one of the sticks to Brandon, who caught it without losing his balance. Patrick mimicked Ewan McGregor's battle stance before adding, "I will do what I must."

"You will try," Brandon replied.

With that, Patrick hopped up on the foundation and began play-dueling with Brandon. They kept it light, neither really trying to hit the other, content to just smack the sticks together, seeing them as the blue laser swords wielded by Jedi Knights. Both boys pursed their lips, doing their best to mimic the unmistakable sounds of the sci-fi weaponry.

After a minute, the combatants separated, each taking a step back and a breath to ready themselves to resume.

"I've failed you, Brandon," Patrick said, still trying to figure out the accent.

"I should have known . . ." Brandon continued the dialogue, but Patrick stopped listening as his attention was diverted elsewhere. Behind his friend, he saw a woman standing by the tree line.

At first, Patrick thought they could be in trouble. The boys had never considered that this might be private property. Maybe it was, but there was something else, though. Something about the woman was *odd*.

She was dressed in old-fashioned clothing. Real old. Like Colonial times. The woman wore a long, blue, collared dress with white frills at the hem and the sleeves. It covered her almost completely, leaving only her hands and head visible.

That was odd enough, but there was something else. Something disturbing.

The woman's face was badly scarred on the left side. The disfigurement ran from the middle of her forehead to just around her eye which was missing its lid, giving it a bulging, unsettling appearance. The deformity continued down her cheek and over her mouth to her chin. It was as if she had been attacked by a very large animal, like a bear or a fricking werewolf. Her eyes were pure white. There were no pupils to be found. She must have been blind, yet Patrick felt like she was staring directly at him.

He was so transfixed that he didn't realize he had lowered his makeshift weapon. Until Brandon whacked him on the side of his left bicep, the sudden sting snapping him to attention.

"Ow!" he blurted, dropping his stick and using his now free hand to rub the affected limb. "What the hell, dude?"

"Why'd you let your guard down?"

The question reminded Patrick that he had, in fact, let his guard down and there was a good reason for it. He craned his neck around to see past Brandon. The woman was gone. But where?

"There was…" Patrick started, but trailed off, unsure of how to tell his friend what he saw without sounding crazy. Ever the opportunist, Brandon whacked his buddy with the stick again, this time just above the left knee. It was light and meant to be playful, but it was enough to send Patrick tumbling off the stones and onto the ground, landing flat on his back.

"Damn it!" Patrick exclaimed, reaching around to rub the point of impact.

Brandon chuckled and held out his arms, still holding the faux lightsaber.

"It's over, Patrick! I have the high ground!"

Patrick groaned as he propped himself up on his elbows and stared daggers into his best friend.

"I was Obi-Wan, dipshit."

"This is the alternate ending," Brandon retorted with a laugh.

Tragically, Brandon wasn't the one with the actual

high ground. Patrick heard a shrill noise amplifying from above. It reminded him of those old cartoons where someone would look up in the sky as an anvil or a piano was about to fall on them. An enormous shadow blanketed his friend and the sound reached its crescendo as something horrific plummeted from the sky.

By the time Brandon registered what was happening, it was too late. A creature landed directly on him, shoving him down onto the stone foundation, a sickening *crunch* accompanying the impact.

Patrick reeled in horror, crawling backward as he watched the thing perch atop his friend. It looked like a gruesome amalgamation of multiple animals. Its head resembled a skeletal horse, but its eyes were bloodred and its mouth was lined with fangs. The beast's legs were inverted like a goat, the hooves pressed into Brandon's shattered spine as it crouched on his prone body. Patrick couldn't place what the arms were from, but they were hairy and punctuated with gnarled claws that looked as angry as its teeth. Of all the blended body parts, the ones that stood out the most were the pair of expansive wings spread as wide as the foundation, the fingers of which protruded into razor-sharp talons.

Brandon was still alive, if barely. His body convulsed, and he opened and closed his mouth but nothing coherent came out, just stunted, choked gasps as blood and drool trickled from his lips, coating the grass below. Patrick's best friend was so gravely injured, he couldn't even cry. Brandon's eyes bulged and Patrick wasn't sure how aware he was of what had happened to him.

The monster stared Patrick down, snorting obscenely through its muzzle, small tufts of smoke escaping. It looked like one's breath did in the winter, only it wasn't caused by the cold air, being that it was almost eighty degrees. It was as if a malevolent fire burned inside the thing, needing to be vented.

Patrick didn't know what to do. He wanted to help his best friend, but couldn't see how that was possible. The smart thing would have been to run, but he was terrified to make any sudden movements, as if he were trying to keep a T-Rex from seeing him. But this monstrosity was not a dinosaur. And it could definitely see him. It remained on Brandon as it lurched its upper body forward, roaring at Patrick who could feel its hot, fetid breath blast his face as it did. The terrified teen braced for it to attack. But it didn't.

Patrick caught the first glimpse of anything resembling recognition from Brandon. It was a subtle twitch of his eye that appeared— a desperate plea to save him from his fate. But Patrick was powerless. He could only watch as the creature reached down with its clawed digits, grabbing his broken friend by the torso, the jagged nails digging between his ribs. He still couldn't scream, and he choked again as a gout of blood spurted from his mouth. The monster roared once more before leaping into the air and flapping its massive wings to gain altitude.

As the thing flew above the trees carrying Brandon's now limp body, Patrick finally found his legs and ran from the woods as fast as he could. He didn't look back to see a single, white sneaker speckled with blood fall from the sky and land in the middle of the house ruins.

Chapter 2

Chicago, Illinois

September 2025

Patrick watched as Nora stepped into her leggings, admiring the way the material molded to the curvature of her ass as she pulled the material up to her waist. She sat back on the bed and slipped on her sneakers, a sheen of light sweat glistening her bare back, a droplet sitting like dew on a petal of the small rose tattoo on her right shoulder. Her shoes secured, she brushed her strawberry blonde hair aside and turned to Patrick, offering him a satisfied, but somewhat awkward, smile. Patrick returned a half-hearted grin of his own, hoping she would get the hint that he was not in the mood for a conversation.

"That was fun," she said.

Damn it.

"Yes, it was," Patrick agreed.

Nora leaned over and picked up her bra and T-shirt from the floor next to the bed, laying the latter aside while she fastened the former. As she continued dressing, a buzzing from the nightstand next to Patrick diverted his attention. He grabbed it and looked at the screen. It wasn't a contact, he didn't recognize the number, and the area code was unexpected.

609.

A small lump formed in his throat as he sent the call to voicemail before placing the device face down on the bedside table.

"Another booty call?"

Patrick returned his attention to Nora, who had finished dressing. She gave him a playful smirk, assuring him she didn't care if it was. Not that she was in any position to judge.

"Spam call," he said.

Nora regarded him skeptically. "Your reaction said otherwise."

"My reaction?"

"Yup," she said, popping the *P* for emphasis. She let that sit with him while she retrieved her purse from the opposite nightstand. Extricating a pale pink vial of lip gloss, she applied it before adding, "You looked like you saw a ghost."

Interesting choice of words, he thought.

Before he could respond, the phone started ringing again. He would have ignored it, but Nora's sardonic expression practically dared him to pick it up. He rolled his eyes and looked at the phone. Same number. This time, he blocked it after declining before tossing the phone onto the bed next to him.

Nora wore a shit-eating grin. "You could have answered."

"I would have if it was someone I knew. It was spam."

"Okay," Nora said, putting her hands up in an "I surrender" gesture as she made her way to the chair in the corner of the room where she'd tossed the hooded sweatshirt that matched her maroon leggings. "It just seemed like it got to you more than your run-of-the-mill spam call." She put it on and zipped it three-quarters of the way up. "You don't strike me as someone who gets rattled easily."

Christ, she's not letting this one go, is she?

"It was an area code from where I grew up. Wasn't expecting it."

Nora sauntered over and sat on the edge of the bed near Patrick. He had hoped giving her some info would be enough to end the conversation, not prompt more. Still, he scooted over to give her—and himself—some space. He caught the scent of her Dior perfume as she got close, the aroma making him consider an encore. Maybe it would get her to stop asking questions.

"You're not from Chicago originally?"

"No."

"Where are you from?"

"Somewhere else."

His evasiveness made her chuckle. "I'm not looking to be your girlfriend, Patrick. I'm just making polite conversation." She gave him a moment to answer, but he didn't. Now it was a game to her, seeing how far she could push. "You ever go back?"

"Where?" he asked with a half-smirk of his own, playing defense.

"Home."

"Don't have one."

Nora furrowed her brow and leaned back, waving her arm around the room like a game show hostess displaying the prizes contestants could win.

"What do you call this?"

Patrick played along, following the gesture as if he wasn't familiar with his own apartment. The floor-to-ceiling window revealed a breathtaking view of the South Loop skyline, the towering skyscrapers dotted with glowing yellow/white portals into the lives of its residents. During the day, the room would be awash in natural light, but now in the late evening, the moonlight merged with the artificial illumination of the city, casting soft shadows on the wide-plank hardwood floors. The motorized shades could provide privacy, but Nora had told Patrick to leave them open, the vibe clearly enhancing her enjoyment of their activity.

"A bedroom," he answered wryly.

Now it was Nora's turn to roll her eyes, conceding the unofficial snark contest. She put her left hand on top of Patrick's right, which was resting atop the navy blue percale sheet.

"You find that ironic?"

"What?"

"You build homes for a living, but you don't have one of your own."

Patrick supposed she was right, but theirs was not a relationship calling for a conversation with that level of depth, so he redirected.

"We should call it a night," he said. "I have a job in

Winnetka tomorrow."

He knew what he did by saying that, but he still felt a little bad watching her squirm.

"I guess so," she said, sounding irked. "Better not keep you, then. Good night, Patrick."

She went to get up, but he grabbed her arm lightly to stop her.

"You forgot something."

Nora instantly forgot her irritation as her mouth turned up into a wicked grin. She ran her tongue across her lips before leaning in and kissing Patrick. The freshly applied lip gloss was flavorless, but he noticed the slippery, if mildly waxy, texture. There was passion and intentionality on Nora's part that Patrick tried to mimic, but his feelings weren't reciprocal. When she broke the kiss, she put her stamp on it by tugging and playfully biting his lower lip.

"Silly me," she said in her best sultry tone.

Patrick was unmoved as he dipped his chin toward her bare left hand. When she realized what he'd *actually* meant, the flirty expression dropped and her demeanor shifted to one of consequence.

"Oh," she breathed as she looked down, suddenly embarrassed to meet her lover's gaze. "Thanks."

She continued to avoid eye contact as she got off the bed and circled back to the other side, retrieving her missing items from beside the lamp. Patrick watched emotionlessly as she slipped the three-carat diamond settled between the platinum nesting band on her naked left ring finger. With the jewelry back in place, she stood fast, twisting it around her digit, fidgeting as her body language shifted from seductive to anxious.

As Nora put the rings back on, Patrick felt an itch a few inches above his palm. He turned it over and scratched the area. It was the tattoo of a goose, part of the sleeve of ink covering the entirety of his left arm from the top of the shoulders to the wrist. But it was only the image of the waterfowl that seemed to itch. He scratched it until the irritation subsided.

Nora, with her head still down, asked, "Do you feel bad about doing this?"

With the question out there, she finally looked back at Patrick.

"Do you?"

"I asked first."

"You have more at stake." Nora didn't know how to respond to that. Patrick thought she might start crying. Despite his desire to remain stoic, he wasn't lacking a heart. "Nora, I don't know exactly what drove you to my bed, but if you don't want to do this anymore, we don't have to."

"It's not . . . simple."

"Didn't think it was."

"I just . . . I . . . I don't have a good answer."

Patrick shuffled over to the other side of the bed and took Nora by the hand. The same one that now wore her wedding rings. "We can end this right here and now. No hard feelings. You do what's best for you."

Nora smiled. It wasn't flirty or sarcastic this time, but rather grateful, if a bit sad. "I don't know what's best for me."

Patrick gave her hand a reassuring squeeze before

releasing it and centering himself against the bed's headboard. "You'll figure it out."

"And what if I figure out that I want to do this again?"

"Then you have my number."

That seemed to prompt something in Nora's mind, and she reached into the bag and checked her phone. When she tapped her finger on the screen and the device came alive, her face registered surprise and it wasn't from the brightness which was set *way* too high.

"Oh fuck!" she said, shooting Patrick a panicked glance that told him all he needed to know. "I gotta go! I'll call you!"

She blew him a kiss and flung open the door, rushing out and around the corner. A second later, he heard the front door open and shut. Patrick shook his head. Maybe he should feel worse about sleeping with a married woman, but it wasn't him who took the vows. If she wanted to step out on her husband, that was her business.

Yeah, but the dude doesn't deserve that. How would you feel?

He didn't really know. Patrick hadn't had a girlfriend since high school. And that was just fine with him. He was better off on his own. Not that he never wanted companionship, but he preferred not to be attached. Can't lose what you don't have. The area over the goose on his arm started itching again.

"Son of a . . ." he muttered as he scratched some more. He looked up toward the bedroom door Nora had left open during her hurried exit. He hung his head in frustration at the prospect of getting up out of bed, but he *hated* sleeping with the door open. "She could have at least shut the—"

Before he could finish, he heard a *creak* toward the front of the room. He looked up to see the door closing by itself. Patrick felt that familiar chill circle his spine as a shadowy figure emerged. At first, it hovered, just out of sight, but soon it stepped forward into the patch of moonlight the sizable window made a path for.

That's when Patrick saw Brandon standing next to his bed.

He looked just as he did the last time he saw him. Not just as a thirteen-year-old boy, but as the mangled victim of a monster. His spine was shifted into an unnatural angle, giving his body a twisted appearance. He still wore the same jeans and New York Giants T-shirt he had on that day. The blue fabric of the shirt was darkened on either rib cage, each side having four jagged holes where the creature's claws had impaled him. He wasn't wearing the matching sneaker on his right foot. A massive chunk of flesh was missing from the right side of his face, along with the eye. Maggots slithered out of the empty socket. His skin was a ghostly white and his remaining eye was clouded over with corneal opacification. His mouth was agape and Patrick could see his shattered front teeth jutting out over shredded lips. Blood stained his chin from that last expulsion before the thing carried him into the sky.

Patrick took a deep breath and settled back into bed, drawing the covers up to his chest before turning onto his side, away from the specter of his childhood

best friend.
    "Good night, Brandon."

37

Chapter 3

"We got a problem, Pat."

Patrick took a break from fighting with the custom-built cabinet that ended up being an eighth of an inch too large to fit neatly in its allotted slot in the kitchen. Wiping the sweat from his brow with his tattooed arm, he rose to his knees and looked at Amari.

"What now?"

He could tell from his site manager's expression that he wasn't going to like the news he was about to deliver. Amari was a hell of a worker and his most trusted employee. He *never* came to Patrick if he could address an issue himself, which he almost always could. Hell, if Patrick were to get flattened by a bus on the way home, Amari Ward could pick up and run Golden Goose Homes without missing a beat.

"Why isn't Jared doing that?" Amari asked.

Patrick braced himself on the installed cabinet behind him and pushed himself off the ground. Jared had called out sick. But that was fine. Patrick ran a lean crew of top-notch construction talent. Fewer bodies meant more money to go around for the team. Plus, he preferred a hands-on approach, so jumping in if they were down a man never bothered him.

"He's got a migraine or something. Quit stalling."

Amari sighed and delivered the news. "Got an email from Milan Marble. The custom flooring is going to be delayed."

"How long?"

"Sixty days. Maybe longer.

"Sixty—" Patrick blurted, unable to finish in his exasperation. "The damn flooring was supposed to be done already! Find—"

"Kendra's already reached out to that shop in Tuscany. They're pricier, though."

"It is what it is. Let her know we'll take a bit of a haircut if it'll get here faster."

"Already authorized her to go up to ten percent."

Patrick peeled off his work gloves and gave Amari a chummy slap on the chest with them.

"Good man." He tossed them on the counter, swapping them for a half-full bottle of Poland Spring which he unceremoniously downed in three gulps.

"I swear, Pat," Amari said, leaning against the stainless steel fridge that had yet to be slid into its alcove. "It feels like it's one thing after another on this project."

"It'd go a lot quicker if Kaminski would stop changing his mind every other day."

"True that," Amari agreed. "But at least he ain't bitching when you jack up the price."

"Spitting facts," Patrick said as he turned the empty bottle completely upside down, capturing the last few drops on his outstretched tongue.

Amari eyed him conspicuously, telling him, "Uh-uh. Don't do that."

"Do what?" Patrick asked with a knowing grin.

"The slang. You sound ridiculous."

"I grew up in Jersey!" Patrick defended.

"*South* Jersey," Amari replied. "My cousin Nelson lived there for a minute. He says if you ain't in Camden or Atlantic City, you may as well be from Iowa or some shit."

Patrick laughed. Amari was the only person in Chicago who knew he was from New Jersey. He'd let it slip one night while celebrating the completion of a particularly lucrative project at The Alibi Room. Too many Don Julio shots. To his credit, Amari kept it to himself. He was a good guy with even better instincts. Hell, he was the closest thing Patrick had to a friend. The first he'd had since . . .

He shut off the train of thought before recollection of the previous night's uninvited guest could rush to the front of his mind. He pushed off the counter and chucked the empty water bottle at Amari, who ducked it easily.

"Well, if I can't use slang, you can't call me *Pat*. You're the only one who does that, by the way."

"Don't work like that."

"How do you figure?"

"Just don't."

"Who works for who here?"

Now it was Amari's turn to deliver a friendly backhand slap.

"You'd be lost without me, and you know it."

"No," Patrick countered, drawing out a pause before continuing, "but I'd have to work a lot harder than I want to, so I keep you around."

They both laughed this time. Amari picked up the water bottle and tossed it to Patrick, who placed it on the counter.

"Better get back to it before Kaminski changes his mind about something else," Amari said.

No sooner did the words leave his mouth than they heard the sound of car doors opening and closing from the front of the property.

Patrick shot his friend a glare before tossing the bottle at him again. This time, Amari slapped it away with his hand.

"Sorry," he mouthed.

Patrick exited through the open portal where the fiberglass front door would eventually go, pulling his well-worn flannel over his dust-stained black tank top.

Aleksi Kaminski walked around the 2024 Dolomite Silver Metallic Porsche Cayenne S Coupé, a midsize hatchback that carried a sticker price north of a hundred grand. A first-generation son of Polish immigrants, he started some fancy fintech company that half the banks in the US had been climbing over themselves to engage with since it launched in 2020. He didn't really know how it worked and cared even less. The important thing was that Aleks had more money than he could spend in a lifetime. That's why he contracted Patrick's company to build him this 6000-square-foot palace in the wealthy village of Winnetka, an hour outside of Chicago.

He was dressed casually in a Saint Laurent button-down with a small check pattern and perfectly tailored ivory chinos, rounding off the look with light brown Ferragamo loafers. His shirt was open enough to display a thin but very expensive gold chain, and his left wrist was adorned with an Audemars Piguet Royal Oak watch while that same hand bore a platinum Harry Winston wedding band.

"Patrick!" he called cheerily, his hand extended. Patrick accepted the handshake, unimpressed as ever at the man's grip.

"Aleks," he greeted. What brings you b-by?" Thankfully, Patrick was almost finished with the question by the time he saw who was with Aleks, because he stuttered slightly on the last word, but not enough for his client to notice.

Nora Kaminski stepped out of the passenger seat and joined her husband, looking stunning in a blue and white striped Veronica Beard Susan minidress and a pair of Valentino calfskin wedge sandals, both of which accentuated her tanned legs. Like Aleks, she wore an array of expensive jewelry, including the wedding and engagement rings she had almost forgotten at Patrick's apartment the night before. He couldn't make out her eyes under her Cartier Trinity sunglasses, but it was probably better that way. As she approached, he caught the familiar scent of her perfume, stirring memories he should not be recalling in this company.

If there was any awkwardness between Patrick and Nora, Aleks didn't seem to notice. He was too busy inspecting the progress the crew was making on his future home. Judging from his furrowed brow and narrowed eyes, it was through a critical lens.

Patrick tamped down his rising irritation. Yes, Aleks was paying him very well, but working for him was a nightmare. He constantly changed his mind about things, was almost never happy, even when portions were completed to his precise specifications, and the project was already 25 percent over budget and completion would take at least four months longer than expected. Now, the way the tech bro was looking at the house, Patrick feared another curveball.

But to his surprise, Aleks simply smiled and said, "Looking good! What do you think, babe?" He didn't turn to actually look at Nora when he addressed her.

She lowered her sunglasses, pretending to look at the house, but actually eyeing Patrick, the hair on his well-defined pecs exposed by the tank top. "Yes, it is, baby."

He surmised she had concocted an adequate cover story for her absence last night and, having gotten away with it, had pushed aside any qualms about her infidelity. Patrick had no such reticence about her being married, but he understood the ramifications if they were to get caught—not just for him but for his crew as well. For someone who had been on their own and unattached as long as he had, it was hard sometimes thinking about how his actions affected others. Now, as he felt Amari's eyes on him, he figured he better cut it off with Nora Kaminski before he put this payday in any more jeopardy than he already had.

"I'm glad you folks like it," Patrick said, keeping his focus on Aleks. "We do have to talk about the marble, though."

"Bro," Amari said, compressing everything he wanted to convey to his boss in a single word.

"It's all good, Amari," Patrick assured. "Nothing's going on."

Aleks and Nora were driving off down the street after a visit that had gone surprisingly well, even with the news about the delay with the flooring. Patrick and Amari had taken them throughout the house—at least the areas that didn't present a hazard—and gave them a detailed explanation of the status of the project. Patrick found people hated not knowing things, especially those with personalities like Aleks. The more detail given, the more comfort received.

Nora had kept giving him the eye whenever she got a chance, the riskier, more playful aspects of her personality on display this morning. Patrick avoided it the best he could, but it was not lost on Amari, prompting his colleague's single-word admonishment.

"She was practically eye-fucking you, Pat."

"I can't help that."

"How many times?" Amari asked.

"What?" Patrick asked back, knowing damn well what he meant.

"How. Many. Times?" Amari asked again, crossing his arms as he emphasized each word.

"Five over the past month and a half," Patrick answered. "Although that's nights, not necessarily how many exact times. That's more like—"

"Maaaan!" Amari said, rolling his head back and drawing out the word. He had a real talent for conveying his message with minimal dialogue. As Patrick pretended to count on his fingers, he added, "I don't want to know. Just tell me you ain't doing that no more."

"I'm not." The assurance seemed to relax Amari somewhat until Patrick added, "Last night was the last time."

"*Last night*?!" Amari exclaimed. "Are you out of your damn mind?"

Patrick patted his friend's shoulder, offering a genuine apology, "I know. I fucked up. I'm sorry. It's done and he'll never find out." Amari searched Patrick's eyes, trying to decide if he believed him. "I'm not going to take money out of your pocket, brother. I'd never do that."

Amari decided he believed him.

"Okay. See that you don't." Then he cracked a smile and asked, "All right, how many *actual* times was it?"

The question made Patrick laugh and Amari joined in too. Patrick never actually answered the question, though, as they were interrupted when Dave, one of their crew members, came into the kitchen. The employee wore a somber expression on his face.

"Patrick," Dave said, "I . . . have a message for you."

Patrick's laughter ceased and his own expression turned serious, matching his employee's.

"I swear to God, if you're going to tell me that the shingles are unavailable, I'm going to lose my mind."

"No, not about the project," Dave answered. "Kendra got a call from a woman named Vivian. Said she was from New Jersey. And that she's your aunt."

Patrick felt that lump in his throat again. He did his best to play it off.

"Trash it," he instructed.

"I really think you need to—"

"I said fucking trash it, Dave!"

"Pat," Amari said, again using the bare minimum phraseology to respectfully tell him to cool it.

Patrick knew he was right. He sighed, composing himself. "I'm sorry, Dave," he offered, evening out his tone. "What's the message?"

"Your mother died."

Chapter 4

May 2005

Patrick sat at the small breakfast nook in the kitchen of the modest one-story home where he lived with his mother in a cul-de-sac in Leeds Point. It was a small space and functional, but Cindy Shourds was not renowned for her cooking skills, so more often than not, meals for her and her son comprised some manner of pasta with store-bought sauce or takeout. It was morning, just after ten a.m. and the overdone scrambled eggs on Patrick's plate were cooling as he jostled them around with his fork. Despite the mild sulfur scent resulting from the overcooking, it wasn't the quality of the food that caused his aversion. It was the consistent lack of appetite in the two weeks since the incident in the woods.

"Patrick," his mother started as she came around the corner from the hall leading to her bedroom, concern written into her tone, "you're not eating."

"I'm not hungry, Mom," he said flatly.

"You still need to eat," she insisted.

Even having just turned fourteen last week, a birthday that he would never count among his favorites, he could understand why his mother was worried. His clothes felt loose, so he was pretty sure he'd lost weight. It wasn't like he didn't eat at all. He forced himself to when he could, but most times, he just felt this swirling vortex start in his abdomen that ascended his esophagus, settling in his throat. On the days when his mind's eye projected Brandon's helpless, terrified face before the monster took him away, he tasted bile and felt as if he might vomit, which he did more than once. Today was one of those days when he felt like he could retch, despite the emptiness of his stomach.

"I know," he acknowledged, scooping a forkful of egg and stuffing it into his mouth, compelling himself to chew past the rubbery texture and ignore the burned, slightly metallic taste as he forced it down his gullet. He closed his eyes, trying to will himself not to regurgitate it.

Cindy came up behind him and wrapped her arms around her son in a comforting hug. He was thankful he was fighting to keep the food down because that helped distract him enough to avoid bursting into tears. He'd shed too many these past fourteen days, and his eyes were constantly dry and itchy. Those same eyes that fell on a prominent bruise on his mother's right forearm. He grabbed her wrist and pulled her arm away to examine the injury.

"What's this?" he asked. "Are you okay?"

Cindy was quick to pull back, moving her arm out

of her son's field of vision. She was wearing a yellow tank top over a light pair of black pajama pants. Even though his initial focus was on that one specific injury, Patrick could see at least two other smaller ones on either arm.

"Oh, this? That's nothing. Stupid bar flap fell and whacked me as I was going to get some cocktail napkins. I've told Ed a hundred times to fix that damn hinge."

Patrick was going to ask about the other marks, but before he got the chance, they were interrupted by a knock at the front door. Cindy's posture tightened, and she froze for a moment before heading to answer it. On her way, she grabbed a hoodie from the basket of unwashed clothes sitting on the dining room table they hadn't used for its intended purpose in months. Pulling it over her head and covering the bruises, she made her way to the door.

On the other side was Leeds Point Sheriff, Paul Alberts. He stood in the doorway, an air of gravitas about him. His broad shoulders filling out his tan sheriff's department shirt, the silver, star-shaped badge glinting in the morning light, and sporting the brown leather utility belt carrying an array of law enforcement tools, including the requisite holstered pistol. He removed his wide-brimmed hat as the door opened, revealing his short brown hair, only slightly matted by the headwear. His face displayed strong features but also had a certain boyish charm, despite his position of authority. He was an approachable lawman who still commanded the respect of the community.

"Good morning, Cindy," Alberts said, a hint of

somberness in his voice.

"Paul," she greeted. "What's going on?"

Patrick noticed the sheriff looking over his mother's shoulder at him. He felt another wave of nausea, but this time it had nothing to do with food. The man whispered something that seemed to give his mother pause. She crossed her arms and glanced back at her son, heartbreak written on her face.

"Give us a second, honey," she said in a cracked voice as she stepped outside with Alberts and closed the door behind them.

Patrick set his fork down next to the plate containing his barely touched meal. He felt like hopping off the chair, pulling the sliding doors open, and running off into the woods behind his house, seeing how far he could get before his body gave out. Of course, given what he knew was *in* those woods, it wasn't a viable escape route. And why should he escape?

He hadn't been back to school since the incident, but he knew how his classmates were. They'd mock him, calling him a liar or maybe even a coward for leaving Brandon behind. Some of them may even think he's the one who killed him.

Was he actually dead, though?

It was a thought that crossed his mind many times since that day. If he wasn't, he'd no doubt be in bad shape and need to go to the hospital. Plus, Patrick knew he was still alive when he was carried away. Maybe he somehow survived? Maybe the thing had dropped him somewhere and he was just holding on, too weak to move, just waiting for someone to rescue him.

The sheriff's department had organized search parties the same evening that Brandon was declared missing. Patrick recalled seeing in movies that someone had to be gone for at least twenty-four hours before the police could start an investigation, but that must have been bullshit because Alberts mobilized the small force and had dozens of citizens combing the woods within a matter of hours. The sheriff accompanied Patrick, along with his mother, to the spot where the attack occurred. Patrick was damn near petrified of going back there, but he knew his best friend was in mortal danger, so he somehow found the courage to go. Alberts and his deputy, both carrying 12-gauge shotguns, helped provide a small measure of security.

When they got to the foundation of the house, they found Brandon's bloody sneaker lying almost exactly in the center of the sunken stones. Copious amounts of blood stained the grass where the injured boy had spat it out before being jerked into the air and on either side of the stones where the monster had impaled him. But there was no sign of a body. The grim expressions on the adults' faces told Patrick they didn't expect a happy outcome, despite not believing his claims that it was the Leeds Devil who had taken him.

Search parties had been deployed every night since then. Leeds Point was not a big town, but the Pine Barrens, the woods themselves, were massive. The forest covered over a million acres in South Jersey, about 20 percent of the entire state. Volunteers were brought in from neighboring towns and the New Jersey State Police sent reinforcements. A tip line was opened and posters with Brandon's face were plastered all over town. It was an all-hands-on-deck effort to find him.

Patrick jumped in his chair when he heard the door open again. Alberts followed his mother into the house and took a seat in the well-worn recliner across from the sectional couch that needed to be replaced a long time ago, the polyester fabric pilled and faded from years of use.

Cindy approached her son, her arms still huddled across her chest. "Patrick, honey," she said softly, "the sheriff needs to talk to you."

Patrick simply nodded and got up out of the chair, following his mother over to the couch, taking a seat beside her. She put her arm around him, and he instantly knew what Alberts was about to say. The first drop fell down his cheek before the lawman even said a word, despite the boy's effort to stay strong.

"Son," Alberts started, taking a second before continuing, as if trying to find the right words. "I'm sorry to tell you that we're calling off the search for Brandon."

"But what if he's still out there? He's hurt," Patrick protested weakly, as if saying the words out loud would alter what he knew in his heart was the reality. He looked to his mom for support, seeing her own dampening, bloodshot eyes.

She tilted her head in sympathy, her heart breaking for her child as she said the words he'd been dreading, "Brandon's been declared dead, sweetheart."

Patrick said nothing in response. He squeezed his eyes shut and melted into his mother, his lids failing to provide a barrier as the tears escaped from underneath. He squeezed her as tightly as he could and she reciprocated, stroking his hair as he broke into sobs.

Alberts, to his credit, allowed them space to process the devastating news. When the initial tsunami of anguish subsided, he spoke, "Patrick, the report is going to classify it as a likely animal attack."

The boy broke away from his mother, a manic fury overtaking his sadness. "I know what it was! I told you what it was!"

"Son, the Leeds Devil is just a myth. I'm not doubting that you saw something, but it was probably a bear."

"It wasn't a fucking bear!" the boy shouted, slamming his fist on the couch beside him.

"Patrick!" his mother admonished.

Alberts put a hand up, telling Cindy that he took no offense to the boy's reaction.

"Patrick," Alberts said, "the woods are a dangerous place. We do our best to keep them safe, but there are predatory animals out there. Not only that, but there are hidden caves and sinkholes that can open up." He paused, defeat in his words. "I wish I could tell you different, but he's gone. I'm so sorry, son."

Renewed sobs broke the teen as he hunched over, burying his face in his hands as his back heaved. Cindy rubbed it in big circles while managing her own emotion as best she could.

"Thank you, Paul," she whispered.

"There's one more thing," Alberts said. "The Murphy family is holding a memorial service on Thursday."

Another pause as Patrick looked up from his hands to see the deadly serious expression the sheriff wore. "They've forbidden you both from attending."

"What?" Patrick blurted, snot and spittle spraying as he hopped off the couch, taking a step toward Alberts. "Why?"

The sheriff rose from the recliner and stood. He was sympathetic to the devastated child, but it was at the point where he needed to exert his authority. Still, he maintained a gentle, even tone.

"They're grieving, too, Patrick. Everything you are feeling, so are they. They lost a child and need to process it in their own way. If having you there is too painful for them, then you need to respect that."

"But . . . but . . . I didn't do anything wrong! I would have helped him if I could!"

Alberts put his hand on Patrick's shoulder. "I'm sure you would have, son."

"He was my best friend," the boy explained in a barely audible whisper.

"I know, baby," Cindy chimed in, doing her best to keep it together. "I know you loved him."

It all became too much for Patrick as he jerked his shoulder away from Alberts's hand and ran to his bedroom, the first door in the hall off the dining room. He slammed the door so hard he heard the picture hung just outside rattle and crash to the ground, glass shattering on impact. He didn't care.

Throwing himself onto the bed, he buried his face in the pillow, unleashing a torrent of sobs. He heard the muffled voices in the living room continue their conversation for a few more minutes until the front door opened and shut. He listened as his mother's tentative footsteps approached his room. They stopped just outside and he expected the door to open, but it didn't. After a few moments, he heard her continue to her own bedroom on the other side of the hall.

Left to himself, he cried himself to sleep.

When Patrick woke up, the room was dark, but it wasn't night.

The sun was obscured by dark gray storm clouds. The steady patter of rain against the windows provided the only sound in the house.

He was still face down on his pillow, the linen cover damp from tears and drool. He pushed himself up slowly, feeling lightheaded from his general lack of nutrition over the past couple of weeks. Once in a seated position, he carefully rubbed the gunk from his irritated eyes, giving himself a moment to let his vision adjust. Before it could, he heard a soft *click*, followed by a *whoosh*. Looking toward the computer desk in the room's corner, he saw the source of the noise. When he did, icy tendrils of fear clasped his spine.

Brandon sat in the chair, his form twisted into an unnatural angle. The entire right side of his face was mangled and painted with blood, flowing freely down his neck and soaking his shirt. The eyeball had popped out and dangled against his cheek, barely hanging by a single extraocular muscle.

"Brandon?" Patrick asked in a confused, choked whisper, his throat not lubricated enough after his nap for the word to come out at normal volume.

His mutilated friend did not answer. Considering the state he was in, Patrick didn't know if he could. Instead, the boy raised a crooked finger to his lips, signaling for quiet.

Patrick found his voice but kept it hushed. "What is it?"

Brandon moved the gnarled digit away from his mouth and pointed to the window. Patrick squinted as if it would help him see better, but all that was visible were the trees behind the rain sluicing down the glass.

He looked back at Brandon, who was still pointing, insistence burned into his remaining eye.

Patrick tentatively scooted to the edge of the bed, keeping an eye on his unexpected visitor while he swung his feet over and stepped onto the carpeted floor. As he rose, he turned his focus back to the window but still saw nothing. He crept closer until his nose was almost pressed against the pane.

He was about to tell Brandon he didn't see anything when two red dots appeared between two trees. They had a demonic glow about them. Patrick realized they were eyes.

The eyes of the Leeds Devil.

Horror-struck, Patrick looked back at the chair,

but Brandon was gone. Ignoring his every instinct not to turn his attention back to the woods, he was still compelled to. When he did, the trees suddenly looked dead, their trunks blackened and the branches needleless. The sky above seemed to have turned darker than he'd ever known. The moon was nowhere to be found, and a thick fog crept along the ground. It was like a new section of the woods opened up behind his house, one he'd never seen. The eyes were gone, but what he heard was worse than what he couldn't see.

A bestial growl shook the trees, the limbs shaking violently as something large hurtled into the sky behind them. The heavy flapping of the monster's wings overpowered the volume of the rain. When the creature that had haunted his nightmares for a fortnight exploded into the sky above the pines, Patrick ran.

He only made it to his doorway, because when he rounded the corner to go to his mother, he saw the strange woman from the woods blocking his path to safety. Her expression was somber, even given her sightless eyes.

"Mommy!" Patrick screamed, using the variation he hadn't uttered since before he turned ten. There was no reply. The only sound was the creature's wings growing louder as it barreled toward the house. Too terrified to look, Patrick braced himself, squeezing his eyes shut as the creature burst through the window, shattering glass and splintering wood as it swooped in on its prey.

Patrick woke up for the second time. This time, it was not a slow ascent into consciousness. Rather, he bolted up, hopping off his sweat-soaked comforter and onto the floor. He stepped wrong and tumbled forward, just barely bracing himself on the desk chair before smashing his nose into the carpet.

He suddenly remembered Brandon and shoved the chair away as if it were on fire, the piece of office furniture smacking into the wall and rattling the shelf next to it, nearly toppling the Lego Luke Skywalker's X-Wing Fighter he and Brandon had built the prior summer.

Disoriented, he frantically looked around the room, taking a moment to register that his window was still intact and there were no ghosts or monsters present. His breathing slowed as the burning in his chest subsided. His pajama bottoms were wet, the terror of his nightmare having loosed his bladder. Slowly, he worked up the courage to get up and peer through the window to inspect the backyard. As with his room, there was nothing there.

Just as he relaxed, a knock at his door startled him.

"Patrick, honey?" his mother's muted voice asked from outside his room. "Are you okay? I heard a noise."

He was thankful she was giving him space, especially since he would prefer not to explain his dampened pants at the moment.

"I'm fine, Mom," he replied.

Even though he was far from it.

Chapter 5

September 2025

Patrick walked through the sliding glass doors and onto the concourse outside Atlantic City International Airport. The first thing he noticed was the humidity. Over the past sixteen years, he'd become accustomed to a milder dampness in the air from Lake Michigan, as opposed to the heavier moisture brought on by the coastal Atlantic influence of New Jersey. It was warmer too. When he boarded the flight a little over two hours ago, the Illinois temperature was slightly above seventy-five degrees. The pilot had announced it was eighty-two here in the southern region of the state. A warm breeze tickled his face, another contrast with the stronger gusts that prompted "The Windy City" nickname.

There was also a heaviness in the air. And not just outdoors. He had felt an unseen weight press down on him the moment the captain announced the plane had begun its descent.

It was the burden of unfinished business. Business that would never be resolved. Patrick left Leeds Point when he was eighteen without saying goodbye to his mother. At least not in person. He'd left a note. He assumed she read it, but was never completely sure because Cindy Shourds had not once tried to contact her son after he fled the only home he had ever known.

Sometimes, the thought made him bitter. His leaving had nothing to do with his relationship with his mother. Having grown up without a father, it always felt like it was the two of them against the world. And even when the world turned against him after Brandon, she still stood by his side. Which is why it was so strange that she hadn't even attempted to find him.

Yet, he did explicitly ask that she not do so. Could he really be upset at her for honoring his wishes? And he certainly didn't make it easy. He left his Motorola Razr—he hadn't yet joined the smartphone club—on the table next to the unmarked envelope, opting for a prepaid phone he snagged at a kiosk in the train station before leaving. Not that he had anyone to call. He was making a completely clean break from everyone and everything. That raised a question in Patrick's mind.

How did his Aunt Vivian track him down?

He had no social media profiles. Never did. Sure, Golden Goose Homes had Facebook and Instagram pages, but Kendra and Amari ran those when they weren't too busy trying to hide the fact that they were dating. And those pages only had company info and photos of projects. There was no mention of Patrick by name anywhere.

Still, 2025 was a different time than 2010. Back then, despite the Internet, a person could still maintain anonymity with a little effort. But now, everything was online. His company was registered with the state of Illinois, and he was listed as the owner under *Meet the Team* on the business web page.

He'd protested, but Amari was adamant about building client trust. And when Kendra had made a crack about how *He must be wanted for murder or something*, he relented. He probably should have changed his name. Even though he considered it more than a few times, he always found an excuse not to go through with it. But no matter what his rationale, the truth was that he wanted to hold on to something of the person he had been. And his name was the only thing he had left.

He pulled the crumpled Post-it note from his pocket and checked the address scribbled on it. After Dave had dropped the bombshell, he left Amari in charge of the Winnetka project and drove back to the office. There, he had called his aunt from the landline, deliberately avoiding using his cell phone.

After a brief, awkward conversation, Patrick had the details. Vivian had gone to pick his mother up for lunch. When Cindy didn't answer the door, she'd used the spare key to let herself in, and that's when she found Cindy dead in her bed. The medical examiner confirmed that she had died in her sleep at sixty-four years old. At first, Patrick had tried to tell Vivian he wasn't coming back and he was okay with her handling the arrangements. The shift in her tone was as abrupt as it was biting.

You abandoned your mother, she'd said, acid

practically oozing through the receiver. *You left us all without so much as an explanation. Now you can't even come back to pay your final respects? She gave up everything for you, you selfish, selfish boy.*

Patrick was not one to be susceptible to guilt trips. In the construction business, he heard a million sob stories about everything from delayed closings to missing deposits. He often sympathized but was rarely moved. Now he was. Because Vivian was right. No matter what his reasons, he had abandoned the woman who gave up so much and worked so hard to take care of him.

So he'd agreed to come back to say goodbye. Plus, while he could handle the estate matters via courier and notary, it would be easier to get the ball rolling in person.

Now, here he was, back in New Jersey for the first time in more than a decade and a half. He checked the signs to see where he needed to go to grab a taxi or rideshare. As he looked up, he felt a sudden, sharp burning sting on the back of his neck. Recognizing the culprit immediately, he slapped at the area but only whacked the irritated skin as he watched the horsefly take flight in a mocking barrel roll motion.

"Damn greenheads are still out in full force."

The man's voice was gruff but familiar. Patrick looked in its direction and saw Paul Alberts leaning against a black SUV with a yellow stripe and *Leeds Point Sheriff* stenciled across the door.

The lawman was sixteen years older than the last time Patrick had seen him, but he still looked mostly the same. His build was thicker, although he appeared to be in decent shape, and his hair had kept its natural brown color outside of some graying around his temples. A short beard was a new addition, that, unlike his hair, was mostly gray. The lines on his forehead and around his eyes had deepened, but he was very much the same man Patrick remembered.

"They still terrorizing the community center?" Patrick asked, recalling many a summer day at the pool under assault from those green-eyed menaces.

"Little bastards are relentless," Alberts confirmed. "Gotta slather on a gallon of Skin So Soft just to have a fighting chance. Wish I'd bought stock in Avon before they sold the company." He paused before opening the passenger door and adding, "Hop in."

"Front or back?" Patrick asked only half jokingly.

"Front. For now," Alberts replied, also not sounding like a joke. "Your aunt asked me to pick you up and give you a ride to her house."

Patrick glanced back at the signs, considering declining the ride, but decided it was for the best to accept. He stepped inside the police vehicle, handing his carry-on to the sheriff as he did. Alberts slid it in the back seat before walking around and taking his place behind the wheel. A moment later, they were on the road.

"Wasn't expecting a welcome committee," Patrick said, breaking the tense silence that had suffocated the car in the ten minutes since they pulled onto South Mill Road heading toward Leeds Point.

"Didn't expect you to come back," Alberts said, keeping his eyes on the road.

"My mother died. Why wouldn't I?"

Alberts side-eyed him. "Don't play cute with me, son."

Patrick contemplated a smart-ass *I'm not your son* quip but suppressed the urge.

"I'm just here to settle her affairs. As soon as that's done, I'm gone. For good."

The men fell back into an uneasy silence as they continued to their destination. The only time either of them spoke was when they passed a road crew hard at work pouring concrete. "Damn sinkholes," Alberts observed. "Been seeing more and more of them lately." It took Patrick back to the day the sheriff had told him Brandon was being declared dead, offering it as an excuse for what might have happened to his body. That old wound tore at his heart, but he stuffed it back down to a place where it couldn't so easily get to him.

Fifteen minutes later, Alberts pulled onto a vaguely familiar dirt driveway. As they approached the house, the largest in the small community nestled on the outskirts of town, his recollection became clearer.

Although he never knew as a child exactly what his uncle, Robert Lumley, did for a living, he did know that he was rich. Everyone in town seemed to know him and Patrick remembered attending several parties at the sprawling estate over the years.

It wasn't often. Patrick was never close to his mother's sister, Vivian, or the man she married. Theirs was the cordial relationship of more distant family.

Alberts parked the car in a row of other vehicles, including an Audi Q8, a Nissan Altima, and a van whose model he didn't recognize, but it looked modified, as if for handicap accessibility.

"I'll wait here," Alberts said after putting the vehicle in park.

"You don't have to," Patrick countered. "I can grab an Uber."

"I don't mind," the sheriff replied, answering a question his passenger didn't ask.

"Sure," Patrick replied, knowing he wasn't being given a choice. Looking over his shoulder, he realized he couldn't get his bag out of the caged-off back seat without Alberts's help. He supposed it would be fine there for now. He gave the sheriff a nod, opening his door and moving to step out. Before he could close the door, Alberts posed a question.

"You're not going to ask me about Megan?"

Patrick chose his words carefully.

"No. Because you don't want to tell me about her."

Alberts gave him a nod as if to say, "Good answer." It was true, but that wasn't the only reason he didn't ask. His return to Leeds Point was opening enough doors. He needed that one to stay shut.

Patrick walked up the driveway, stepping onto the cobblestone path leading to the front door. The rocks were sunken into the dirt, and weeds invaded the spaces where the mortar base had worn away.

It wasn't just the path that had fallen into disrepair. As Patrick got closer, he noticed the sorry state of the house. Even if he didn't have a construction background, the need for renovations was obvious.

The once-pristine Tennessee stone façade was eroded and crumbling at the edges. Dark patches of moss took up residence beneath the leaky gutters. The twin marble columns that framed the entrance remained epic in scale, but hairline fractures spiderwebbed their way up and down the length like varicose veins. The windows on either side were clouded over with trapped moisture from broken thermal seals, the surrounding trim warped and peeling.

With all their money, his aunt and uncle couldn't get the place fixed up? What had happened since he'd been gone?

Stepping onto the porch, Patrick reached for the doorbell but didn't need to ring it, as the faded fiberglass doors opened and a man stepped out. Patrick had never seen him before. He looked to be in his mid-forties and was wearing an impeccably tailored navy blue suit with a magenta silk tie, providing a splash of color against a crisp, pristine white dress shirt. He had a look about him that Patrick was familiar with from his dealings with bankers and real estate investors. His dark hair was precisely styled, framing his features in a way that gave off a youthful appearance, one that could easily be underestimated in negotiations, giving him an edge.

Although, judging by his current expression, whatever tête-à-tête he had just engaged in did not go his way.

Following immediately behind him was his mother's sister, Patrick's Aunt Vivian. A tall, wispy woman with severe features, hardened further by age, she was three years Cindy's senior and miles ahead of her younger sibling in assertiveness. If Suit Guy's expression was one of frustration, Vivian's face had disdain written all over it.

"We will not be discussing this matter any further, Mr. Savila," Vivian said, practically spitting the man's name from her mouth in a voice carrying a cracked inflection Patrick remembered.

Vivian and Mr. Savila stopped when they saw Patrick standing on the porch. Savila used the distraction to attempt one last pitch. He reached into the inner pocket of his jacket and produced a business card. Patrick couldn't make out what it said, but it was black with gold lettering on premium stock. The guy looked like he had some real funding behind him.

"I'm sorry you feel that way, Mrs. Lumley," Savila said, maintaining an air of professionalism. He held out the card. "In case you change your mind."

Vivian crossed her arms, refusing it. "Perhaps you should reconsider shoving that card up your ass," she said with a vicious sneer.

Shocked at the vulgarity, Savila gave Patrick a look that asked, "Is she serious?" To which Patrick only shrugged. He was not getting involved in whatever this was. Understanding that the woman would not be swayed, he returned the card to his pocket with a sigh. "Have a good day, Mrs. Lumley."

Vivian watched intently as Savila walked to the Audi, got in, and drove away. With the businessman gone, her demeanor immediately shifted, an unusually warm smile stretching her wrinkled face.

She opened her arms for a hug and Patrick tentatively accepted the woman's musty, nonenal scent filling his nostrils.

"Patrick, dear!" she exclaimed with the nuance of a first-year high school drama student. "Welcome home!"

There was a distinct inauthenticity about the whole interaction, but Patrick wasn't going to call her out on it. He wanted to get in and out as quickly as possible. Debating the genuineness of a relative he hadn't seen in years, and probably never would again once he left, would not serve that purpose.

"Thank you, Aunt Vivian," he said cordially before offering the requisite, "I wish it were under better circumstances."

Vivian stayed in character, bringing her hand to her chest and tilting her head as she pursed her lips.

"My poor, sweet sister. She'd always hoped you'd come home one day. Such a shame you missed out on saying goodbye."

Every word felt like a thinly veiled dig, but Patrick

continued to let it slide.

"I wish I'd had the opportunity."

"Yes, I'm sure you do," Vivian agreed. "Come in, say hello to your Uncle Robert."

That wasn't high on Patrick's list of things he wanted to do, but when Vivian stepped aside to grant him access, he entered the house.

The interior was in better shape than the outside, but not by much. The tile floors were scuffed and cracked in spots. A once-majestic chandelier hung overhead, now rusted and fitted with mismatched bulbs mingling to give off a diluted yellowish glow. The grand, bifurcated staircase was still impressive in design, but time had faded and frayed the runners. The left side was home to a motorized chair on a track leading to the second floor. A tuft of cotton peeked out of a small tear in the cowhide seat.

Who is that for? Patrick wondered.

"Come, dear," Vivian said, waving her arm at the opposite staircase. He stepped aside at the base to let his aunt lead the way. As they ascended, the wood creaked and groaned under even the old woman's slight frame.

At the top, they turned down a hall lined with corroded sconces and dust-laden furniture. A console table pressed flush against one wall and a bench with a cracked leather top sat against the opposite, next to a bookcase lined with untouched tomes and wilted plants. An ornate maroon rug with gold etching lined the path to the double doors at the end of the corridor. A faint clicking sound came from somewhere behind it.

Vivian led her nephew down the hall silently.

Something about it felt like a funeral procession to Patrick. Paintings and old photographs lined the walls. About halfway down, he recognized one. It was Cindy and Vivian in high school in the 1960s when his mom was a freshman and her sister was a senior. His mother had the same one framed in their house. Patrick had always found their expressions in the photo fascinating. His mother smiled, but it looked forced. Pained even. Vivian, on the other hand, was the picture of stoicism, as if she'd never cracked a smile a day in her life.

"Patrick?" Vivian called to him. The woman had reached the end of the hall. He hadn't even realized he'd stopped to look at the photo. He gave it one last glance before joining her.

While he didn't know what he expected to see on the other side, it wasn't what lay before him.

Sunlight filtered into the master bedroom through sheer curtains, shining on the hospital bed in the center of the room. The mattress was elevated and Patrick could see the roller pattern under the sheet. He'd worked on enough handicap-accessible homes to know it was designed that way to relieve pressure.

Robert Lumley lay in the center of the bed. Patrick's uncle, once strapping in stature, looked like a shell of his former self. His facial features were sunken into saggy skin and his hair had thinned considerably. A stringy, patchy beard covered his typically clean-shaven countenance, and a nasal cannula delivered oxygen through his nostrils. Robert's frail body was mostly covered by the sheet drawn up to his neck, but Patrick could still make out his gaunt, twisted frame.

Twisted like Brandon's spine.

Patrick shook off the intrusive thought and focused on his surroundings, sad as they may be.

A ceiling-mounted patient lift system with a track similar to the stair seat was installed above. The tube from Robert's nose ran to a mechanical ventilator beside him. The sound he had heard from the hallway was the rhythmic *hiss* and *click* of the machine as it delivered the oxygen. On the wall opposite the bed, a sleek monitor with a camera attached to its bottom exhibited an unusual interface. In the top left corner, there was a display that captured Robert's dark eyes next to a window that looked like a text box. Below were several green, red, and blue command buttons sandwiching a gray on-screen keyboard.

"It's an eye-gaze computer," said a soft, feminine voice with a slight Italian accent.

Patrick had been so shocked by the state of his uncle that he hadn't noticed the woman enter the room from the door off to the right. She was stunning.

The woman, who looked to be in her mid-twenties, carried a confidence beyond the years her youthful appearance presented. She moved gracefully into the room, her long, raven hair cascading down to the small of her back in waves. Her expressive brows and full lips looked as if they were perpetually on the verge of some private amusement. She wore a pristine white V-neck shirt offering a tantalizing view of her ample cleavage. The black yoga pants acknowledged her curves without apology, creating a striking contrast with her top and matching sneakers. Her eyes—amber at the pupils, giving way to rings of honey brown—had a chameleon quality to them as she gave Patrick a look that told him right away she was going to be trouble. He practically felt Amari glaring at him from eight hundred miles away.

"Caterina," Vivian said to her, "this is my nephew, Patrick. Patrick, this is Caterina Esposito."

Caterina sashayed over to them. Patrick couldn't tell if it was intentional or if that was just her natural glide. She offered a handshake that Patrick accepted as she put a hand over her heart in much the same way Vivian had earlier, except appearing more genuine.

"I was so sorry to hear about your mother," she said. "I met her a few times and she was always very nice."

"Thank you," Patrick acknowledged, releasing her hand but not her gaze.

"Caterina was one of the exchange students we housed a few years back," Vivian said, interrupting. "She studied nursing at Stockton. Now she works as a home health aide and has been very helpful in assisting with Robert."

"What happened?"

Vivian again grew somber, and again it felt somewhat performative.

"ALS."

Patrick was speechless. He was familiar with the disease but had never met anyone afflicted by it.

"This device is called an Eyegaze Edge," Caterina explained, bringing his attention back to the display. "Mr. Lumley can use his eyes to control the keyboard and communicate."

"Hello, Patrick," the device sounded in a natural tone as the words populated the text box. Patrick expected the synthesized, robotic intonation from the movies, but though the inflection was not perfect, it sounded human.

Patrick turned to the frail man. "Hello, Uncle Robert."

They spoke for a few more minutes, mainly light small talk. As much as possible under the circumstances. The whole time, Patrick was keenly aware of the looks Caterina was giving him. He tried to ignore them. A fling was far from the reason he came home. He just wanted to say goodbye to his mother and keep his aunt at arm's length to the greatest extent possible. It's not like he ever planned to see them again after this.

Focus, Patrick.

Thankfully, Vivian pulled him away and brought him down to the living room to talk in private, leaving Caterina to attend to her husband. As Patrick took a seat on the quilted chesterfield, his aunt asked, "Can I get you something to drink?"

"No, thank you, Aunt Vivian," Patrick declined politely. "I'm so sorry about Uncle Robert."

"Thank you," Vivian said, actually sounding like she meant it. "It's been three years since he was first diagnosed. Unfortunately, the end appears to be drawing near."

Patrick tightened his lips and nodded, not wanting to repeat, "I'm sorry."

Vivian changed the subject.

"I've made the arrangements for the viewing and funeral. Your mother kept her circle . . . small. I felt it best to have calling hours at St. Mark's on the morning of the funeral. I don't expect a large crowd. It's set for Thursday, two days from now."

Patrick wasn't surprised. His mother didn't have a robust social life from what he remembered. And that was before the Shourds became the town's punching bag.

"That's fine. Thank you for doing all of that." Vivian nodded her acknowledgment. "May I have the key to her house? Sheriff Alberts told me you kept the spare."

Her posture stiffened slightly. "Patrick, why don't you stay here? Being alone in that old house. So many memories. So many ghosts."

I'm used to ghosts, he thought.

"Thank you, but I want to be able to say goodbye. Not just to her, but to our home. Properly this time."

Vivian's brow narrowed, annoyance creeping back into her expression. The way Patrick left town was always going to be a sore spot with her. But it was what it was. He made the choice he had to. No one would ever truly understand that.

"Very well," Vivian said as she rose from the couch. "I'll get you those keys."

Chapter 6

The stones crunched under the SUV as Sheriff Alberts pulled into the gravel driveway of Patrick's childhood home on Hawk Hill Road next to Cindy's silver 2002 Hyundai Elantra. Patrick was surprised she'd maintained it this long. But considering she rarely ventured out of town, he guessed she was able to keep the mileage low.

The modest cottage-style house looked much as he remembered it, nestled beneath a canopy of trees. Its blue-gray siding appeared to still be in decent shape and dappled sunlight filtered through the leaves, casting gentle shadows on the white trim framing the windows.

The small Japanese maple his mother had loved stood sentinel near the entrance, its delicate, red leaves offering a splash of color against the subdued palette of the dwelling. A carefully cultivated garden bed lined the foundation, the low-growing shrubs and perennials unaware that Cindy had tended to them for the last time.

"You sure you want to stay here?" Alberts asked. "It might dredge up some unpleasant memories."

Too late for that, Patrick thought.

"I'll be fine," he said, stepping out of the car. "Thanks for the ride."

Alberts exited the car as well, unlocking the rear driver's side door and retrieving Patrick's bag before walking around and handing it to him. The men said nothing more to each other. Patrick didn't look back as the sheriff backed out of the driveway and drove off.

Patrick slid the key into the lock, meeting no resistance as it unlatched, granting him access to the home he'd left sixteen years ago. He pushed the door open and stepped inside. He wasn't alone.

Brandon stood directly in front of him, next to the same couch Patrick had sobbed on the day his best friend was declared dead. He still didn't quite know what the thing was, even after all these years. A ghost? A revenant? A vision? Whatever it was, the mangled, rotting reminder of the nightmare that was his adolescence stood before him, welcoming the prodigal son home.

"Not in the mood, Brandon," Patrick told the silent specter as he passed it, rounding the corner into his old bedroom.

It was exactly as he had left it, a memorial to an eighteen-year-old who may not have been dead but was thought to be gone forever. *Star Wars* sheets had long given way to a neutral black and gray comforter set, but the *Revenge of the Sith* poster still hung on the back of the door. Patrick could never bring himself to take it down, even though it was an outlier among the rest of the wall décor. The others were a snapshot of his musical taste back then, bands like Breaking Benjamin, Seether, and My Chemical Romance.

As he set his bag on the bed, he glimpsed the framed photograph on the nightstand in his peripheral vision. He reached over without fully taking it in and gently placed it face down.

He unzipped his bag, then stopped when he heard a noise from down the hall. It sounded as if something had fallen. And it came from the direction of his mother's room.

Patrick steeled himself to go investigate. He doubted the Leeds Devil was lightly knocking over objects in his mom's house, but he was acutely aware that there were things in this world that defied explanation. Some of them deadly. For a person who had been haunted—figuratively and literally—for twenty years, investigating a noise was never a mundane task.

He crept down the hall slowly, carefully stepping to minimize the groaning of the old floorboards. As with Vivian's house, the walls were lined with pictures, but none were from the past sixteen years. The most recent of them was his high school graduation photo. It captured Patrick at eighteen years old, adorned in his navy blue graduation gown, holding a matching cap in front of him. A wide, genuine smile lit up his younger self's face.

Patrick remembered the day it was taken. Since that horrible afternoon in the Pine Barrens, much of his life had been clouded by darkness. But that photograph captured a moment in time when he had found true happiness. It was a feeling he hadn't experienced before. And certainly hadn't since.

Although Patrick officially graduated from Leeds Point High School, he never got to wear that cap and gown again. There was no walk across the stage, no handshake with the principal or celebratory tossing of the cap. Shortly after his diploma arrived in the mail, he was already long gone. He wondered if his mother still had it somewhere.

But that was a question for another time. Right now he wanted to find out what had made the noise. At the end of the hall, he tentatively reached for the knob and slowly twisted, hesitating partially out of caution and partially from not wanting to see what awaited him. When the door slowly pushed open, Patrick probably should have been shocked by what he saw, but at this point, a ghost was not high on the list of things that surprised him.

The bedroom was well-kept and organized, as was his mother's way. Against the wall on one side of the room was a mirrored dresser lined with skin care products, deodorant, and perfume, set for easy access while getting ready. The shades were drawn on the window opposite the entrance but cracked enough that a ray of sunlight squeezed through, throwing a bright line across the unmade bed where his mother had taken her last breath.

Despite that, Cindy Shourds stood in the corner of the room next to the sliding doors of her closet. Unlike Brandon or the strange woman in colonial dress, she wasn't mutilated or scarred. She was just . . . older. The sandy brown hair Patrick inherited from her had thinned and grayed. Once long, she had often kept it up in a ponytail, but now it was styled in a short bob stopping just below her jawline. Heavy circles surrounded her eyes, giving her a permanently fatigued appearance. Her blue eyes were dulled as the initial stages of opacification had set in, but they were still somewhat clear, at least in relation to the one Brandon had left.

"Mom?" Patrick asked. He didn't expect an answer, nor did he get one, but he had to ask.

Cindy regarded her son pensively, almost sorrowfully, but remained silent. She slowly tilted her head toward the closet.

"What's in there?" Patrick asked, again, more rhetorically than anything else.

The apparition righted her head and continued to stare wordlessly. Patrick tentatively made his way to the closet, giving his mother a wide berth. Neither Brandon nor the other woman had ever done anything except stand around mostly, so he didn't feel like he was in danger. But there was a first time for everything and he wasn't keen for this to be it. As he inched around, he spoke again, continuing the one-sided conversation, "So, I guess you're going to be joining Brandon and Helena in haunting me?" he asked.

Helena was the name he'd given to the woman. He had no idea who she was or when she'd died, but her clothing made it seem like she had lived hundreds of years ago. Either that, or she was one of those reenactment folks who performed at state fairs. Regardless, Helena was what he settled on.

"The more the merrier, I guess. I guess you're not going to talk to me either?"

Cindy's continued silence answered the question as Patrick stopped in front of the closet.

"I had to leave. You know that. Right, Mom? I couldn't stay after what happened."

He felt his eyes moisten. He couldn't remember the last time he cried, having sometimes felt like he expended his supply of tears during the fucked-up days of his youth, so it surprised him that he felt them coming on now.

"I'm sorry I wasn't there to say goodbye."

The guilt finally compelled him to look away and he opened the sliding doors, temporarily blocking his mom. Once open, he saw that the tension rod holding the hangers full of Cindy's clothes had fallen. Shirts, pants, and dresses lay sprawled on top of shoes and handbags. Patrick sighed and lifted the rod off the ground, many of the hangers still wrapped around the cylindrical piece of plastic rising with it. Once it was in place, he went to work picking up the few stragglers left on the ground. He didn't know why he bothered. He was just going to toss them in a box to donate to the Veterans Association.

When he was down to the last shirt, he saw it was one he recognized. It was a black polo shirt that had been washed so many times it was looking more grayish. The sleeves were tattered and there were more than a few grease spots spattered on it. The yellow lettering on the left side of the chest read *Parkhill's.*

Parkhill's. The pub his mother had worked at his whole life. It was a roadside bar off Highway 9. It was mainly a beer and shots joint, but folks in town always said it had some pretty good food. Football Sundays were especially popular with discount beer and buckets of twenty-five-cent wings. At least back then. It would likely cost a good deal more here in 2025.

Patrick couldn't attest to the quality of the food because he'd never been there. Although families could patronize the restaurant, his mother never took him. Even for lunch. Her excuse was always that she spent so much time there working, the last thing she wanted to do was go there during her off hours. But as Patrick got older, he suspected it was something else. Especially when he noticed the whispers at school when he would walk down the halls. He supposed it didn't matter now. His mother was gone and he was an adult. Maybe it was time to see what the place was like.

"I think I'm going to go to Parkhill's for dinner, Mom. You going to come?"

He closed the closet door and saw that his mother's ghost was gone.

"Guess not."

Chapter 7

May 2005

Cindy pulled her car up to the curb outside Daniel Leeds Middle School, joining the line of parents dropping off their children. While those kids exited their rides immediately—whether bounding with enthusiasm or reluctantly shuffling toward their academic prison—Patrick sat frozen in the passenger seat, belt buckled and head down.

"Patrick, honey," his mom said, her voice soft and sympathetic, "it's time."

The boy bobbed his head in a weak nod and drew out the process of unbuckling his seat belt. Free of the strap, he fell still again. His mother sighed.

"I'm sorry, Patrick. You have to go back to school." She paused before asking a silly question, "Are you going to be okay?"

Patrick turned to her, feeling as if he were on the verge of tears.

"Does it matter?"

"Of course it matters!" Cindy replied emphatically. "But I've kept you home as long as I could. Mr. Hendry said if you didn't come back today, you'd have to repeat eighth grade. Do you really want that?"

He didn't, but he also really didn't want to set foot in that building either. Middle School for Patrick had always fallen somewhere in the range between *barely tolerable* and *total suckage.*

Whoever thought it was a great idea to round up kids from all over the district and jam them into a crowded building amid the hormonal chaos of puberty was either ignorant or psychotic. Every day felt like anarchy between disruptions in class, congestion in the halls, and the physical fights that seemed to break out daily. The teachers were overworked, and the administration seemed defeated, powerless to control the disorder that ruled its corridors.

And that was all *before* Patrick became a pariah.

He had not been back to school in the four weeks since Brandon's death. Not one of his other friends had called or come by to check on him, so he had no idea what to expect walking in there. Would they be cold to him? Sympathetic? Mocking? Knowing the casual cruelty that permeated the halls here, sympathy was the least likely.

The only kid his age he'd seen the past month was Brandon.

After that terrible dream he'd had the day the sheriff delivered the tragic news, Patrick had seen his friend—or more accurately, his friend's ghost—on half a dozen occasions. Each time, he looked worse, like his soul itself was rotting.

At first, Patrick was terrified. He ran to his mother's

room, forgetting she was at work, but when he calmed down, he saw that the thing did little more than stand there. He tried talking to it, but never got a response. Now whenever it showed up, it was just *there*.

He'd only seen the woman from the woods one other time. He woke up in the middle of the night, his bladder screaming for relief. After making it to the bathroom and back without incident, he saw her through his window, pacing the edge of the forest. Patrick was seized with fear. Her two appearances prior had both heralded the arrival of the Leeds Devil, once in his dream and once in the waking nightmare of his reality. He bounded to his bed, drawing the sheets to his chin as he trembled in terror, expecting the abomination to fly toward his house at any moment. But it never did. The woman just continued pacing until Patrick succumbed to exhaustion. When he woke up, it was morning, and she was gone.

Now, sitting in his mother's car, faced with the prospect of going back to school, those apparitions didn't seem as frightening. Hell, at this point, they may be his only friends.

"Are you sure I can't just do homeschool?"

"You know we can't."

Patrick had brought the idea up to his mother when the administration contacted them to mandate that he return. To her credit, Cindy looked at the requirements, then told her son that she didn't have the time or qualifications to provide an *academically equivalent* program. He asked about a tutor, but he knew before she even answered that they couldn't afford it.

With his last-ditch effort unsuccessful, Patrick resigned himself to his situation and gathered his backpack and water bottle.

"Patrick?" his mother prompted before he exited the car.

"Yeah, Mom?"

"I'm sorry."

A tear slid down her cheek as she apologized.

"For what?"

"For everything," she answered as another fell from her opposite eye.

"You shouldn't have to deal with this. You should be a kid, playing with your best friend not mourning him."

"Mom . . . ." Patrick started, not sure what to say. She was full-on crying now. Her words were choked and a small snot bubble ballooned from her left nostril.

She continued. "I'm sorry I haven't given you a better life. And I'm sorry you don't know your father. You deserve so much more than I've given you."

She gripped the steering wheel tight and sat up straight, pressing back against the headrest, letting her supply of tears run out.

Patrick was surprised at her mention of the word "father." Mom had always skirted around that subject. All he knew was that he was long gone from Cindy's life before she even knew she was pregnant. He didn't even know the man's name. It clearly made her uncomfortable to talk about it, so he'd stopped asking questions years ago. Answers probably wouldn't stop the taunting whispers some of his more malicious classmates uttered just loud enough to hear.

Patrick may have given up on ever knowing his father, but his mother, despite her perceived failures, was all he needed.

Seeing her beat herself up when all she ever did was her absolute best spurred a resolve in the boy. His own guilt and fear pushed aside. He wasn't going to let her believe she hadn't done right by him.

Without warning, he reached over and wrapped his arms around her, squeezing as tightly as he could. She leaned into the embrace, bringing her hands up to Patrick's arms, pulling him in tighter, mother and son unleashing a torrent of pent-up emotion as they cried.

The tender moment was interrupted by a blaring car horn. They broke the embrace and saw a white Lexus jerk out of the spot behind them and move around. The vehicle stopped beside theirs and a snooty-looking woman with shoulder-length auburn hair and expensive sunglasses shouted at them with her passenger window down. Even though Cindy's was up, they still heard her clearly.

"Drop off and go!" the obnoxious woman spat. "This isn't a parking lot!"

Cindy's face twisted into an expression of apoplectic rage as she rolled down her window.

"Eat a dick, Melissa!" she screamed back. The other woman fell into stunned silence, much of the anger on her face giving way to fear, knowing she'd fucked with the wrong woman. Her mouth opened and closed several times as her haywire brain failed to formulate a response. Unable to come up with anything, she drove off.

Oh shit, Patrick thought. For two reasons.

One, he recognized the woman as Melissa Gideon, Cameron Gideon's mother. Cam was in Patrick's class and was the biggest asshole in school. If he found out their moms were beefing, it would not be great for him.

But on the other hand, his mom didn't care who that woman was. She refused to take shit from her. It was pretty badass. He looked at her in admiration as she took a cleansing breath before offering Patrick an apologetic smile.

"Probably shouldn't have done that. Sorry."

The temporary burst of determination drained the moment Patrick stepped through the doors. It felt like every student stopped what they were doing just to stare at him. He wasn't an expert at reading facial expressions, so he couldn't determine if his classmates' looks were steeped in pity, anger, or disgust.

He fought the urge to turn and run back out of the school and all the way back home. Instead, he put his head down and pushed forward, the other kids moving aside as if he were afflicted with some type of plague.

As he rounded the corner into *B* hall, he caught sight of Brandon's abandoned locker, and it stopped him in his tracks. Taped to the front was a large piece of white poster board with a color printout of Brandon's yearbook photo pasted on it.

The smiling, carefree boy in the photo was a far cry from the mutilated husk that popped up for random visits. Above the photo, it read *We love you, Brandon!* in colorful letters.

Below, in the same handwriting, were the first and last dates of his life. *August 18, 1992–April 30, 2005.*

Displayed all around the poster and up and down the length of the locker were sympathy cards.

The memorial display stirred an anger inside Patrick. Most of these assholes didn't give a shit about his best friend. Neither one of them would be mistaken for the most popular kid in school, but Brandon was significantly less so—his short, stout stature making him an easy target for bullies. Whoever did this didn't really care about him. It was all performative bullshit.

He wanted to rip the whole fucking thing down, but he gritted his teeth and fought the urge, walking past the memorial while trying to block out the whispers.

"I didn't think he was coming back."

"My sister told me he was in a mental hospital."

"He probably was the one who killed him."

By the time he got to his locker, he was fighting tears. His hands fumbled with the combination, taking him three times to unlock it. He had just opened the door when he felt a shove from behind. It knocked him off-balance and he barely managed to brace himself on the sides before he face-planted. Whoever had pushed him didn't give him a chance to recover, as Patrick felt the back of his shirt being tugged before his attacker spun him around.

He found himself face-to-face with Cameron Gideon. They were the same age and around the same height, but Cam was more muscular and, judging by his grip, stronger. The boy's light blue eyes burned with anger as he berated his target through gritted teeth, so close that Patrick could smell the onion bagel he'd had for breakfast lingering on his breath.

"You got a lot of nerve showing your face here, Shourds. We all know what you did!"

Patrick gripped Cam's wrists and tried to pry himself free, but the other boy was too strong.

"I didn't do anything!" Patrick yelled as he struggled. "Get the hell off me!"

Cam was unmoved. "You killed Brandon and made up that bullshit story about a monster to cover it up! You're a fucking psycho! A fucking psycho with a whore mother!"

"She is not!"

Cam smirked. "Sure she is. She takes guys home from that shithole bar all the time. Everyone in town knows she's a slut. Shit, she probably doesn't even know who your father is."

"Shut the fuck up!"

"Aw, did I hit a nerve, you fucking psycho? You going to try to kill me like you killed Brandon?"

"I didn't hurt him! He was my best friend. Ask Tyler!"

Tyler was Brandon's older brother and a freshman at Smithville High School. Despite being a year older, he and Cam were tight. The mention of the elder Murphy boy's name made him laugh.

"Tyler? You should feel lucky it's me here and not him. Tyler would put you in the fucking ground! Even worse than what you did to Brandon!"

A crowd had gathered; the throng of students watching the confrontation with rapt attention. Patrick felt a desperate anger rise from the pit of his stomach. Humiliation and accusation fueled his fight-or-flight response.

"I didn't . . . Fucking . . . Do ANYTHING!" Patrick bellowed as he found the strength to shove Cam off him, sending him stumbling back as their audience parted.

Despite the force behind the push, Cam maintained his balance and positioned himself to charge. Patrick braced for the assault, but it didn't come as a booming voice interrupted the proceedings.

"What is going on here?"

The boys turned to see Principal Hendry storming toward them. The onlookers rushed away, not wanting to be part of the fracas now that an authority figure was involved.

"He shouldn't be here!" Cam said unapologetically, looking as if *he* might actually be the one to start crying. "He's a killer!"

"Enough of that talk, Mr. Gideon!" Hendry ordered, "Get to class."

Cam gave Patrick a look, letting him know this wasn't over, before picking up his books and stomping off down the hall.

Patrick was flabbergasted that the principal would just let him go like that. Hendry was young to be the head of a school, only in his late thirties. With blond hair and a chiseled jaw, the moms, and even a dad or two, were falling over themselves to get involved with the PTA.

But to his students, he was affable and approachable. That's not to say he couldn't effectively lay down discipline when he needed to, but he always came off as the type of educator one could believe in.

That's why the way he regarded Patrick right now—with an accusatory disdain—was so confusing.

"You're just letting him go?" Patrick asked incredulously. "He attacked me!"

Hendry stared at him stone-faced as if he wanted to say something to the boy his position wouldn't allow.

Patrick lowered his voice to a whisper. "I didn't do anything." It was a dual defense, both today's altercation with Cam and denying his involvement in Brandon's death.

Like Cam, the principal's reaction was cold. "You've only been back for minutes and there's already trouble around you," Hendry said. "Watch your step, Mr. Shourds. This is your first and last warning."

Patrick was stunned. He couldn't believe this was the same guy who'd always greeted him with a smile and a high-five. Did he actually believe Patrick was a murderer too?

Hendry said nothing else as he walked away, leaving Patrick in the now-empty hall as the bell sounded, signaling the start of the school day.

Patrick stood at his locker, devastated that his reception upon returning to school was even worse than he'd feared. He took several minutes to compose himself, gathering books for his first class that he was already late for. When he had what he needed, he shut his locker, letting out a startled yelp and dropping his books when he saw Brandon, his broken body having been hidden by the door.

The ghost kept its clouded eyes on Patrick as he bent down to retrieve his things, maintaining contact until he was back upright.

Patrick sighed heavily. "Any chance you want to tell them it wasn't me?"

The specter remained silent as ever.

"Didn't think so."

Chapter 8

September 2025

Patrick's mother had worked at Parkhill's for his entire life, as far as he knew. Yet he only just set foot in it for the first time at thirty-three years old.

The bar and grill looked pretty much as he expected. It wasn't going to be mistaken for a Michelin-rated fine dining establishment, but it was clean, and judging by the redolence of grilled meat in the air, probably had a decent burger.

A polished oak bar gleamed under pendant lights, reflecting off rows of pint glasses lined in front of a variety of liquor bottles on stepped shelves. Two taps, each containing eight spouts offering a variety of draft beers, framed each end. The iron stools were topped with shiny, maroon leather upholstery, free of blemishes or rips. A row of televisions played a selection of sporting events and national news networks.

The place had a sparse crowd, even for a Tuesday. No one was seated at the bar and only about a quarter of the tables were occupied. The few patrons engaged in conversations that were lively but not rowdy, and the soundtrack of classic rock tunes was at the perfect volume so as not to be overwhelmed by—or to overwhelm—the diners, even if the place got closer to capacity.

The way his mother kept him from coming here, Patrick would have thought it was a hovel, but the place was actually quite nice.

"Grab any open table or a seat at the bar," a friendly male voice called from the left.

The bartender was a man in his forties with a warm, inviting smile that crinkled the corners of his eyes. The lighting, though soft, caught the enthusiasm he seemed to exude. His close-cropped hair and clean-shaven face gave him an air of professionalism. He wore a black polo in the same style as Cindy's.

But while hers was old and faded, his was relatively new. Plus, the lettering looked to be a different font in a more vibrant shade of gold. They must have updated it at some point, prompting Patrick's realization that he didn't actually know when his mother had stopped working there.

He nodded and took a seat at the center of the bar, leaving plenty of space on either side. The bartender approached, placing a black cocktail napkin with the pub's logo and a laminated menu in front of Patrick.

"What can I get you, friend?"

"I'll have a Stella and a Black and Bleu Burger, well done, with bacon."

"Man knows what he likes. I'll put that right in for you."

The bartender shuffled over to the double doors with

circular windows toward the rear of the establishment. He pushed one open and shouted, "Order up, Teddy! Black and Bleu, well done with bacon!"

With the order placed, he grabbed a clean pint glass and poured a damn near perfect Stella Artois with only a small crown of foam. He placed the drink in front of his new patron. "Sorry, a little short-staffed and the one waitress I have on for tonight is late. Again."

"Business slow?" Patrick asked

A little of the bartender's enthusiasm faded at the question.

"Yeah, but could be worse," he admitted. "Lots of places in Leeds Point are struggling right now. I'm lucky we're on the highway. Gets us a lot of travelers passing through. Keeps us afloat even if I'm not buying a yacht anytime soon."

"Hopefully, things get better for you so you can get one," Patrick said, raising his glass before taking a sip, enjoying the cool sensation of the slightly bitter liquid.

Before he could ask about his mother, the front door opened, prompting a brief expression of relief from the bartender before it quickly vanished.

The new arrival was a thin man who looked to be in his thirties dressed in casual attire and a Philadelphia Phillies baseball cap. A table full of men around the same age nestled in the corner got his attention. He dipped his chin, acknowledging them as he moved to join their party.

"Where the hell is she?" the bartender muttered, stealing a glance at his watch.

Patrick barely registered what the man was saying

because something else caught his eye when he looked toward the entrance. A frame hung on the wall. Encased within was a sketch on aged, yellowed paper. The drawing was a crude, but fairly accurate depiction of the thing that had started his nightmares two decades prior. Three jagged tears ran the length from the top right corner to the bottom left.

"You familiar with the Jersey Devil?"

"Huh?" Patrick asked, taking a second to register that the bartender was talking.

"The Jersey Devil," he repeated, nodding in the picture's direction. "You heard of it?"

I wish I fucking hadn't, Patrick thought.

"Yeah," he replied, taking a bigger gulp of his beer. "Who hasn't?" He hoped he was playing it cool enough.

"The guy who used to own the place apparently had that drawing framed and hanging on the wall for years. Claimed it was made in the 1800s."

"That's pretty old."

"No kidding." The bartender continued. "Story goes that one night, a bunch of people were in here drinking and whooping it up when that thing came bursting in the front door. Scared the shit out of everyone. But all the damn thing did was claw at the picture before flying off. Can you believe that?"

No, because if that thing actually burst in here, no one would be left alive.

"I guess anything's possible," Patrick said before quickly changing the subject. "How about a shot of Jameson?"

The order shifted the bartender to a more jovial

mood.

He poured the shot and Patrick downed it instantly, wincing at the burn, eliciting a laugh from the bartender.

"Damn, man. You downed that like you were on a mission." He wiggled the bottle, which was still in his hand. "Want another?"

"Sure," Patrick said, pushing his glass forward. "You can't fly on just one wing."

The bartender looked like he'd just seen a ghost. Patrick regarded him curiously.

"Where did you hear that?" he asked.

"Sometimes my mom would drink too much, but then still go for another," Patrick explained. "When I would ask why she needed more, she'd say, 'You can't fly on just one wing.' Never mind the fact that it was five or six wings at that point." He paused before asking, "That mean something to you?"

"Yeah," the bartender replied. "That was something my stepdad, Ed, used to say back when he owned this place.

"That makes sense because my mom used to work here."

"No kidding? Who was your mom?"

"Cindy Shourds."

The bartender thought about it for a moment before he was able to place her.

"Oh yeah," he said. "I remember her. Nice lady. How's she doing?"

"She passed away a couple days ago."

"Oh man," the bartender said with genuine sympathy. "I'm so sorry to hear that . . ." he trailed off in the form of a question, prompting an introduction.

"Patrick," he offered. "Patrick Shourds."

"Chris Boland," the bartender said, wiping his hand and extending it.

Patrick accepted. "Good to meet you, Chris."

"You too. Ed passed about six years ago and I inherited the business. Never saw myself as a bar owner, so we shut down for a few months while I sorted things out. I *think* your mom may have still been working here when he died, but a lot of the old staff didn't come back when we reopened. I offered everyone their jobs back, but I guess most figured it wouldn't be the same without Ed. Feels like I've been short-staffed ever since."

He grabbed an extra shot glass and poured two, one for Patrick and one for himself, raising it to his guest.

"To Cindy."

"To Ed," Patrick said in return.

The men tapped glasses and downed the shots. Chris collected the glassware and deposited both in the sink.

"I'll check on that burger for you." Then he muttered under his breath, "Looks like I'm on my own tonight."

As if on cue, the front door opened and Chris eagerly looked up, anticipating reinforcements. Judging from his expression, that wasn't what he got. Whoever it was caught damn near everyone's attention because most conversations stopped midsentence, leaving Santana and Rob Thomas's "Smooth" as the only background noise.

Patrick turned to see who had caught the room's attention. He understood why instantly.

Caterina, his uncle's exchange student-turned-home health aide, had entered the bar dressed to kill. While the beautiful woman would no doubt turn heads in most scenarios, her attire especially stood out in Parkhill's casual atmosphere.

She wore a silky, black, spaghetti strap dress. In a way, it was a simple garment, designed to place the focus on the wearer's assets rather than the article itself. The bodice accentuated her bust, even though no enhancement was necessary, and cascaded into tiered ruffles that barely extended to mid-thigh, swirling around her tanned legs.

She smiled at Patrick when she saw him at the bar, her ruby red lipstick framing her perfectly white teeth. Her makeup was more pronounced than what she'd been wearing at the Lumley residence, but still managed subtlety, her natural beauty evident underneath. Before Chris could offer her a table or seat at the bar as he'd done with Patrick, she was already on her way over to them.

With the gorgeous new arrival's destination clear, the rest of the room resumed their conversation. Patrick half expected her to take a seat farther down the empty bar, but she sat on the stool directly next to him, already seated when she asked, "Do you mind?"

"Not at all," Patrick said. He didn't mind, but his brain screamed at him that she was trouble.

He knew she was. Caterina was stunning, no doubt, but she worked for his aunt and uncle who he was very much trying to keep at arm's length while in Leeds Point. Still, he didn't plan to be here very long and a little company other than his ghosts wouldn't be the worst thing. Especially company as sexy as Caterina.

His internal debate was interrupted as Chris placed a cocktail napkin in front of her along with a menu, asking, "What can I get you?"

"I want a VO Manhattan. Extra cherries." She pushed the menu back toward the bartender. "No food."

Chris nodded and went to work on her cocktail while she engaged Patrick.

"How long are you staying in Leeds Point?"

"Just for the funeral and to get the ball rolling on the estate. Hope to be out of here by next week."

"Back to Chicago?"

Christ, Aunt Vivian had a big mouth.

"How long have you been in New Jersey?"

Caterina smirked at Patrick's lack of subtlety in changing the subject.

"Six years, she replied. "I came over in the third year of my laurea triennale."

"Is that like your version of college?"

"Sì. The laurea triennale would be like your bachelor's degree. Only we do it in three years instead of four." She punctuated the last sentence with a wink. "When I had the opportunity to come to America, I jumped at the chance. Your aunt and uncle were very kind to host me. They even helped me through nursing school when I decided to stay."

"That's very . . . generous . . . of them.

"Why do you say it like that?"

Because the cheap bastards never lifted a finger to

help when Mom was struggling, he thought.

"No reason," he replied, taking another healthy swig of his beer. Chris came over and placed the Manhattan in front of Caterina, providing a welcome interruption.

"Can I get you anything else?" he asked.

Caterina shook her head while keeping her gaze locked on Patrick. "No, thank you," she said. "I have everything I need."

Chris read the room and pushed the flap up to exit the bar to check on the tables. Patrick observed the hinge worked perfectly fine, but still reminded him of the times it attacked his mother. At least based on what she'd told him.

"To your mother," Caterina said, raising her drink with care not to let it spill out of the conical glass. Patrick raised his own, bringing it 90 percent of the way to gently clink hers.

They each took a sip, with Patrick downing the rest of his beer. Caterina gently placed hers on the bar and licked her upper lip. She plucked one of the three cherries by the stem and opened her mouth, sticking her tongue out ever so slightly to draw in the fruit before severing it at the stem with her teeth.

Patrick cocked a suspicious brow.

"Let me guess," he said wryly, "you're going to tie the stem in a knot with your tongue?"

Caterina played it coy. "Why would I do that?"

"It's the next logical step, the way you're flirting with me."

"What makes you think I'm flirting with you?"

Patrick waved to Chris and pointed to his empty

glass. The bartender, who had been professionally keeping his distance, grabbed a fresh pint to fill as Patrick answered, "Because I have eyes and ears, Caterina."

That made her laugh. Patrick joined in too.

"You're a very direct man," she noted. "Doesn't seem like you're big on games."

"Depends on the rules."

"I prefer to make them up as I go," she said, placing her hand on his thigh.

The broken touch barrier ended up being the first in a convergence of events. Chris brought the fresh beer over, swapping out the empty glass. As he did, the front door opened again, a female voice accompanying it.

"Sorry, Chris! I know, I know!"

This time, the bartender's expression was a mix of relief and irritation. Mostly the former. He addressed the new arrival, his voice laced with sarcasm as he pointed at his watch, "Thanks for showing up, Megan."

The sound of that name hit Patrick like a freight train.

Chapter 9

October 2005

Patrick stepped into the courtyard at Smithville High School. Students were permitted to eat their lunches outside during the warmer months, and it being early October, the weather was still mild enough to accommodate it. He had tried to get out early so he'd have a chance to grab a seat at an unoccupied picnic table, but with freshman lockers being on the far end of the building, he had no shot at making it on time.

The tables were all filled with classmates who, only a month into the school year, had already cliqued up. Seeing as there wasn't a kids-everyone-thought-killed-their-best-friend group, Patrick was on his own. He exhaled deeply and scoped out an area against the fence just past the basketball court. Hopefully, it was isolated enough for him to eat in peace.

He hurried over and took his spot, reaching in and grabbing the peanut butter and jelly sandwich his mom had packed him, stretching the limits of her culinary ability to do so. Still, he was thankful she made the effort, allowing him to avoid the lunch line. He took a bite and leaned his head back against the chain-link fence.

High school was pretty much going how he had expected.

After gritting through the last few weeks of eighth grade, Patrick spent much of the summer in his room. His mother had tried to get him out to help him socialize, offering to take him to the community center pool, but he refused. If Brandon were alive, they'd have gone just about every day, but without him, he knew he'd continue to be the target of suspicious glances and accusatory sneers.

Cindy had forced him to go to the movies one time, taking him to see *Fantastic Four*, a film he would've found lame even if he wasn't depressed. After the movie and suffering through a silent meal at TGI Friday's, she didn't press him anymore about going out, even though she let him know the offer was always open.

So he embraced solitude when he'd normally be out of the house from sunrise to sundown. But he wasn't totally alone. His mom was home when she wasn't working and did her best to spend time with him while not pushing him to do anything outside of his comfort zone. And he had Brandon. He didn't see the rotting specter every day, but at least a few times a week. Patrick gave up on the thing ever talking to him. It would usually just stand there and stare at him. It didn't attack, didn't even look like it was judging him. Mostly, it just looked sad—and more for Patrick than for itself.

The woman in the old-time garb showed up a few times, too, though not as frequently as Brandon's ghost. She would materialize at night, always on the edge of the woods, pacing back and forth. While Patrick had somehow gotten used to the phantom in the shape of his best friend, the colonial woman never failed to stir a sense of dread, especially when the surrounding trees shifted into dark, dead variations of themselves while blotting out the night sky, no matter how bright the moon. It was as if she brought twisted doppelgangers from an alternate dimension. On the nights she appeared, he would huddle in fear before crashing into a tense, restless sleep. In the morning, she would be gone and he would spend the next day completely exhausted.

When it came time to start his high school experience, Patrick didn't argue or beg to be homeschooled. He knew he was going to have to power through. A small, naïve part of him thought maybe his incoming freshman class would have largely forgotten about him by now, and those who hadn't would be lost in the sea of upperclassmen.

No such luck.

Patrick had made it through his first morning of high school without incident. However, as he searched for a place to sit in the cafeteria, he didn't see the attack coming.

Someone had come up behind him and slapped his tray, sending his hot dog, yogurt, bag of Doritos, and bottle of water crashing to the floor. The yogurt container splattered his sneakers and the cuffs of his jeans. While Patrick was recovering from the shock, he felt himself being turned and came face-to-face with Tyler Murphy, Brandon's older brother. It was the first time he'd seen anyone from Brandon's family since before the incident.

Tyler was a year older than Patrick and Brandon and had always been pretty cool with his brother and his best friend. They were Irish Twins, being less than a year apart in age. It wasn't uncommon for Tyler to spend time with the duo playing video games, messing around in the woods, and even going with them on one of those trips to see *Revenge of the Sith.* Until a few months ago, Patrick thought of him like his own older brother. But now, seeing the rage burn in his eyes, he knew Tyler didn't reciprocate that sentiment.

He was flanked by an unwelcome reminder of his middle school days in the form of Cam Gideon. While Tyler was clearly driven by fury, Cam's expression was one of disdain.

Tyler's body was tensed and his jaw clenched, looking like he wanted to beat Patrick into the ground. The younger boy braced himself, but no attack came as Tyler continued to stare, his eyes reddening as wetness pooled at their base. He was angry, but it was an anger born of unimaginable loss. If he just knew that Patrick felt the same way, then they could grieve together. But

Tyler was in no mood to commiserate.

"What did you do to my brother?"

"Nothing," Patrick said, his voice barely above a whisper.

"What did you fucking do to him?" Tyler screamed, blood rushing to his reddening face, emphasizing the veins that bulged in anger.

"I didn't hurt him, Tyler! It was . . . it was . . ."

"I swear to God, if you say the Leeds Devil, I'll fucking beat your ass, you little bitch," Cam chimed in. Tyler shot his friend a look for the audacity to get involved, taking the wind out of the bully's sails.

"I didn't hurt him, Tyler. I swear to God."

Tyler stepped forward. He was a few inches taller than Patrick, so he had to look down to get eye to eye, addressing the smaller boy with a menacing glare.

"I'm going to make your life a living hell until you admit what you did. You're going to regret the pain you caused my family."

Patrick opened his mouth, then stopped. It was futile. Tyler, Cam, every fucking student here. None of them would ever accept that he had nothing to do with Brandon's death. If things were this hostile on day one, how the hell was he going to do this for four years?

"Is there a problem here?"

A heavyset woman in her sixties with gray hair tied in a tight bun approached them. The card held by the lanyard draped around her neck read *Mrs. Rhodes*, clearly a faculty member assigned to supervise this lunch period.

Tyler continued to stare daggers at Patrick, months

of mourning and anger superseding any concern about the presence of an authority figure. Cam looked a little more nervous but kept his mouth shut out of fear of his friend.

Patrick was the one who answered, "No, ma'am. I dropped my tray and Tyler and Cam were checking to see if I was okay."

She didn't seem to buy it but clearly wasn't in the mood for this on the first day of school.

"Clean up and get something else to eat. You can't just stand here blocking everyone."

"Yes, ma'am," Patrick said, bending down to gather his toppled lunch.

Mrs. Rhodes walked away, and Tyler bent down to help. The gesture wasn't benevolent because he whispered in Patrick's ear, "You're going to pay for what you did to my brother."

Patrick got back to his feet, and Tyler stood with him. Just as he righted himself, Tyler slapped the tray again, this time from underneath, sending the contents onto Patrick's chest, the yogurt spattering his dark blue T-shirt. He didn't say another word as he walked away. Cam followed, getting in one last dig.

"Now it looks like one of your mom's shirts."

That was day one of high school for Patrick. Tyler and Cam, along with their growing friend group, accosted him every chance they got, usually accusations of Patrick killing Brandon and obscene comments about his mother. Nothing had gotten physical since that initial encounter, but sometimes that felt even worse. Like they were using the anticipation of a future beating as a method of psychological torture. But that may be giving them too much credit. They probably didn't want to risk getting in trouble.

He uncapped his water bottle and took a swig before capping it again. As he set it down, he was shocked to see a girl coming his way across the basketball court holding a lunch tray.

She had an alternative style. Her hair was cut just above her shoulders and was as dark as a raven's feathers. Probably dyed that way. She wore dark, dramatic eyeshadow that contrasted with her jade green eyes. A small hoop in her nose glinted in the sunlight, surprising Patrick since she looked to be his age and fourteen was too young to legally get your nose pierced. Probably a clip-on. She wore dark, ripped jeans and a black hoodie emblazoned with pink skulls.

As she passed the threshold of the court, he recognized her. It was Megan Alberts, the sheriff's daughter. He hadn't seen her since middle school ended, but she had undergone quite the transformation. Patrick remembered her hair being a similar shade of brown as her father's, so it was definitely dyed. And there was *no way* uptight Sheriff Alberts would allow her to pierce her nose. Not to mention that her style was more Hello Kitty than goth. She looked like a totally different girl.

Whoever she was now, she must not have known Patrick because she sat down next to him, crisscrossing her legs with a tray over her lap. Without even acknowledging him, she took a bite of the square monstrosity that passed for pizza there at Smithville High, followed by a sip of Cherry Coke.

"Why are you sitting here?" Patrick asked, hoping it didn't come off as rude as it sounded to him.

"You look all mopey," Megan said through a mouthful of pizza. "It's bumming me out."

"You know who I am, right?"

"Patrick, we've been in school together since kindergarten. I know who you are."

"And you're still sitting next to me?"

"Why not?"

"Ask around."

She turned to him for the first time, her expression quizzical.

"What will they tell me?"

Patrick shrugged and lied, "I don't know."

"They'll tell me you killed Brandon Murphy and ditched his body in the Pine Barrens, then blamed the whole thing on a mythical creature. Am I warm?"

"If you know, why do you ask?"

"Has anyone ever asked you what your side of the story was?"

No, Patrick thought. *No one but her dad and my mom. All the kids just assumed I had something to do with it without ever asking me.*

"You're the first one."

"So, you want to tell me?"

He considered it, but that would probably only scare away the one kid his age who'd actually spoken to him without a threat in almost six months.

"Not really."

She regarded him curiously. "Why not? Are you some kind of serial killer or something?"

"Maybe I am . . ." he said, playing along, but regretting it almost instantly.

"If you are, you have to be the worst serial killer I've ever heard of."

Patrick saw the opening and took it, unable to control the smirk that stretched his lips.

"But you *have* heard of me."

Megan smiled, wide and bright. It was antithetical to her gloomy attire.

"Holy shit! I love *Pirates of the Caribbean*! I'm a total Disney nerd!"

Patrick raised his eyebrows at that. "You look more like a metalhead."

She looked offended. "Two things can be true, Patrick. And I'm more emo than metal. I think Captain Jack Sparrow would appreciate MCR."

"What's MCR?"

"My Chemical Romance! Jesus! Have you been living under a rock? You should check out their album *Three Cheers for Sweet Revenge*. It'll probably help you through whatever you're dealing with right now."

"Maybe . . ." he said, trailing off as his mood dampened against his control once he realized he was enjoying their exchange. He knew reality would eventually slap him in the face. May as well self-sabotage. "What would your friends think if they saw you sitting with me?"

"Do I give off the vibe that I care what other people think?"

"Not really. What about your dad?"

"Maybe he sent me to get close to you. Gain your trust so he can build a case."

"Did he?" Patrick asked sarcastically.

"Of course not. And no, I don't care what these dipshits think of me. And I'm certainly not concerned with Daddy Law's opinion."

"Well, I think his opinion would be that you shouldn't talk to me."

"See? That just makes me want to talk to you more. I have ODD."

"Um . . . ODD?"

"Oppositional Defiance Disorder. It basically means I'll do the opposite of anything anyone tells me to do. It's especially annoying to my father."

Patrick mulled over their interaction for a moment. Megan was a frenetic ball of contagious energy and somehow, even her talking about his *situation* put him at an ease he hadn't felt in months. Not to mention that Patrick had always thought she was very pretty. They had never really talked beyond an occasional interaction in class, but her carefree attitude made her even more attractive to him. He had no illusions that she would be interested in someone as messed up as he was, but it was nice to have someone treat him like a human being for a change.

"Go away."

She looked offended and Patrick felt his chest tighten, thinking he had just royally fucked up. But Megan couldn't hold it in and let out a hearty laugh, slapping Patrick playfully on the shoulder.

"I like that!" she said through her residual chuckles after the laugh subsided. "Maybe you're not such a weirdo after all!"

Patrick smiled, a gesture that seemed almost foreign to him by now. It faded when he saw Brandon staring at them from across the court. He'd be almost perfectly in line with center court were it not for his twisted spine.

"Don't be so sure."

"What'd you think?" Megan asked eagerly as Patrick handed her iPod back to her.

They were walking home from school and she insisted he had to listen to the song "Until the Day I Die" by Story of the Year. Patrick had never been too into music outside of movie soundtracks and he'd certainly never heard anything like this. From the muted intro to the explosive guitar riffs underscoring a combination of clean and screaming vocals, it really took him on a journey. Maybe this emo music was for him!

"It was . . ." he started, trying to think of the right words. "Wow. I never really heard anything like that. It was awesome!"

Megan squealed with delight. Patrick found it endearingly cute.

"I knew it!" she exclaimed as she scrolled through her music library. "What should I have you listen to next? Oh! Check this one out! It's called 'The Kill' by Thirty Seconds to Mars.

She handed the iPod back to him, but before he could put the earbuds in, the quick *beep boop* of a police siren startled them.

A Leeds Point Sheriff's Department SUV pulled up to the curb beside them. All the good feelings Patrick had been gathering since lunch evaporated in an instant, the police vehicle stoking the memories of the fear and sorrow that had dominated his life for the better part of this year. The weight crushed him like he was drowning in a lake with cinder blocks chained to his ankles.

The window rolled down, and Sheriff Alberts removed his sunglasses. Patrick swallowed hard when he saw just how displeased the man was at his daughter's choice of company.

"What's going on here, Megan?"

"What do you mean? I'm walking home from school." The sheriff kept his gaze locked on Patrick, letting his silence do the talking for him.

"You're being weird, Dad."

Alberts slowly shifted his focus to Megan.

"Get in."

Her face wrinkled in genuine confusion.

"I'm fine walking."

"Get in the car, Megan," Alberts repeated. His voice remained even, but his tone was insistent.

"Ugh!" Megan blurted, tossing her new friend an apologetic look.

"I'll catch you later, Patrick."

As she walked around the passenger side, the sheriff returned his glare to Patrick. His eyes countered Megan's words.

No, she won't.

Settled in the car, Megan leaned forward to see around her dad.

She gave Patrick a smile and a wave. As Alberts pulled back onto the road, he rolled the window back up, leaving Patrick once again dejected and alone.

Just after six p.m., Patrick was sitting at his computer listening to "Helena" by My Chemical Romance. He'd been on YouTube all afternoon, soaking up music by emo and alternative bands, falling more in love with the genres with each new song.

Alberts would probably never let Megan talk to him again, but he'd always be grateful to her for expanding his musical horizon.

He had just clicked play on "So Cold" by Breaking

Benjamin when he heard a knock. He froze at first, not expecting anyone. His mother was at work until midnight. Maybe she forgot her keys?

When he went to the front door and looked through the small window, he felt like his heart leaped into his throat. He opened the door to reveal a grinning Megan Alberts. She held a bag of Wise brand buttered popcorn in one hand and the familiar blue, yellow, and white DVD case bearing the *Blockbuster Video* logo.

"Hi," she said cheerily.

Patrick was happy to see her—thrilled, actually—but his return greeting was more skeptical.

"Uh, hi," he said. "What are you doing here?

"Don't you mean, 'Hi, Megan! Come on in!'?"

He'd only talked to this girl in any meaningful way for the first time that afternoon but, man, did she already have a way of throwing him for a loop.

"Sorry," he said. "Hi. Come in."

"See? I knew that was what you meant."

She stepped past him into the house and surveyed the environment.

"Cute place. Just you and your mom?"

"Yeah," he answered before redirecting. "Does your dad know you're here?"

"Ha! No way! He didn't outright say it, but he *does not* want me hanging out with you!"

"So, you came here anyway?"

She plopped down on the couch, setting the DVD and bag of popcorn on the coffee table.

"Remember . . . ODD," she said with a wink. "If he keeps it up, we may as well start wedding planning!"

Patrick felt heat radiate across his cheeks and hoped they weren't as red as they felt. Meagan's giggle confirmed they were.

"Aw! You're cute when you blush!"

"I'm not!" Patrick protested.

"Surrrre," Megan said, drawing out the *R*. "You must be part tomato."

"What's the movie?" Patrick asked, desperately changing the subject.

Megan held up the DVD case and he saw *Pirates of the Caribbean* written on it. "You quoting it made me want to watch it again. I figured I already improved your musical taste in record time, so now I'm going to bring you into the wide, wonderful world of Disney! *Pirates* is a great gateway drug to ease you in!"

She held the DVD out to him. He hesitated, but took it, bringing it over to the player, popping it in the tray. Megan had already opened the bag of popcorn and stuffed a handful in her mouth.

"Hit the lights!" she said as Patrick made his way back over to the couch. He flicked off the overhead illumination and took a seat next to his new friend, the TV glow becoming the only light source as the sun continued its descent outside.

As Patrick sat there watching Johnny Depp do his thing on-screen, he felt like they were being watched. He hesitated to look around, not wanting Brandon or the woman—he decided to call her Helena from now on—to rear their intrusive heads. Finally, he looked around and to his relief, the living room was ghost-free.

When he turned to Megan, she wore that smirk that

was seemingly ever present.

"This ain't a date, Romeo. Eyes on the screen."

Chapter 10

September 2025

Patrick found himself lost for words. He knew there was certainly a chance he would see her again, but he just wasn't prepared in that moment. If he thought about it, he would have realized there wouldn't be a time when he was.

Megan had changed quite a bit since he had last seen her. She had grown out her hair, which was tied back in a tight ponytail. While her habit had been to dye it a variety of shades over the years, now it was closer to her natural brown, albeit with some blonde highlights. Her outfit was simple: blue jeans, sneakers, and the familiar Parkhill's polo shirt.

Judging by her expression, Patrick wasn't the only one who had been smacked in the face by a blast from the past. Those green eyes looked as if they had lost some of their spark over the years. It broke his heart knowing the role he had played in dimming it.

"Patrick . . ." she started, breaking the awkward silence. It took her a beat to formulate a follow-up. "I was so sorry to hear about your mom. I didn't know you were coming back."

Patrick could feel Caterina's stare, but Megan was the only thing in the world that could draw his attention away from the sexy Italian.

"I'm here for the funeral and to handle the estate," he said, fumbling his words like he did as an awkward fourteen-year-old the night she showed up at his door. "I'm not staying long," he added, answering an unasked question.

"Oh," Megan replied, letting another few moments of silence hang in the air. She glanced at her boss behind the bar. To Chris's credit, he didn't let his impatience interrupt the impromptu reunion. Still, she used him as her out. "It's . . . nice to see you. I gotta get to work." With that, she hurried around the bar and into the kitchen.

Curiosity was written all over Chris's face, but the man excelled at reading the room. He simply said, "Let me check on your food."

Patrick turned his attention back to Caterina, who also showed interest in his connection to the woman, but unlike the bartender, she came right out and asked, "How do you know her?"

"She's . . . an old friend."

"You seem pretty rattled by someone you just consider a *friend*."

"We were close. Best friends, in fact. I haven't seen her since I left Leeds Point."

"Well, if you two would like to catch up, I can go talk to those men over there." She pointed to the table of guys in the far corner. Some of them wore vests and pants with reflective stripes, and a few hard hats sat under the table. Patrick recognized the attire from the road crew he'd seen when the sheriff drove him into town. Needless to say, Caterina had not gone unnoticed by them. She put her hand back on Patrick's leg, giving it a subtle caress to drive her point home. "But you'll probably regret it in the morning."

Patrick's body was at war with itself. His baser instincts told him to focus on the beautiful woman in front of him, who lacked any type of subtlety in conveying her intentions. His heart screamed at him to go talk to Megan, to tell her everything. While his brain said he shouldn't involve himself with either. That he should focus on the task at hand and get back to Chicago ASAP.

Chris came back from the kitchen, providing a welcome interruption. The bartender placed a plate in front of Patrick. On it was the burger he had ordered, thick and juicy with melted bleu cheese spilling out from under the toasted bun. A silver cone stuffed with hand-cut french fries sat to the side next to a dipping container filled with ketchup.

"Here you go, bud," Chris said. "Can I get you another?" he asked Caterina. Patrick hadn't even noticed that she was downing the rest of her Manhattan.

Caterina ignored him and focused on Patrick. "Are you going to be a gentleman and buy me a round?" she asked, irritation slipping into her tone.

"Sure," Patrick agreed. "Another Manhattan for the lady, please." Back to Caterina, he asked, "Extra cherries?"

"Of course," she replied, the iciness unmistakable. "Where's your restroom?"

"Back and to the left," Chris said, pointing toward the table with the road crew.

"I'll be back in a minute," she told Patrick before sauntering off to the back, sending the table full of men into awed silence as she passed.

"You got a way with the ladies," Chris whispered, even though she was out of earshot.

Patrick laughed and took a bite of his burger. "I got a way of getting myself into trouble," he said through a mouthful of grilled meat. "This is a damn good burger, by the way."

"Thanks," Chris replied. "Kept all the old recipes once Ed passed. If it ain't broke, don't fix it, ya know?"

"I build houses for a living. Believe me, I know."

"So how do you know Megan?"

"We went to high school together."

"Did you guys date?" Patrick supposed Chris wasn't always great at reading the room after all. Chris must have seen Patrick's expression because he put his hands up. "Didn't mean anything by it. You both just seemed a little shocked to see each other. I'm just trying to make sure my customers and employees are comfortable, is all."

"It's complicated," Patrick said, "But we're good. Nothing that's going to cause you any trouble."

As he said that, Megan came out from the back, actively trying not to look in Patrick's direction. She went to the touch screen in the opposite corner and tapped it a few times before grabbing an order pad and heading over to check on the workers.

"Flag me down if you need anything else," Chris told Patrick before getting to work on Caterina's next drink. He swapped the full glass for the empty one before heading back into the kitchen.

Alone for the first time since he walked in, Patrick focused on eating. The burger really was good. He wasn't just blowing smoke. But the food provided little distraction from the tidal wave of thoughts and emotions flooding through his body. He had known that seeing Megan was always a possibility. Shit, in a town as small as Leeds Point, it was practically an inevitability. But he really didn't expect to see her here, of all places.

"You clear your head?" Caterina's sultry voice asked as she came back around, brushing her hand across his shoulder, lightly raking it with her perfectly manicured nails.

Patrick resolved to focus on the woman in front of him. A beautiful distraction while in town was one thing. Opening up old wounds with Megan would cause far too many problems for both of them. Closure was overrated anyway. Of course, the universe has a way of forcing you into situations, whether or not you want to get involved.

Just as Patrick started to ask Caterina about her home in Italy, he heard Megan raise her voice.

"Fuck off, Zach!"

Patrick and Caterina turned toward the commotion. He saw Megan wrench her wrist away from the guy in the Phillies cap while the road crew snickered.

"C'mon, Meg," he said in a drawn-out mock plea with a bit of a slur, "give me another chance. We had fun, didn't we?"

"Nah. I'm good, Zach," Megan rebuffed with a sneer. "Why don't you just order?"

"If I recall, you liked it when I gave you orders."

The workers found that one hilarious and erupted into laughter, with some men slapping the table in emphasis.

"I liked when you left so I could finish myself off properly," she shot back. "Shit, I added two extra *Z*'s in front of your name in my phone, you were so fucking boring."

Patrick felt an odd twinge of jealousy at the thought of Megan sleeping with someone else—not that he was in any position to pass judgment—but as much as he hated the idea of her being with that clown, he was happy to see she still had a bit of that old fire in her. The table found her witticism even funnier. The clapback dialed up their amusement to a riotous level. One of the guys reared back so hard, it looked like he was going to fall out of his chair.

"Fucking bitch," Zach muttered as he slapped the order pad out of Megan's hands.

Patrick felt his face flush, not unlike that day she made the crack about them getting married to defy her father. But this time, it wasn't out of bashfulness. The red in his cheeks bled into his vision as well. By the time Caterina asked, "What are you doing?" he was already halfway across the room.

A guy at the far end of the table saw him first.

"Hey, Zach!" he called to his friend. "Look at this fucking guy."

They turned to see who he was talking about. Megan's eyes widened as Zach's narrowed.

"You got a problem, bro?" Zach asked.

"Patrick . . ." Megan said, putting her hand up to stop him.

"He a friend of yours, Meg?"

Patrick stepped up to Zach, close enough that he could smell the Miller High Life mingled with the lingering odor of tobacco on his breath.

"What did you call her?" Patrick asked, jaw clenched and fists balled.

"What's it your business what I call my girl?" Zach asked as he shoved Patrick, pushing him back.

"I'm not *your* girl, you fucking prick!" Meg interjected as she put her hand on Patrick's chest, blocking him from retaliating. Even under the circumstances, feeling her touch was electric. "Patrick, it's okay. He's harmless."

Zach looked as if he were getting ready to make a crack, but a sudden realization hit him. He tilted his head, sizing Patrick up, a wicked smile forming.

"Patrick? Shourds?" Zach asked. Megan glanced up, eyes pleading with Patrick to just walk away as the man continued to taunt him. "Yeah. I remember you. You're that fucking psycho. You come back to Leeds Point to finish the job? How many people did you kill?"

Patrick stood fast. He would have to push Megan aside to get to the prick, and he didn't want to do that.

"Let me ask you this, *Zach*," he said, placing extra

emphasis on the man's name. "If I did what you think I did, wouldn't it be in your best interests to watch your fucking mouth? And I certainly would think twice about putting your hands on me again."

Zach's smile dropped. He tried to maintain a façade of toughness, but Patrick could see apprehension creep across his face. His beer muscles may have put him in the path of somebody dangerous. He was regretting the decision but had also come too far to back down. Patrick could see the calculus going on in his head, determining if he should back down at the risk of looking like a coward in front of Megan and his friends.

"What the hell is going on here?" Chris asked as he shoved himself between the men, extending his arms to create separation, his friendly demeanor replaced with a no-nonsense, stone-faced look.

"He was harassing Megan," Patrick said without hesitation.

Chris looked at Megan. She stayed quiet, but he knew. He turned to Zach and pointed to the door. "Get the hell out of here, Zach."

"I didn't do shit!" Zach protested. "You're going to listen to *him*? Do you know who he is? What he did?"

"I know what *you've* done in my bar before and I've warned you one too many times. Get out and don't come back. You're banned."

Zach stared daggers at Patrick, fear forgotten and replaced with false bravado. It didn't intimidate him, so he turned his focus to Megan.

"You two fucking psychos deserve each other," he spat. "You guys coming?" he asked his friends.

The table didn't rush to answer as Zach searched each of them for support. Their hesitation told Patrick all he needed to know about Megan's belligerent former fling. Finally, one guy still wearing his road crew gear answered, "We still got food coming. We'll catch up with you later."

Zach couldn't believe it. His jaw practically hit the floor when no one showed any solidarity. Finally, he threw his hands up and exhaled dramatically.

"Fuck you guys!" he shouted as he stormed out of the bar.

With the instigator gone, Chris focused on Patrick.

"Do I have to worry about you causing trouble in here?"

Patrick shook his head and reached into his pocket, retrieving his wallet and pulling out a hundred-dollar bill. He handed it to Chris.

"No trouble. Thanks for having me. Keep the change." He didn't give Chris the chance to protest as he walked away, pausing only to tell Caterina, "Have a good evening," while keeping his pace toward the door, not even stopping to see the stunned expression on the woman's face.

He stepped outside, half expecting Zach to be waiting for him, but there was no sign of the drunken asshole. His mom's car was parked around the side of the building, so he started toward it when he heard a woman calling his name, stopping him in his tracks.

"Patrick!"

He turned and saw Megan approaching him, looking pissed.

"What the hell was that?" she asked.

"What was what?" he countered, knowing damn well what she meant.

"I haven't seen or heard from you in *sixteen years*. Sixteen fucking years, Patrick! Now you want to come act like my knight in shining armor?"

"No one else was sticking up for you," he said. "Those guys—"

"I deal with drunk idiots all the time. I can stick up for myself."

"Fine, Megan," Patrick acknowledged, holding his hands up in a gesture of surrender. "I'm sorry I got involved."

Megan's eyes went up to the right, looking at his tatted left arm. The anger drained, and she let out a small, incredulous huff. He could see tears pooling in the corners of her eyes.

"Nice goose tattoo," she said in a venomous tone. "What's the story behind that one?"

Patrick put his arms down, hiding the ink from her view.

"Megan, I . . ."

"Save it," she said, not even giving him the chance to respond as she stomped back inside, getting one last word in before she disappeared behind the doors. "Asshole."

Chapter 11

Patrick's heart continued to beat out of his chest as he pulled into the driveway of his mother's home. This was a man who had seen a monster fly away with his best friend and lived with him and other ghosts throughout the years. He'd become numb to horrors the average person couldn't fathom and never allowed himself to get attached to anyone or anything. Yet, ten minutes of being back in Megan Alberts's presence dug up a cache of emotions that had been buried so deep for so long, he'd forgotten he was capable of them.

He had been reticent to get involved with Caterina and she would have been nothing more than a quick fling. Megan was something else entirely. If anything could keep him in Leeds Point . . .

Patrick pushed the thoughts out of his mind. He knew staying wasn't an option. Besides, her reaction to seeing him again wasn't exactly enthusiastic. The wave of longing and regret subsided, temporarily replaced by anger and resentment.

Why the fuck is she still here? Why are any of these

people, with that thing in the woods? I can't be the only one who's ever encountered it. All the sightings reported over the years, the shows, the movies, and goddamn podcasts. Why am I the only one who's ever seen it kill up close? How did I become the fucking chosen one?

He slammed his palm against the top of the steering wheel, the sting sharp and instant. A slow learner at times, he smacked it again and again, each time harder than the last, until his palm was too numb to sting anymore. Despite the horrors he'd seen throughout his life, Patrick was usually even-keeled. At the urging of his mother, he'd seen a psychiatrist for years and been prescribed multiple SSRIs and SNRIs to deal with his *hallucinations* and *false memory*. Not that he ever took them. Cindy trusted him, and even though he felt bad for deceiving her, those pills always ended up in the toilet. He knew he wasn't crazy and he didn't care what his shrink, the sheriff, or anyone else thought.

If they want to risk their lives by living in this goddamned town, that's on them.

He took a deep breath, calming himself before getting out of the car. As he approached the door, he noticed a plain white envelope sticking out of the small black mailbox affixed to the side.

Pulling the parcel out, he saw there was a logo in script lettering in the upper left corner. It read *Casa Bella Developers*. Despite this, there was no address or postage. It had been hand-delivered.

Inside was a folded piece of letter-sized paper and a business card bearing the same logo with the name

Peter Savila, President & CEO along with contact information. Savila. That was the guy Vivian had unceremoniously expelled from her home earlier that day.

Patrick unfolded the letter and read the simple handwritten note:

I'm very interested in acquiring this property. If you're looking to sell, I've enclosed my card. I'm prepared to make a cash offer.

Perfect! Patrick wanted to unload the place quickly. He'd been in construction long enough to know that cash offers were almost always lowball, but he didn't care about making money. All he wanted was to be free of all ties to Leeds Point as soon as possible. He'd call Savila first thing in the morning.

Patrick opened the door, having every expectation he'd see Brandon waiting for him, but there were no ghosts inside this time. He tossed the envelope and card on the table before heading to the bathroom.

There were no ghosts waiting for him there either, and he was able to shower and brush his teeth in welcome solitude. By the time he got into bed, the exhaustion from traveling, confrontation, and reunions—both expected and not—overtook him and he was asleep in minutes.

"Patrick . . ."

Drip.

Drip.

"Patrick, honey . . ."

Drip.

Drip.

"Patrick, honey, it's time to wake up."

Patrick shot up with a gasp, the sheets falling around his waist as he released a disoriented breath. He ran a hand through his sweat-dampened hair as he got his bearings, recalling that he was back in New Jersey in his childhood room. Being there felt like a dream of its own, but the reality became clearer by the second.

He surveyed the room. The voice calling his name that had roused him was unmistakably his mother's, but it had to be a dream. None of the apparitions that made regular visits throughout his life had ever spoken to him. They never did much beyond staring. Besides, he imagined a spirit's voice would sound more ethereal. The one he'd just heard was as clear and vivid as any of the times his mom had to nudge him awake for school.

Drip.

Drip.

The sound of water caught Patrick's attention, reminding him that his mother's voice wasn't the only sound he had heard.

Easing himself out of bed, making sure he had fully regained his faculties, Patrick went to investigate. His first stop was the bathroom halfway between the two bedrooms. He checked the sink and the shower, but both faucets were closed off with no signs of leaks.

Drip.

Drip.

He backtracked toward the kitchen. While he wouldn't explicitly say he was avoiding his mother's room, he was trying to rule out other areas of the house first. The kitchen sink was also free from leakages, as were the dishwasher and refrigerator. With all other options ruled out, the bathroom in the master bedroom was the last place he could think of as the source.

Drip.

Drip.

Patrick shifted into higher alert. He wasn't exactly sure why, having long since gotten used to Brandon and Helena. Maybe it was because those two had been around for two decades, while his mother, whom he hadn't seen or spoken to for almost as long, was a new member of the ghostly group. Her being there was as unexpected as it was disquieting.

He entered the room and flipped on the light, embarrassed to admit how relieved he was that she wasn't there. He entered the master bathroom off to the right and checked all the plumbing, finding no damage. Perplexed, he listened carefully, trying to pinpoint the source.

Drip.

Drip.

He heard the sound, but couldn't ascertain where it was coming from. While focusing on his hearing, he found another sense unexpectedly stimulated. A familiar scent crept into his nostrils.

It only took a moment to place it as the Elizabeth

Arden Green Tea Scent Spray his mother wore. It was Patrick's perennial birthday and Christmas gift to her, not really ever knowing what else to buy. Thinking back, he wondered if she actually really liked it or was just playing up her enthusiasm so her son didn't feel bad. Either way, she wore it just about every day.

And right now, Patrick could smell it as clearly as if she were there with him in the bathroom. As he stepped back into the bedroom, the scent became stronger. He expected to see her, but she remained absent. The smell intensified further as he exited the bedroom into the hall. The assignment became clear: follow your nose.

So that's what he did. He tracked the augmented scent into the living room and toward the kitchen. The odor was becoming so potent that Patrick's eyes watered and stung. He didn't even think pouring out an entire bottle would produce such an overpowering fragrance, but by the time he reached the basement door, he felt like he might get sick.

He pulled it open and the smell dissipated rapidly. There was no opportunity for relief, however, as the ghost of his mother stood at the bottom of the stairs.

Cindy's expression was neutral as she stared up at her son. Patrick stood frozen, unsure how to proceed. After several moments of charged silence, he addressed her, "Mom?" The apparition remained silent. "Mom," Patrick said again, "what are you trying to tell me?"

Cindy still didn't respond verbally, but she turned and walked off to the left. Her movement spurred Patrick, who descended the stairs to go after her, flicking the wall switch as he did, flooding the cellar with light.

He turned at the bottom and saw her standing in the far corner. His mother continued to focus on him for a few more moments before she tilted her head upward. Patrick followed her eyes and saw what she was trying to show him.

The drywall ceiling was soaked through. Moisture pooled in the center, forming into droplets. Patrick watched as one formed anew, dangling precariously for a beat before hitting the concrete floor.

Drip.

Another formed in rapid succession and plopped down a split second later.

Drip.

Shit, Patrick thought. *The culprit must be up there.*

He would need to fix that ASAP, especially if he was going to sell the house. Even an expedited cash closing would still require the house to pass inspection.

Patrick took his eyes off his mother long enough to locate the valve to the water supply and turn it off. He could always put it back on temporarily to shower and use the sink as needed. Next, he grabbed a large bucket placed next to some wire shelving on the other side. He hurried to retrieve it, planning to place it under the leak. While that would keep the floor dry, it wouldn't stop the annoying dripping, so he emptied a cardboard box in the corner before searching the shelves. He located a roll of duct tape. That would do just fine temporarily.

With the proper items to resolve the problem, at least for now, Patrick returned to the area. He wasn't even surprised to find his mother was gone.

He went to work, using a generous amount of tape to secure the flattened cardboard to the affected area to stem the slow drip. At least for the time being, so he could get a decent rest. He'd fix it properly tomorrow. When he was done, another drop of water hit the ground. Only this time, it wasn't from the faulty plumbing.

Patrick wiped away the next tear before it could fall, but he ended up in a losing battle as he felt a cramp in his abdomen before it warmed over. The sensation spread throughout his body and soon his legs shook. He stumbled back against the wall and slid down.

He was halfway to the floor when the dam broke and emotion overwhelmed him. Patrick could not remember crying a single time since the day Sheriff Alberts told him Brandon was dead. He'd spent his entire adult life running from his past, but tonight, everything caught up.

Brandon. Mom. Megan. For the first time in a long time, Patrick Shourds was acutely aware of everything he'd lost. Of the life he'd once had and the chance at the life he could have.

In the solitude of his mother's basement, he sobbed, mourning them both.

Chapter 12

"Fucking bitch," Zach Torres grumbled under his breath, despite being very much alone as he walked the shoulder of the county road leading toward his house. It was a little after ten p.m. and traffic was practically nonexistent. This wasn't a road like the Turnpike or Parkway, where there was always at least some traffic no matter what time of day. At this hour, it wasn't unusual to go long stretches without seeing a vehicle.

Kenny had dropped him at the bar on his way home. He didn't stay because he had a new baby at home and Darla would hand him his ass if he went out drinking till all hours of the night. Of course, those disloyal, worthless sons of bitches he worked with couldn't be bothered to show any kind of solidarity and walk out with him. They just let that asshole Boland toss him out of the only decent bar in town. It wasn't his fault that Meg's psycho ex-boyfriend was back in town.

Fuck her. If that's the kind of dude she's into, he can fucking have her. He remembered Shourds from high school. He was a year younger, but he heard all about him when he got to Smithville High. The nut job had killed his friend out in the woods when they were thirteen and he hid the body, so no one ever found it and couldn't pin anything on him. Zach couldn't believe it at first. He looked like a normal kid, but what do they say? It's always the ones you least suspect.

What he had done senior year . . . Jesus. He didn't even want to think about it. Everyone knew it was him, even if the cops still didn't have enough evidence to charge him.

What the hell is he doing back here? Zach thought. *Probably here to finish the job. Meg wants to fuck around with him, that's her funeral.*

It was that time of year in New Jersey when the days were hot, but the nights got significantly cooler. The wind whistling through the pines and slapping Zach in the face didn't help relieve the cold that was spreading throughout his body. He had planned to walk no farther than from Kenny's car to the pub, then from the vehicle belonging to whoever gave him a ride home to the small house where he still lived with his dad.

Raul Torres had worked the same road crew as his son. In fact, it was Raul who got Zach the job. Zach knew his dad wanted more for him, but the boy liked booze and chasing girls. He was never one to take his education seriously. When he asked his dad what was wrong with working manual labor, seeing as the elder Torres had done so his entire life, his father had told him, *Nothing at all. It's honest work. But I did it because it was what was available to me so I could support my family. You do it just to drink and smoke your way through till the next pay period. Seek something more from life, son.*

Yeah. And what did all that hard work get his father? It got him paralyzed from the waist down when some asshole veered off the road texting while driving. Now Dad was in a wheelchair and living off disability while Zach covered the difference in their ever-mounting expenses. Mom had died of a heart attack last year, so it was just the two of them.

It wasn't just the bills. The work had been drying up the past couple of years and shifts were getting harder to come by. There wasn't much work elsewhere in town either. Even for folks who went to college.

So, yeah, it didn't matter how Zach had spent his life up to this point. He was stuck in this shithole town same as everyone else, whether they went to college or not. And with Dad in the condition he was and Zach having no love life to speak of, it didn't look like that was going to change anytime soon.

Zach's personal pity party was interrupted by the snapping of a twig. It sounded close. He turned and peered into the darkness, posture tightening. It was probably a deer. Damn things were a menace on this road. His crew had scraped more splattered venison off the asphalt than he thought possible in a lifetime.

Another *snap*, followed by a rustle of leaves. Zach still couldn't see anything, but he felt something. A presence. He couldn't pinpoint exactly what, but it felt *big.*

"Hello?" he called into the darkness, his voice shaky. "Someone there?"

The woods fell silent, even though he still felt as if he were being watched. Whatever was hiding in the darkness was still there. It just wasn't moving.

Zach took a tentative step forward, cringing when he heard the *snap* of the twig he stepped on himself. He froze, remaining still for nearly a minute, scared to move for fear something would snatch him from the darkness. He pulled his phone from his pocket and turned on the flashlight, pointing it toward the trees to investigate.

Finally, he heard something scurry behind him. He whirled around in time to see a raccoon running across the road. Small though the animal was, he still jumped back, startled at the sight of it, dropping his phone in the process.

"Jesus Christ!" he exclaimed as he watched the diminutive mammal scuttle away.

A surge of relief seasoned with embarrassment coursed through Zach. He knew he'd drunk too much and, whether or not he wanted to admit it, the whole incident with Meg and Shourds rattled him. It was really stupid to get into it with someone as dangerous as that guy.

"Fucking hell, Zach," he said to himself as he bent over to retrieve his phone. "You need some—"

He didn't finish his advice to himself because a low growl rumbled from the trees where he was originally looking. He snapped back up and around in time to feel something swipe across his midsection, causing a white-hot jolt of pain.

It took several seconds for Zach to register what had happened. The initial ache gave way to a more pronounced pulling in the area. A sensation that he was unaware was from layers of skin and muscle separating. Time became distorted and his head spun as an instantaneous cold sweat broke out on his forehead. His ears pulsed as he could hear the blood rush throughout his body, sounding like a washing machine several rooms away.

As darkness encroached from the corners of his eyes, he felt a strange coldness over his midsection. When he finally looked down, his mouth opened into a soundless scream as he saw a length of intestine spill out of the gaping wound, bodily fluids gushing down his body and pooling at his feet. The wind again blew in his face, this time carrying with it the metallic scent of blood draining from him. He could feel his organs shifting unnaturally within his abdominal cavity, which was enough to make him vomit as his legs buckled and he fell to his knees.

As his vision continued to darken and the world tilted around him, he saw red eyes pierce the dark void between the pines. His sight failed him as he felt stabbing pains on both sides of his rib cage.

The last thing Zach Torres experienced before he died was a muted flapping sound, followed by the sensation of his body leaving the ground.

Chapter 13

February 1749

Samuel stood before the grave behind his family's cabin. The ground was blanketed with a fresh coat of pristine snow, marred only by the footsteps he had taken to get to the site where he had buried his beloved one year ago today. The surrounding forest bore witness to the man's grief, same as it had the day he lost her, bare branches etched into the pearl-gray sky. He brushed the snow from the horizontal beam of the wooden cross marking his wife's final resting spot.

Despite the multiple layers he wore—made up of a linen shirt and a brown, woolen waistcoat—the cold invaded Samuel's body, coating his bones and stiffening his joints, which had worn down over years of hard labor on this modest property. A wide-brimmed felt hat and knitted gloves provided some additional protection from the elements, but not nearly enough to stave off the brutal northeastern winter.

The widower mouthed a silent prayer, asking God to watch over his family and praying for the soul of the woman with whom he had made it.

Tears stung his cheeks, freezing almost as soon as they escaped his eyes. Life had been harsh since their banishment to this godforsaken place, but the love he and his spouse had shared was enough to warm them through winters, even harsher than the one he was experiencing now. Still, he was not totally alone. He had his children.

Abner and Anna, twins who both bore an uncanny resemblance to their mother, were thirteen and both were an immeasurable help—Abner with the chores and Anna had taken on much of the responsibility in helping to care for his younger children. Mary was ten and almost as capable as her older sister. It was six-year-old Nathaniel who required the most care of his brood.

Samuel finished his prayer and made the sign of the cross. He wiped the frosty tears from his cheeks.

"My darling wife," he said, "I hope you are finally at peace. Though you experienced unimaginable horror throughout your life, I hope that I and our children brought you a measure of happiness. I love you and will miss you until the end of my days."

Samuel took a step forward and placed his hand atop the marker. It was only a piece of wood, but it was as close as he could get to his love now that she had passed on. It was so unexpected, the way she had keeled over while preparing dinner one evening. One moment she was singing while stirring the stew, the next she was sprawled on the floor, eyes open but unseeing. Even though their family was banned from ever setting foot in the town proper, he would have risked it had he a chance at saving her. But there was no doubt she was no longer alive. After corralling his children, he wrapped up her body and said an approximation of what he thought a priest might when delivering the last rites. It had been so long since either of them had set foot in a church that he did not even know if he did it correctly. All he knew was that he wanted to offer one last plea to God to accept her into his kingdom.

"Nathaniel!" Anna's panicked voice interrupted Samuel's sorrowful rumination.

He could see none of his brood from the gravesite, but it sounded as if his eldest daughter's voice was coming from the front of the cabin. Without hesitation, the alarmed father hurried toward the commotion, kicking up mini squalls under his boots. As he rounded the side to the front of his home, he saw a sight so unholy, it made him question the God he had just petitioned.

Nathaniel sat in a pile of snow about ten feet from the cabin. He was dressed warmly in clothing smaller but similar to his father's. His cheeks were flushed red and he cried softly, trying to hold back a louder outburst out of fear of provoking the thing in front of him.

A monstrosity, over seven feet tall, stood equidistant from the boy. It was an obscene menagerie captured in a single, corrupted creature. Glowing red eyes burned with malice, set into the head of a horse. Its legs were twisted and capped with goatlike hooves, and a shock of thick, dark fur blanketed its body. Its hands formed into gnarled claws at the fingers, outstretched as were the massive wings protruding from its back. Samuel knew beyond the shadow of a doubt that he had finally witnessed the Leeds Devil.

The abomination took a step forward, keeping its eyes on its tiny prey. It was taking its time, stalking the boy and savoring the fear its very presence drew from him. A second step prompted a scream from Nathaniel, agitating the monster. The thing reared back and roared, its wings flapping twice in rapid succession. The howl subsided into a hungry grumble as the devil crept forward once again, stooped and ready to pounce.

"Nathaniel!" Samuel shouted as he sprinted to his son, desperately aware that he had too much distance to cover to reach him before the creature snatched him up. That desperation turned to sheer terror when he saw Anna rush forward ahead of him. "Anna! No!"

The brave girl stepped in front of her younger brother, shielding him. Samuel pushed his body to its limits as he forged ahead toward his children, ignoring the biting wind that slapped at his cheeks. The creature bellowed again, drawing fresh screams from Nathaniel and Anna. But it stopped. Instead of advancing, it took a step back. Then another, a frustrated hiss squeezing through its jagged fangs.

Anna stood fast, her body shaking from the fear and adrenaline. Nathaniel had gotten to his feet and now stood behind her, clutching at the worn, cuffed sleeve of her dress. Samuel was only a few feet away when he heard his older son's voice call to him from the porch, "Father!"

He turned to see that the boy had brought his blunderbuss out. Abner tossed it to his father without prompting. Samuel caught the shotgun as his son added, "It is loaded!"

"Get down!" Samuel screamed. Anna understood and threw herself on top of Nathaniel, wrapping her arms around the boy's head to shield his vision from whatever was about to happen.

The creature roared again and pounced, but Samuel got the shot off before it could close ground. Lead pellets exploded from the barrel and found their way home in the left side of the Leeds Devil's chest. A gout of darkened crimson erupted as the monster wailed in inhuman agony. It fell backward and writhed in the snow, its wings separating the powder into the form of a demonic angel.

As soon as it was subdued, Anna quickly rose, helping Nathaniel up and pulling him toward the cabin. Samuel rushed back to join his family and, despite the terror of the moment, was proud to see Abner emerging from the doorway with the gunpowder, lead shot, and ramrod needed to reload the weapon.

"Inside! Now!" Samuel ordered as he went to work pouring the gunpowder into the flared barrel. As he stuffed the cloth in after it, preparing to load the shot, he looked at the predator only to see it was back on its feet. A wave of panic coursed through him as he watched the thing take shaky steps forward, its wound dripping a trail of dark, oily blood as it advanced.

Samuel picked up the already frantic pace, pouring the pellets in and shoving the ramrod down as fast as he could to ready his weapon to fire. He completed the process and aimed again, but the devil leaped into the air, narrowly avoiding another round of lead shot. It continued ascending, its wings cutting through the swirling winds. Instead of doubling back toward the cabin, it disappeared over the thicket of barren trees, the sound of flapping fading until it was gone.

The shaken man lowered his weapon and leaned against the exterior wall of the cabin. With the thing gone, Anna tentatively pushed the door open just a crack, peeking her head through.

"Father," she whispered, "is it gone?"

A demonic screech answered the question as it echoed through the pines, rattling the trees and scaring the birds into the air. The creature was gone. But not far. Samuel saw the direction in which it had fled. If he was correct, it was to a place he dare not follow.

Chapter 14

September 2025

"I'll be honest, Mr. Shourds, I didn't think I'd hear from you."

"Patrick," he said to Pete Savila as he took a seat in front of his desk.

The offices of Casa Bella Developers were modern yet cozy. The reception area where he first walked in was clean, lined with comfortable-looking chairs interspersed with small end tables offering real estate trades and home renovation magazines. Photos of beautiful—if perhaps a bit cookie-cutter—homes lined the walls along with historical photos of the greater Galloway area. Patrick had been drawn to the coffee station on the far side of the room by the aroma of high-quality dark roast permeating the air. Next to it was a bulletin board pinned full of a local map, several area photographs, and a sample blueprint for what must be their most popular design.

He only had to wait a few minutes before Savila came out to greet him personally, ushering him back into his office. It had a similar relaxed yet contemporary aesthetic with a large pine desk set in front of a picture window as its centerpiece, with certifications, plaques, and more photos to the left and right of the glass. Patrick could see that the businessman was well-educated and credentialed. There was a framed diploma from Seton Hall University, his real estate license and broker certification, and pictures of what looked to be several landmark deals with a younger version of Savila standing in front of buildings wearing a suit with a hard hat and holding a ceremonial gold-plated shovel.

Several frames sat on opposite corners of his desk, turned away from anyone sitting across from its occupant. Their angle told Patrick they were personal family photos and that Mr. Savila was a private person. The one visible image of the man was a framed photo of him playing the saxophone on stage as part of a seven-piece band. Underneath was an image of an album called *He's on Fire*. The cover depicted the band, whose name was Some Chill Dude.

"That you?" Patrick asked.

Savila looked at the frame and chuckled. "Yeah. That was a ska band I played in back in college."

"No shit? And now you do real estate?"

"Yup, life takes us on different paths. A few of the guys still play in different bands, but most of us moved on to other ventures."

Patrick nodded. "Speaking of those ventures, what's your offer?" he asked.

"Very direct," Savila acknowledged. "We have to take several factors into consideration when putting together a proposal. For instance—"

"I know how it works, Mr. Savila. I'm in construction. Look, I'm not trying to be rude here. I'm really not. Let's just say I'm a motivated seller."

"Pete," Savila said, offering Patrick the same first-name courtesy. "And I can see that. I can also see that you appreciate direct talk, so that's what I'll do. Being in the business, you probably know that you're not putting yourself in a strong negotiating position."

"I don't care," Patrick replied. "Again, not trying to be rude, I'm just trying to settle things and get back as soon as possible."

"Where are you from?"

"Out west."

Savila's eyes narrowed ever so slightly, realizing this wasn't going to be the typical back-and-forth deal where neither party walks away completely happy.

"I appreciate the candor. And I'm going to make you a fair offer. Two fifty."

"Done," Patrick said, extending his hand.

Despite all signs to the contrary, Savila seemed surprised Patrick didn't even attempt to counter. Patrick had estimated he could get two ninety-five if he put it on the market, but why bother? It was all found money to him. Savila paused for a beat to let it sink in before accepting the handshake.

"That's great news, Patrick," he said. "We can get a letter of intent signed and can close as soon as thirty days after the estate settles. Do you have a timeframe yet?"

"Not yet," Patrick replied. "But it should be relatively

quick. She didn't have any other kids. I just need to double-check her will to make sure the property is transferable on death. Even if not, the house is free and clear. I found the canceled mortgage from twelve years ago in her filing cabinet. Didn't look like she had much debt, so I should be able to pay the taxes and speed it through probate, if that's the case."

"But the will wasn't there?"

"No," Patrick said. "I'll see my aunt at the funeral tomorrow. I'll ask her about it then."

"If she doesn't have a TOD, it could take up to a year before you're able to sell it."

"Is that a problem for you?" Patrick asked.

Savila shook his head. "Not at all. I have long-term plans here in Leeds Point."

Patrick shouldn't have cared, but the confrontation with his aunt and the man's eagerness to make an offer piqued his curiosity. "Such as?"

Savila turned and rolled his chair away from the window so Patrick could see. "This town has been on the decline for years now." He looked at his watch, then back at Patrick. "It's twelve thirty in the afternoon. Those streets out there should be lined with people walking up and down on their lunch breaks or days off. But it's practically a ghost town. Half of those shops are closed permanently."

"I didn't know that," Patrick admitted.

"People are out of work. Incomes are limited. Their houses are falling apart and they don't have the money to fix them. This town is only twenty minutes from Atlantic City. It has so much potential as a resort destination."

"Why not develop in Atlantic City directly?"

"Aside from the mountain of red tape in that town?" he asked rhetorically before continuing. "Because it's a city founded on vice. It's not ideal for families. But building out here is close enough to accommodate folks who want to hop over to the casinos without paying five hundred dollars a night for a hotel room with a shitty view and sheets and bedding you wouldn't want to look at under black light. Here, they have the Smithville Village, the community center, and if we can acquire the right parcel, we have plans for a hotel and entertainment complex.

"You're talking about my aunt and uncle's property."

Savila nodded. "They own a lot of acres. It's the perfect spot. I've made them some very lucrative offers, but Mrs. Lumley is adamant that she won't sell. I don't understand why she'd rather the bank take it."

Patrick arched an eyebrow. "The bank?"

Savila looked surprised now. "Listen, Patrick, I'm just a businessman. I'm not looking to get involved in your family affairs, but this is all public record. A notice of foreclosure was filed last week. That's why I went to see her. I wanted to make one last offer."

"Why not just wait for the sheriff's sale?"

"I prefer a sure thing rather than chance getting outbid. Plus, I've been here in Leeds Point long enough to understand that Alberts has history with your family. I'm not saying he would sabotage the process, but again, I'm just trying to remove variables."

This was all shocking to Patrick. Sure, the house

needed a lot of work, but he had chalked that up to his uncle's illness. Maybe the treatments and equipment weren't covered by insurance. He had no great love for his uncle or aunt, but part of him felt sympathetic to their situation.

"My uncle isn't in any condition to move out," he told him.

Savila was taken aback. Patrick watched his eyes go to the frames on his desk before he answered, "I wasn't kicking them out," he defended, seeming genuine. "I don't have to tell you how long a project like this takes to come together. We're talking twenty-four to thirty-six months to break ground." He paused, trying to say the next part diplomatically, "You don't have to be a doctor to know your uncle doesn't have long. I offered your aunt an eighteen-month use and occupancy agreement with no rent provision. She would just have to maintain the property. There was even a six-month extension option. With foreclosure, she'll be evicted in twelve months with nothing to show for it. I promise you, Patrick, I threw her a lifeline and she outright refused."

Patrick had dealt with a lot of developers in his career. To be successful in his line of work, he needed to be able to read people, and there was nothing about Peter Savila that seemed anything other than authentic. He appeared to be the rare real estate guy who thought big picture instead of just looking to cash out on fix-and-flips.

"Did she give you a reason?"

"She doesn't seem too fond of Italians and had a few

choice words about my heritage, but that's as close as she got to a rationale."

"Don't feel bad. From what I remember, she pretty much hates everyone."

The men laughed as Patrick stood, Savila following a moment later.

"Thanks for coming in, Patrick. Looking forward to a smooth transaction.

I'm going to have to fix that leak ASAP, Patrick thought as he rounded the corner onto Hawk Hill Road. *And find out where the hell Mom's will is.* He had no doubt his aunt had it somewhere. Hopefully, Cindy hadn't named her executor. That would make things way more complicated than they needed to be. As he got closer, he saw another wrinkle waiting for him in the form of a Leeds Point Sheriff's SUV parked in front of his mother's house. It looked like the same one Alberts had picked him up in. *What the hell is this about?*

Patrick pulled into the driveway and got out of the car, not bothering to head to the house. Instead, he walked toward the police vehicle. As he approached, the passenger side door swung open and out stepped a face as familiar as it was unwelcome.

Cam Gideon.

He looked like he'd spent every day in the gym since Patrick had last seen him. As an athlete, he'd always been in good shape, but back in high school, his face had a slightly rounded look. Now, his chin looked carved out of granite. He was also noticeably bigger and more defined, straining the fabric of his black button-down shirt affixed with a sheriff's department badge. The one thing completely unchanged was the look of utter disdain he shot toward Patrick.

Alberts exited the driver's side, also wearing a black button-down matching Cam's. The department must have swapped the old tan uniforms for these sleeker black ones. The only difference outside of the men's physical appearance was that Cam's badge was silver and read *Deputy*, while Alberts's was gold with his official title as *Sheriff*.

"Patrick," Alberts addressed as Cam mean-mugged him. "We need to talk."

"About?"

Cam spat out the question before Alberts could reply, "What happened between you and Zach Torres last night?"

"The drunk idiot at the bar?" Patrick asked. Cam's face reddened and his nostrils flared, and for a second, Patrick thought the cop might lunge at him. He opened his mouth to say something, but Alberts put his hand up, silencing the younger officer.

"Was there an altercation?" the sheriff asked calmly.

"Kind of," Patrick said, choosing his words carefully. "We had some words and he pushed me, but the server broke it up."

Patrick watched Alberts's expression. He had to know his daughter was the server in question, but how did he feel about Patrick running into her? It wasn't intentional, but he knew the man, and when it came to Patrick and his daughter, he didn't always think rationally. But to his credit, he remained stoic.

"Why did you have words with Mr. Torres?"

"He was harassing the server."

"You were compelled to intervene?"

"He was being openly hostile, Sheriff."

"How so?"

That was a question that was going to get Patrick into trouble, no matter how he answered. What was he going to say? This Zach guy had fucked his daughter and was upset she wouldn't let him do it again? The thought of them together produced a bitter taste in the back of his throat, but if he told Alberts that, the sheriff would think that Patrick was trying to reinsert himself into Mcgan's life. And he knew damn well that wasn't going to fly with him.

"He was making inappropriate comments. Then he slapped her pad out of her hand. That's when I stepped in."

Alberts remained calm, but a flicker of anger danced across his irises. Although he didn't react outwardly, he paused long enough for Cam to jump back in.

"And what did you do to him, Shourds?"

Patrick had put up with a lot of shit from these two men over the years. It was for different reasons and it manifested in different ways, but he was just about at his limit with both of them. Cam may be some juiced-up gym rat, but Patrick wasn't a slouch himself, having built considerable strength from years of working construction. He'd love to beat the smugness off his face, proving that physique was nothing more than showy muscles. Still, the prick was a cop now and Patrick did not want to extend his stay in Leeds Point by getting arrested.

"Nothing. He got kicked out," he said, staring directly at Cam as he continued. "So why don't you stop pussyfooting and tell me what the hell *you* think I did?"

"Zach Torres is missing," Alberts said. "And there's evidence of foul play."

Patrick didn't expect that. Surprise overtook his anger and he turned his focus from his old bully to the sheriff. "What do you mean, 'foul play'?"

"We found his phone on the side of the county road," Cam said, not even trying to mask his contempt. "His phone and a shitload of blood. What do you say to that, Shourds?"

The bastard was baiting Patrick. That pissed him off enough, but what made him even angrier was that it was working.

"What do I say? Why don't you just fucking say what *you* want to say, Cam?"

The deputy stepped forward, the veins in his sizable neck bulging. Alberts held out his arm to block him. Both lawmen focused on Patrick. The elder stood fast and composed despite obvious irritation at both men, while the younger seethed, impulse and emotion overriding rationality.

"Cam," Alberts said, "wait in the car."

"Sheriff," Cam protested.

"Now."

The deputy remained incensed, but not insubordinate. His jaw tightened as he stepped back. Patrick half expected him to say, "Fuck it" and charge him anyway. But he didn't. As ordered, he got back in the car, slamming the door behind him.

Alberts put his hand out as if he were going to grab Patrick's shoulder, but stopped short, hovering instead.

"Walk with me, son," he said.

Patrick watched Cam stare him down from inside the vehicle as he took several steps back before turning to walk with Alberts toward the house, stopping just in front of the door.

"Am I a suspect here, Sheriff?"

Alberts didn't answer, posing a different question instead.

"What were you doing at Parkhill's last night, Patrick?"

"Are you serious? I was hungry. I went to get a burger."

"You could have gone to Wendy's."

Patrick couldn't help but roll his eyes. Every goddamn move he made in this town was scrutinized like he was running for fucking mayor.

"I didn't know she worked there, okay, Paul?"

Patrick had never addressed Alberts by his first name, but the cop didn't fall for the transparent attempt to turn the tables. Even when Patrick felt he was close to getting under the sheriff's skin, the man's heartbeat never even seemed to jump.

"Listen to me carefully, Patrick," Alberts said. "I don't think you're a killer. But bad shit follows you. And you make choices that make that bad shit worse. You chose to come home. You chose to go to Parkhill's last night. Now, I've got a missing person and a pissed-off deputy that wants to nail your ass to the wall."

"What about you?"

"I told you. I don't think you're a killer. But word is out now that you're back. And sixteen years isn't that long in the scheme of things. Folks haven't forgotten what happened that night. They're not going to be receptive to you being here. You need to bury your mom and get the hell back to wherever it is you went."

"Aren't you supposed to tell me *not* to leave town?"

"This ain't the movies, son. If I'm not charging you, you're free to leave."

Both men fell quiet, tension suffocating the air in the space between them. It was finally Patrick who broke the silence.

"Trust me, Sheriff," he said emphatically. "I'm not staying a second longer than I have to."

Chapter 15

Cindy Shourds looked like she was sleeping. That was the thing that first struck Patrick when he saw his mother lying in state in the mahogany casket at the center of one of the two viewing rooms in Bousman's Funeral Home. There was a light waxy sheen to her face, but otherwise, Patrick would not have been surprised if her eyes fluttered open and she asked what he wanted for breakfast.

When he first entered the funeral home, a strong sense of apprehension overcame him. At thirty-three years old, this was his first wake. When he was a child, it was just him and his mother. His grandparents had passed before he was born and with no other family, he hadn't lost anyone until Brandon and he was forbidden to attend his memorial, just as he was at the others years later. Once he left Leeds Point, he kept as much distance as possible from anyone else who entered his life from that point on.

He saw the casket in the distance as his foot fell on the burgundy carpet. A lump settled in his throat and goose bumps erupted from his arms, spurred by the air conditioning that was set several degrees too low. As he approached, the lifeless husk lying on a bed of pleated white satin revealed itself as his mother, not as he had last seen her in life, but bearing the visage of the ghost that had now visited him twice.

She wore a simple navy dress with a modest neckline and three-quarter-length sleeves. The hemline extended just past her knees and brass buttons lined the front, disappearing momentarily under folded hands mapped with more wrinkles than Patrick remembered and holding a strand of translucent rosary beads, before reemerging and lining the dress to the collar. Her feet were covered with a pair of simple, black flats. None of the attire reminded Patrick of his mother's style, but people change, he supposed.

Or maybe Vivian dressed her how she wanted her to look.

Patrick tamped down the brewing resentment of how his aunt had handled all the arrangements. Could he really be that upset? He had skipped town and left her alone. While Cindy and Vivian never seemed to be the closest of siblings, he had no idea how their relationship evolved while he was away. Vivian mentioned she was going to pick her up for lunch when she found her dead. Maybe Cindy's relationship with her sister had become stronger in her son's absence.

He tried to arrive early, but Vivian was already there. Caterina too. The aide was dressed more modestly than their previous meetings, but even the most conservative dress could only do so much to hide her figure. At least she was making an attempt at propriety. Her presence here surprised Patrick. Wasn't she supposed to be watching over his uncle? Especially since his aunt was here.

Vivian was clad in the requisite black dress and matching funeral hat, its lace veil interwoven with tiny black pearls draped over her face. She stood by Cindy's casket, her hand atop her sister's while another clutched a crumpled tissue. Something about her mannerisms reminded him of the way she'd expressed her condolences when they met the other day. It felt less than authentic.

Patrick took a deep breath as he approached his mother. Caterina saw him enter and offered him a muted smile. Vivian either didn't notice him or pretended she didn't.

"Aunt Vivian," Patrick said softly, putting a hand on her shoulder.

The woman jumped ever so slightly, as if she had not heard his approach. Again, Patrick doubted that was the case.

"Oh, Patrick!" Vivian declared as she hugged her nephew. "She's with the angels now."

Who talks like that? Patrick thought.

He tried to shake it off. Who was he to judge? He didn't really know this woman. Everyone handled grief differently. Maybe this was just who Vivian was.

"I know, Aunt Vivian. Thank you for taking such good care of her while I was away."

She squeezed him tighter. The length of the embrace was bordering on uncomfortable, but Patrick wasn't going to force his way out of it. Finally, Vivian broke away but kept her hands on his arms.

"She missed you every single day, sweetie."

There's that dagger.

"It was . . . a complicated situation," Patrick said.

"I'm sure it was, dear. I know you had your reasons. It was just so hard on my poor sister."

Thanks for driving that point home.

"I know. And I'm sorry for that."

Vivian nodded and went and took a seat in a cushy accent chair with a floral pattern. It was one of three such seats in the first row. She took the center one. In between each was a small table equal in height to the armrests. Placed on each was a metal tissue box and a small bowl with wintergreen Life Savers. The rest of the chairs in that and subsequent rows were foam-padded funeral chairs set on black steel chassis. Outside of the one his aunt occupied, the rest of the seating was empty.

Caterina approached and offered Patrick a hug, which he tentatively accepted, her subtle perfume slinking into his nostrils, offering the scent of vanilla with a hint of almond. Had his past not come bursting through the door of the pub the other night, he was pretty damn sure she would have come home with him. Embracing her at his mother's funeral now felt a little awkward. Unlike Vivian, she didn't let the hug linger. She did, however, lean in and kiss him lightly on his cheek, her soft lips warm against his freshly shaven skin. She let her hands slide down his arm and squeezed his hands gently before releasing them.

"I'm so sorry for your loss, Patrick," she said. Unlike Vivian, there was a legitimacy to her condolence.

"Thank you, Caterina," he replied. "And thank you for coming."

"Of course. Your aunt and uncle have been so kind to me since I came here. It was only right that I pay my respects."

"Who's with Robert right now?" he asked, sounding more interrogatory than he wanted. She didn't seem offended.

"The agency I work for has other aides. I'm his primary, but even I need to have some time off for myself."

She punctuated the last part by reaching forward and hooking Patrick's index finger with her own, tugging it lightly before letting it fall back, the implication obvious.

Guess we're not using that *much decorum.*

"Thank you," Patrick said, not reciprocating the flirtation. Her forwardness surprised him. At any other time and any other place, he'd let it play out, but as with everything in Leeds Point, nothing was as simple as it seemed on the surface. He couldn't get a read on this woman and he knew it was best that he steer clear.

He went and took a seat next to Vivian who was sitting off to one side of the chair, elbow perched on the armrest with her fist holding the wadded-up tissue near her eyes. The veil was still down, so he couldn't see if she was actually crying.

"Aunt Vivian," he said gently, "can I ask you something?"

She lifted the veil, draping it back over her hat. Patrick saw that her eyes were indeed watery and bloodshot. So there was some legitimate emotion there. That made him feel better. Maybe his mother *did* have someone to fill the void he left.

"Yes, Patrick?"

"Did Mom have a will?"

Vivian reeled back as if she'd been struck.

"Is that really an appropriate question at a time like this?"

"I'm sorry, but time is not on my side. I have work in progress and I can't stay here for too long. Of course, I'm not saying we need to address it today. I'm just trying to line things up so I can get back as soon as possible."

"What things are you trying to line up exactly?"

"There's someone interested in buying the house. They're motivated and I want to know what I'm working with legally."

"Let me guess," Vivian said superciliously, "your *motivated* buyer is that Mr. Savila, am I right?"

"He has some good plans, Aunt Vivian. He can really help turn things around here."

Vivian scoffed. "The only thing that guido is looking to turn is a profit. We can talk about this another time," she said snidely. "We can have lunch next week and go over all the finer details about the estate."

Next week? he thought. He wanted to get that letter of intent signed as soon as possible. Still, there was no way Vivian was going to be receptive before the funeral was over. He'd drop by on the weekend.

Before he could say anything else, the door behind them opened and he heard the funeral director say in a hushed tone, "Right this way."

Patrick turned and saw Paul Alberts enter the room, clad in a simple black suit. He stood, ready to approach and greet him. In a way, he was glad to see the man. Despite the tension and their extremely complicated relationship over the years, he was a familiar presence, and right now, despite the mystery surrounding Zach Torres's disappearance, a welcome one. As he stepped around the row of chairs, his breath hitched, stunned to see who walked in behind him.

Megan finished signing the guest book and placed the pen beside it on the small podium before following her father into the room. Patrick tried to keep his focus on Alberts but found his attention continually diverted to his daughter. She was dressed in a knee-length, sleeveless black dress and her hair was tied back in a neat ponytail. She didn't wear too much jewelry but one piece stood out, hanging over the garment's high neckline—a silver necklace with a goose pendant. Even more so than Megan, the sight of that particular charm punched Patrick in the gut.

"I'm sorry for your loss, Patrick." Alberts offered a handshake.

Patrick accepted and said, "Thank you. I appreciate you coming."

"Of course," Alberts replied without offering anything else. He let a look linger for a second. Not necessarily a glower, but it was the type of expression Patrick had long since learned the sheriff was adept at. A simple, understated look that simultaneously conveyed guidance and warning. His point made, he stepped aside and Megan took his place, the familiar scent of her Ralph Lauren Romance perfume taking him back to high school. It was an understated aroma, but infinitely more potent than the expensive, seductive brand Caterina wore.

Patrick felt like his throat was packed with setting cement, but fortunately, Megan spoke first.

"I'm so sorry about your mom, Patrick."

"Thank you," he replied, slightly cracked as he found his voice. "And I'm sorry about the other night."

Megan's face scrunched. "Thanks."

"I hope your . . . friend is okay."

Her expression shifted again. But this time, it looked more like embarrassment than any type of deep worry for Zach Torres. Her detachment was more that of a person who heard about a tragedy on the news than someone who was concerned for a missing loved one.

"Thank you, but we weren't close. He was . . ."

Patrick saw her blush as she trailed off and understood her discomfort at the topic. He knew his own feelings about what little he knew of their relationship were unearned.

"No explanation needed," he said. "I gave up that right a long time ago."

"You did," she agreed, as her features shifted again with a mix of longing and regret.

If Vivian's words felt like a dagger to the heart, Megan's felt like a broadsword. But what could he say to that? All he could do was nod.

"Thank you for coming."

No other guests attended the wake. Maybe Patrick shouldn't have been surprised, but he was. It broke his heart that his status as the town pariah had impacted his mother's life in such a way that almost nobody showed up for her funeral. Patrick and Alberts had to serve as pallbearers, with the funeral home providing additional bodies. They offered four men, but Megan insisted on being one, so three employees stepped in to help. The glare Megan gave Caterina when she didn't offer did not go unnoticed.

The procession made its way to the small church just down the street from the Smithville Village. As they drove by, a memory popped up inside Patrick's head. It was Megan, laughing at something silly while they played miniature golf back in high school. He remembered how she put her arm on his shoulder. How they looked at each other as their laughter subsided, replaced by a silence that spoke louder than any words. That was when . . .

He shook the memory away. It was too painful on a day already filled with it, and which was only going to cause him more.

The ceremony at the Methodist church was brief.

The Shourds were not a religious family and had never belonged to any denomination as far as Patrick knew. Maybe it was Vivian's choice, or maybe it was just the closest one. It didn't matter. The minister gave some generic remarks about life and death and God's kingdom, but none of it resonated. There were graves outside the church, but from what Patrick could see, they were all from the nineteenth century and earlier. Patrick's mother was going to be interred at Ashton Memorial Park a few miles west.

The small cadre of mourners stood before the grave as the clergyman delivered the final blessing. When he was finished, they took turns placing roses on the casket before dispersing. Vivian offered an invitation, "We can return to my house if you'd like to have a repast luncheon. Caterina is an excellent cook."

"I can make you some fettuccini al burro. You call it 'Alfredo' here, but that's actually an American invention. We Italians do it with a more delicate *technique*."

Patrick wondered if he should offer this girl a glass of water, the way she was acting so thirsty. It was almost over-the-top.

"Thank you," he declined politely. "I have to get back and fix a leak in the ceiling. It won't pass inspection if I don't."

"Inspection?" Vivian asked.

"Yeah. The house has to pass inspection to sell," Patrick reminded.

"You're going to just let some developer knock down your childhood home?"

Of course he was. This place held nothing but dark memories for him. The sooner it was gone, the better. But this was an emotional day for his aunt, and he wasn't going to get into it now.

"Like you said, Vivian, this isn't the time. We can talk about it when we talk about the will. I'll stop by this weekend."

He didn't give her a chance to protest before he turned and walked toward Alberts. He shook the sheriff's hand.

"Thank you for coming. I mean that. I'm going to finish up as soon as possible and I'll be out of here. You have my word."

Alberts seemed to accept that. "Sorry again for your loss, son."

To Patrick's surprise, Alberts moved aside, allowing Megan to step forward as he walked toward his car.

"You're leaving soon?" she asked.

"Yeah," Patrick said. "I have work in progress back in Chicago."

"Chicago, huh? How's it there?"

"It's okay. It's . . . different."

"Well, I'm glad you found somewhere to call home," she said.

Patrick thought back to his conversation with Nora. Shit, that was less than a week ago, but it felt like years at this point. He still stood by what he'd told her: Chicago wasn't his home. It was a place he lived. *Home* was somewhere else. When he had said it, he really thought he meant Leeds Point. But now, looking at Megan, he grasped what he really meant. He also understood that home was a place to which he couldn't return. No matter how much he wanted to.

"That necklace looks good on you," he told her.

"It felt appropriate."

"Do you wear it often?"

Patrick cringed at the question. Why the hell would he ask that?

To his surprise, she answered without hesitation, "Every day." Forget a broadsword. That one hit his chest like an artillery shell. She stepped forward and hugged him. Patrick couldn't help but put his arms around her and hold her tighter than the situation called for, savoring the moment that filled an absence he'd felt for sixteen years. "I'm so sorry for your loss, Patrick."

He fought back tears as he continued to hug her. Guilty as it made him feel, they weren't for his mother. When he broke away, he saw that everyone else's eyes were on them. Vivian was stone-faced while Caterina registered irritation and Alberts had the now-familiar look of disapproval. Despite all that, Patrick's attention fell on three new spectral observers.

Cindy stood behind her casket, her expression forlorn as she watched her son and the pitiful congregation of mourners that had shown up for her funeral. Brandon was in front, his shattered visage as neutral as ever. And behind Alberts's car, Helena paced the edge of the forest.

Patrick's stomach churned at the sight. If the colonial woman was here, something bad was not far behind.

Chapter 16

July 2007

"Happy graduation day!" Megan squealed as Patrick stepped out of the office building, registering genuine surprise when he saw her.

"How long have you been out here?" he asked.

"Since you went in," she replied.

That was an hour ago. Patrick had his regularly scheduled appointment with his psychiatrist, Dr. Sharif Hassan. He had been seeing Dr. Hassan regularly for the past two years at the urging of his mother. What followed were multiple appointments of intensive therapy at least twice a week and a seemingly never-ending supply of medications to help Patrick deal with his trauma and depression.

Of course, Patrick hadn't actually taken the meds. He would simply pretend to in front of his mother, stealthily sliding them into the side of his mouth and flushing them at the first opportunity. Part of him was surprised that Mom always just seemed to trust he was doing what he was supposed to do, but she had a host of her own issues, having to pick up extra shifts to pay for her son's mental health care.

Sometimes, Patrick felt guilty for rejecting his prescriptions, but he knew the things he saw weren't delusions or hallucinations. They were as real as that monster in the woods. He may have been a teenager, but he wasn't stupid. He knew dulling his senses to the very real danger that existed in the Pine Barrens was not in his best interests, especially since he seemed to be the only person who knew the truth about what was out there. If he was going to be haunted, he wasn't going to let a pill tell him he wasn't.

So, Patrick got really good at masking. He would tell Dr. Hassan exactly what he wanted to hear in the sessions. While the doctor, being good at his job, was skeptical, after a while he started to believe his young client. Their sessions continued to be an exploration of the root cause of his issues, going back even before his best friend died. They spent a lot of time on his feelings about not knowing his father. Truthfully, he didn't feel like he had any. You can't miss what you never had. Still, he went along with the topics his psychiatrist wanted to explore.

That's not to say Patrick didn't improve throughout the process, because he did, but he didn't take the pills and it wasn't the therapy either. About a year and a half earlier, the ghosts stopped coming to see him. While he had only seen Helena on a handful of occasions—sometimes accompanied by the twisted vision of the darkened woods, other times not—Brandon had been a frequent presence in his life, even though his appearances had never adhered to a schedule. There reached a point where Patrick realized it had been almost three weeks since he last saw the ghost of his best friend. Once he did, he began actively looking for him. Before he knew it, months had gone by without disturbance. Thinking back, he realized the visits became less frequent once he started hanging out with Megan. Yes, there were moments when Brandon would pop up unexpectedly, ruining an otherwise fun time, but those incidents happened less and less as the years passed.

It was much easier to tell Dr. Hassan he hadn't seen ghosts when it was the actual truth.

Patrick had told Megan the doctor had been strongly hinting that he was going to be discharged from therapy at his next appointment. Like many of the businesses in Leeds Point, the office was within walking distance. With Cindy working so much, that was pretty much Patrick's only option to get to and from his appointments. Megan would often walk with him after school, and truthfully, talking with her did infinitely more for him than anything he discussed in therapy.

Of course, Sheriff Alberts was not too pleased when he found out that his daughter defied his wishes to keep spending time with Patrick, but surprisingly, he backed off after some initial resistance. Megan must have just plain worn him down. Still, they didn't end up spending too much time at her house for fear of quickly expending that goodwill. It's not like they were dating after all, they were just really good friends.

Patrick's mom was much more supportive and gave

Megan an open invitation to come over for dinner, although she spared her son's friend from being subjected to her cooking and usually just ordered a pizza or Chinese. She told Patrick early on that they weren't allowed to be behind closed doors and it wasn't appropriate for her to spend the night, but other than that, she let them be, grateful for the lifeline Megan gave her boy.

On their walk over today, Patrick had expressed some doubt that Dr. Hassan would actually discharge him, but Megan was adamant that he would.

"You could always just stop going if he doesn't," she told him with a mischievous glimmer in her eyes as they arrived at the doctor's office.

"Sure, my mom would love that."

"I don't think she'd care."

"She would. Believe me."

"Whatever you say, dude." She'd gotten a little more serious and added, "I've got a good feeling this is it." What she did next threw him off. She lurched forward and kissed his cheek. "Good luck!"

Patrick was stunned. She'd hugged him a couple of times, but this was a first. He felt his face flush instantly, but stuttered out, "T-thanks."

Megan giggled at how uncomfortable he looked. "That was just for luck. Don't read too much into it, bud."

Don't read too much into it.

Easy for her to say when Patrick analyzed her every gesture and shift in body language trying to determine if she had any interest in him beyond friendship. He had been crushing on her since they started hanging out but never tried to break out of the zone for fear of ruining what they already had. It had been two years now and they were both sixteen. Megan had only grown more attractive in his eyes. Her hair was still dyed black, but it was now streaked with purple. The nose ring she'd been wearing when they first met was indeed a clip-on and had since been replaced by the real thing, having visited a less-than-diligent establishment that performed the piercing despite her being underage. But it didn't matter how she styled herself, Patrick saw the beautiful woman she was becoming. And those looks were secondary to her generous heart.

She came into Patrick's life when he needed her the most, and he would always be grateful for that.

Turns out Megan was correct. He and Dr. Hassan talked as they always did. Patrick told him about how he was focusing on his schoolwork and steering clear of kids like Tyler Murphy and Cam Gideon as much as possible. The doctor praised the progress Patrick had made and told him that while he should continue his medication, regular therapy appointments were no longer necessary. He did caution, however, that if the visions or any other issues arose, he should call him immediately. Patrick nodded in agreement despite having no intention of taking the medication. They shook hands and Patrick left the building, no longer under the psychiatrist's care.

"Soooo," Megan said, "is it official?"

"Yup!" Patrick replied, not doing a great job of hiding his enthusiasm.

"Yay!" she exclaimed and threw her arms around him. The hug was disappointingly quick as she broke away and lightly punched his shoulder. "This calls for a celebration!"

"A celebration?"

"Yes! You should take me mini golfing at the village. Then we can get ice cream."

"I'm celebrating the end of *my* therapy by taking *you* mini golfing and buying *you* ice cream? That sounds more like a celebration for *you*."

"Yeah, but you get to spend the day with me. That's the best gift you could get!"

The mischievous smile stretched her face, and her eyes twinkled. Who was Patrick kidding? There was no other way he'd rather spend his day.

They were on the fifth hole and both had brought their A game. They were currently tied and Megan just hit a birdie, putting her ahead.

"Oof. That's gotta sting," she told Patrick with a smirk.

"Please, this is the easiest hole. Watch this."

He tapped the ball and tried not to act surprised when it just skirted under the windmill blade and out the other side. The friends watched in anticipation as the blue golf ball rolled almost painfully slow up the slope, barely vaulting over it before picking up speed on its descent. It hit the cup, swirling around once before settling inside.

"Fuck!" Megan exclaimed, genuinely surprised that his called shot had worked.

Patrick winked at her. "Who's stinging now?"

She lightly shoved him on her way past.

"You're up by one. Don't get cocky, Shourds."

They moved to the next hole, an L-shaped section with a small wooden bridge over some water. As they set up, Megan asked, "What did you talk about at therapy?"

Patrick shrugged. "Brandon, mostly."

He felt uncomfortable talking about it now. They were here to celebrate him being discharged from therapy. He didn't want to rehash it.

"By talking it out, you were able to understand that it was a bear that attacked you guys that day?"

No, but as far as you, Dr. Hassan, and the rest of the town are concerned, that's what it was.

"Yeah," he said instead of voicing his thought. "The doc called it a 'trauma-intrusive hallucination.'" He paused. "Why are we talking about this now?"

Megan's cheery façade dropped. Patrick had seen her get quiet like this once or twice before, but she never voiced the reason and he never pushed. This time he was going to.

"What's wrong?"

Megan didn't answer right away. Instead, she set the ball on the marker and tapped it. The putt was haphazard and the ball clinked off the side of the little wooden bridge.

"Shit!" she blurted.

"Megan," Patrick said.

She ignored him. "You're up."

"Megan," he said more insistently, "what are you thinking about?"

She closed her eyes and breathed in deep before exhaling slowly.

"Sometimes I hear my mom singing at night."

Patrick was surprised. In the two years they'd been friends, she had never mentioned an experience like that. She'd told him the story of how her mother had died after she was born. Her father was sparing with the details, but Megan, ever persistent, found the case file while snooping around. Apparently, Georgia Alberts had suffered from something called "peripartum cardiomyopathy," a weakening of the heart muscle during pregnancy. It somehow got missed during the prenatal term. During delivery, Georgia's blood pressure became dangerously low because of the condition, requiring an emergency C-section.

Unknown to the hospital staff, the obstetrician they brought in had developed an opioid addiction after back surgery six months prior. He'd hidden it from his colleagues up to that point, but he was called in unexpectedly, having already taken a dose of painkillers earlier that evening. While delivering the baby, he misjudged the depth of the incision, inadvertently cutting into a major uterine artery. Distracted by withdrawal symptoms, he did not recognize the excess bleeding until it was too late. Despite emergency transfusion efforts, Megan's mother died from hypovolemic shock less than an hour after giving birth.

The resulting investigation had several eyewitness reports that Dr. Eric Chase appeared erratic during the procedure, but before he could be brought in for questioning, he skipped town, denying Megan and her father justice and closure for Georgia's death.

While Patrick knew the tragic story, this was the first time he'd heard his friend describe any type of supernatural experience.

"Why didn't you tell me this before?"

"I knew you were struggling," Megan said, her eyes reddening. "I didn't want to make what you were dealing with worse. It was kinda my job to take your mind off of it, ya know?"

She had. And she was likely the reason his own ghosts had finally left him alone.

"I get it," he said. "What do you hear her sing?"

"My dad showed me a video he took back when she was pregnant. Mom was sitting in a rocking chair in the nursery they had just finished. She looked so beautiful. So happy." A tear slid down Megan's cheek. "She was rubbing her belly and singing 'The Rainbow Connection.' You know, the one Kermit the Frog sings in *The Muppet Movie*? It's a little before our time, but once I saw that video, I had to watch it."

Patrick smiled. "Yeah, I know it. My mom loves that one. We watched it all the time when I was little."

"Sometimes I wake up at night, but I can't move. It's like I'm paralyzed or something. It's kind of scary. You're awake, but not in control. Whenever that happens, I hear her voice singing 'The Rainbow Connection' and then I'm not scared anymore."

"I get it," Patrick said, "But I gotta ask, why bring this up now?"

She shrugged and looked down at the green. "I guess now that you're done with therapy, maybe you learned something you could share to help me." She took another breath and lifted her head, meeting Patrick's eyes. He saw another tear had fallen down the opposite side. He stepped toward her.

"You want to know a secret?"

"Sure."

"Therapy didn't do shit for me. Neither did the meds."

"But the doctor said you were better."

"He did."

"So what was it?"

He took another step forward.

"You."

Her eyes widened, not expecting him to say that. "Me?"

He gently raised his hand and carefully swiped his thumb under her eye, wiping the tear away. It surprised him that he would do something so bold, but it was like he wasn't in control anymore, like the universe had taken the wheel and he was just along for the ride. With the tear gone, he kept his palm resting gently on her cheek. When she tilted her head, trapping his hand between her face and shoulder, he felt his insides swirl.

"Yes. You," he said. "When you sat down and talked

to me when everyone else would have been happy to see me end up just like Brandon, it meant the world to me. Even if you never said *anything* else to me, I would have been happy just in that moment. But then you showed up at my house and we had movie night and we laughed. I don't think I'd laughed in months before that."

A smile started to form. "You are kind of cute when you laugh. In a dorky kind of way."

Patrick ignored the wisecrack.

"You've been there for me ever since. Every time I felt down or scared or lonely, you were always around the corner. Talking to you on our walks from school or to those appointments did more for me than a psychiatrist ever could. You saved my life, Megan Alberts."

"I am kind of a big deal."

Megan quoting *Anchorman* in that moment caught him off guard. The heavy, emotional weight of the surrounding air dissipated in an instant. They both tried their damndest, but Megan cracked first. The nascent smile expanded and Patrick could feel her shaking with impending laughter under his palm. Patrick's own body convulsed as he tried to stifle his chuckle. Both failed and erupted into a fit of giggling that doubled them over.

Patrick kept his hand on Megan's cheek and she brought her opposite one up to cup his shoulder as they released the needed laughter. As it faded, they straightened and locked eyes, each welled with the rare tears of happiness. Then Patrick saw her look change to something else. Something he'd either never seen, or never noticed before. She slid her hand from his shoulder to the back of his neck, applying a gentle pressure to urge him closer. Patrick reciprocated and before either of them fully grasped where the moment was taking them, their lips touched.

Patrick let his club fall to the ground and Megan did the same, allowing the teens to wrap their arms around each other as they shared their first kiss.

Chapter 17

September 2025

In all the confusion and chaos of the past few days, Patrick had completely forgotten about the leaking pipe. Losing his mother, getting interrogated by the police, and running into the long-lost love of your life will do that to a guy. So when he woke up the day after his mother's funeral to hear a more pronounced, consistent dripping coming from the basement, he was not thrilled, to say the least. Not to mention confused when he saw the water valve was turned back on. Had he forgotten to turn it off after he showered?

He supposed it was possible. It's not like he didn't have a million thoughts and emotions smacking around in his brain like bumper cars. Whatever the reason for his negligence, things had gotten a lot worse because the water spot had expanded quite a bit and the drywall ceiling was already buckling.

He made a quick trip to the hardware store to pick up supplies. It was a small mom-and-pop shop, but it had everything he needed. There weren't a lot of customers milling about, and the few present all kept their eyes glued to Patrick the entire time he was in the store. Leeds Point was a small town and word traveled fast that one of its most infamous residents—well, infamous *human* residents—was back in town. And now another person had gone missing. The clerk barely said two words as he rang him up.

With the appropriate tools procured, he returned to the car, half expecting to walk out to a group of townspeople wielding pitchforks. The sun was out, so torches wouldn't be necessary. Thankfully, he made it to his car without incident.

During the short ride back, the phantom scent of Megan's perfume lingered in his nostrils. He remembered that was the gift he had given her for her seventeenth birthday—her first after they'd started dating. It was an aroma that would occasionally invade his senses, bringing him back to the lone bright spot of his time in Leeds Point. Of all the ghosts that haunted him, that was the only one he welcomed, no matter how much it hurt.

Back at the house, he went right to the basement, ready to fix the leak. It should have been a simple matter of cutting into the ceiling, locating the source, sealing it, then putting up a piece of fresh drywall. Some sanding and painting and it'd be as good as new. But, as was typically the case in Patrick's life, it wasn't going to be that simple.

Cindy was waiting for him in the basement, looking much the same as she did the other times Patrick had encountered her. Only now, she was wearing the dress Vivian had picked out for her to be buried in. She stared down her son without saying a word.

Patrick's chest tightened. He felt an overwhelming need to say something to her. He knew she wouldn't respond, but he had to address her.

"Mom . . ." he started, but before he could finish, he heard the groan of the ceiling immediately before a chunk of sodden drywall collapsed.

Patrick jumped back, startled, taking his eyes away from the ghost for a split second. In that minuscule amount of time, it disappeared, leaving him with a hell of a mess. He looked up and saw the exposed pipe, the water gathering and sluicing off the fitting.

What the hell? he thought as he went back to the valve and found that the water was back on. Maybe he forgot to turn it off yesterday, but he knew damn well that he had turned it off this time. *How did it get back on?*

The mystery would have to wait as he heard another *crash* on the floor, this time accompanied by the sound of something metallic hitting. He turned to see that another section, just below the first, had crumbled away. Among the wreckage, he saw a medium-sized metal lockbox. It had landed with the front end facing down, jarred open from the impact.

Patrick approached cautiously, as if a rattlesnake were about to jump out and bite him. Bending down, he turned the box over and gathered the contents off the floor. Why the hell did his mom have this sealed in the ceiling? She must have hidden it under the floorboards in her room, but the leak caused it to crash through down here.

The items inside were random, to say the least. There was a Movado watch with a cracked crystal face, a pair of cuff links, a monogrammed handkerchief with the initials *BG* on it that still smelled of cheap cologne, a Jeep key fob, and a pocket knife with a scuffed handle—thankfully, nothing resembling blood on the blade. But it was the last item Patrick picked up that caught his attention.

The laminated ID card was from Leeds Point Memorial Hospital. On it was the picture of a smiling man who looked to be in his mid to late forties. His head was as clean-shaven as his face and a distinctive mole sat under his right eye. Even though Patrick didn't recognize him, he knew exactly who he was based on the name inscribed on the card.

Eric Chase.

This ID belonged to the doctor who botched Georgia Alberts's surgery. He was the one whose negligence killed Megan's mother.

But why did *Patrick's* mother have it?

Chapter 18

March 1749

The rain pelted Samuel's face as he loaded the saddlebag onto his horse. What had started as a light drizzle had intensified, the blackened sky above threatening to unload its fury at any moment. But he had no choice. He had to venture into Leeds Point. The cabin where he had lived with his family these past fourteen years was technically part of the jurisdiction, but it was far removed from the town itself—a place Samuel and his family had been forbidden from setting foot inside since that dark night years ago.

But the situation in his home had become dire, leaving him no other option than to risk incurring the wrath of Daniel Leeds.

It had been one month since the incident with the creature in the woods. The beast had not since returned, and Samuel prayed every day that it would succumb to its wounds. But more than that, the monster's attack appeared to be the harbinger of much more severe problems.

The day after, Abner had fallen ill. At first, it was

just lethargy. The boy had trouble performing his chores, and Samuel had told him to rest. He slept for several hours before awakening in a stupor. When he rose from his bed, his balance was unsteady and he froze in the center of the room, voiding his bowels before collapsing. Samuel had rushed him back to his bed, cleaned him up, then covered him with blankets as violent shivers coursed through his body. The fever broke, but every time the boy started to improve, the sickness would intensify. Samuel had tried every remedy at their limited disposal, to no avail.

And it was not just Abner who was afflicted. Samuel and his family were completely self-reliant, forced to grow crops and raise livestock year-round. In the winter, when conditions were not too harsh, he grew squash, turnips, and cabbage. The family would harvest and store these, but inexplicably, their supply spoiled rapidly after the monster's appearance. He had worked feverishly to plant more once the snow cleared, but there was nary a sprout to be seen weeks later. Even worse, the small flock of chickens they raised fell victim to a predator. It could have been the creature, but the thing did not appear to favor stealth. More likely it was a wolf or coyote, but there was no way to know for sure. Nor did it matter. Their food sources were dwindling and their situation had become desperate.

Yesterday, Abner's condition worsened to the point where the boy could no longer walk. His skin was a pallid shade and he could barely speak, a low rattle in the back of his throat. Cut off from civilization, Samuel's only option to save his boy was to return to the town that had expelled him and his wife.

"Father," Anna said from the porch, her voice shaky, "he is barely conscious."

"I know," Samuel replied. "It will be half a day's ride into town. I hope to return by evening with help."

"You have told us our whole lives we are forbidden to go there. Why would they help us?"

Samuel stepped up onto the porch and set himself on one knee in front of the girl, placing his hands on her shoulders, steadying her so she could see his determination.

"There is a boy's life at stake. No matter what grievances Mr. Leeds may have with our family will not supersede that."

"What do I do if that monster comes back?"

"I have loaded the blunderbuss. If you have to use it, hold the stock in the crook of your shoulder and point the barrel toward the creature's center mass. Brace yourself before you squeeze the trigger, because there will be a reverse impact as it fires. Do this and your shot will land true, driving it away."

Anna nodded, her lip quivering, trying to remain strong.

"Do not fear, Anna," Samuel said reassuringly. "The abomination has not returned since I wounded it. It is either dead or it has been scared away. Focus on caring for your siblings. I will be back posthaste."

Samuel planted a light kiss on the girl's forehead and squeezed her shoulders before rising. He mounted the horse and looked back one last time, giving her a pained smile before snapping the reins and rushing toward Leeds Point.

At first glance, it looked as if the town had been abandoned. The torrent of rain that drenched the desperate man on his frantic ride through the Pine Barrens had slowed to a drizzle. While that may have accounted for the dearth of residents in the streets, there was a distinct emptiness about the buildings.

Many looked to have fallen into disrepair with chipped wood, cracked glass, and sunken roofs. Grass was overgrown and snaking its way up through gaps in the road. It was midafternoon, but the clouds suffocated the sun, preventing nary a single ray of light from breaking through. Despite this, less than half the buildings in Samuel's field of vision had any type of light glowing within the interiors.

What had become of this place in the years Samuel was away?

That was a mystery that would have to wait. He urged the horse forward, hoping the physician's office was still where it had been. Thankfully, it was.

Samuel hastily dismounted and secured his horse to the hitching post. Wasting no time, he pounded on the door, praying the doctor was inside. After several minutes of trying to attract attention, a sinking feeling overtook him as the possibility that the physician was not available became very real.

Just as he was about to abandon hope, the door creaked open and a round face appeared from the darkness within. The woman looked to be in her sixties. She was short and stout, her countenance grim.

"What in God's name are you making such an infernal racket about?" she asked, eyes brimming with annoyance.

"Apologies, m'lady," Samuel said. "Is the doctor available? My boy is in desperate need of medical attention."

The harshness in the woman's features gave way to a more melancholic expression.

"The doctor you are seeking was my husband."

"I'm sorry, m'lady, *was*?"

"He was. Until the Lord called him home three days ago."

Samuel's heart sank, and it took him several moments to process what he had just been told.

"The doctor has passed on? I'm terribly sorry, m'lady, and I feel vulgar posing the question, but is there another physician in town?"

The widow regarded him as if the question was among the most foolish she'd ever heard.

"Alas, good sir, there is not."

What was happening here? A town without a doctor? When he'd been forced out of his home in Leeds Point, it was one of the more prosperous burgs in the New Jersey colony, but over fourteen years, it had become a desolate shell of its former self. With no other options, he had to find the one man he thought he would never seek out.

"Where can I find Daniel Leeds?"

The tavern, like most of the other buildings, looked to be falling apart. The heavy oak door groaned on leather hinges as Samuel stepped into the dimly lit interior. A fire sputtered in the massive stone hearth on the far side of the room, smoke curling upward through a crumbling chimney. An acrid scent wafted into Samuel's nostrils as he entered, a mix of burning pine, spilled ale, and the stink of unwashed bodies mingled with the aroma of mutton stew.

Smoke-blackened timber beams stretched across the low ceiling from which hung dented pewter tankards alongside strings of onions. The surface of the establishment was equally worn, the wooden floor bearing the scuffs of boots, spurs, and the occasional brawl. All the planks were warped and stained, some were in worse condition than others. Around the room, a handful of trestle tables surrounded by mismatched stools and benches were arranged, the surfaces marred by knife points and mug rings.

The bar was a basic counter made of varnished oak. Like the tables, it was blemished by years of serving rowdy patrons, although today's crowd was sparse, to put it generously. A solidly built man in his thirties wearing a yellowed apron stood behind the bar as he wiped down a tankard. Cracked earthenware jugs lined the shelves behind him, alongside a scant collection of glass bottles, the liquor within having long since turned cloudy.

With the minimal clientele, it was easy for Samuel to spot the man he was looking for. He had not seen Daniel Leeds in fourteen years, his limited communication with the town facilitated through proxy. The state of the man stupefied him.

The town's founder had once carried an unmistakable air of authority, his face etched with intensity. Now he wore a veneer of defeat and apathy. His hair, once a rich chocolate brown, was now faded and streaked with gray, falling in loose waves that framed his gaunt appearance. Samuel recalled how he had kept his beard neatly trimmed. Now it was overgrown and bordered by stubble. The man who had built this settlement had fallen into ruin along with it. Nursing his drink, he did not see the tavern's new arrival.

"Daniel Leeds!" Samuel called.

Daniel turned lethargically in his chair, uninterested until he saw who had addressed him. When he did, his eyes bulged and a sneer curled his lips.

"Samuel Shourds," the man addressed in his most disdainful tone. "What business do you have showing your face around here?"

Samuel removed his hat and approached, having caught the attention of the other patrons as well.

"I would speak with you, sir."

"And I would have you swing from the gallows for your audacity."

"Believe me, sir, I would not set foot in this accursed town if I were not in a desperate situation. One I imagine you would prefer we discuss in private."

Daniel considered the man as he stood steadfast, willing to risk the statesman's wrath given what his family had at stake. He drained his tankard and slammed it on the bar, the decomposing wood shuddering under its impact.

"Outside," he said.

Samuel turned on his heels and exited the tavern, not waiting for Daniel. The founder followed moments later. The men took shelter under the jetty. Although the overhang provided some relief from the steady rainfall, leaks had formed, allowing the occasional drop to seep through and spatter their heads or shoulders.

"Speak quickly, Shourds," Daniel insisted.

"My family was attacked. By the Leeds Devil."

Daniel bristled at the mention of the monster. He lunged forward and grabbed the man by the collar, slamming him against the side of the building, getting close enough that Samuel could smell the flat ale on his breath as he delivered an admonishment in a harsh whisper.

"Hush your tongue, fool! Do not speak that name!"

Samuel slammed his own arms down on Daniel's, breaking the hold. He followed up with a shove, creating space between them.

"Call it what you wish!" he exclaimed. "We both know what it is and where it came from. If you wish to deny that, it is your business. That is not why I am here."

"Then why are you here, Shourds?" Daniel asked, stepping back underneath the jetty but staying out of striking distance. "You were warned not to return."

Samuel smoothed his coat and looked around him, taking the moment to calm his anger while also observing the state of his surroundings.

"And what exactly have I returned to, Mr. Leeds? Your town has seen better days."

Daniel scoffed at that. "We all have, Shourds. What is your point?"

"When the . . . creature attacked my home, I wounded it. Since then, my boy Abner has fallen ill."

"Your boy?" Daniel asked.

"The eldest," Samuel replied. "His condition has worsened over the weeks and all available remedies have failed. I came to town to seek a doctor, but I have been told he has died. There are no other physicians in this town?"

Daniel laughed sardonically. "There is no one of any stature left. Look around you. My town was once prosperous, a jewel of the colonies. Now it is a desolate wasteland."

"How did it decline so?"

"I do not know. Much of this has been in the last year. For reasons unknown, the harvest has failed to yield sufficient crops, our natural resources have dried up, and our most skilled, valuable citizens have either fled or died. I have no explanation."

"Perhaps I do."

"*You*? What could a simple carriage driver offer by way of explanation?"

"I know a curse was placed on your family fourteen years ago. And I know that the beast born of that bewitchment attacked my home one month ago. Since then, we have experienced similar calamities as you have described here. Do you not see the happenstance?"

"You are saying the beast brought this misery upon us?"

"I am," Samuel said, as clarity washed his mind. "I have been seeking a solutions in medicine and science, but perhaps we should be looking to the supernatural."

"Damn it, Shourds! Stop speaking in riddles and say what is on your mind!"

"I'm saying, in order to save my boy and your town, we need to kill the Leeds Devil. And I think I know where to find it."

Chapter 19

September 2025

Pete Savila did not know where he was. The last thing he remembered was getting out of his car at Parkhill's. He went there because he'd gotten a text from Patrick Shourds saying he needed to get back to Chicago but wanted to meet before he did so they could sign the papers. He suggested the pub because he was going to grab a quick meal before heading to the airport. Seeing as Patrick was one of the few folks in Leeds Point willing to make a deal without endless negotiation, Savila was fine meeting him. Besides, he could go for some wings from Parkhill's.

As soon as he stepped out of the vehicle, he felt a sting on the back of his neck. He assumed it was one of those damn horseflies, but immediately he felt woozy. His vision blurred and his mouth dried instantly as his legs buckled. He was dimly aware of the sensation of falling and then his world went black.

Now he struggled to sit up. The surface on which he lay was mushy and his hands sank in as he tried to push off them. Armed with that knowledge on the second attempt, he managed to brace himself enough to get to a seated position. As soon as he was upright, his head spun and he pivoted to his side just in time to prevent the resulting stream of vomit from landing in his lap. He wiped the foul chunks from his chin with the sleeve of his sport jacket, then turned his head to spit traces of bile onto the ground.

With the scant contents of his stomach emptied, his focus went to a pain in his head. He reached up and gently probed his forehead with his fingers, recoiling as he felt a stabbing sensation when the tips grazed a certain spot. Holding his fingers out as his vision came into focus, he saw they were covered in blood.

Disoriented and terrified, he surveyed his surroundings to find that he was in the woods. He didn't know exactly where, but this section looked different. It was like something out of a horror movie, as it was littered with bones. Many looked to be from animals, but some seemed very much human.

At this time in September, it was still technically summer. The pines should have been bursting with greenery sprouting from healthy branches. But here, the trees were as barren as the forest's moniker. The needleless branches were jagged and blackened at the edges as if burned. Large pieces of bark were torn from the trunks and unidentifiable insects wriggled in and out of the resulting holes.

The area in which Savila sat was in front of a large pool of water blanketed by a coating of dense fog. The liquid looked black, almost ink-like, the surface unreflective. Lifeless trees circled the body of water. As

Savila's sight continued to sharpen, he saw that they were all carved with strange symbols. There was no identifiable pattern, just a series of geometric shapes interspersed with formless squiggles and odd symbols. The suffocating humidity carried an acrid aroma that reminded him of spoiled meat. It hit his nostrils and caused him to retch, dry heaving with nothing left to spill from his empty stomach.

When the episode passed, he breathed through his mouth, doing his best to avoid the pungent stench. He struggled to his feet and looked around, searching for a path out of this odd place. With no apparent exit directly ahead and nothing but trees to his sides, his only option was to find a way out behind him. He turned, only to find his progress impeded.

Two figures blocked his exit. They stood side by side, wearing long hooded robes and gloves, completely obscuring their features. The heavy garments looked ceremonial, made of a heavy material Savila couldn't place. They were dark red, accented with black trim, and adorned with symbols not unlike the ones carved into the decaying trees.

"Who the hell are you?" Savila shouted at them. "What the fuck is going on?"

They didn't answer. Nor did they move.

"People are going to be looking for me." He continued. "My wife was expecting me hours ago. She's probably already called the police."

It was a bluff. He told his wife he was going to meet his client at Parkhill's, but he didn't know how long it had been since he was brought here. Wherever *here* was. For all he knew, he hadn't been gone long enough for her to worry. He just hoped *they* didn't know that.

"I'm serious!" he persisted. "Step aside!"

They remained motionless, but the figure on the right started chanting. It was gibberish, but something about it chilled Savila. After a moment, the second person joined in, chanting in unison. The voices were unidentifiable in the short time he had to think about it before a bigger problem presented itself.

Behind him, he heard something wading through the water. He spun in time to see what looked like a horse emerging through the dense fog. Only it wasn't like any horse he had ever seen. It wasn't devoid of flesh but it had a bony quality to it, like the biblical steeds of the horsemen of the apocalypse. Most terrifying of all were its eyes. They burned red, an otherworldly, demonic glow. As the thing rose from the muck, its body emerged and two enormous, leathery wings expanded from its back, sending the dark liquid splattering in all directions as they unfurled. Some of it hit Savila's gaping mouth, the sour taste of spoiled earth assaulting his tongue.

Savila reeled back as the beast stepped out on strong, angulated legs that resembled a goat's. It raised its thick, fur-coated arms, razor-sharp claws ready to strike. It was enough to spur the terrified man to take the risk.

He twisted around to run past the two figures, ready to shove past if needed, but he didn't get the chance as he rushed into a large knife blade held by the one on the right. Searing pain radiated from his abdomen and he looked down to see that it was buried to the hilt, blood blossoming around it, painting his white dress shirt crimson.

The pain dissipated into numbness and cold permeated his body as he went into shock. He stared into the blackened voids under the hoods but saw nothing. The robed figure withdrew the knife, part of the man's insides squeezing through the gash. A trickle of blood spilled from Savila's mouth as he staggered back on shaking legs. After a few steps, he met resistance behind him, backing into something large.

He looked up to see the creature's fiery eyes staring down at him. The figures continued to chant as it unhinged its jaw. Savila barely managed a final scream before the beast clamped its teeth into his skull.

Chapter 20

It occurred to Patrick that, like Parkhill's, he had never seen Sheriff Paul Alberts's office before. He and Megan had dated for almost two years, but given their propensity to evade her dad at home, they were *absolutely* going to avoid him at the station.

Patrick wasn't really sure what to expect, but he didn't picture what he was looking at now. The Leeds Point Sheriff's Department occupied a squat brick building on a corner, its tan façade weathered by New Jersey's ever-increasing bouts of high winds and summer storms. Alberts' office sat in the back corner, past the reception area that hummed with the din of fluorescent lights and smelled of stale coffee, and the four metal desks comprising the bullpen, each topped with an outdated desktop computer and stacks upon stacks of paperwork.

The glass walls gave the top lawman a clear view of his squad. Like Savila, Alberts's walls were lined with commendations, a mounted largemouth bass that he probably caught at Lily Lake or Reeds Bay, and a framed, autographed photo of New Jersey Devils Hall of Fame goaltender, Martin Brodeur. Patrick had no idea the sheriff was a hockey fan, but his choice of team to root for was ironic, to say the least. There were also several framed photos of himself and Megan and one of him and his wife, Georgia, from their wedding.

Megan had shown him photos of her mother before and there was no doubt that was where she got her looks, a fact that Patrick was grateful for. The thing that struck him most about that photo, however, was the smile on Alberts's face. He'd seen him crack one a time or two, but never one that genuine. He must have truly loved her.

"Gotta say, Patrick," Alberts said, taking a sip from a mug painted with the slogan *World's Okayest Dad*, a gift bearing Megan's trademark sarcasm. "I didn't have you showing up at my office on my bingo card for this week. What can I do for you?"

"Any idea why my mother would have this?" he asked, reaching into his pocket and retrieving Dr. Eric Chase's hospital identification card, holding it up for the sheriff to see.

Patrick knew what it was like to see ghosts. While he'd never stopped to look in the mirror or take a selfie to see what his face looked like, he didn't need to know the specifics to understand that Paul Alberts had just seen one. He tried to hide it, but this was the first time Patrick had ever seen the man look rattled.

"You say your mother had this?" he asked, a slight crack in his voice.

Patrick searched Alberts's face. He appeared

legitimately surprised. The question was whether that surprise was because Cindy had the badge in her possession or because Patrick had found it?

He held it out further, allowing Alberts to take the laminated card. The sheriff accepted it gingerly, almost as if it were going to burn him to touch it. He leaned back in his chair, turning it over in his hand and then back, studying it like the small object held some deeper meaning behind just the surface level. Patrick allowed him the time to process uninterrupted. After a few moments, Alberts straightened his posture and placed the ID on the worn leather blotter atop his desk.

"I take it you know who this man is."

Patrick nodded. "The doctor who botched your wife's surgery."

Alberts turned in his chair and looked up at the wedding photo, the smiling groom a distant memory.

"Megan told you."

"She did. Said he had a drug problem and was high when they brought him in. She also said he skipped town before he could be charged with anything."

"That's right," Alberts replied, turning back to Patrick. "Where exactly in your mother's house did you find this?"

Patrick hesitated, but withholding information would do him no favors, especially considering he was one to regularly be accused of violent crimes.

"In a box, with a bunch of other random items. Items belonging to a man. Or men. I don't know. That was the only thing identifiable."

"Your mother never mentioned this man?"

"Sheriff, she never even told me about my father, let alone anyone else she may or may not have been involved with."

Alberts arched a brow. "You think she was involved with him?"

Patrick didn't know what to make of that. His mother was at least acquainted with Alberts over the years. If she had any type of relationship with the man whose negligence killed his wife, wouldn't the sheriff be aware of that little detail?

"I have no clue. Was she?"

"How would I know that, son?"

"Isn't that your job?"

"The sex lives of the citizens of Leeds Point don't fall under the purview of the sheriff's department, Patrick."

Patrick seethed internally but kept his cool.

"So that's it? You think my mom was keeping souvenirs from the men she took home?"

Alberts let out a heavy sigh and took another sip of his coffee. Something about his response to this situation wasn't adding up. This was the man who ruined his life. That robbed Megan of a relationship with her mother. He had been missing for over thirty years and Patrick just handed him what was potentially a piece of evidence, yet he was brushing it off using Cindy Shourds's alleged extracurricular activities as an excuse. The math wasn't mathing.

"Far be it from me to speak ill of the dead, but your mother had a reputation. I'm not telling you anything you don't know here. Why else would she have a bunch of men's items in a box? Sure sounds like souvenirs to me."

Now it was becoming a challenge to stay calm.

"Fine," he said through gritted teeth. "I'll take this and the rest of that shit and put it in a fucking time capsule."

He reached for the ID, but Alberts slapped his hand on top of it, preventing Patrick from taking it back. The men locked eyes, each trying to get a read on the other. Finally, it was Patrick who relented and let the sheriff have the card. Alberts took it and tossed it in a basket on the credenza behind his desk.

"Okay, Patrick. I'll come by later and take a look at the rest of the things you found. I don't think it'll add up to much, but I will look. Fair?"

Patrick still didn't like it. The sheriff's attitude about the whole thing was far too nonchalant for his taste. But what other choice did he have? Alberts was the law in Leeds Point, so this was his responsibility.

"Fine," he said as he rose from his seat. "It's your show, Sheriff. I'll see myself out."

Everything that needed to be said had been said. Patrick left the office and crossed the bullpen into the reception area. As he exited, he heard Megan's voice before he actually saw her at the reception desk.

"Okay if I steal the old man for lunch, Carole?"

"Fine with me," the receptionist, a pleasant-looking woman in her seventies, said. "If you get him out of the office, I can put on some BTS instead of this god-awful elevator music they always have on in the background."

Megan was chuckling at the older woman's affinity for K-pop when Patrick stormed out, giving her only a brief acknowledging glance on his way to the exit.

"Patrick?" she asked, confused.

"Have a nice day, sir!" Carole called after him.

He was halfway to his car when Megan caught up to him.

"Patrick!" she shouted, forcefully enough to compel him to stop. "What are you doing here? And why do you look pissed off?"

Patrick wanted to tell her, but despite everything, it wasn't his information to disclose. He had told the sheriff what he knew. It was on Alberts if he wanted to share it with his daughter. It wasn't like she and Patrick had a relationship anymore.

He sighed.

"Ask your father."

Chapter 21

April 2009

"Check this out!" Megan exclaimed excitedly, her voice rising above the strains of My Chemical Romance's epic emo anthem "Welcome to the Black Parade."

"Huh?" Patrick asked, having been lost in the music, air drumming along with the band while lying on Megan's bed.

Sheriff Alberts was pulling a double shift that day, so it was nice to hang out at Megan's house for a change. Her bedroom matched her personality. The walls, painted a dark lavender with black accents, were adorned with band posters. There was MCR, The Used, Paramore, Three Days Grace, and A Day to Remember. In between, her favorite lyrics were written on the wall with a silver paint pen. She also had some movie posters mixed in, including *Pirates of the Caribbean* and *The Little Mermaid*—the Disney flicks providing a quirky contrast with the darker aesthetic of her musical taste.

As Patrick was lounging on the bed, a simple twin with a black comforter and metal rails, Megan was sitting at the small desk opposite the vanity littered with makeup bottles and brushes. Her workspace was cluttered with notebooks, pens, and some scattered college brochures that Patrick had no doubt were left by her dad, yet she never opened. The wall behind her was lined with photographs, mostly of the young couple. From looking at the happy memories captured in time, one would think they'd never experienced a bad day in their lives.

She excitedly pushed back from the desk, bringing her Dell laptop with her, half the pile of clothes she'd tossed over the back sliding off in the process. She had that "I have a great idea" smile that Patrick both loved and dreaded because he knew he was about to be a participant whether he wanted to be or not.

Megan brushed the loose strands of her hair behind her ears. She had been growing it out since they started dating and now it was down to the small of her back. It was still dyed dark, but the purple had given way to streaks of red. She had ditched the nose hoop in favor of a small stud, and while she briefly had an eyebrow ring during her Evanescence phase, she kept the piercings to her ears and nose now. Patrick also noticed she'd lightened up her wardrobe a bit. She still leaned toward dark clothing and band T-shirts, but he noticed she'd been mixing in some brighter colors. It had even become a bit of a joke between them.

Uh-oh! Your emo card is gonna get revoked if you go out like that!

Patrick, to his credit, had also grown quite a bit over the years. A growth spurt at the start of his junior year put him just over six feet tall. He'd also started exercising regularly, finding he enjoyed using the equipment at the community center. Despite feeling good physically, he never tried out for any of the sports teams. High school had improved, but things only got better once Tyler graduated. Cam would hit him with the occasional sneer in the hallway, but never anything more than that. Even though things were better, people still mostly avoided him and he had no friends outside of Megan, but truthfully, that was just fine with him. He figured trying out for a team would only put him at risk of butting heads with other students who may still harbor ill will toward him. He did find that he enjoyed shop class, though. Maybe he'd do something with woodworking one day.

"It's a company that analyzes your DNA!" Megan said, turning the laptop so Patrick could see the advertisement. "You sign up and they send you a kit. You like . . . spit in a cup or something and they can tell you all kinds of stuff about you!"

"And probably start an FBI file on you."

Megan playfully backhanded his shoulder.

"Oh, please. I'd be more worried about them monitoring your browsing history. Which they totally are, by the way."

Patrick laughed, but an intrusive thought crept its way in. Not about his aforementioned browser history. His was surely no different from any other high school senior's, but he was part of a police report years ago. Did they keep tabs on you after that?

Probably not, but Patrick realized he hadn't

thought about what happened to Brandon in a while, nor seen his ghost in over three years. He never went too long without the memory of the traumatic incident slithering its way to the front of his mind, but this current stretch was as long, if not longer, than it had ever been. Part of that made him feel guilty, like he should be thinking about Brandon every day. But another side of him was glad that his life was at a point where the good outweighed the bad. And the reason for that was grinning from ear to ear in front of him.

"Why'd you get so quiet, Patty Boy? Oh! Now I *really* want to see your browser history."

"Oh, shut up!" he said unseriously. "Feel free to look anytime."

"I'm calling your bluff and I am absolutely going to Sherlock your shit next time we're at your house—and remember, a clear history is just as incriminating—but let's focus on my thing right now."

Patrick rolled his eyes. "What kind of things can they tell about you?"

"All kinds! Like your ancestry, types of foods you're allergic to, what color your kids' eyes are going to be, what kinds of diseases you're at risk for . . ."

Her tone changed as she trailed off on the last one. She looked away from him and back at the screen, pretending to read over the disclaimer language on the ad. It all made sense to Patrick.

"Your mother," he said. "You want to know if you're at risk for the same condition."

She stopped pretending to read and stared blankly at the screen. Patrick gently curled his index finger under her chin and nudged her to look at him. When she did, he saw her eyes had reddened. She nodded.

"I don't know. I kinda think I might want to be a mom someday. But not if it's going to kill me."

Patrick felt for her. She'd absolutely want to know that. But he also didn't want to discount what she said about having kids. They'd talked about their future somewhat, but only to the extent of where they might want to go to college and maybe do for a living. But as far as family and what their lives as a couple would look like, they never got into it. Was she even talking about *with him*? He knew he loved her, but he also knew that high school relationships weren't usually ones that lasted. He desperately hoped that wouldn't be the case here, but did she feel the same?

"I get it. Completely."

She hesitated before asking, "Do you want to be a dad?"

Patrick didn't expect that, nor had he really thought about it. People would occasionally say how hard it must have been growing up with only one parent, but honestly, Patrick never had a basis for comparison. It was all he knew. Would he even know how to be a father? Still, something about it appealed to him. Maybe through a child of his own, he'd understand the man he never knew. That wasn't a good reason to become a parent, but with the topic broached, he looked at Megan and saw a future in her eyes. A life that he could have, that they could have together, giving their children the things they may have missed out on. A piece of their puzzles they could finally complete together.

He knew he took too long thinking about it because he saw disappointment creep into her expression.

"Yes. I want to be a father someday."

Megan brightened up at that and grinned!

"Awesome! When you find that right girl, you'll be a great dad!"

Patrick caught his jaw as it dropped because he realized she was doing her trademark deflective sarcasm whenever a topic got too serious. He shot her a "Cut the shit" glare.

"Uh-huh," he muttered.

Megan hoisted herself out of the chair and grabbed the back of his neck, planting a kiss on his lips.

"Baby, we're geese."

"Geese?"

"Yeah. They mate for life."

"Isn't that penguins?"

"Fuck those waddling bastards. We learned in science that Canadian geese mate for life! So yeah. Geese. Besides, they're so much cooler than stupid fucking *penguins*!"

"Aren't geese aggressively violent? And have you talked to a therapist about your unhealthy disdain for penguins?"

"Yes! Geese are *badass*! Just like you and me! And if a goose and a penguin ever got into a fight, the goose would fuck that penguin up!"

They both cracked up. She could make him laugh like no one else. When it faded, Patrick turned the laptop toward him so he could get a good look. He read the description and thought, *Why the hell not*? Maybe he'd finally be able to learn something about his father.

"Okay, my little goose, let's do it!"

"Yay!" she shouted as she ordered two kits.

"Holy shit," Patrick said. "That's like three hundred bucks for both! We can't afford that!"

"It's fine," she said nonplussed. "I memorized my dad's credit card number."

"That doesn't sound fine."

"*Shh!*" she hissed, waving him off as she finished up. "Annnnnd done! The kits will be delivered in seven to ten days! Sweet!" She closed the laptop and tossed it on the bed.

She rolled in closer and put her hands on his legs, her expression turning serious.

"There was something else I wanted to talk to you about?"

Oh boy, Patrick thought. *That's never good, right?*

"Uh . . . what's up?" he asked tentatively.

"How would you feel about actually going to prom?"

Chapter 22

September 2025

"What was that all about?" Megan asked her father as she burst into his office.

"Hello to you, too, sweetheart."

"Cut the shit, Dad! What was Patrick doing here and why did he leave all pissed off?"

Alberts sighed and clasped his hands on his desk.

"You'll have to ask him that, Megan."

"Ugh!" she groaned. "Why is every man in my life so fucking infuriating?"

Her father furrowed his brow.

"Didn't think he was still in your life. And watch your language in here."

"Fuck, fuck, fuckity, fuck-fuck-fuck!" she exclaimed. "How's that, Dad?"

"Never did get that ODD figured out, did we?" Alberts said, more to himself than to his pacing daughter. He gestured toward the chairs in front of his desk.

"Would you like to sit?"

"Nah. I'm good," she said petulantly.

"Megan," Alberts said calmly but forcefully enough

to be qualified as using his Dad voice. "Sit. Please."

She calmed herself, understanding that she'd pushed her father to the brink of losing his cool. It was a rare occurrence, but when it happened, watch out. Megan was an expert at pressing him just enough to get under his skin but pulling back before incurring his wrath. She plopped herself in the chair on the left, placing her handbag on the one next to it.

Father and daughter remained in a silent standoff for several tension-laden moments. Alberts waited for Megan's expression to soften before he finally spoke, "I know Patrick being back here is bringing up all kinds of emotions for you."

"You think?" she replied, again unable to curb her acerbity.

"Megan . . ." her father said, using just the tone of his voice to illustrate his thinning patience. She got the hint.

"Sorry."

"I know him being back is hard for you. I hoped he would have just stayed away altogether. But if he had to come back, I would have preferred that he not dredge up your past relationship."

"But why?" she asked calmly, albeit with a hint of creeping frustration. "Why have you always been so against him? You said you believed he didn't have anything to do with Brandon Murphy . . . or the others."

"I said he wasn't a killer. Not that he didn't have anything to do with the things that happen around here."

"What does that even mean?" She struggled to

keep her composure. It wasn't just a simple question. This conversation was the culmination of years of frustration bubbling under the surface, a nagging, unanswered question of why she couldn't be with the only man she'd ever loved.

"It means you don't have to be a bad person for bad things to follow you. Patrick isn't a bad person, but people get hurt around him. People get killed. I couldn't have you around that. I knew then, as I know now, that you're going to do whatever you damn well please. But it doesn't mean I have to like it."

"Jesus, Dad. You make it sound like he's cursed."

"Maybe he is."

Megan couldn't believe what he was saying. But was he right? Brandon was one thing, but the incident senior year? No. Fuck that. They weren't there when it happened. It was only after they left. If they hadn't, they might have ended up dead too. Patrick was as *cursed* as the Jersey Devil was real.

"Are you hearing yourself right now?" she asked.

"I am. And you can believe whatever you want, but if you want me to apologize for protecting my little girl, you're going to be waiting a long time."

Megan didn't know how to respond to that. She hated her dad's overprotectiveness, but could she blame him? She looked at her parents' wedding photo. At her mother and her truly happy father. There were two people in the photo. She'd never met either.

Dad gave her an out from continuing the tense conversation.

"Still up for lunch?"

Megan cracked a smile. This was never going to be a point of agreement between them, but they were all each other had. If they were going to have a relationship, they'd have to accept each other, warts and all.

"Sure, Dad," she said. Feeling like that was too blasé, she rephrased her answer, "Of course I am."

"Lucille's?" he asked, offering the only approximation of a grin the man seemed to possess.

"Sounds great!"

As they got up to leave, there was a knock at the door. Megan turned and saw that prick Cam Gideon through the glass. He was standing with two men in suits. One was tall, solidly built but with gentle features. In contrast to the other, who was shorter with a boxer's frame and a face akin to a bulldog.

She looked at her father for his reaction. It was not positive.

Cam didn't wait for approval to open the door and poke his head in.

"Got a minute, Sheriff?"

Dad's face went beet red. Megan had never seen the men before, but her father seemed to know who they were, and he wasn't happy they were here.

Again, Cam didn't wait for permission to swing the door open and step in. The men followed. Megan saw that they each had badges clipped to their belts. They were shaped differently from her dad's and his deputies. They weren't from Leeds Point.

Dad placed his fists on the desk. Megan knew how far she could push him before he blew his top, so she *definitely* knew that Cam had just shoved him over by bringing these men in here. To her father's credit, he still kept his cool.

"Excuse me, gentlemen," he said. Megan could hear the strain in his voice. "My deputy here clearly needs a training refresher. Would you mind stepping outside while I finish my conversation with my visitor?"

Now Cam's face was flushed. He hadn't expected Dad to call him out like that. He could have simply had them stay where they were while he escorted her out, but he wasn't going to let Cam's audacity go without a response. She was half tempted to sit back down and watch the fireworks.

The men in suits were unbothered and left with nothing more than acknowledging nods. Cam went into damage control.

"Sorry, sir. Sorry, Megan."

"Eat shit, Gideon," she said without hesitation.

Cam's jaw dropped. He gave her father a look that asked, "Are you really going to let her speak to me like that?" The sheriff's lack of response confirmed that he was. Incensed, Cam left the office, shutting the door behind him.

Alone again, Megan asked the obvious question, "Who are those guys?"

"Staties," Dad answered, keeping his eyes on Cam and the two men through the glass.

"Why are the state police here?"

"I got a pretty good idea."

Before Megan could ask what that idea was, the desk phone buzzed and her father finally lost his cool.

"Goddamnit!" he blurted as he yanked the receiver

from its cradle. "Yeah?"

Dad listened as the caller delivered their message. Frustration was written across his face. "Okay," he said, shutting his eyes and rubbing the bridge of his nose. "I'll be right there."

He hung up and gave his daughter an apologetic look.

"Duty calls?" she asked.

"Going to have to rain check that lunch, sweetheart."

She gave him a smile, showing that it was okay. "Anytime, old man."

She stood and met him as he walked around the desk, giving him a peck on his cheek.

"Oh, whatever Cam did wrong here . . . you should definitely fire him."

Dad couldn't hold back a slight chuckle. Megan was pleased she got that much because it dropped as soon as he looked through the window at the deputy.

"He's moved up the shit list for sure."

They left the office, Megan walking in front of her father and giving Cam her best bitch face as she passed.

"Bye, Dad," she said, turning back and blowing him a kiss as he stopped to talk with the state policemen. She kept her arm outstretched and curled all her fingers but one that she pointed in Cam's direction. She continued to flip him off as she traipsed through the bullpen and out the door to the reception area.

Megan made it all the way to her car by the time she realized she had left her bag in her dad's office.

"Shit!" she hissed as she began the trek back to the station.

On the way, she saw her father, Cam, and the staties leave the building. They headed around to the other side where they kept the department vehicles. Cam kept a healthy distance from the sheriff, which was wise because Megan could practically see the steam shooting out of her dad's ears.

Carole was already shuffling at her desk to a BTS song when she walked back in. Megan couldn't name a single one of their tracks, but the septuagenarian seemed to be enjoying it.

"Sorry, Carole," Megan said. "I forgot my bag in Dad's office. Is it okay if I run back and get it?"

"No problem, honey!" she replied. "You ever listen to this one? It's called 'Butter.' It's bangarang!"

"I'll put it on the playlist," she said with a laugh, not having any intention of doing that. "Enjoy, Carole!"

Megan hiked back through the bullpen and into her father's office. Man, she really hoped he was tearing Cam Gideon a new one right now. Her bag was right where she left it. She snatched it up, slung it over her shoulder, and was ready to head out when something caught her eye.

There was a laminated ID card thrown on a stack of papers behind the desk. It first caught her attention because it looked out of place, but the second she got a look at it, she saw a face that had haunted her for years. She'd first seen it when she snooped into the file on her mother. There was a photocopy of that very ID on the report. Megan had gone back to that file often over the years. Each time, she stared into the xeroxed eyes in the photo. She was trying to understand, trying to see into the soul of the man responsible for her mother's death.

Why did Dad have this here and now?

Chapter 23

"Just what the hell do you think you're doing, Cam?"

Alberts laid into his deputy the moment they pulled out of the sheriff's department parking lot. The call that came in while he was with his daughter was about an abandoned car found in the lot at Parkhill's. Dana Savila had gone looking for her husband, who hadn't come home last night. The last location on his phone showed he was at the pub, so she drove out there and found his car abandoned in the parking lot. Normally, a husband not coming home after a night at the bar wouldn't warrant a police investigation, but Savila's phone was found next to his vehicle. It, and the surrounding asphalt, were splattered with blood. The similarities to the Zach Torres case couldn't be ignored.

Now they were on their way to the scene. The state detectives, who had introduced themselves as Stermak and Masters, were following behind in their unmarked vehicle.

"I could ask you the same thing, Sheriff."

"Excuse me?"

"Why are you protecting Patrick Shourds?"

"Goddamn," he scoffed, "you got some balls, you know that?"

"I'm just doing my job, Paul."

"By going over my head? You forget all about chain of command?"

Cam shook his head and looked out the window, his demeanor completely different from when he interrupted Alberts and Megan. After a moment of contemplation, he said, "I didn't want to do this, Paul. I didn't want to have to bring in the state boys, and I wasn't trying to embarrass you in front of your daughter. I didn't know she'd be there."

"Well, ain't that just fucking magnanimous of you?"

"Yeah. It was," he replied before taking another moment between thoughts. "You remember Jim and Angie Murphy?"

Alberts clutched the steering wheel tightly. Of course he remembered them. How could he forget? The only thing worse than telling Patrick Shourds that Brandon Murphy was declared dead was delivering the same news to the boy's parents. Angie had collapsed before he finished the sentence, and the howl that Jim unleashed would haunt the sheriff for the rest of his life. When he had to do it a second time four years later, it was damn near unbearable.

"Tread carefully, Cameron," he warned.

"Angie Murphy died of a sudden cardiac arrest in 2011. She was only forty-eight years old, but I guess a broken heart will do that to a person. And I'm sure you remember the headlines when Jim Murphy slit his wrists in the bathtub of his room at the Tangiers in Atlantic City. You were probably glad AC police had to handle that one and not us."

"You think I don't know any of this? What's your point?"

"My point is, the Murphys were my friends. I grew up with them. Now they're all gone and there's one common thread. Patrick fucking Shourds. But you constantly refuse to investigate him. Daughter's boyfriend or not—"

"Enough!" Alberts yelled. "I don't know what you think you know, but we *thoroughly* investigated Patrick. Both times. He came up clean. Now, I know you like to run on emotion and an inherent sense of justice, but in the real world, we need evidence. And there was none connecting Patrick to those deaths."

"How hard did you look?"

"You've officially crossed the line into insubordination. Consider yourself suspended."

Cam huffed a laugh. Not the reaction Alberts expected.

"Sure. Tell the staties that. Not going to look at all suspicious that I called them here and got suspended for it."

Alberts seethed. The bastard was right.

"What's the endgame here, Cam? You got your eyes on my office?"

The deputy was genuinely taken aback. "The endgame is that I'm trying to solve cases and save lives. How many people have disappeared from Leeds Point over the years? More than most towns, I'll bet. Now we've got two missing persons cases with signs of foul play in less than a week. And for whatever reason, you don't want to see that Patrick Shourds is the link. You don't think clearly when it comes to him."

"Me?" Alberts countered. "You've had a bug up your ass about him since you were kids. Maybe that grudge is clouding *your* judgment."

"I lost a lot of friends because of him. Brandon. Tyler. The others. Did you know Zach Torres and I played Little League together?"

"Torres is missing. We don't know if he's dead."

Cam sat flabbergasted. Alberts knew he was playing a dangerous game of semantics with his deputy.

"You don't believe that, Sheriff. How could you? Either you're blind or you're hiding something. And I've worked here long enough to know you're not blind."

Alberts didn't respond to that. They had arrived at Parkhill's. He pulled into the parking lot and parked across from the abandoned Audi. Deputy Sullivan was talking to Chris Boland, the proprietor. Behind him, a frantic Dana Savila was chewing her fingernails, intently hanging on every word.

Alberts killed the engine. Cam went to open the door, but the sheriff grabbed his arm.

"You got anything else you need to say to me, Cameron?"

Cam shook his head. "No, sir. I'm just trying to do my job."

He nudged his arm out of Alberts's grip and the older man let him go so he could exit the vehicle. The sheriff exhaled deeply before doing the same.

Stermak and Masters were waiting for them. Alberts gave the detectives a courteous nod as he exited his SUV. Dana Savila did not wait for them to get to her, running in the officers' direction instead.

"Sheriff!" she shouted, fear cracking her voice. "You need to organize a search party! Please! My husband is hurt!"

"Calm down, Mrs. Savila," Alberts said, regretting the words as soon as they came out of his mouth. In his years of law enforcement experience, the words *calm down* seldom had the intended effect. He had long since trained himself to avoid it, but he was clearly off his game today.

"Don't tell me to calm down!" the frantic woman shouted. "We have to find Pete!"

"I know, Mrs. Savila," Cam said, stepping in and gently creating distance. "And we're going to do everything we can to help him, but we need to make sure we know where to look. Would you mind going over your statement with us once more?"

Dana groaned in frustration but started again. As she went over the events of the day leading up to her husband's disappearance, Alberts examined the car. It seemed mostly intact, but a splatter of blood coated the side of the front fender diagonally from the wheel well. Other than that, you'd have thought he just got drunk and took a rideshare home, leaving his car at the pub.

While Cam took Dana's statement, Alberts took a moment to speak to the state police detectives.

"I'm sorry my deputy dragged you fellas all the

way out here. Leeds Point is a small town surrounded by woods, right on the way to Atlantic City. Stands to reason that we'd have a few more missing persons cases around here."

"Hrm," Stermak grunted. His voice was as gruff as they come, matching his hardened exterior. "Maybe. But that Torres case. That was a lot of blood for a simple drunk getting lost in the woods. Now we got more on this car here. That don't strike you as peculiar, Sheriff Alberts?"

"Unfortunately, animal attacks are quite common around here. Folks toss food out the windows. Attracts bears. Hungry bears are dangerous."

Masters laughed. "Sounds like this town is just one big hazard!" He presented it as if in jest, but Alberts knew it was more probing than the detective made it sound.

"We've had our share of misfortune here."

"It would seem so," Stermak agreed. The detective pointed at Chris. "He work here?"

"The owner," Alberts confirmed.

"Let's have a chat with him, shall we?" Masters suggested.

"Sure thing," Alberts said. "Chris! We need a word."

Chris nodded and excused himself from Deputy Sullivan to join Alberts and the detectives.

"Chris, this is Detective Stermak and Detective Masters from the New Jersey State Police. They'd like to ask you a few questions."

"Morning, Sheriff. Detectives," he greeted pleasantly. "I'll tell you anything I can."

"The deputy showed you a picture of the missing person?" Stermak asked.

"Yes, sir. I've seen him around. He comes in every now and then. Nice guy. One of the few Giants fans down this way, so we'd always commiserate about how shitty they've been."

"Did he make his way in last night?" Masters followed up.

"No, sir. I was at the bar all night. We only had a handful of folks, and I can tell you one hundred percent that he wasn't one of them."

"Did you hear anything out in the parking lot? A scuffle maybe?" Alberts asked.

"No. It was a quiet night."

Alberts nodded. There was so damn little to go on here. None of it made sense to him.

"Were any of the others here at the bar last night regulars?" Stermak asked.

"Yes, sir. Just about all of them," Chris answered.

"Going to need their names, Mr. Boland," Masters instructed.

"I'll go write them down for you. Don't have their numbers or anything like that, though."

"We'll be able to track those down," Masters assured. "Just the names will be fine."

"I'll get right on it. Unless you guys have any other questions for me."

"We're good for now, Chris. Thanks. You'll hear from us if anything else comes up."

Chris nodded and went back inside. Stermak and Masters moved in opposite directions, circling the car, looking for anything that might have been missed. Sullivan joined the sheriff, holding a plastic evidence bag with a cracked iPhone inside.

"It dead?" Alberts asked.

"Yes, sir," Sullivan replied.

"Dust it for prints. Once you got what you can, get it plugged in so we can see if it turns on. If not, we'll contact the provider to get the records. Going to need to know who he was in communication with."

"I already know, Sheriff," Cam said, as he approached with Dana Savila by his side. "Please tell the sheriff who your husband was coming here to meet."

"He was bringing a contract for a client to sign. He didn't say why, but it seemed like it needed to be done urgently."

"Did he mention the client's name, Mrs. Savila?"

"Yes, it was Patrick Shrouds."

"I believe you mean *Shourds*, Mrs. Savila," Cam corrected before locking eyes with the sheriff. "He was coming here to meet Patrick Shourds."

Son of a bitch, Alberts thought. *You just can't stay out of trouble, can you, Patrick?*

"Bring him in."

Chapter 24

March 1749

Anna sat at Abner's bedside. Her twin brother was delirious, slipping in and out of consciousness. She read to him from a weathered copy of Benjamin Franklin's *Poor Richard's Almanack*. It was the only book they had in the house and the one their mother had used to teach her to read. She did not know if he could even hear her, but if it was not providing comfort for him, it was at least presenting a distraction for her.

Nathaniel and Mary sat on the floor in front of Abner's sickbed. They played with marbles Father had made them by rolling and firing clay. She remembered how he said wealthy families bought glass ones for their children, lamenting that he could not do the same. But none of the Shourds children cared. They were happy enough with the clay versions.

While Anna's younger siblings were lost in their activity and her twin trapped in the throes of delirium, she was the only one aware of the scene unfolding in the center of the large, open room.

Father had been gone nearly a day when he returned.

Only he was not alone. Five men accompanied him. The first, whom he referred to as Daniel, looked weary and unkempt, his graying wavy locks matted to his forehead and cheeks from their journey through the rainstorm. While all Father's companions wore serious demeanors, the face of this one seemed etched with a permanent scowl. From the way he spoke to the others, especially Father, it was apparent that he fancied himself a figure of authority. He was armed with a smoothbore musket in his hands and a flintlock pistol hooked at his side.

The rest of the men formed a motley crew indeed. Anna could discern their names as she eavesdropped.

Thomas stood tallest, and outside of Daniel, looked to be the eldest. His own graying hair was tied back, revealing a forehead etched with deep lines. His dark brown coat extended to his knees over breeches tucked into large leather boots. He held a musket in his hands, the stock worn from years of use, and a large hunting knife hung in a leather sheath at his side.

Jonathan was closer to Father's age, possessing the broad shoulders and thick arms of a tradesman. A blacksmith, perhaps. His dark hair was cropped short, most of it concealed by a wool cap. He wore a leather jerkin over a linen shirt and canvas breeches. He carried a shorter carbine rifle, similar to the one Father used when he hunted fowl, like those accursed geese. Sheathed in his belt was a heavy-looking iron-headed hatchet.

Ezra looked better suited to working in a tavern than joining a hunting party. He possessed an ample gut that tested the integrity of his wool coat, which was holding strong for now. His skin bore a pale hue, a telltale sign that his vocation was conducted indoors. His weapon of choice was a blunderbuss.

William was the youngest of the crew, barely more than a boy. His thick auburn hair fell loose to his shoulders and his unblemished face, shaven and with no wrinkles to speak of, left no distractions to hide his anxiety. He wore a fringed buckskin hunting shirt and wool leggings and opted for moccasins over boots. Anna surmised they would allow for more stealthy movement. The young man carried a Pennsylvania rifle, its long barrel making it an ideal choice for firing on prey at a distance. Unlike the others, he carried no blade, betraying his intention to avoid close-quarters combat.

Father, for his part, was clad in the same attire as when he had departed for town. He was loading his blunderbuss, and while he did not carry a blade either, his antique flintlock pistol, a gift from his own father, dangled by a hook at his side. He readied himself in silence as Daniel prepared the men.

"We have gathered you here tonight under the direst of circumstances," he began, trying to use volume to compensate for the unsteadiness in his voice. "I do not have to tell you that our beloved Leeds Point has suffered plague upon plague of misfortune for the past year. Our crops have rotted, our livestock have spoiled, and our townspeople have died!

"It is a bloody curse!" Ezra shouted in a thick brogue, divulging his Irish heritage.

"Yes!" Daniel agreed with the enthusiasm of one who had just solved a perplexing riddle. "A curse has befallen our town." He paused as if trying to create a dramatic moment before waving his arms around the cabin. "A curse that began *right here!*"

"Here?" William asked nervously, the younger man's voice lacking the gruff affect of his elder companions.

What started as a rallying speech had become a performance. Daniel answered, "Fourteen years ago, in that very room!" He pointed at the door to the bedroom Father had shared with Mother before she passed away. "In that room, an abomination was born! An affront to God himself! A devil! All the misery that has come upon this town is the fault of that unholy beast!

The men exchanged looks and grumbles before Thomas spoke up, his voice deep as darkness, "If so grave a danger this beast poses to your town, why have you not taken precautions to keep your citizens safe?"

Anna observed the panic in Daniel's eyes as his rousing speech betrayed his folly. Though the young lady had never met the man prior to today, it did not surprise her when he took the coward's way out.

"I did!" Daniel protested. "I entrusted Samuel Shourds to keep watch over these woods." Father arched an eyebrow at the politician as he spoke out of both sides of his mouth.

Anna knew they were forbidden from traveling to town, but it was not because her father was chosen for the solemn task of serving as its protector.

"Samuel has done an exemplary job up to this point. But the devil has grown in power. It will require our combined efforts to hunt it down and end this curse once and for all!" He fell silent as if he were expecting the men to applaud his fervor. They did not.

"Where do we find the beast?" Ezra queried.

Anna watched Daniel's internal struggle as the man realized he did not know the answer. This time, it was Father who allowed him to save face.

"The Hollow," Father said.

At the utterance of the words, fear fell over the older men. William looked around, confused by their reaction.

"What is The Hollow?" he asked.

"A myth. A ghost story," Thomas replied, though his weighty voice lacked confidence. "No such place exists."

"I believe it does," Father countered. "There is a path behind this very house. It will take you into the trees, then disappear without warning. But if one were to continue forward, the woods become almost impossible to navigate. When the beast attacked my family, that was the direction in which it fled. I believe The Hollow is part of the untraversed forest."

"Again I ask, what is this Hollow?" William looked as if he might leap out of his skin as he posed the question.

"Legend tells of a cursed section of these woods," Father replied. "Some even claim it is a doorway to hell, an area where dead trees sit under a blanket of perpetual darkness. Light will not penetrate, even in the daylight hours."

"Impossible!" Thomas protested, still short on

conviction. "How do you know this?"

Father gave Daniel a sidelong glance before answering, "It is the only possible location. Perhaps it is just a darker part of the woods, or it could be the portal to hell. Either way, we must venture beyond where no men have dared before."

"If that is where you believe the devil resides, why have you not gone there and put an end to the beast once and for all?" William asked.

"It is not a task suited to a lone man," Father replied. "If the very land and air are corrupted, then that is where the devil is most powerful."

"But—" William started before Father cut him off.

"The time for discussion is past." His eyes met Anna's before turning back to William. "Time is not on our side. You volunteered to join this hunt. If you now have reservations, you may return to town, but we need to leave *now*."

Anna watched William swallow hard and steel himself before declaring, "I volunteered to accompany you, and that is what I shall do."

"I will ready the horses," Ezra said.

"No. Horses cannot navigate the path," Father explained. "We go on foot."

Murmurs rose before Father quickly shut them down. "Step outside and I will join you in a moment. I would have a word with my children before we depart."

The men did as instructed and Father kneeled in front of Mary and Nathaniel. The two youngest of the brood ceased playing with their marbles as Father addressed them, "Mary. Nathaniel. Mind your sister while I'm gone. She will care for you in my absence."

"What if the monster comes back?" Mary asked, her voice trembling.

Father placed his hand on her shoulder. "It will not return," he said. "After tonight, it will hurt no one again."

He placed a kiss on her forehead and then did the same with Nathaniel before standing and putting his hands on Anna's shoulders. She spoke before he could, "Is that really the reason our family is banished from Leeds Point? Were you charged with protecting it from that monster?"

"No, Anna. The true reason is . . . complicated."

"Then why did you not contradict that man?"

Father sighed. "I do not have the luxury of being selective about who accompanies me on this task. Dealing with a man like Daniel Leeds requires a degree of strategy." Anna saw his gaze drift to her brother, who was writhing under the covers. "All that matters is destroying the creature and saving Abner. If achieving that end requires stroking the ego of Daniel Leeds, so be it." He stood and kissed Anna's forehead as he had done with her siblings. "When I return, I will answer any questions you may have about our family's history with this town and its founder. But for now, I must make haste." Father quickly hunched over the bed and planted a final kiss on Abner's sweat-speckled brow. "Do not heed God's call, son. Your time here is not finished."

With that, he left the cabin, joining the men on the porch.

He spared one last glance at Anna before she closed the door, sliding the wooden bolt into the slot embedded in the frame. She rested her head against the rough-hewn oak, mouthing a silent prayer for her father's safety and success while fighting back tears.

When she felt she was composed enough to rejoin her family, she turned. When she did, she saw something that turned her blood to ice, sending her reeling back against the door.

"Mother?"

Chapter 25

September 2025

Patrick had just gotten out of the shower when he heard the doorbell ring. He was still stewing after his tense visit to Paul Alberts's office and was definitely not in the mood for company. Who could it even be anyway? Maybe Savila had the papers ready for him, but he figured he would have called first. He tapped his phone screen, bringing it to life. No notifications. The bell rang again.

Looks like they're not just going to go away.

He finished toweling off and threw on a pair of basketball shorts and a black tank top. By the time he rounded the corner from the hall, whoever it was had transitioned to knocking on the door. Insistently.

"Okay, okay!" he said as he pulled the door open. "What—"

"You tell me," Megan said as she pushed past Patrick into the house, not waiting for an invitation.

"Come on in," Patrick said sarcastically, shutting the door behind him. He truly had planned to avoid seeing Megan during his time at home. Looked like he was doing a shitty job of that. Face-to-face now, Megan started to say something, but the words didn't come out. She blinked, her train of thought temporarily derailed as she really looked at him, caught in the sudden realization that this was the first time the two of them had been alone since Patrick's homecoming. "What are you doing here, Megan?"

"What is this?" she asked, taking her phone out of the bag and holding it out so Patrick could see the picture she took of Dr. Eric Chase's ID badge in her father's office.

"I told you at the station. You'll have to—"

"I swear to Christ if you tell me to *ask my dad,* I'm going to kick you in the fucking balls."

Patrick fought to suppress a smile. This wasn't a joke, especially to Megan. But he was overwhelmed by a wave of nostalgia. She always had an unintentional humor about her. That quick-witted sarcasm felt like it could break up even the tensest of situations, even if that wasn't what she was going for. It took him back to the almost four years they'd been together, first as friends, then as something more. The only time he'd felt any kind of genuine happiness in the past twenty years.

"Fine. You want to sit down?" he asked, gesturing to the couch.

Megan rolled her eyes. "You are so much like my father sometimes. Maybe you two should date."

"Doubtful. He's never been a fan of mine. Not many around here are."

That tugged on her heartstrings. Patrick could see

her jaw unclench and relax, along with the rest of her posture. She sighed and took a seat on the sectional. Patrick considered sitting next to her but chose the recliner instead.

He decided to be honest. What did he have to lose? He tried to do the right thing and go to her father and he blew him off. Megan was the only other person who seemed to want answers. Why not open up to her?

"My mom had that in a lockbox hidden in the floor. I found it when I was fixing a broken pipe in the basement."

"Why would your mom have it?"

"I don't know. That's why I went to your father."

"And?"

"He was evasive." Patrick expected Megan to get defensive, but she didn't. She looked sad, dipping her head down as she looked at the picture on her phone. She didn't respond until he prompted, "Megan?"

"He was with me, too," she said, looking up. She adjusted her posture, leaning back on the couch and rubbing her hands through her hair. "Looks like both of our parents had issues with the truth."

"My mom had other things in the lockbox too."

"Like what?"

"Random shit. All the items looked like they belonged to a man. Or men."

Megan's face relaxed a bit more and she tilted her head, her eyebrows drawing upward. "I'm sorry, Patrick," she said, taking a beat before adding, "that doesn't mean the things those assholes at school said were true." Another pause. "Maybe they belonged to your dad?"

Patrick shook his head. "I don't think so. Why would she have them hidden like that? And with the doctor's ID?"

"You don't think Dr. Chase was . . ."

She trailed off, the question too gross to even give voice to.

"No. I really don't."

"So what do we do now?"

Patrick considered the question for a moment. There was someone else he could ask, but he had to weigh how badly he wanted answers.

"I could ask my aunt," he suggested.

"You think she'd fill you in about your mother's . . . extracurricular activities? Assuming she even knew?"

"Not really," Patrick admitted. "The truth seems to be a rare commodity in Leeds Point."

Megan's eyebrows that had turned up in sympathy now dipped in anger. She put her head back down and clasped her hands over her phone. Patrick couldn't figure out what he'd said to make her react like that until he heard the words, soft but pointed.

"You're one to talk."

"What?"

"How about you be honest with me?"

"About what?"

She threw her hands up in exasperation. "About why you left."

"You know why. I told you."

"No, Patrick," she countered, getting pissed off. "You didn't *tell* me. You left me a fucking letter."

"And I said why in the letter. You knew I couldn't stay here. The whole town blamed me for everything. I had to go."

Megan's emotions surged, shifting from growing anger to bubbling sadness.

"I was supposed to go with you," she said, her voice shaky. "Why did you leave without me?" Patrick didn't answer right away, but he didn't shy away from looking her in the eye. He could see years of hurt brought on by lack of closure reflecting inside. Silence wasn't good enough for Megan. "Why?!" she yelled as she hopped off the couch.

"Because I'm fucked-up," he said calmly. "You wouldn't have wanted that kind of life. You don't deserve it!"

"Who the fuck are you to tell me what I want?"

Patrick stood and put his hands out, trying to defuse. "Megan—"

"The only life I wanted was with you!"

Patrick couldn't respond. What was he going to say? That he didn't want that? That it killed him every day since he left Leeds Point? What would that matter to her if the result was the same?

"It's not that simple."

Megan scoffed and shook her head. "You and my dad. Peas in a fucking pod."

Maybe she was right. For all the shit he'd put up with from Paul Alberts, when it came to Megan, they both ended up hurting her in similar ways no matter how much they loved her. But that didn't change the fact that Patrick seemed to put the people around him in danger. Better to lose her love than to lose *her*. No matter how much it broke his heart.

"We were in high school. How many people do you know from high school that are still together? I wasn't going to take you away from your home only to break up a few months later."

She was tearing up now. And she was well and truly pissed off as she took a step forward.

"You really believe that? You think we'd have broken up a couple months after leaving?"

"It's what happens with people."

"And that's us? People?" She was seething.

"What else are we?"

She stomped toward him, the familiar scent of her perfume disarming. She grabbed his left wrist, yanking his arm upward and jabbing her finger into the goose tattooed on his inner forearm.

"Then what the fuck is this?" she screamed. She reached inside the top of her shirt with her free hand and pulled out her necklace. "Our stupid little high school fling was so unlikely to last that you chose to get it permanently inked on your skin?" She gave him a second to respond before changing her mind. "You know what? Fuck you, Patrick. I do deserve better."

She let go of his wrist and tried to shove past him toward the door, but he flipped his arm and grabbed hers, pulling her back toward him. They locked eyes, silently communicating years of guilt, regret, and longing. The air magnetized between them and their lips crashed into each other. Megan pulled Patrick tightly into an embrace and he reached down, cupping

the backs of her thighs and lifting her off the ground.
She responded by wrapping her legs around his waist
as he carried her to the bedroom.

Chapter 26

May 2009

Patrick couldn't help but be nervous as he knocked on the door. If someone had told him on the first day of school freshman year that he'd be standing on a girl's doorstep wearing a simple black tuxedo and holding a wrist corsage to give to his girlfriend on prom night, he'd have told them they were as crazy as he was. But here he stood, outside Megan's house, waiting for the door to open.

When it did, it was Paul Alberts on the other side. He was dressed casually, a sight Patrick rarely saw since most of the time he and Megan spent together was at his house or somewhere around town. The sheriff wore khaki pants and a dark blue short-sleeved button-down shirt with gray moccasins. He looked like a different person. Hell, there was even an approximation of a smile on his face.

"Patrick," he said in his typical dry tone.

"Hi, Mr. Alberts," he greeted. "I'm here to pick up Megan."

"Really? I thought that corsage was for me."

Holy shit, was that an actual joke?

"I can get you one tomorrow if you'd like, sir," he replied, still unsure if banter was permissible.

"I'm good," he said, stepping aside to allow Patrick entry. "Come on in."

Patrick nodded and accepted the invitation. The Alberts house, while not the couple's preferred spot, was still familiar and dare he say, comfortable. Its layout wasn't too different from his own. The living room was the first area that greeted visitors upon arrival. While Patrick's was eaten up by the large sectional, the sheriff's living room was furnished with a three-seater couch perpendicular to a love seat. He and Megan had made out there once, but he was uncomfortable the whole time, expecting Alberts to come bursting in and tase him or something. An end table rested in the nook between the sofas, a simple bronze lamp casting a soft glow on a framed photo of Megan and her father at what looked like a dance recital.

Across the room was a recliner next to the same style end table and lamp. On it were two remote controls and a coaster holding a rocks glass filled a third of the way with an amber liquid. Alberts took a seat on the lounger and gestured for his young guest to do the same. He opted for the couch over the love seat.

Patrick looked at the staircase. His house was only one story, but the ones he saw on TV were usually lined with photos. This one was bare. Alberts clearly wasn't big on interior decorating, and Megan would have lined it with band and movie posters if she had her way. A soft light emanated from the hallway along with the muffled strains of The Used's "I Caught Fire" playing from behind closed doors. He felt his palms sweat as he waited for Megan to come down.

"You looking forward to tonight, Patrick?" Alberts asked, drawing him from his thoughts.

"Uh, yes, sir," he replied, clearing his throat. "Very much so."

"I don't think I have to lecture you about being safe, right?"

"No, sir. I'll make sure we wear our seat belts and I'm not going to drink or anything like that. I promise."

Alberts nodded slowly. Patrick felt like he was missing something. The sheriff took a sip of his drink and leaned forward, resting his wrists on his knees and clasping his hands.

"Listen, son," he said, "I know you think I've given you a hard time over the years, and honestly, you're probably right. But it was never personal. That girl up there is all that matters to me in the world, and it's my job to keep her safe. Do you understand?"

Patrick felt a lump in his throat, unsure of where this was going. "Yes, sir. Of course."

"She's chosen to be with you, and even if I've been hesitant to accept it, I respect it. And I believe you do too. So, tonight I'm entrusting her to your care." He stood and Patrick followed suit. "Don't gloss over how difficult that is for me."

He offered his hand. Patrick accepted immediately, not wanting to offend with any type of hesitation. "I promise, Mr. Alberts. She's safe with me."

As they shook hands, Bert McCracken's voice

abruptly cut off mid-lyric, followed by the sound of a door opening. Patrick's heart skipped a beat. Both men, young and old, turned their attention to the stairs as they heard heels echo from the second floor. A moment later, Megan appeared on the steps and Patrick lost the power of speech. To him, she was always the most beautiful girl in the world, but the vision before him truly took his breath away.

Her emerald green gown cascaded around her as the bodice hugged her delicate frame. The neckline was adorned with beadwork that reflected off the light from the hallway. Her hair was freshly dyed but instead of being streaked with an array of colorful accents, it was a solid raven black, hanging in spirals that framed her face outside of a few strands held back with pearl-tipped pins. Her makeup was tasteful and understated, going for a more natural look as opposed to her usual dramatic eyeshadow and dark lipstick. A string of pearls wrapped around her neck where a choker would typically be her preference, and a matching bracelet hugged her wrist. She had kept her nose stud in, but most of her earrings had been removed in favor of a set of solitaire danglers that perfectly matched her dress and a silver-plated ring set with a faux emerald.

She stopped at the landing and pulled the sides of the skirt out slightly before letting it fall back into place. Her smile was more vulnerable than Patrick was used to. Megan, who never cared what anyone thought, looked very much like she did right now, having not stepped out of her comfort zone but jumped headfirst from it.

"Can I assume your silence and gape-jawed expressions are a good thing?" she asked, a touch of nervousness behind the quip.

Patrick somehow managed to peel his eyes away to glance at her dad, and he was shocked to see a small tear swirling in the corner of the man's eyes as he regarded his beautiful daughter in tight-lipped silence. Compelled to once again stare at her in awe, he found his voice.

"You look beautiful!" he blurted.

Megan stepped off the landing and approached the two men in her life, walking up to Patrick first and sliding her hands up his lapel before planting a featherlight kiss on his cheek, careful not to smudge her lipstick.

"You clean up pretty good yourself," she said, her jade eyes betraying that she was more impressed than she let on before she gave voice to it. "You look very handsome." With the genuine compliment out of the way, she moved her hand to stroke his tie and added, "Dare I say, even *hot.*"

"Megan," her father started in a neutral yet no-nonsense admonishment as Patrick cringed internally. She angled her head to the side as she smirked at him. Alberts couldn't resist a smile of his own. Patrick wished he had one of those camera phones so he could capture the rare occurrence. "You look beautiful, sweetheart."

"Thank you, Daddy," she said with a little curtsy. "It's been a long time since I had a princess phase. Kinda wanted to remember what that felt like."

After exchanging the corsage and boutonniere, they

spent a few minutes taking the obligatory pre-prom photos and then they were ready to go. Megan kissed her father goodbye, and Patrick shook his hand again. Before Alberts let go, he told Patrick, "Remember what I said."

"You ready for this?" Megan asked Patrick as they stood outside the doors leading into Smithville High.

"Ready as I'll ever be," he replied, sliding his hand into Megan's, interlocking his fingers with hers. He took a breath and smiled, shaking his head in disbelief. "I never would have thought we'd be here."

That was an understatement. Considering how middle school had ended and high school had begun, prom was never something Patrick considered a possibility. But here they were. More than that, they were going to graduate in a few weeks. Neither of them had thought too hard about what they wanted to do with their lives, but they had both enrolled in the local community college. He figured he'd find what he wanted to do somewhere along the way. The important thing to him was that he was still going to go to school with Megan. But that was months away. Right now, he was about to attend his first real social event of high school.

Things on that front had improved exponentially

over the years, especially since the visions stopped. Even better, Tyler Murphy graduated last year, removing one of the last holdovers who truly resented Patrick. Cam was neutered with his buddy gone and was too focused on sports and being a prick to the girls who thought his looks were enough to compensate for his shit personality. Megan also had a small circle of acquaintances that they would occasionally spend time with so as not to be *total* outcasts. Walking into the gymnasium four years ago would have been impossible. Now it was exciting.

"Let's do it."

The doors swung open and the couple observed their school gym—that only yesterday was filled with the sound of squeaking sneakers, bouncing basketballs, and coach's whistles—now draped with silk runners extending from the ceiling to the floor while streamers stretched across the walls over arrangements of balloon columns in the school colors of navy blue and white. The center of the room was open for dancing, but tables covered with blue tablecloths and centered with floral arrangements were organized around the edges of the makeshift dance floor. Off to the right was a refreshment table with a large bowl of punch in the middle.

The typical odor of commercial floor wax and old sporting equipment was overpowered by a strong, but not unpleasant, wave of perfume and cologne interspersed with the light musty scent from the fog machines that were working hard to create a dreamlike atmosphere for the students.

Said students had all, to paraphrase Megan, cleaned up nice. The typical sweatpants, jeans, T-shirts, and hoodies set aside in favor of tuxedos and glamorous gowns. The colored strobe lights bouncing off their faces showed the effort just about everyone had put into their hair and makeup. In a lot of ways, this night was these kids' first taste of the adulthood knocking at their doors. Patrick stole a glance at his gorgeous date and a quick burst of sadness hit him—the piece of his childhood he'd lost after Brandon died—but that was quickly followed by a glimmer of hope. Hope that his best days were ahead of him. And hope that he and Megan truly were geese.

As they made their way toward the center of the room, Kevin Rudolf's "Let It Rock" was fading out, only to segue into Taylor Swift's "Love Story." Megan wrinkled her nose at the selection.

"Well, this was a fucking mistake."

Patrick laughed and put his arm around her. "I don't think Escape the Fate is making it onto too many prom playlists."

"No accounting for taste, I suppose. Let's get a drink!"

The couple proceeded to the refreshment table, where Patrick ladled them each a cup before taking a big chocolate chip cookie and breaking it in half, keeping one side for himself and handing the other to Megan, who happily accepted.

"You know," Patrick said, "there's something I never considered when we agreed to come here."

"Oh yeah?" Megan asked, raising a brow. "What's

that?"

"That I might actually have to dance."

Megan let out a hearty laugh mid-bite of her cookie, crumbs spilling out of her mouth. "Oh, yeah you do, buddy. We're just going to wait for the next one."

"Fine with me. Knowing you, you'll find a problem with every silly little pop song they play and I won't have to shake my ass even a millimeter."

The next song ended up being "Swing, Swing" by The All-American Rejects. As soon as the opening notes rang through the gym, Megan lit up.

"I can work with this!" she said, grabbing Patrick's hand and tugging him toward the dance floor.

What followed was a noble, but less than optimal attempt to mimic the other students' dance moves. While Patrick didn't come away feeling like he embarrassed himself, he had no illusions that he was going to be on one of those TV dance competitions anytime soon. Megan couldn't wipe the smile off her face as they reveled in being normal teenagers for a change.

Sean Kingston's "Fire Burning" was up next and Megan looked disappointed, but Patrick didn't let her leave the dance floor, and soon she was as into it as the last song. It wasn't the music that mattered. When that one ended, the DJ announced that they were going to "slow it down," and a familiar acoustic guitar melody replaced the heavy electronic beats. Patrick and Megan smiled as Paramore's "The Only Exception" brought the couples together, swaying slowly in rhythm with the music.

They remained silent, eyes locked on each other through the first verse and chorus. As the second started, Patrick asked, "Are you glad we came?"

Megan nodded and pecked him on the lips. "I am. Are you?"

Patrick tore his gaze away to peek around the room, noticing just how little tension he was carrying at the moment. He felt light as a feather.

"I am," he replied. "Nowhere I'd rather be."

They kissed again, this one lingering.

"Hey, you two! Get a room!" a girl's voice said from their right.

It belonged to Crystal Paxon, one of Megan's aforementioned acquaintances, now dancing next to them with her boyfriend, Josh Harris. He was cool. Patrick wouldn't call them *friends*, but Josh was never anything but cordial to him.

"Nope!" Megan said. "I'd rather make you uncomfortable."

She was joking, but Patrick felt that familiar tug of uneasiness. He'd made enough people *uncomfortable* over the years. He quickly brushed it off as he realized no one else had made that connection.

"Oh, shut up! I almost didn't recognize you!" Crystal exclaimed. "You look *gorgeous*!"

"Thank you!" Megan said. "You too! I love that color on you!"

Patrick and Josh gave each other a cursory upnod; the male of the species being less prone to gushing compliments.

"You guys have plans after this?" Crystal asked.

Megan glanced at Patrick to gauge his reaction to the question. He shrugged.

"No," she replied. "You know me. Never think too far ahead."

Crystal laughed as Josh chimed in, "My folks rented a cabin at Swan Lake for us to use. We're doing an after-party. You guys are welcome to come."

"Cool," Megan said, trying not to sound hesitant. "We'll try to swing by."

"Awesome!" Crystal replied. "Okay, you two can go back to making out now."

"Ha ha," Megan said.

Patrick felt bad. He knew she'd jump at the opportunity to go to a prom after-party, but he knew she was noncommittal thanks to him. The cabins at Swan Lake were in the Pine Barrens. She was right to be skeptical of his desire to go. He'd spent so much time getting past the trauma he'd experienced there. Would going back undo it all?

"We don't have to go, Patrick," Megan said, reading his mind.

"It's not that . . . I just . . ."

"What? You can tell me. It's okay. Really."

Patrick contemplated. He felt like he was at a crossroads. He'd come so far, but getting there had cost him most of his high school experience. With only a month left, this could be his last chance to fully embrace it. What was the worst that could happen?

"You know what? Let's do it."

After a night filled with dancing and smiles, prom came to an end. It was everything the young couple had hoped it would be. They'd even done a good job avoiding Cam Gideon, only entering his orbit on a couple of occasions and without incident. A few times during the evening, nagging doubt crept its way into Patrick's mind, trying to tell him going to an after-party in the woods *wasn't* a good idea. But he suppressed the concern, telling himself he was overreacting. By the time he turned onto the access road to Swan Lake, he had completely put it out of his mind, focusing instead on Megan.

"Did you text your dad?" he asked her.

"Of course."

"Where did you tell him we were going?"

"An after-party. He was totally cool with it."

Patrick side-eyed her skeptically.

"What did you really tell him?"

"That we were going to DeLorenzo's for pizza with Crystal and Josh."

Patrick sighed. "It's like you want me to get shot."

"Oh, please," she scoffed. "He'd just graze you as a warning. You'd be fine. And have a sexy scar as a bonus."

"You say that now, but . . ."

He trailed off and his stomach tightened as he caught a glimpse of something behind the trees. While he couldn't see it clearly, it appeared to be the shape of a woman. It couldn't be.

Megan was still going on, saying something about how scars were rugged, but Patrick was focused on figuring out if he saw what he thought he did.

"Earth to Patrick!"

"Huh?" he asked, returning his focus to Megan. She could tell something was wrong.

"Are you okay?"

Patrick looked back in the direction where he may have seen something, but couldn't find anything this time.

Your mind's playing tricks on you, Patrick. Knock it off. Don't ruin the night.

"Yeah," he said, forcing a smile. "I'm great!"

"We can turn back," she offered.

"Nope! All good!"

He continued glancing toward the trees as they approached the cabin, but he didn't see anything else, determining it must have been his eyes playing tricks on him.

Patrick parked at the end of a row of cars belonging to the partygoers who had already arrived, turning off the engine.

"Last chance to back out," Megan offered.

"No backing out," he assured. "Let's go have some fun."

The cabin sat nestled among the pines whose dark silhouettes created jagged patterns against the starry night sky. Warm light spilled from the windows, casting bright rectangles on the wraparound porch, itself illuminated by string lights woven around the railing. Inside, shadows moved, preceding the growing throng of revelers who navigated the interior. A mix of laughter and hip-hop blaring from the speaker system provided the evening's soundtrack.

As they stepped onto the porch ready to enter, the front door opened and Patrick saw something. Unlike whatever had been in the woods, it was very real.

"Cam stopped off to sneak some beers from his dad. He'll be here—"

Tyler Murphy stopped in his tracks when he saw Patrick. He had one arm around Keisha Hudson while holding a beer can in his other. He'd been hooking up with Keisha while he was still at Smithville High. Patrick hadn't seen either of them at prom, but it didn't matter because they were here now and this was definitely going to be a problem.

Tyler's face curled with anger when he realized who was in front of him.

"What the fuck are you doing here, Shourds?" he asked, a hint of a slur in his voice.

Patrick didn't advance, but he didn't back down either. He'd always taken a more passive stance with Tyler, partly out of a lack of support, but mostly because he did sympathize with his anger. He'd lost his brother and Patrick was there. But tonight was different. Patrick had moved past what had happened, and while he still felt a measure of compassion, he was no longer going to take the blame for something he didn't do.

"I don't want any trouble, Tyler. I'm just here to hang out."

"Well, you're not fucking welcome," Tyler spat.

"That's not your call," Patrick said, taking Megan's hand and leading her up the stairs, trying to angle past his antagonist. He didn't make it as Tyler took his arm away from Keisha and shoved Patrick back, almost toppling Megan in the process, but Patrick held his grip on her hand and kept her upright as red clouded his vision.

Once he was sure Megan was steady, he charged up the steps, bumping chests with Tyler who dropped his beer and tried to push Patrick again. But he was drunk and Patrick was faster, hitting him with a shove of his own that sent him backward through the open doorway.

"Motherfucker!" Tyler bellowed as he lurched forward.

Patrick was fully prepared to defend himself, no longer willing to be Tyler's—and Leeds Point's— punching bag. Turns out he didn't have to as Josh stepped in, pushing Tyler back while holding out his arm to keep Patrick at bay.

"Dude, what the fuck?" he asked of Patrick rather than the instigator.

"He fucking pushed *me*," Patrick explained.

"He don't fucking belong here!" Tyler shouted. "That fucking psycho killed my brother! He'll kill us all if he gets the chance!"

"I didn't kill Brandon!" Patrick bellowed. "I never fucking hurt anybody!"

"Get inside, Tyler," Josh ordered. "I'll handle this."

Tyler turned his attention to Josh. For someone throwing out accusations about Patrick being a killer, he certainly had a look of murder in his own eyes.

"You fucking better," he threatened. "Or I will." He shoved himself free and Keisha put her arm around him, guiding him back inside, but not before he threw one last warning to Patrick. "If I see you again, Shourds, I'm going to fucking kill you."

"C'mon, Tyler," Keisha said, "let's go."

They disappeared behind the door, but Patrick could still feel his heart beating out of his chest as adrenaline surged through him. The door opened again and he truly believed that if Tyler were to come back out, he would charge him. But it was Crystal who emerged.

"Hey, Josh," Patrick said, calming himself, "I'm sorry, but—"

"You need to leave," Josh interrupted.

Patrick couldn't believe what he was hearing. Megan stepped up and joined him at his spot on the porch.

"Are you serious right now?" she asked. "You're telling us to leave, but letting that fuckwit stay?"

"That's what I'm telling you. And I'm not telling you again."

"Crystal?" Megan appealed. "For real?"

"You heard him, Megan," she said. The message came out unsteady, but it was delivered loud and clear.

Patrick scoffed. He supposed that's what he got for thinking he could actually fit in with the people who had ignored him at best and shunned him at worst. Again, he took his girlfriend's hand, this time nudging her toward the car. And, in typical Megan fashion, she had to get the last word in when they were halfway there, turning back and shouting to Crystal, "Enjoy getting herpes tonight, bitch!"

"I guess that's what we get for trying to be normal teenagers," Patrick lamented as he and Megan sat in the backseat of his car.

They had driven to Pilot's Point, a clearing in the woods overlooking a cliff. They called it that because one could easily get a view of the planes departing from and arriving at Atlantic City Airport. Even though their attempt to go to the party was a disaster, they still had a bit of time before Megan had to be home, and she suggested this would be as good a spot as any. So there they were, sitting in the back, Patrick's arm around her as she cuddled up to him while they listened to Megan's meticulously curated playlist.

"Normal's overrated," she said.

"Probably," he agreed. "I'm just sorry you didn't get to do the whole prom after-party thing."

"Don't be. That wasn't the point of tonight anyway."

"So what was it?"

Megan seemed surprised that he had to ask.

"The point was for me and you to have a special

night. And we did. That little failed side quest didn't take away from that." She paused. "It didn't for me, at least. Do you feel like it did?"

He squeezed her and kissed her forehead.

"No. Not at all. Being out there with you was amazing. It was an experience I didn't think I'd ever have. And it was perfect."

He kept his head down, so she tilted hers upward. What started as a small kiss escalated into something more as their lips parted and passion overtook them. They'd made out plenty of times over the past two years and had explored different ways of expressing their physical connection, but they'd never fully consummated it.

In the back of his mind, Patrick had thought tonight would be the night. Prom seemed like the appropriate time, but they never actually talked about it so he didn't want to assume. As she started to unbutton his shirt, he cursed his lack of preparation and broke the kiss.

"Wait," he said, catching his breath. "Are we . . ."

She nodded, her eyes burning with an intensity he hadn't seen before. She clasped her hand around his neck and pulled him in for a truncated kiss before breaking away. Her voice was breathy as she said, "Yes. It's time. You want to, right?"

"Of course! I just didn't . . ."

Megan smiled and reached into her bag, showing Patrick that while he may not have been prepared, she was. That was all the incentive he needed.

Patrick hadn't realized they'd fallen asleep, so when he heard the light tapping on the window, he was disoriented at first. He was lying across the backseat of the car, Megan on top of him, her soft breathing telling him she was still asleep. Their discarded clothes lay on top of them, forming a makeshift blanket.

As the tapping continued, Patrick suddenly felt a wave of panic when he realized he didn't know what time it was. Had they been gone too long? Was it Megan's dad ready to beat Patrick's ass?

He twisted around so he could see who was trying to get his attention and saw Brandon's mutilated visage for the first time in years. From what he could see through the fogged-up glass, his friend's ghost looked as if it had decayed even more since last he saw him. The thing's finger rested on the glass, dirt and blood dripping down into the window well.

Feeling Megan stir on top of him, he looked down at her, only to see that she was gone and the colonial woman, whom Patrick had named Helena, was resting atop his chest. Ever silent, her scarred face registered the same lack of emotion it always did. When she opened her mouth, he thought she might finally speak, finally tell him what all this had been about. Instead, a black viscous sludge spilled out, coating his chest in a substance that smelled as foul as it felt.

Patrick shoved her off and sat up in time to see a demonic pair of eyes burning into him through the front windshield. As the Leeds Devil smashed through the glass, Patrick screamed.

"Patrick!"

Megan's voice sounded like it was far away. Everything was dark, so he did his best to locate where she was calling to him from. The next thing he knew, his body was being jostled. When she called his name again, he snapped awake.

Patrick breathed a sigh of relief when he found that he was in the car and the windshield was intact. It was an even bigger relief that Megan was the one who was with him. Until he saw her face. It was etched with fear.

"What is it?"

"Look," she said, pointing out the back window.

It was a bright night with a nearly full moon, so Patrick could easily see the thick, black smoke billowing above the pines. Following it down, he could see the flickering glow of flames burning in the distance, too big to be a simple bonfire. It was coming from the direction of the after-party.

They dressed quickly. Megan called her father as Patrick sped back to the cabin.

Something terrible had happened.

Chapter 27

September 2025

Patrick was awake but didn't want to open his eyes. That was the one sense that could betray him right now, that could reveal Megan actually *wasn't* here with him. He felt her head and hand resting on his chest while his fingers traced the smooth skin of her bare back. The taste of her honey-vanilla ChapStick lingered on his lips as he listened to her breath, soft and steady. He'd caught phantom whiffs of her perfume so many times over the past sixteen years, but now it was a steady aroma that soothed him as he took it in.

If he opened his eyes, he was afraid he'd see it was all in his mind. That he was alone again. He always thought he was okay with that, happy to keep everyone in his life at a distance. But being back here with Megan dispelled that idea. If he opened his eyes and she wasn't really there, he didn't know if he could handle it.

Unfortunately for Patrick, his bladder compelled him, so he bit the bullet and looked. To his relief, Megan was indeed still there, sleeping on him, the cool silver of her goose necklace resting on his chest.

The late afternoon sun invaded the windows, forcing Patrick to raise his forearm to shield his eyes. He carefully extricated himself from underneath Megan. While she mumbled something incoherent and rolled onto her side, she didn't wake up. Able to move freely, Patrick stepped out of bed and into his shorts. He closed the blinds, blocking out the intrusive light before making his way to the bathroom.

With his business conducted, he returned to his room and found his mother standing over his bed looking down at Megan. This newest haunting had quickly become the most awkward.

But there was also something different about it. Brandon and Helena always wore stoic expressions, bordering on sadness. The few times he'd seen his mother since his return, she'd had a similar look. This time, though, a small smile crossed the ghost's lips. She regarded Megan as a mother would a sleeping child. When Patrick reentered the room, she looked up, the smile remaining as she lovingly observed her son.

They stood like that for several moments, emotion coming dangerously close to overwhelming Patrick. Finally, Cindy walked toward him, her steps slow and deliberate. She stopped briefly in front of him and raised her hand gently, hovering it just over his cheek without making contact, even though Patrick desperately wanted her to.

"Mom . . ." he whispered.

The spirit's smile remained, but she lowered her hand and moved around Patrick, leaving his room. This time, he understood she wanted him to follow her.

By the time he stepped into the hall, she was gone, but he saw the door to her bedroom slowly creep open. He headed that way without hesitation, yet she was still absent when he entered. Looking around, he didn't see her hiding in the corner, but there was something different. A drawer in the dresser was open, and he was certain it hadn't been before.

The contents seemed innocuous at first—some makeup, a small tin filled with assorted coins, and a pile of stationery. Patrick sorted through the papers and found photos, birthday cards, and a piece of macaroni art he'd made in elementary school. There were also envelopes bearing logos of the utility company, car insurance, and some medical bills. The tops had all been torn open and the statements stuffed back in unevenly. But there was one envelope that remained unopened. It took Patrick a second, then he realized what it was. His DNA results from the tests he and Megan had taken senior year.

He'd forgotten all about them. Especially after the chaos following their prom. He checked the postmark and it was mailed toward the end of the first week of June. Either it had arrived after he'd left town, or Mom had intercepted and hidden it from him. Whatever the reason, he found it odd that she had never opened it and taken a peek. Was it because she already knew what was in there? Or because she didn't *want* to know?

He tucked his finger under the flap, ready to tear open the envelope, when the doorbell rang.

Who the hell is here now?

He returned the envelope to the drawer and pushed

it shut. Not bothering with a shirt, Patrick navigated the hall to the front door, opening it and knowing immediately he was in trouble. In more ways than one.

Sheriff Alberts and Cam Gideon were on the other side, their SUV parked at the curb in front. Behind them was another car that, while unmarked, was almost certainly a police vehicle. He could see two men sitting inside.

Patrick stepped into the frame, trying to block off as much as he could.

"Sheriff," he greeted. "What's going on?"

"Catch you at a bad time?" Cam asked snidely.

"Anytime I see you is a bad time, Cam," Patrick shot back.

"Enough," Alberts said. "Were you supposed to meet Peter Savila last night at Parkhill's?"

"No, why?"

"He's missing," Alberts replied. "There's some evidence of foul play."

"Just like Zach Torres," Cam added.

Patrick was shocked. He didn't know what he expected to hear from the lawmen, but not that.

"I'm sorry to hear that, but I'm not sure what it has to do with me?"

"His wife said he was on his way to meet you last night to talk about some real estate deal. Were you doing a deal with him?" Alberts asked.

"Yes," Patrick said. "He's going to buy the house once the estate is settled."

"Uh-huh," Cam chimed in. "What'd he lowball you?"

"He made a fair offer. I accepted. Why would I want

to hurt him?"

"You tell us," Cam said.

"I didn't. What else do you want?"

The sheriff produced a printout of what looked like a text message exchange and showed it to Patrick.

> It's Patrick Shourds. I need to get back to Chicago ASAP...problem with a project I have to deal with. You got those papers ready?

> I can. We still good with the terms?

> We can talk about it. Can you meet me at 8 p.m.? Parkhill's?

> Sure, but if we need to amend the terms, I'll need to know before I draft the contract

> We'll talk tonight. See you then.

"I didn't send those," Patrick said, dumbfounded. "That's not my number."

"They came from a prepaid phone," Alberts clarified.

"Patrick," Megan's voice sounded from behind him and his stomach dropped. This was about to get way worse. Megan stepped around the corner, having slipped on his Chicago White Sox T-shirt before coming to see who he was talking to. When she saw her father,

her eyes bugged out, and before she could stop herself, she blurted, "Oh shit!"

Alberts's eyes burned with fury as he looked first at his daughter, then at Patrick. How the man kept his composure, Patrick would never know. Even Cam looked uncomfortable.

"Let's go, Patrick," the sheriff said through gritted teeth.

"Am I under arrest?" Patrick asked defiantly.

"Not yet," Alberts replied. "But it'd be in your best interests to come with us. Now."

Chapter 28

March 1749

Anna stood frozen by the door, scarcely able to believe what she was seeing. Her mother had passed away a year ago, yet there she stood by the fireplace, the flames casting a soft glow on the scarred left side of her face. She looked much as she did the last time Anna had seen her, even wearing the very dress she was buried in. The only thing different was her eyes. Her left, on the scarred side, had always been covered with a leather patch, but now it was bare, the lidless orb bulging from its socket. Both irises were clouded with a milky sheen. Despite that, Anna felt as if she were looking through her, into her very soul.

"Mother?" she asked again. "How are you here before me?"

The specter remained silent, its purpose unannounced. The only acknowledgment it provided was a slight tilt of the head.

Anna willed herself to step forward, despite her trepidation at approaching her dead mother, who had inexplicably returned to their home. As soon as she moved, so did Mother. The spirit moved purposefully to the far side of the room, stopping briefly in front of the door to Father's bedroom before disappearing through it.

Keeping a cautious distance, Anna followed. Hesitant to open the door but deciding the phantom was her mother, at least in form, she had to see what it was trying to convey to her. Slowly turning the knob, she felt her breath catch in her throat as she pushed the door open.

Mother was waiting for her inside, standing next to a heavy oak chest beneath the window.

"Mother," Anna said, "what are you trying to tell me?"

The spirit remained silent as Anna strained her eyes to see through the dark room. As if sensing her difficulty, the room gradually illuminated. Startled, she turned to see the candle by Father's bedside now flickered with a tiny flame, providing the means she needed to find her way.

Turning her back only for a moment to pick up the candle was long enough for the specter to vanish. Anna was as confused as she was fearful, but she knew she had to see what it was Mother was trying to tell her.

Anna was surprised to find the chest was not locked, and it opened without resistance, carrying the scent of the wood as the lid rose. She examined its contents, removing them one by one, seeing nothing that Father would deem necessary to keep secret. Most of the things were Mother's personal items. They included an apron, lengths of fabric she used to sew, pillowcases and cloth, and recipes written on yellowed scraps of paper. None of it was anything Anna hadn't seen before, so for what purpose her mother drew her to this box would seemingly remain a mystery.

That was, until she went to put the apron back in the chest. As she picked it up to return, it unfurled and a leather-bound book tumbled from inside, hitting the floor with a *thud*.

What is this? she thought.

She opened the tome and read the inscription on the first page:

The Journal of Jane Sharp

Who was Jane Sharp? Why would Mother have this?

Her ruminations were disturbed when she heard Abner moan. Keeping the book with her, she hurried back to the common area and took her seat by her brother's sickbed. She placed the back of her hand on his forehead, feeling the heat radiate across her knuckles before they even made contact with his skin. He moaned a second time and writhed momentarily before falling still once again.

Anna took one of the cloths she had previously laid at the foot of the bed and dipped it in the pail of water set beside it. She wrung it out, letting the excess drip back into the bucket. Once damp, but not soaked, she gently dabbed Abner's forehead, the boy again moaning in his delirium as she tried to curb the fever. When he fell still, Anna felt a moment of anxiety, but the shallow rise and fall of his chest alleviated the immediacy of it, although she knew her brother was far from saved.

She settled back in the chair and paged through the journal. Jane Sharp lived in Middlesex County with her sister Abigail. In 1727, a man named Abraham Shotwell accused Abigail of witchcraft, claiming he had seen her take on the shape of a cat roaming his rooftop and bewitching his horse, which died shortly thereafter. Abigail was tried and convicted of witchcraft and sentenced to death. She urged Jane to flee Middlesex, which she did, ultimately ending up in Leeds Point.

The diary detailed Jane's dalliances with witchcraft, although by her own admission, she was not as powerful as her sibling. Though she attempted to maintain a low profile, eventually she was accused of witchcraft herself. She claimed Daniel Leeds offered to protect her from standing trial, but in doing so, she would be betrothed to his brother Japhet.

Daniel Leeds? Anna thought. *The man who accompanied Father tonight?*

The subsequent entries describe Jane's life with Japhet in their cabin out in the Pine Barrens. As Anna read, it became clear that the home she spoke of was the very one in which she had resided her entire life. The journal painted Japhet as a drunken oaf, loud and belligerent, with a penchant for whoring. Jane alleged that it was not uncommon for her husband to force himself on the young women his wealthy brother sent from town to assist with various household chores and to care for their growing brood.

Much of the next part was spent talking about Jane's numerous pregnancies, each one more trying than the last. She had a dozen offspring, laboring away to care for them while Japhet drank and philandered. Her final entry tells that she had recently found she was pregnant for the thirteenth time. The anger in her written word was palpable. She spoke of her desire to see Japhet and Daniel Leeds dead, along with, she wrote, *the denizens of this wretched town.*

While that was the last of Jane's entries, there were further writings, only now they were signed differently. Her mother's name practically leaped off the page:

Delphia Shourds

Jane's writings contained allusions to witchcraft and dark magic, but Mother's entries read like a tale of horror. Anna flipped through the pages frantically, doubting her own eyes as to what she had read. She scanned one harrowing passage after another, the true breadth of the situation at hand becoming dangerously clear.

She dropped the book and checked on Abner. Her brother was sleeping as peacefully as possible given his state. She rushed to Mary and pulled her away from the game she played with Nathaniel, much to the younger girl's dismay.

"Listen closely, Mary," she said with urgency. "Father is in danger. There are forces at play in this land that he is unaware of. I must make haste to catch him before it is too late. Do you understand?"

"No, sister," Mary replied innocently, "I do not."

"You do not need to in this moment," Anna said. "All you need to do is watch over Nathaniel and, should Abner's fever spike, dab his head with a cool rag. Can you do that?"

The ten-year-old nodded, although fearful.

"I will return as soon as I can. Nathaniel, heed your sister while I am away."

Anna donned her wool coat and leather boots and rushed off into the woods behind her family's home, praying she would not be too late.

Chapter 29

September 2025

Patrick shifted in his chair in front of the metal table ringed with coffee stains in the interrogation room of the Leeds Point Sheriff's Department. It was squeezed into the back, almost like it was added after the building was already completed, as if an afterthought. Nestled between the evidence locker and a small supply closet, the room carried the slight odor of disinfectant. Patrick would never consider himself easily distracted—years of persistent hauntings will do that to a person— but even he couldn't ignore the irritating *buzz* of the flourescent light that cast an oversaturated glow on the room's occupants. It was only slightly worse than the rattling air conditioner that did nothing to cool down the stifling environment.

Alberts stood in the corner of the room, leaning against the wall with his arms crossed, looking none too pleased about deferring the questioning to the two state police detectives who currently sat across from Patrick with open file folders laid out in front of them. He wondered if that was by choice or mandate from the higher-ranking cops. He'd seen the sheriff range from mildly annoyed to downright pissed off over the years, and Patrick could say with 100 percent certainty that this was the angriest he'd ever seen him.

The detectives were polar opposites of each other. Stermak, the shorter one, looked like he'd gone many rounds in the boxing ring during his time. The bridge of his nose was flattened, the result of more than a couple of breaks. His voice sounded like he gargled gravel, reminding him of the boss in *Reservoir Dogs*. Masters was taller and looked like somebody's favorite uncle. Patrick could tell that he was playing the "good cop" role here. A small recorder sat at the center of the table, the green light showing its *on* status.

"When was the last time you were with Peter Savila?" Stermak asked.

"I met with him at his office on Wednesday."

"You're sure?"

"It was the day before my mother's funeral. I'm sure."

"Have you communicated with him by any other method since then? Phone? Text? Email?"

"No."

Stermak held up the printout of the text chat Alberts had shown him at the house.

"You're telling us these didn't come from you?"

"They did not."

"Then who did send them?"

"You tell me. I'm not a detective."

"No, but you're certainly a smart-ass," Stermak growled.

"Are you aware of anybody who may want to impersonate you?" Masters asked.

"I don't know," Patrick replied. "Deputy Gideon out there used to try to get me in trouble by telling the teachers I did things I didn't do. Maybe it was him."

"That's a serious accusation to level against a law enforcement officer, Mr. Shourds," Stermak said, still irritated.

"I didn't text him," Patrick said. "I don't know who did, and I can't think of anyone who would."

The detectives exchanged glances and Masters posed the next question.

"What can you tell us about an altercation with Zachary Torres on . . ."—he paused to double-check the file—"Tuesday at Parkhill's Pub?"

Patrick looked up at Alberts. The sheriff met his eyes but didn't betray his thought process.

"He was harassing the waitress. Slapped a pad out of her hands. I felt obliged to come to her aid."

"The bar didn't have other staff to handle it?"

"The owner was in the kitchen checking a food order. No one else seemed interested in helping her."

"What's your relationship with the waitress? Miss Alberts?"

Again, Patrick turned his attention to the sheriff, the lawman's expression advising him to tread carefully.

"We're friends."

"Friends?" Stermak scoffed. "That wasn't her standing in *your* doorway wearing *your* shirt before you drove here?"

Alberts was boiling. Patrick was thankful the state

detectives were in the room right now because he remained unconvinced that the sheriff wouldn't shoot him right then and there. And he sure as shit wouldn't just graze him.

"We have a . . . complicated relationship," Patrick answered, now avoiding eye contact with Alberts. "Tuesday night was the first time I'd seen her in sixteen years. We dated in high school and it ended without closure."

"Did you get your closure?" Alberts asked, surprising Patrick.

"Working on it," he replied, knowing he risked sending the sheriff into orbit. He didn't care. Alberts had some explaining of his own to do concerning the missing doctor's ID badge.

"What can you tell us about the incident in May 2009?" Masters asked.

Patrick didn't answer. He looked down at his hands, trying to somehow recall and block out that night at the same time.

"Twenty-seven people died in the Pine Barrens that night," Stermak said. "Report says you were there."

"I was," Patrick agreed. "But I wasn't there when they . . . I wasn't present for the incident."

"That's what it says," Masters admitted. "According to this, you had an alibi. You were with Megan Alberts at the time. Is that correct?"

"It is," Patrick confirmed, still avoiding the sheriff's glare. "If this is all in the file, why are you asking me about it? Am I a suspect in these recent disappearances?"

"You're a person of interest," Stermak said. "Unless

you have an alibi for Tuesday or Thursday nights?"

"I was at home . . . at my mother's house both nights."

"Alone?"

Now he looked directly at Alberts as he said emphatically, "Yes." Back to the detectives, he asked, "Am I being charged with anything?"

"Not at the moment," Masters admitted.

"Then I can just get up and leave?"

"You can," Stermak replied. "But it's not advisable."

"Well," Patrick said as he stood, "I advise you to coordinate all future correspondence through my lawyer. His name's Richie Aguilar with Aguilar and Thompkins in Chicago. I don't have a card on me but feel free to Google the firm. Have a good day, gentlemen."

Patrick walked around the table and offered handshakes to the lawmen. Masters accepted. Stermak did not. Alberts stepped in front of the door and issued a warning.

"Tread carefully, son."

"I'd like to leave now, Sheriff."

Alberts stepped aside and let Patrick open the door.

Stermak called after him, "Don't leave town, Mr. Shourds."

"'This ain't the movies,' detective," he said, pausing briefly after he used Alberts's words from the other day against the cop. "You want me to stay? Charge me."

Chapter 30

May 2009

Patrick saw the flames ahead as he drove the path to Swan Lake. The closer he got, heat radiated into the car as it was invaded by the acrid stench of smoke.

"Yes, Dad! Swan Lake! Hurry!" Megan yelled into her phone before hanging up.

"Is he on his way?" Patrick asked.

"Yeah," she replied, leaning forward over the dash, terror growing as they approached the inferno. "He already knew. Someone had seen the smoke before us and called it in. Fire and EMTs are on their way."

Patrick gave it as much gas as he could, barreling toward the cabin as fast as possible without sacrificing his ability to navigate the winding path. Motion in his left peripheral vision caught his attention and he took his eyes off the road long enough to see a large shadow move through the sky. Or at least that's what he thought it was. For the first time in almost four years, he didn't trust what he was seeing with his own eyes.

That was, until they reached the end of the path and pulled onto the cabin's lot. The sight before him he couldn't deny.

"Jesus Christ!" he shouted, as if the Lord had anything to do with the carnage he witnessed.

The fire spread from the center of the cabin, the blaze having pushed through the ceiling was dancing around the stone chimney. Flames peeked out from cracked windows, the wood frames blackening rapidly. Patrick felt the heat lick his face as soon as he was in the open air, the smell of smoke overpowering. The inferno was scary enough, but the light it cast on the surrounding environment revealed the true horror that had occurred.

Mutilated bodies were scattered across the area, blood splattering the dirt, turning it into a canvas of death.

A headless corpse was folded over the railing. Patrick couldn't tell if it was a boy or a girl because the body was on fire and had already been burned beyond recognition. He identified it a second later when he saw Josh's head resting on the grass below, eyes bulging and mouth agape. The girl lying face down near the head had to be Crystal, recognizable by the few areas of her ivory dress that weren't covered in blood. Deep gashes ran the length of her back and her neck was twisted into an unnatural angle.

Flame erupted from the windows, sending shards of glass hurtling in all directions, and a fresh wave of intensified heat barreling into them.

Patrick grabbed Megan by the hand and led her around to the front of the house. The scene there was even worse. More bodies were strewn across the ground and porch, many missing limbs, some of which lay nearby while others were nowhere to be found.

Keisha Hudson was sprawled across the steps where, not long ago, Patrick and Megan had been unceremoniously expelled from the party. Her throat was completely torn out and her midsection ripped open, with things that should be on the inside bulging out and sliding down her legs. Like Josh, her eyes were frozen in her final moment of unimaginable terror.

Megan screamed, finally registering the carnage before her. Patrick pulled her in and held her head against his chest, shielding her from seeing what had become of their classmates. He felt her heaving against him as she sobbed and screamed, having witnessed something no person should ever have to see.

A weak groan from the right drew Patrick's attention.

He turned and saw Tyler Murphy, face down, his clothes tattered and bloody. His left leg was missing below the knee, but he tried dragging himself forward, trailing a carpet of blood.

"Tyler!" Patrick shouted as he released Megan from his embrace, rushing over to check on the injured teen. "Hang on, I got you!"

Patrick rolled him onto his back and nearly recoiled at his condition. Tyler's face was gashed with deep diagonal lacerations crossing from the right side of his forehead to the left side of his jaw and vice versa, forming an *X* across his visage. Like Keisha, his abdomen was sliced open and he pressed his hands against the wound, trying in vain to keep his guts where they belonged.

"Oh shit!" Patrick exclaimed, pressing his hands over Tyler's, not knowing what else he could do. "Megan! Get my belt off, wrap it above his knee, and pull it as tight as you can!"

He didn't know if that would work. That's what people did in the movies when someone lost a limb. They couldn't all be lying, could they? Patrick felt Megan's hands reach out and unbuckle the belt, pulling it through the loops. Once it was free, she did as he instructed, wrapping the leather around the knee above Tyler's stump and pulling it through the buckle until she couldn't wrench it any further. Tyler screamed, a gout of blood spurting from his mouth, the result of his grievous injury.

"Tyler! What happened? What did this?" Patrick asked.

The dying boy looked up at Patrick. He tried to speak, but doing so only produced more blood and a choked gurgle. His eyes bulged, conveying every emotion he was feeling at that moment—terror, agony, regret, sadness. But most of all, Patrick believed he saw a glimmer of understanding. As though he finally realized that Patrick had been telling the truth all these years about what happened to Brandon that day in the Pine Barrens.

"I'm sorry," Patrick said to his best friend's brother as he died in his arms.

Tyler's arms fell limp and Patrick lifted his own, letting the dead boy's limbs drop to his side. Patrick kneeled on the ground, his own emotions fading as he went numb. He looked at his hands, coated such that it looked like he was wearing crimson gloves. Forgetting his surroundings, he breathed in deep, inadvertently taking in a mouthful of fire-choked air, the mingled scent of smoke and copper snaking into his nose. He heard Megan crying softly down by Tyler's missing leg.

As the couple sat among the carnage, unsure of what to do next, red and blue lights suddenly spiraled around the area, mingling with the flames to give a hectic glow to the surroundings. The blare of an approaching fire truck echoed down the path as Paul Alberts stepped into view. He was still dressed in his street clothes and wore a badge on a chain around his neck. His gun was holstered, but he kept his hand on the butt, ready to draw.

He wasn't the only one who had arrived. Just ahead of his car was Cam Gideon's Ford Mustang. With the cops on-site, Cam got out of the car and ran up to Alberts, pointing at Patrick.

"It was him, Sheriff!" Cam insisted. "Shourds did this!"

"He didn't!" Megan protested. "He was with me all night! We weren't here when this happened!"

Alberts studied the trio, determining what he believed.

"Step back, Cameron," he ordered. The teen complied immediately. "Megan, come to me."

She did as her father said but took her boyfriend's hand, pulling him with her.

Patrick felt as if he were an observer outside his own body, the conflagration overwhelming his senses. The heat was still overpowering, but he felt like he couldn't smell the smoke anymore. The sirens were still there, but they sounded muted and distorted. As he saw the fire truck and ambulance coming down the path, something to the right caught his attention, just in front of a cluster of trees.

Helena and Brandon stood side by side, observing the mayhem in silence. Even amid all the chaos, Patrick knew that what he was seeing was real. The ghosts were back. The evil red eyes penetrating the darkness behind the specters told him they were not alone.

Chapter 31

September 2025

P atrick was both surprised and excited to find Megan still at his mother's house when he got back. Her Jeep was parked in the driveway next to his mom's Hyundai and when Patrick opened the door, she was pacing the living room, having changed into her own clothes. She stopped in her tracks when she saw him.

"Patrick!" she shouted, running over and giving him a hug. He reveled in the brief comfort of her embrace, but Megan released it quickly, eager to know the details.

"What did they say? Do they think you did something?"

"C'mon," Patrick said, placing his hand on the small of her back, "let's sit."

They went over to the couch and took their seats next to each other. Megan clasped Patrick's hand as he started to explain, "You know Pete Savila? Casa Bella Developers?"

"He came into the pub every now and then, but I wouldn't say I *know him*."

"Apparently, he went missing last night. They found

his car in the parking lot at Parkhill's, along with his phone. And blood."

Megan connected the dots, registering shock. "Just like Zach?"

"Yeah," Patrick said. "They called me a 'person of interest.'"

"Holy shit," Megan muttered. "Why?"

"Because Zach and I got into a fight the night he disappeared, that doesn't surprise me. But Savila . . . someone texted him from a burner phone claiming to be me. Asking him to meet at the bar."

"Why would anyone do that?"

"I don't know. He was going to buy this house. We'd agreed on a price. I was just waiting for the papers."

"That doesn't make any sense."

"I know."

"How'd you leave it?"

"The state detectives told me not to leave town."

"Can they do that?"

"No. I called my lawyer. That's just movie bullshit."

"What about my dad?"

"Pretty sure he wants to murder me."

"Sorry," Megan said sheepishly.

"I'm surprised you didn't march down there and badger him while they were interrogating me."

"Oh, I thought about it. Even I can only push him so far. And seeing me come out of your room in my underwear and your T-shirt was the upper limit. I figured it was better for you that I stay out of it."

"I think that was the right move," Patrick agreed. He paused, then added, "You hungry?"

"How are you still so wrong after so many years?" Megan asked, her mouth still full of her bite of DeLorenzo's famous tomato pie. That was always the couple's go-to pizza place, sausage and extra cheese being their meal of choice. And the current conversation, spirited debate that it was, provided a welcome reprieve from the multitude of questions surrounding missing doctors and real estate developers and what their parents may know about them. At least for now.

"*Die Hard* is *not* a Christmas movie!"

Patrick washed down his latest bite with a sip of Stewart's Birch Beer—in his opinion, the perfect soda to pair with the pizza they were eating at the dining room table. The restaurant's quality he and Megan agreed on, unlike the current debate about a movie Patrick considered a Yuletide classic.

"Yes, it is!" Patrick countered. "The trailer starts out with Christmas music, the Christmas aesthetic is present throughout the entire movie, *and* the guy who wrote the movie *said* it was a Christmas movie!"

"Fuck writers!" Megan said dismissively. "What do they know?"

"Uh . . . the story? Are you serious right now?"

"Everyone knows writers don't really matter. Look

at *Jurassic Park*! Everyone knows Steven Spielberg directed it. No one knows who wrote it."

"David Koepp," Patrick stated without hesitation. "From the book by Michael Crichton."

"How the hell do you know that?"

"When you don't have a big social life, movies and books are your friends."

"I was the only social life you needed," Megan said as she leaned forward, a telltale sign that the conversation was getting intense on her part. "Christmas movie is a genre in and of itself. It needs to be about the holiday, not just a bunch of shit that happens at Christmas."

"No way," Patrick retorted. "There is no specific *Christmas* genre! There are Christmas *action* movies like *Die Hard*—and *Die Hard 2,* for the record—and there are even Christmas horror movies, like *Gremlins* or *Silent Night, Deadly Night*!"

"You have truly lost your goddamn mind, Shourds."

"Me? You are defending an indefensible position. I seriously think you would argue water isn't wet just to be stubborn."

Megan laughed through another mouthful of pizza. "What can I say? Being obstinate is in my DNA!"

"Holy shit!" Patrick blurted. "I completely forgot!"

"What?" Megan asked, but Patrick was already up and heading down the hall. When he returned, he held up the unopened envelope from the genetics company.

"I found this in my mother's room," he said. "It must have come after I—" He stopped himself, not wanting to ruin the evening by dredging up memories of his departure. "I never got to open it." He sat down and placed it on the table in front of him. "Did you ever get yours?"

"I did," Megan said, turning somber.

"And?"

"I'm clear. There are no markers for my mother's heart condition."

That should have been good news, but Patrick was not blind to the greater ramifications. Megan's whole impetus for taking the test was because she wanted to have children. As far as he knew, she hadn't. His arm itched. He didn't even need to look to know it was his goose tattoo.

"That's great!" he said, trying to keep it light.

Megan was on the same wavelength, preferring to focus on the here and now.

"Well? What are you waiting for? Afraid you'll find out you're at risk for Horrible Movie Take-itus?"

"It'll probably say I'm allergic to people with ODD," he said as he tore into the envelope.

"Didn't seem that way this afternoon," Megan shot back.

Patrick waved her off playfully as he extracted the report. It contained several pages of data. The first detailed his family's origins, which were unsurprising: mostly English, with some traces of Scottish and Irish. The rest was a bunch of information ranging from his traits like eye color, hair color, and personality to the amount of DNA he inherited from Neanderthals, which was less than he would have guessed.

It was the last page that was the most eye-opening. It went into what illnesses he may have been genetically predisposed to. There weren't many, but one leaped off the page at him. At first glance, he thought maybe it was a coincidence, but Patrick couldn't shake it. He stared at the three letters, wondering if that was what his mother's ghost was trying to tell him when she led him to the envelope. Could that really be the case?

"What is it?" Megan asked, genuinely concerned.

"It says what diseases run in my family."

"And?"

"It says I'm genetically predisposed to ALS."

Chapter 32

March 1749

The path had long since disappeared as the hunting party made its way through the overgrown thicket of smaller trees dwarfed by the looming pines that blocked out the moonlight. It felt as if the deeper they ventured into the woods, the colder it became, resembling the harsh conditions of the prior month more with every step. Samuel had only a short time to warm and dry himself after his journey to and from Leeds Point. Now, his clothes stuck to his skin as a chill permeated his bones. But he had no choice. The beast must be destroyed.

"We have not gone so far for the temperature to drop in such a manner," Ezra noted in his thick Irish accent. "How is this possible?"

"It means we are getting close," Samuel said.

"What makes you so certain?" Thomas asked.

"Because unholy land will have an unnatural environment. That is the only explanation."

"So you do not actually know this," Daniel observed, snideness dripping from his tone.

"Were you to present an alternative, I would gladly hear you out," Samuel replied acerbically.

Jonathan took the lead on Samuel's direction, using his hatchet to cut through the dense tangles of branches and brush. The deeper they got, the more effort it took him to clear the path. Fortunately, the work now should allow them an easier walk back to the house once the deed was done. Assuming God willed it to be so.

"These bastards are getting difficult to cut through," he noted.

"Perhaps your axe has dulled?" William asked innocently, though the query immediately raised Jonathan's ire.

"Perhaps you should stay your tongue, boy. I will test my work against any other blacksmith in the colonies. My blades do not dull so easily."

"Apologies, sir, I meant no disrespect."

Samuel patted the young man's shoulder reassuringly. "We are all tense in this moment, son. Pay it no mind."

The crew continued in silence. Samuel noted that the ground softened as they went. Solid, packed dirt turned to mud, their boots sinking in deeper with each footfall and requiring greater effort to extract. The surrounding air thickened, carrying an increasingly foul odor.

"Smells of spoiled meat," Ezra observed.

William gagged, and Thomas shot him a look. The youngest of the group fought to suppress a second retch, only partially successful in hiding his revulsion.

Daniel caught up to Samuel and got close to

whisper in his ear. Samuel found the man's proximity as unpleasant as the stench in the air.

"Is he going to be a problem?" Daniel asked.

"You tell me, Daniel," Samuel replied. "You've relegated us to these woods for well over a decade. These are your recruits. If there were more able bodies available, you should have brought them. There is no turning back now."

"Well," Ezra said, "then how are we going to get past that?"

Distracted by talking to Leeds, Samuel had not seen the massive blockage revealed as Jonathan cleared another overgrowth. This one would not be felled by the tools the men carried. Rows of pines stood before them, trunks squeezed together, preventing even the slimmest of creatures from getting through. Trees did not grow in such an unnatural manner, but the structure looked too large to be man-made. The symbols carved into the trunks, however, very much appeared to be the work of human hands.

"God in heaven . . ." William muttered.

Samuel knew God had nothing to do with this place. If the stories were true, beyond that barrier lay a cursed place known as The Hollow. People had spoken of it in hushed tones, dating back to the very settlement of the colonies. It was said that an early band of explorers stumbled upon an unnatural place where the rules of the surrounding forest seemed not to apply. The tales varied, but the common description was of a barren landscape permeated by the stench of death. Some even claimed it was a doorway to hell itself.

While Samuel had heard the stories throughout his life, he had not lent credence to them until his banishment to this accursed land. The path they had taken warned of something evil, the supernatural essence of The Hollow leaking into the natural world, giving even the most intrepid explorer pause. When the creature fled in this direction, Samuel knew that the legend was true. What he did not know was how to pass the barrier.

"What the bloody hell are we supposed to do now?" Thomas asked in frustration.

"Yes, Shourds," Daniel added, "what is your grand plan now?"

Samuel ignored him, approaching the wall of pines cautiously. He slowly reached out and traced his fingertips along the markings. He observed that some were made more recently, whereas others had been distorted as bark fell away, the result of weather or rot. The rest of the party kept their distance as Samuel walked the perimeter, searching fruitlessly for a way in.

"Is there no entrance?" William asked, his penchant for redundancy on full display.

"There would seem not," Daniel said, his voice cutting. "Mr. Shourds has brought us on a fool's errand!"

Samuel had reached the limits of his tolerance for Daniel Leeds.

"You speak of me as a fool? Look at what has become of your town! Your own folly and failure far exceed mine!"

"Hold your tongue, Shourds," Daniel said, stepping

forward with the confidence of a man believing he has reinforcements. "You know nothing of my town!"

Samuel stood his ground. "And why is that, Daniel Leeds? Shall we tell these men?"

Daniel's mask of false bravado slipped, but ever the politician, he attempted to worm his way out of it.

"That is a private matter that does not concern them."

"It does not concern them that the monster they hunt is your brother Japhet's child? Your nephew?" He watched Daniel's face drain of color. "Or perhaps you can tell them why you imprisoned my wife and I in the godforsaken home where the abomination was born."

"Bastard!" Daniel shouted as he charged, anger superseding good sense.

Samuel easily sidestepped him, extending his foot as he did. Daniel, slowed by age and years of drink, tripped over his foot and landed face-first in the mud. Samuel did not give him a chance to recover, grabbing him by the collar and shoving him into the blockade.

As Samuel reared back to strike the man, he felt the ground shift beneath him. A low rumble escalated in volume as the tremors intensified. Miraculously, the two center trees parted, shedding needles and debris as the path revealed itself.

Startled by the sudden development, Samuel released his grip on Daniel, who fell onto his back, coating his other side in mud to match his front.

As Leeds Point's founder squirmed and squealed with frustration and fear, the others watched as the path to The Hollow revealed itself. No one spoke until the trees settled once again.

"What sorcery is this?" Thomas asked, fear weaving into his gruff voice.

"The darkest kind," Ezra said without pretense.

Samuel took the lead, stepping over Daniel as he entered the cursed section of woods. Ezra followed. Then Thomas. It was only William who offered to help their fallen companion stand. Daniel begrudgingly accepted the assistance.

The hunters readied their weapons as they ventured into The Hollow. It was everything that Samuel had pictured and yet, somehow worse. The pines were as tall or taller as the ones on the other side, but whereas those were sprouting new needles after winter's end and the bark was a rich brown color, these were as black as ink, the branches gnarled and bare, dead sentinels circling a pit covered in a blanket of fog so dense it was impossible to see what lay underneath. The area was littered with bones, leaving no doubt that this was the lair of the Leeds Devil.

Samuel inched forward as the viscous mist swallowed his legs up to the shins. He took care with each step, slowly testing the integrity of the ground before completing the footfall.

"Stay on my path," he commanded. "We do not know what hazards this fog obscures."

The men did as they were told, even Daniel, who now looked more frightened than William. Samuel thought the man may even soil his breeches. But between the mud that coated his clothing and the rot that permeated the air, it would likely go unnoticed.

The entire party was now within the confines of The Hollow, venturing deeper into the unknown with every step. Samuel felt his next footfall sink deeper as wetness enveloped his boot.

"Take care," he told the others. "We are entering a body of water. I cannot discern how deep it goes."

Continuing onward, the party entered the mist-covered pool. The water felt thicker than any lake Samuel had ever bathed or swum in. Colder too. It leveled off when it reached his waist, allowing them to continue wading forward. Daniel was the last to enter the water. As he did, another rumble emanated from behind them.

The men turned to see the trees shifting back toward each other, blocking the exit.

"No!" Daniel shouted, trying to wade fast enough, but he didn't even make it to the edge of the water before the barrier closed, trapping the hunting party inside The Hollow.

"What do we do now?" William asked, dropping any pretense of bravery, unaware that the water behind him began to churn and foam. When a whooshing sound became audible from behind, he turned to see the emerging horror before him.

The crown of the Leeds Devil's equine head surfaced first, its eyes of blood penetrating the darkened water, then the fog. Foul liquid cascaded down its demonic form as it rose to full height, standing more than a foot above Thomas, the tallest of the men. A low rumble arose from its throat and it blew mist from its nostrils as its chest heaved, injured and furious.

Samuel observed the damage from his blunderbuss on the left side of the beast's chest. The wound remained open, a crater of blistering red that oozed around the maggots slithering within. Blood and mucus ran down its chest, matting its fur, which appeared to have grayed since the last encounter. What skin was visible through its hair had wrinkled and taken on a pallor that had not been there before. It was hurt, and that meant it could be killed.

But it did not mean it was not dangerous.

Tremors of terror wracked William's body. He shook so violently that the water churned beneath him. Muted by fear, he did not speak another word as the beast swung its claw, decapitating the young man with one clean swipe. The head traveled an impressive distance, hitting the water with an obscene *plop*, sinking beneath the surface instantly. William's body stood upright for a long moment, a geyser of blood spurting into the air, matching the monster's evil eyes.

When what was left of the boy sank into the pool, the devil turned its attention to the remaining hunters. With an ungodly, screeching howl, it flapped its wings and lunged at Ezra. Even with its bulk and injury, it was still impossibly fast. He lifted the blunderbuss but had no time to aim properly as the thing speared him, shattering his spine on impact. It took him off the ground and drove him against a tree, splintering the trunk as a branch penetrated the man's head, killing him.

Thomas got off a clean shot from his musket but it went wide, blowing a hole in the wing. The devil screeched in pain but was not hampered as it whirled to face its attacker.

"Damn it!" Thomas yelled as he reached into his shot pouch for the powder horn. It would take him several moments to reload. He hoped one of the others would provide cover as he did.

Fortune was on his side as Daniel fired his musket, a terrible shot that sailed over the creature's head and bounced off a tree, sending a shower of darkened bark into the night sky. Though the shot failed to land true, it drew the monster's attention. It lumbered toward the town's founder, who almost certainly soiled his breeches.

Samuel came to his aid, aiming the blunderbuss. Given the gun's short range, he had to let it get closer, but when it sped up, he no longer had the luxury of waiting. He squeezed the trigger and the buckshot exploded from the barrel. The beast was not close enough for a kill shot, but the projectiles tore into its stomach, staggering it.

Jonathan followed from behind, firing his carbine and hitting the thing's back, sending it reeling before it collapsed to its knees. While Samuel's shot did not have enough impact due to the distance, Jonathan's gun was best suited to smaller game. Something the Leeds Devil was decidedly not.

With the creature momentarily incapacitated, the surviving men went to work reloading their weapons. All save for Thomas, who charged, wielding his hunting knife overhead. He leaped onto the abomination's back and drove the blade into its shoulder just below its neck, spraying his face with the thing's darkened blood.

Unfortunately for the man, the creature still had more fight in it than should have been possible with its level of injuries. He continued stabbing at it, but without warning, the monster burst into the air. Thomas instinctively held on, a mistake that would prove fatal. Samuel fired on it with his flintlock, but he missed as it disappeared into the ink-black sky.

"Where did it go?" Daniel shouted. "Do you see it?"

"No!" Jonathan replied. "It is as if it vanished into the night!"

As suddenly as the creature had ascended, something came back to Earth, but it was not the beast. It was Thomas. A guttural scream followed him on the way down before the impact silenced him forever.

"Dear God!" Jonathan shouted. Unlike William, he did get last words of a sort before the Leeds Devil hurtled back to Earth, smashing into the blacksmith before he knew what happened. The collision broke him beyond repair, but it did not kill him. It was the beast's jaws tearing into his throat that took care of that.

The men's sacrifice had allowed Samuel and Daniel time to reload their weapons. Daniel landed his second shot, though it was not ideal, just above the right side of the creature's pelvis, sending it off-balance. Samuel, however, got the shot they needed from his blunderbuss, hitting the thing center mass and toppling it onto its back.

Despite all of it, the monstrosity was still not dead.

"What will it take to kill this blasted thing?" Daniel

asked. Samuel did not answer, but a glance to Leeds's left did. Ezra's body remained impaled on the tree, but lying in a pool of his blood was the man's unfired blunderbuss.

Daniel navigated around the felled monster, giving it a wide berth as he retrieved the weapon. He held it out in front of him as he approached slowly from one side while Samuel moved in from the other. He raised the weapon, pointing the barrel at the thing's head. Before he could pull the trigger, however, the trees leading out of the accursed place opened inexplicably.

Samuel was shocked to see his daughter come running toward them, a look of panic on her face.

"Anna?" he called to the girl. "What are you doing here?"

"Please, sir!" she cried desperately. "Stay your hand! All is not as it appears!"

"I will do no such thing," Daniel spat defiantly. "This curse ends now."

With that, he pulled the trigger, exploding the creature's head.

"No!" Anna screamed in despair as she fell to her knees.

Samuel rushed over to her and dropped down beside her, grabbing her by the shoulders.

"Why have you followed us here? You were supposed to care for your siblings!"

The mention of siblings triggered something in the girl.

"Abner!" she blurted. "We must return home at once!"

Samuel had never seen Anna run so fast as they hurried down the path to the cabin. Daniel had fallen behind, his breath laboring as he tried to keep up.

"Anna," Samuel said, "tell me, what is going on?"

"We must hurry," was all she could say, her own breathing erratic.

When they reached the cabin, it seemed at first that nothing was amiss, but when Anna burst through the door, flanked by her father and Daniel Leeds, they saw that was not the case.

The Leeds Devil growled at the sight of the trio. It stood high in the center of the room as it stalked toward Nathaniel, who was sprawled out and crying in terror. Mary stood in the far corner of the room, huddled against the wall with her knees drawn up to her chest, tears streaking her reddened face.

"How?" Samuel blurted.

Not only was the creature alive, but it appeared unscathed. There were no gunshot or knife wounds. Its fur was thick and its skin had regained its color, no longer the complexion of the dying. There were also some anatomical differences. The fingers of its wings had jutted into sharp talons and its head, still resembling a horse, had taken on a more skeletal, almost demonic structure. What hadn't changed at all were its glowing red eyes.

Samuel fumbled for his flintlock, but in his bewilderment did not unhook it cleanly, the weapon tumbling to the floor. Before he could retrieve it, the creature snatched Nathaniel and hurtled into the sky, crashing through the roof as it disappeared, taking the youngest of the Shourds children with it into the night.

"No!" Samuel screamed in anguish, mirroring Anna's reaction back in The Hollow. He rushed out the door and looked around the sky, aiming his flintlock as if he had any chance of shooting the beast out of the sky while also saving his son. He saw and heard nothing, not even the flapping of the obscenity's wings.

Rushing back inside, he ran to the cabinet where he kept his guns, retrieving his carbine.

"We must return to The Hollow at once!" he cried.

"Father!" Anna said, trying to get his attention, but Samuel paid her no mind, focused on trying to rescue Nathaniel.

"Anna," he said desperately, "please heed my words this time. Stay and look after—"

He cut off his own words as he realized something. Looking to the corner of the room, he saw that his eldest's sickbed was now unoccupied. A sickening sensation twisted his gut. Mary was still crying in the corner, but there was no one else to be seen.

"Abner?" he asked. "Where is Abner?

Anna stood frozen as tears spilled down her cheeks.

"Where is your brother?" Samuel shouted. "Where is Abner?"

Anna closed her eyes and told him the horrible

truth, "That *was* Abner."

Chapter 33

September 2025

"If you're here to talk about your mother's will, I'm afraid I haven't located it," Vivian said as she took a seat on the chesterfield.

"That's not why I'm here," Patrick said, sitting on the opposite side. "I'm actually here to see what you know about my father."

"Your father?" Vivian asked, genuinely surprised. "I have to say that wasn't a question I was expecting. What prompted that?"

"I don't know," Patrick lied. "I guess losing Mom and coming back here got me thinking. Mom was always kind of . . . evasive about it. I thought maybe you could tell me something about the man. Did you know him?"

He watched her face. She kept it neutral, but he thought he saw something beneath the surface. A slight pause as she searched for an answer to the unexpected inquiry.

"I did not. I'm sorry, dear."

He didn't believe her.

"Did she ever talk about him? I thought she would have told you *something* after you found out she was pregnant."

"I thought she would have, too, Patrick, but she kept pretty quiet about it other than saying . . . ugh, it's so distasteful to even utter the words so I do apologize . . . it was just a one-night stand. My sister was somewhat . . . less than selective when it came to her choice in men."

Was she? Patrick thought. Despite the rumors and all the bullshit he had heard over the years, he'd never actually known his mother to ever bring a man home, much less date one. Of course, there were the bruises that she would show up with after a night at work, but that was it. For someone with such a reputation for promiscuity, there was very little evidence to prove it.

Then there was the reason he came here—the DNA test. After he had seen the genetic results and his potential risk for ALS, he wondered if maybe it was just a weird coincidence. A quick search showed that the disease is somewhat rare, only affecting about one out of four hundred people. But familial ALS, like the report showed Patrick may be at risk for, accounts for only 5 to 10 percent of those cases. That was too rare to be a coincidence. Still, it was quickly becoming obvious that Vivian wasn't going to be forthcoming if Robert was somehow his father.

Caterina stepped into the room, carrying a polished silver serving tray with a porcelain teapot adorned with intricate patterns that matched the delicate cups on either side. She was dressed similarly to how she was the first time he met her, wearing blue leggings and a tight white T-shirt. She made it a point to exhibit how well it showed off her cleavage when she bent over to place the tray directly in front of him, remaining bent at the waist while pouring both cups. It would have been impossible not to notice, but Patrick was unmoved. Any thought of a dalliance—using his aunt's vernacular—with the beautiful Italian woman disappeared the moment Megan walked into Parkhill's and back into his life.

"How is Uncle Robert?" Patrick asked, changing the subject as far as his aunt would know.

Vivian slipped into her melodramatic persona, replete with her signature move of placing her hand over her heart. "My poor husband," she said, exhaling deeply. "I fear he does not have long left."

"I'm sorry to hear that, Aunt Vivian," Patrick said. "There's nothing they can do?"

"Unfortunately, no," Vivian replied. "Soon, I'll be left all alone in this big house."

She didn't know that he knew about the foreclosure. Now, with Savila missing, she'd missed a window to unload it before the bank took it. Why was she trying so hard to hang on when she clearly couldn't afford to stay here, let alone maintain it? It didn't make any sense.

"You'd stay here by yourself?" he asked.

"Where else would I go?"

"There are plenty of nice retirement communities. You could be around others in a similar situation."

"Ha!" Vivian said, the snide corner of her personality taking over. "I'd sooner blow my brains out on my husband's deathbed."

She was already pissed, may as well add to it.

"How come you and Uncle Robert never had children? Did you want them?"

It was another question that threw her off. The irritation drained from her face, replaced with a mix of sadness and regret. She put her head down and took her tea from the tray, taking a sip. Patrick cringed at how loud she slurped it.

"We did. But it was not to be. Turns out we couldn't conceive."

"I'm so sorry," Patrick said. "Was Uncle Robert infertile?"

Vivian narrowed her eyes.

"That's an odd and . . . borderline inappropriate question."

"I'm sorry. I was just trying to understand his condition better. Perhaps the two were related?"

"We never determined if it was him or I that couldn't conceive. He developed the ALS many years after we stopped trying." She took another sip of her tea, again grating on Patrick's nerves given the loud way she sucked down the hot liquid. When she placed the cup back on the tray, she shifted back to a more congenial demeanor. "I'm sorry, Patrick. I sincerely was not expecting you to come over and ask all these questions. Especially about your father. Perhaps we can look into them together?"

"How would we do that? You said you didn't know who my father was."

"I don't," she replied. "But we can take our time

and go through your mother's house. Perhaps she had something that could tell us who he was?"

Patrick sat back in the chair, watching as the last hints of steam faded from his untouched cup of tea. He understood he was at a crossroads. The DNA test had hinted that Robert Lumley may have been his father. But if that was the case, Vivian would not just come out and admit it, which meant one of two things.

Either she didn't know, and Cindy and Robert had an affair behind her back. If that was the case, did she need to know that now? Her husband was about to die, leaving her alone in a house she was mere weeks from losing. Patrick had no great love for his aunt, but he also had no ill will toward her. Why ruin what little of her life was not troubled?

Or, she did know, which begged several questions: Why would she allow it? Was it some weird type of open relationship? Was it a way for them to see if he could conceive a child? But if that was the case, why her sister?

Everything about this situation just raised more questions. But one stood out above them all. Did he even want the answers? The ghosts? His parents? The missing people? The monster in the woods? So, yeah, did he need answers, or did he just need to get far the fuck away from here?

Patrick had spent his entire adult life away from Leeds Point. His time in this town had brought him nothing but sorrow and pain. In all that time, there were only two people he truly loved.

The first was his mother. She wasn't perfect and

clearly there were things she never told him, but the one thing he never doubted was how much she loved him. He knew she would have done anything for him and had worked so hard to give him a good life, even under tragic circumstances. Whether he was the result of a one-night stand or Robert Lumley was his father didn't matter, and the truth, whatever it was, may make him see his mother in a negative light. He didn't want that. He must have broken her heart the way he left town without so much as a word. Who was he to stand in judgment now? Better to let the woman finally rest in peace, remembering her as the loving soul she was.

The other was Megan. While Patrick couldn't repair the relationship with his mother, he still had time to make things right with the girl he loved, yet abandoned sixteen years ago. Maybe that was why this all happened: to bring him back here, to give him a second chance with her. Just like his mother's ghost had led him to the lockbox and then the envelope with the test results, perhaps it was her death that lcd him back here to what he really needed to find.

Fuck it. The mystery of his parentage could remain in this haunted town.

"It's okay, Aunt Vivian," Patrick said as he stood. "I'm going to head out."

Vivian stood with him, her expression suddenly anxious. "So soon? Would you like to stay for dinner? Caterina is making chicken Française." She turned and shouted toward the kitchen, "Caterina! We have enough for Patrick, right?"

After a moment, Caterina stepped back into the

room, a wicked grin on her face. "Of course," she said. "I'd love to have him for dinner."

Subtle.

"Thank you, Caterina, but I'm going to have to pass," he said before taking his aunt's hand in his. "I have to pack, but thank you for taking care of Mom all these years."

Now the old woman looked downright spooked.

"You're . . . leaving town? For how long?"

"I have things to attend to back in Chicago. I'll handle any estate matters via courier and notary."

He started toward the door. Vivian hurried after him.

"What about the sheriff's daughter?" she asked. When he turned back to her, he saw Caterina over his aunt's shoulder. If she held the sneer that currently twisted her face too long, it might very well freeze that way. "You seemed like you had some type of connection at the funeral. Were you thinking of giving it a second chance?"

Patrick tried not to show the confusion he was registering. Why was Vivian so hell-bent on him staying in Leeds Point? Enticing him first with this Italian vixen, then by appealing to his heart by bringing up Megan. She seemed awfully invested in his love life. It was strange, to say the least.

"Respectfully, Vivian, my personal life is my business." He gave her shoulder a gentle squeeze. "You can have any estate documents forwarded to my lawyer, Richie Aguilar, in Chicago. Take Care."

Vivian did not protest further as Patrick left and

made his way to Cindy's car. As he pulled away from the old house and onto the highway, he saw more than asphalt before him.

He saw his future.

Chapter 34

Chris Boland did not look happy to see Patrick come through the door of Parkhill's. It was just after four p.m., so the dinner crowd—if any—hadn't arrived yet. There was only a table of four guys wearing purple and red football jerseys with Greek letters identifying their fraternity as *Sigma Phi Epsilon*. Having seen *Animal House*, Patrick could tell the names embroidered on their backs—*Snarf, Dizzy, Phlegm,* and *Jem*—were pledge names. They were having a spirited discussion about someone in the frat deleting their custom football league in the latest version of *Madden NFL Football*. Seeing them reminded Patrick that college was one of the many things he missed out on in life. It only reinforced his desire not to live in regret any longer.

"Hey man," Chris said from behind the bar, "I'm not trying to be a dick, but trouble seems to follow you, and most of it here, so can you maybe go somewhere else to eat?"

"It's okay," Patrick said, understanding his trepidation. "I just need to talk to Megan, then I'll be out of here. In fact, I'm leaving town tomorrow. I won't be a problem for you anymore."

"Sure. Just please don't cause any trouble."

"Scout's honor," Patrick promised. "Is she here?" He posed the question, even though he knew she was.

"She's in the kitchen," Chris answered. "I'll go grab her."

Before he could, the door swung open and Megan came out, wearing jeans and a Parkhill's polo, wiping some buffalo sauce off her chin while she stuck out her tongue as if trying to cool it down.

"Hey, Chris, you gotta tell Teddy to chill on the cayenne pepper. I nearly burned my damn tongue off!"

She stopped when she saw Patrick and a smile stretched her face.

"Hey!" she said, stepping out from behind the bar and making her way to him. They took their seats on two stools as Boland went back to work reloading ice and cutting fruit, releasing a hint of citrus into the air as he worked. She rubbed his arm and asked, "Did you talk to your aunt?"

"Yeah, it was a waste of time."

"She didn't have any answers about your dad?"

"Oh, I think she did. She was just lying about it."

"Do you think Robert is your father?"

"I don't know. And honestly, I don't care."

"Just like that?"

"Yeah. Just like that. I've gone this long not knowing and truthfully, any answers would just raise more questions about my mom. And I want to remember her like I do now. Whoever my father is, he was never in my life. And he's not going to be."

"Wow," Megan said, taking in his explanation. "That makes a lot of sense. You're good with it?"

"I am. Really."

"Speaking of dads, did you talk to yours?"

"Fuck no!" Megan blurted. "He needs six to twelve months to cool down."

"What about Dr. Chase? The ID? Are you going to press him on it?"

She thought for a moment. Dealing with the aftermath of him finding her with Patrick was the more immediate concern. She looked like she hadn't thought much more about it.

"It may answer some of those questions you don't want answered. About your mom. You just said you didn't want that."

"True, but I don't want to deny you closure either."

"Maybe that's not the closure I was looking for."

"No?"

His hand was resting on the bar. She put hers on top of his and looked deep into his eyes, her jade green irises looking as vibrant as ever.

"No." She paused, really contemplating what she wanted to say next. "We're both chasing answers about people who are long dead. Who we never even met. Should that prevent us from living?"

Patrick knew now, more than ever, that he was making the right choice.

"You're right. None of it matters. Our parents, this town. You know, Vivian was practically begging me to stay for dinner with her and my uncle's aide. The

Italian girl."

"Oh, I fucking remember her."

"You're very cute when you're jealous. You know that, right?"

"Whatever, dude," she snapped back, but Patrick knew she was also playing it up. "Why didn't you stay? I'm sure she would have made you fettuccini Alfredo or some bullshit."

Patrick rolled his eyes. "I'm not a big pasta guy."

She smacked him. "Oh, *that's* why?"

It was amazing how easily they had fallen back into their old banter. Patrick tried not to think about how much his decision sixteen years ago had cost him. Never again. He took her hands in his and got serious.

"I'm leaving town," he said. "Tomorrow. I'm going back to Chicago."

Megan's face dropped and her shoulders slumped. She pulled her hands away as if they'd been burned like her tongue from the wings.

"Oh," she said, her voice dropping. "So, that's it?"

Patrick took her hands back in his. She didn't resist.

"No, that's not it. I want you to come with me."

It didn't sink in right away. He tried to read her, which, considering how Megan typically wore her heart on her sleeve, was unusually tough right now.

"You want me to just pick up and leave Leeds Point?"

"It's sixteen years later than it should be. But it's not *too* late. So, yes. I want you to come to Chicago with me."

"I . . . I don't know. I have an apartment and a job . . ." Chris turned from cutting the limes and shook his head, letting her know not to use her employment as an excuse. Patrick could see the thoughts racing around her mind until finally, she came out with it.

"Fuck it!" she said, grabbing his face by the cheeks on both sides and pulling him in for a kiss, drawing a round of applause from the frat boys. "Let's move to Chicago!"

She turned to Chris, cringing as she offered him an apologetic smile.

The bar owner sighed. "I'm not getting two weeks' notice, am I?"

Chapter 35

June 2009

Patrick dipped the sponge into the bucket and wrung it out before wiping it up and down. He'd gone out to cut the grass but was greeted by a word written in red spray paint across the white garage door.

It was the third time his house had been vandalized since the prom night massacre. Patrick had been questioned, of course. He knew that would have been the case even if Cam Gideon wasn't accusing him to everyone who'd listen.

The cops questioned him in the emergency room where he and Megan were being treated for smoke inhalation. Alberts was there, but it was the state police who took the lead. They were not overly antagonistic in their queries. Patrick had a solid alibi in Megan, and the injuries suffered by the classmates were consistent with an animal attack. They presumed it was a pack of bears that attacked the party. They even floated the possibility that they were rabid.

But Patrick knew the truth. The Leeds Devil was still out there. Why it had lain dormant for so long and why it chose prom night to attack was a mystery, but he knew it was the creature that was responsible for the death of twenty-seven students that night. Not a pack of fucking *bears* that somehow they were unable to track. Just like the *bear* that killed Brandon.

The following weeks passed in a surreal blur. There were funerals and memorials that, while Patrick was not explicitly told he was banned from attending, he didn't dare show up. Brandon had once again become a steady presence in his life, showing up just when he thought maybe he'd seen the last of his best friend's ghost. He thought often about the look in Tyler's eyes as he'd died in his arms. He believed Brandon's brother had finally seen the truth. Maybe he even forgave Patrick. But that provided little comfort.

One thing somewhat welcome was the fact that he hadn't seen Helena or the Leeds Devil since that night. Brandon had never been more than a silent spectator. Helena was a dark omen of tragedy to come. While he couldn't be sure, he hoped the woman's absence signaled an end to this cycle of killing. Maybe the creature had been satiated and would not return. It hadn't been seen in the four years since Brandon died. With over two dozen dead, maybe that would multiply.

Somehow he doubted it.

Mom was supportive, but there was little she could do other than give him space. She urged him to go back and see Dr. Hassan again, but Patrick was not going to play that game. He knew what he saw. He wasn't going to run and shout it in the streets like the town crier, but he wasn't going to sit in a psychiatrist's office and pretend the monster wasn't real. And he sure as hell wasn't going to go on medication.

The only thing that brought him a semblance of normalcy was Megan.

Unsurprisingly, her father had told her she shouldn't see him anymore, and just as predictably, Megan summarily ignored that edict. She came over every chance she got and they'd hang out in his room, listening to music and watching movies, keeping it to light fare like comedies and Disney flicks. They didn't talk much about what happened that night, often preferring to lie down, holding each other in silence.

While it was rooted in sadness, it was never awkward. Her warm body and steady breath beside him were the only things that kept him from losing his mind some days. More than ever, he felt like they truly were geese.

They had plenty of time since school shut down for two weeks in the aftermath. There had only been a month left and the administration had contemplated letting the students finish from home, having assignment packets they, or their parents, could pick up so they could do the work to complete the curriculum, especially the seniors who were on the cusp of graduating. Ultimately, they reopened but provided the homeschooling program as an option. It was a no-brainer for Patrick, and Megan's father had surprisingly allowed her to do it as well. While Sheriff Alberts had given up on trying to keep her from going to Patrick's house, he insisted she, at minimum, do her schoolwork on her own and finish before she saw him.

"Patrick?" Cindy called as she exited the house. "You've been out here a long time and I didn't hear the lawn mower. Is everything—"

The sight of her son scrubbing the accusation off the garage was enough to answer the question before she finished asking it.

"Sons of bitches!" she screamed while pulling her robe tight. It had been a late night at Parkhill's and she slept in. Patrick knew she'd be getting up soon, which is why he figured it was a good time to cut the grass without disturbing too much of her sleep. "I'm so sorry, honey. Let me get changed and I'll help you." She let go of her robe and it fell aside a bit. Patrick saw a fresh bruise by her collarbone, but he didn't mention it. He'd long since given up on asking about her injuries.

"I got it, Mom. Really."

"Honey, I can help."

"No, you worked all night. They did this because of me. I can clean it up."

She walked up and gently stroked his cheek. He let the sponge fall into the bucket, the water splashing over the side as it was displaced. Cindy pulled her son into a hug as he tried to hold back tears.

"You didn't do anything, Patrick. These assholes

don't know what they're talking about."

A solo tear broke through as he squeezed his mother tight. He knew she believed him and she believed *in* him, and that meant the world to him. Without her and Megan, he didn't know how he would have made it to this point.

"I'll go get lunch ready for when you're finished," she conceded. "What do you want to eat?"

"I'm not hungry, Mom."

"Honey, you have to eat something. How about I order Chinese and go pick it up? Does Megan want anything?"

Patrick furrowed his brow. "She's not here, Mom."

Cindy smiled and pointed behind him before stepping back into the house.

Patrick turned to see Megan walking up the driveway wearing a sympathetic expression. She shook her head at the vandalism.

"At least they spelled it right this time. Remember when they forgot the *C* in motherfucker?"

"Yeah. You went around for two days calling everyone 'motherfewker.' I'm not even sure that's how it would be pronounced."

"No one corrected me," she said with a smirk, before leaning in and giving him a quick peck. "Got another sponge?"

With the garage cleaned off, Megan and Patrick joined his mother in eating takeout from Great Wall, their favorite Chinese restaurant. Cindy offered to leave them be, but they insisted she eat with them. It was a nice meal. It almost felt normal, if that was even possible anymore.

When they were done, it was getting late, so Patrick was ready to excuse himself and say goodbye to Megan so he could actually cut the grass. But Mom gave him a look and said, "The lawn can wait until tomorrow."

The young couple went to Patrick's room, leaving the door cracked. Patrick put on music and they sat together on the bed, Megan holding his hand in her lap.

"You okay?" she asked.

"Sure," Patrick replied. "Just the town psycho cleaning graffiti off the garage." He couldn't even tell if it was sarcasm or levity. He fell quiet as Megan rested her head on his shoulder.

"This is so unfair," she said softly. "Why can't they just see what's in front of them? How could you have even done any of that realistically?"

"It doesn't matter," he replied. "The town wants their boogeyman and I'm it. As long as the police don't have any interest in finding out what really did this, they're going to pin it on me. Because it's easy."

"I believe you, you know."

Patrick stayed silent. Megan lifted her head and nudged his face to look at her, her green irises registering sincerity.

"I know you do," he said. "We were together the whole night."

"No," she countered. "I believe you. About *everything*."

"Everything?"

"Yes. I know there's been weird shit in this town as long as I've been alive. Everyone knows and no one wants to talk about it. I think my dad is trying to keep people from panicking, but I saw those bodies too. There's no way a pack of bears did that."

"So, you believe in the Jersey Devil."

She stared at him, taking her time before answering, "I don't know about the legends, but I know there's something out there. Something only a few people have ever seen. So, I believe you. I've *always* believed you."

"It doesn't scare you, living here with a monster in the woods?"

"Fuck yeah, it scares me!" she said. "But our parents don't seem as concerned, so what can we do? It's not like we can just pick up and run away."

"Why not?" Patrick asked, giving voice to the thought before it was even fully formed in his head. Megan sat up and grabbed him by his wrists, pulling him up to a seated position opposite her. The sincerity gave way to a glimmer of something mischievous. And hopeful.

"Are you serious right now?" she asked.

"Yeah. I am," he said. He got off the bed and paced, the idea spurring him forward. "We're eighteen and about to graduate high school. It's not like I can show my face at the community college now. Why not make a fresh start somewhere else?"

"What about money?"

"I've got some saved. Mom started an account for me when I was born. She didn't put much in there, but I haven't touched it, so there's a few thousand dollars. Now that I'm an adult, I can access it. There's enough to get us started."

Megan lit up. "Yeah! Dad did the same for me! Plus, I got a bunch saved from working at the mall the past few summers. Like six grand in total! If we combine our money, we can rent an apartment and get jobs!"

"Exactly!" Patrick said eagerly. "It'll be a lot easier for me to get hired somewhere outside Leeds Point!" He paused, then added, "This can work."

"Where will we go?" Megan asked, her enthusiasm mirroring Patrick's.

"Anywhere!" he said. "Arizona? Colorado? Montana? You name it!"

"Arizona sounds nice!" she said. "It'd be awesome to not freeze my ass off in the winter!"

"Arizona it is!" Patrick replied as they hugged and kissed, their strategy cemented.

"When should we leave?" she asked.

"The letter from school said that anyone who does not attend the graduation ceremony will get their diplomas mailed within a week. We may need those to get jobs. As soon as we get them, we leave the next day."

"Holy shit," Megan said, letting the plan sink in. "We're really doing this, aren't we? We're really leaving Leeds Point?"

Patrick kissed her again.

"Fuck yeah, we are."

Chapter 36

September 2025

Patrick saw Alberts through the glass wall of his office as Carole escorted him through the bullpen. He looked like he was holding something in his hands, but they were below the desk, so he couldn't see the item. When the sheriff heard them approaching, he opened a drawer and put it inside before closing it. Patrick had a good guess as to what it was.

Alberts stood as Patrick entered his office. "What are you doing here?" he asked.

Patrick thanked the receptionist as she excused herself. He stood behind the chairs rather than sit.

"I came as a courtesy to let you know I'm leaving Leeds Point tomorrow. I won't be coming back."

Alberts looked conflicted. Patrick knew that his leaving was exactly what the sheriff wanted, but the state police detectives weren't going to be happy about it. And now there was another layer to complicate things.

"You talk to Megan about this?"

"I did."

Patrick could see the man's jaw clench.

"She's going with you," he said. It wasn't a question.

"It's not for me to say. I'm sure she'll come see you."

The lawman rolled his chair back from the desk and stood. He took a long look at the framed photos of his family. For a second, Patrick wondered if he had forgotten he wasn't alone. Finally, Alberts broke the silence.

"Do you remember our conversation before you left the first time?"

"I do," Patrick replied.

Alberts turned his attention from the pictures back to Patrick. "I stand by everything I said then. You need to think about this carefully."

Patrick snorted a punctuated laugh. "I've had nothing but time to think about it, Paul. You were wrong back then. And you're wrong now."

"Am I?" he asked, fighting to keep his cool. "Why is that?"

"I think you know there's something more going on in Leeds Point. I think you know there's something in the woods and it sure as hell isn't a rabid fucking bear."

"That's what you and a bunch of drunken Pineys claim. I haven't seen any evidence to say otherwise. How is it that no one credible has ever seen your Leeds Devil?"

"I'm not credible?"

"Don't misconstrue me, son. I'm saying you were traumatized. That can fuck with even the best of us. But there's no evidence other than your word, and I've told you before, police work relies on *evidence*."

"Like an ID badge for a missing person?"

The sheriff rested his knuckles on the desk. He was pressing them down so hard, Patrick could see them turn white.

"I have two *active* missing person investigations. I'm not going to prioritize a cold case from damn near twenty years ago . . . no matter how close it hits to home."

"That seems to be the problem with Leeds Point, Sheriff. *Everything* here hits close to home. That's why I'm leaving."

Alberts pushed off his desk and sat back down in his chair.

"And what if the problem isn't the town, Patrick? What if it *is* you? You really want my daughter to be a part of that?"

Patrick laughed again. "The only bad things that have ever happened to me have happened to me in Leeds Point. There's no reason to think that wouldn't be the case if I leave. And Megan? She can make her own decisions."

"Then I guess we've said everything we need to say."

Patrick eyed the sheriff, his inability to get a read on the man infuriating to the end.

"I suppose so," Patrick agreed. He grabbed a Post-it note and a pen from Alberts's desk and jotted down a name and number on it. "I know I told the detectives to look up my attorney's info, but I have nothing to hide, so I'm going to make it easy on them. Here is his name and phone number. If they have any other questions, they can go through him."

He stuck the note with the information on the center of the sheriff's blotter. Alberts didn't try to take it.

"I'll let them know."

"Goodbye, Sheriff."

Chapter 37

Megan couldn't believe they were really going to do it. Just a week ago, she'd never thought she'd see Patrick Shourds ever again. Now, he was back in her life and they were back together.

We are together, right?

The thought was odd. Patrick had just asked her to drop everything and move to Chicago with him. That was as together as it gets. When she really thought about it, she never felt like they weren't. There was a reason she hadn't dated anyone seriously since he left the first time. Sure, there were some poor decisions with guys like Zach Torres, but no one else ever had a piece of her heart. It may have started as a silly joke, but they really were geese.

How many poor decisions did Patrick make out there? Was he ever serious with anyone else? I'll have to ask him. No. Scratch that. I don't want to know.

She told herself to knock it off. Whatever happened in their time away from each other didn't matter. For whatever reason the universe brought them back together, she wasn't going to let jealousy fuck that up.

That's why she was driving to his house now. Everything she needed was packed into a suitcase and a carry-on bag she'd bought years ago with an eye on travel that never happened. Her rent was paid through the end of the following month, but she'd call her landlord about ending the lease early. He was always reasonable, so she was hopeful. Patrick had told her not to worry about it. He would buy out her lease if need be.

Until he said that, she had never considered what his financial situation might be. But she knew he owned a construction company and had built some pretty extravagant houses from what she saw when she looked up his website. He was obviously doing well. She thought back to when they'd first planned to run off to Arizona with less than ten thousand dollars between them. They were willing to go anywhere as long as they were together. And that hadn't changed. He could live in a penthouse or the poorhouse and Megan would still be all in.

There were things she'd need to take care of. She took the necessities, but she had left a good amount of things in her apartment. Patrick told her they could hire a company to pack it up and haul it out to Illinois for her. She would just have to coordinate with her landlord to give them access. That was one potential area of disagreement, though. Patrick made it clear he would never return to Leeds Point, but Megan didn't know if that would be the case for her. After all, her father would still be here.

Which, of course, was the biggest problem of all. Megan loved her father despite his quirks. She knew there were things he didn't tell her, but she also kind of accepted it because of his career in law enforcement. If movies or TV were anything to go by, they were supposed to be evasive. Whatever his reasons, she knew he did his best for her and she had no plans to just abandon him forever. Patrick knew that and would never try to stop her from having a relationship with her dad.

The only question was: would Dad want a relationship with *her* after this?

She always suspected that he had something to do with Patrick ghosting her the first time around. She had even called him out on it, but he never admitted or denied it. He just talked around it in typical Paul Alberts fashion. But, like every other secret this town held, the truth didn't matter as much as escaping the lies.

The plan was to stay one last night at Patrick's childhood home and then head to the airport in the morning, but when she pulled into the driveway, Cindy's car wasn't there. Megan knew he was going to the sheriff's office about the investigation before they left. She probably should have called him first, but she thought the conversation would be best conducted face-to-face. Dad deserved that much, at least. Patrick promised her he wouldn't say it, but he also wouldn't lie about it. She knew her father would realize what was going on the moment Patrick said he was leaving town.

She sighed, deciding that she would drop her bags off

and then go see Dad when he got off work, not wanting to have this conversation at his office. After she ripped off that Band-Aid, she would pick up another pie from DeLorenzo's for her and Patrick's last night in Leeds Point. Sure, they'd eaten pizza last night, but Megan knew that deep-dish stuff they had in Chicago couldn't come close to a good old New Jersey tomato pie.

Shit. Maybe I should rethink this whole thing.

Even in her inner monologue, she couldn't help being a smart-ass.

Megan had been at Patrick's house for about a half hour when the doorbell rang. She paused the *Vanderpump Rules* rerun she was watching to kill time and leaned forward to try to make out the shape through the front door sidelights. Patrick wouldn't ring the bell and he hadn't told her he was expecting anyone. The silhouette she saw was small and thin. It looked like a woman. The bell rang again.

Flipping off the television completely, Megan got up and went to the door. Once she was closer, she saw that the unanticipated visitor on the other side was Vivian Lumley, holding an unmarked manila envelope.

The old woman greeted her pleasantly enough when she opened the door, but something about it seemed disingenuous. Like some *Stepford Wives* shit.

"Megan, dear!" Vivian said. "How nice to see you!"

"Um, hi, Mrs. Lumley. Nice to see you too."

"Oh, pishposh," Vivian said with a wave of her hand. "We're practically family. You can call me Vivian."

Who the fuck says 'pishposh' in New Jersey?

"Okay," Megan said tentatively. "What can I do for you, Vivian? Patrick isn't here right now."

"He's not?" Vivian asked as if she already knew that. "Well, it's certainly nice of you to look after the place while he's away."

"Yeah," Megan said. "Just trying to help in any way I can."

Vivian stood there for several long, awkward moments, maintaining a level of eye contact Megan found unsettling. Finally, she asked, "Aren't you going to invite me in, dear?"

"Does Patrick know you're coming?"

"I called him and let him know I'd be stopping by."

"He didn't tell me that."

"I left him a voicemail. I know you younger people prefer text messages, but I could never come around to those things. Too impersonal. He must not have heard it yet."

Megan narrowed her eyes. Patrick was always fond of telling her, *If your mouth doesn't say it, your face will.* Most times, she had no problem using her words, but here she was trying to restrain herself, even though her expression couldn't hide her skepticism.

"What's that?" she asked, nodding toward the envelope.

"Oh, this?" Vivian asked, sounding as if she forgot she had it. "This is the copy of my sister's will. Patrick was looking for it."

"Great!" Megan replied, trying to convey enthusiasm as she held out her hand. "I'll be happy to give it to him."

Vivian maintained her creepy-ass smile even as she disagreed.

"It would be better if I wait and give it to him personally. There are some . . . finer details I need to discuss with him."

"Well, I'm not sure how long he's going to be. So how about you leave it and I'll have him call you when he gets home?"

The old woman's smile closed into a tight-lipped variation, her mask slipping. It was only a moment before she widened back into the pod-person grin. Again, she let an uncomfortable silence hang in the air for several tense moments. This time, instead of speaking, she reached out and stroked Megan's brown hair. It took everything the younger woman had not to recoil.

"You are such a beautiful woman, Megan. You know that, right? My nephew is very lucky to have you."

"Um, thanks," Megan said, shifting, trying not to appear too uncomfortable. As she moved, Vivian saw the suitcases and her phony smile dropped completely.

"Are you going somewhere, dear?"

"That's not really your business."

"I don't understand why you don't convince him to stay here," Vivian complained with a disappointed shake of her head. "You two could get married and live in this very house. Think of what a great place Leeds Point is to raise your children."

With predators in the woods, either a pack of rabid bears at best or a murderous mythical creature at worst? No thanks.

"What is this about, Vivian?" Megan asked, dropping pretense. "Why are you so insistent on keeping Patrick here?"

"Because it's important, dear."

"Important for *who*?"

"For all of us. Without him, we have no future."

That was it. This was too weird.

"I don't get it. I just don't get anyone in this fucking town," Megan said. "And you know what, Vivian? I don't *want* to get it!"

She snatched the envelope out of the old woman's hands before she could react, slamming the door in her face with the other.

"Bitch," she muttered once the barrier was between them.

She watched as Vivian stood on the porch for a few more minutes. What? Did she think Megan would reconsider and let her in? Finally, she scowled as she turned and walked to a van parked at the curb. The woman got in on the passenger side, but Megan couldn't see the driver.

What the hell is she doing? Megan thought as she watched the van idle.

Suddenly, Megan's nostrils flared as she caught a whiff of something different in the air. It was the scent of a woman's perfume, but one that was unfamiliar.

She turned just in time to see Caterina. The medical aide was wearing latex gloves and a sinister smile as she jabbed a syringe into Megan's neck.

She barely registered the pinch of the needle breaking her skin before everything went dark.

Chapter 38

Patrick felt a warmth course through his body when he saw Megan's car in the driveway. This time tomorrow, they would be picking up their bags at O'Hare International Airport. By evening, they'd be at his apartment. At *their* apartment. The anticipation of what life could be going forward made him feel better than he had in years. Maybe his entire life.

So when he opened the door and didn't see her, he was confused, but not concerned. Maybe she was in the bathroom or taking a nap? He headed to his bedroom and pushed the door open. The bed was made and untouched. No Megan. The bathroom door in the hallway was open. Patrick reached in and flipped on the light, seeing it was empty as well. Same thing in the master bedroom and attached bathroom.

Where the hell is she?

Going back toward the kitchen, he planned to check out back, then stopped in his tracks when he saw he wasn't alone. And it wasn't Megan who was with him.

Brandon stood in front of the breakfast nook. Mom

stood behind it. Patrick didn't need to look out the window to know what was there, but he did anyway. Helena was pacing the edge of the woods, the trees in her immediate vicinity dead and twisted. He turned back and saw that Brandon was still there, but he had moved to the side. Patrick could see an unmarked manila envelope on the table. Given the trio of ghosts present, he didn't need to open it to know whatever it contained wasn't good.

He didn't hesitate to tear the seal, extracting the handwritten letter inside. Rage bubbled through him as he read it.

Patrick,

Megan is with us. Have Alberts bring you to The Hollow. Involve no one else.

If you do, Megan <u>DIES.</u>

Ten minutes later, a Leeds Point Sheriff's Department SUV screeched to a halt in front of the house. Patrick was already outside waiting for Alberts with the note. He got in and immediately handed it to the sheriff, who was in plain clothes as opposed to his uniform. This was not going to be official police business.

"Son of a bitch!" he yelled as he crumpled the note in his shaking hands. He stomped on the accelerator and the police vehicle whipped around the cul-de-sac.

"What the fuck is going on, Paul?" Patrick demanded.

Alberts hit the lights as he approached the turnoff from Hawk Hill Road and didn't even slow down as he turned onto the main road, nearly clipping a pickup truck and leaving skid marks in the process.

"Paul!" Patrick shouted insistently, not needing to repeat the question.

Alberts took a deep breath.

"It's time to tell you the truth."

Chapter 39

March 1749

"What do you mean, 'That was Abner'?" Father shouted as he held Anna by the shoulders. "What madness do you speak?"

Mary was still trembling in the corner as the men tried to make sense of what had happened. A light rain had started up again and drops fell through the hole created by the creature during its escape. She could feel the cold droplets even through her nightclothes. The frantic panic in her father made her wonder if he even heard what her older sister was telling him.

"I speak the truth," Anna said through her tears. "Mother showed me."

Father's eyes went wide. Daniel Leeds came up behind him and grabbed his shoulder, spurring him to stand.

"Of what does she speak, Shourds?" the angry man asked. "You told us your wife had passed."

"I spoke true!" Father declared as he wrenched himself free, pointing toward the front of the house. "She has lain buried in that ground for over a year."

"Then what is your daughter saying? That she knows something she has been withholding from you?"

"No!" Anna insisted. "Mother came to me after you left." She paused. "At least, her spirit did."

Father crouched down to her again, his confusion growing with each word rather than diminishing.

"Anna," he said, "that is not possible."

His words made her angry. "You killed a winged demon tonight only to encounter another minutes later, yet you question the existence of a spirit realm?"

He did not respond, knowing her logic was sound.

"What did this *spirit* show you?" Daniel asked dismissively, despite all he had witnessed that night.

"A book," she said, getting to her feet and rushing to the bed where her sick twin once lay. "Mother appeared just after you left and led me to the chest in your bedroom. Among her possessions, there was a journal. The journal of Jane Sharp. Or as she came to be known—Jane *Leeds*."

Daniel was pale to begin with, but he went as white as a ghost at the mention of the name. The irony was not lost on Anna, even at her young age.

"What did you say?" he demanded.

"I said I found a woman's journal. A woman I assume you know of . . . Uncle."

Father—*Or perhaps I should call him Samuel?* Anna thought—already had experienced an abundance of horrors this night, the scars of what he had seen etched into his countenance. But this revelation hit him equally as hard. Not because he didn't know. But because he was well aware of Anna and Abner's true parentage.

"What did you call me, girl?" Daniel spat.

"I call you Uncle!" Anna screamed defiantly as she threw the book at him. He failed to catch it and it fell open on the ground. "My brother and I are bastards, the result of your drunken brother forcing himself on our mother while she was attending to his wife's pregnancy!" She turned to Samuel as tears spilled down her face. "Why did you not tell us?"

She saw the man who, until mere hours ago she knew as her father, break down, falling to his knees and embracing her tightly. Anna wanted to resist, but could not remain angry with him. From what she had read of the diary, she knew he was the one who nursed their mother back to health after he found her, the sole survivor of the creature's attack.

It was also he who stayed with her when Daniel banished them from ever setting foot in Leeds Point again. Though he knew she carried another man's child, he fell in love with her and married her before God, even if not formalized by the church. And when Delphia Shourds née McNeal gave birth to twins, he loved them as his blood. Even when Mother gave him two children of his own.

Seeing her sibling and father embrace, Mary rushed over and Samuel held out his arm to pull her in as well.

"I am so sorry, my daughter," Samuel said to Anna, defiant of the truth. "There was . . . too much for young minds to be forced to comprehend. You *are* my daughter even though we may not be connected by blood. I am bound by my love for you . . . and your brother."

He sobbed at the mention of Abner, and she squeezed him back.

"It is *I* who am sorry, Father," she said, choosing to see him as she always had. "Were I to find the journal sooner, we could have prevented this."

"What?" Daniel Leeds bellowed, interrupting the sharing of sorrow. "What does this blasted book say other than libel against my brother?"

Father let them free from his embrace and stood. Mary huddled against his side and he put his arm around her. He put his other hand on Anna's shoulder.

"Pay him no mind," Father said. "But do tell what the journal said and quickly. We must know what we are dealing with if we are to save your brothers!"

Anna felt a wave of sadness overtake her, but she suppressed further tears. Father was unaware of the folly of his words. There was no saving Nathaniel. Or Abner.

"Jane Leeds was a practitioner of witchcraft."

"You raise my ire with every word you speak, child," Daniel said, stepping forward. Father did not let him get too close as he shoved the angry man to the ground.

"You will keep your distance and stay your tongue when it comes to my daughter! Do you understand me, Leeds?"

"Bah!" Daniel blurted as he stood, not even bothering to brush himself off as he was still caked in copious amounts of mud and, judging by the foul stench that surrounded him, something else.

"She admits as much in her diary, Mr. Leeds," Anna

said. "She fled here from Middlesex after her sister, Abigail Sharp, was convicted of witchcraft. When *you* discovered she was also a practitioner, you blackmailed her into marrying your brother!"

Though Daniel wore a scowl, he remained silent, offering neither confirmation nor denial.

"What does this have to do with your brother?" Father asked.

"Jane Leeds cursed her thirteenth child. More than that, she cursed the entire town. The beast and Leeds Point are doomed to be forever intertwined."

"That is why we are here!" Daniel interjected. "The thing's very existence plagues my town!"

"No!" Anna countered. "The creature must survive or the town dies!"

This latest revelation had both Father and Daniel reeling. Everything they believed about the creature dispelled in an instant.

"I don't understand . . ." Father said.

"That is the curse: if the beast dies, the town dies. For the town to live, it must live with a monster. A monster that needs to be fed."

"Fed?" Daniel asked.

"While Mother was convalescing after being attacked, she read the journal, same as I have now. Mrs. Leeds told of cursed spots scattered throughout the world. Places born of ancient evil that only evil could access. She knew of the curse she planned to inflict on her child and the town. She knew once the monster was born, it would seek The Hollow and make that its home."

"What does that have to do with your mother?" Father asked, fear rising in his voice.

"When Jane Leeds died, Mother took over writing in the journal. She studied the spells and sigils she would need to protect us all. She knew the creature was still out there and that as long as it was, it would pose a threat to her family. So, one day, while you were out hunting, Mother searched for The Hollow. And she found it. And the creature."

"Impossible!" Daniel said. "It would have killed her on the spot!"

"It did not because she was carrying my brother and I! It sensed its bloodline within. *Your* bloodline! If what Mother wrote was true, it will not attack its own." She turned to Father. "That is why it stopped advancing on Mary when I stepped in front of it."

"Anna," Father said impatiently, "I do not understand and we are short on time. How do you know that creature was your brother?"

She hung her head. "As long as the Leeds live, so will the creature. Should the creature die, it will pass to the next in the bloodline."

"Then why did it not pass to me?" Daniel asked.

"While the cursed blood courses through your veins and allows you to enter The Hollow, it does not afford you the same protection. Nor does it place you at risk for transformation. The affliction only passes to descendants. It does not fall in reverse."

"What are you basing this on?" Daniel countered.

"That you are standing here and my brother is gone, you foolish man."

Daniel's face reddened and he looked as if he wanted to slap her. Then Father stepped forward, backing him off before turning his attention back to Anna.

"Continue, daughter."

"Mother followed the spells in the book, carving the sigils into the trees surrounding The Hollow to keep the beast at bay. She taught herself to hunt, satiating the beast with small game and scraps of our own food supply while performing rituals to keep it docile. As the mother of children with Leeds blood, the monster never attacked her."

"I saw the woman's face after the child was born. The thing nearly ripped it off! How do you explain that?" Daniel sneered.

"Mother did. In the journal. The creature did not attack her directly. She tried to save her colleague by pushing her out of the way of the beast's strike, putting herself in the path of its claws. Once she fell, it did not advance for the kill."

The pieces started coming together in Father's mind.

"When your mother died, there was no one to keep the beast fed and contained." He surmised.

"I believe that to be the case," Anna said. "The creature was trapped in The Hollow without sustenance. It grew weaker with each passing day."

Samuel turned to Daniel. "That coincides with the start of Leeds Point's decline."

Daniel remained stone-faced but agreed. "It does . . . but how did it get out?"

"The spells need to be maintained. With Mother

dying suddenly and no one to carry on, the barrier weakened, allowing it to get out. That's when it came here. It must have sensed its blood in my brother and I."

"But why attack Nathaniel?"

"Mother carried Japhet Leeds's offspring," Anna said, seeing how Father's face twisted in revulsion. His love for Anna and Abner was true, and so was his distaste for the Leeds family. "There must have been a part of us, of our blood, that remained with her which is why she remained protected and able to enter The Hollow. But that does not appear to be the case with Mary and Nathaniel. It was hungry. And Nathaniel . . . Nathaniel was easy prey. Just as the Leeds children were for the first incarnation of the monster."

Daniel's frustration was at its apex.

"So you say that when I killed the creature in The Hollow, the curse passed to your brother because he was the eldest of the direct bloodline?"

"Yes," Anna said bluntly.

Daniel followed up. "What happens if the bloodline dies out?"

Anna looked at her father, Mary still huddled at his side, her face buried in his ribs. She turned back to Daniel. "As I said, if the creature dies . . . the town dies."

"I see . . ." Daniel said as he drew his flintlock and stepped forward. Father did not have time to react before the man shot him point-blank. A mist of blood sprayed from his forehead, splattering the white linen of the girls' nightclothes. Father fell to the ground, eyes wide at the betrayal that ended his life.

"Father!" Anna screamed. Mary did as well, but hers was an unintelligible wail of anguish.

Daniel grabbed Anna by the arm and yanked her away from Samuel Shourds's body. He did the same with Mary. With the girls on their feet, he reached into his shot pouch, reloading the pistol.

"Gather your things, my dears," he said with a sneer. "You two are going to save my town."

Chapter 40

September 2025

Patrick Shourds first encountered the Leeds Devil twenty years ago, right before he started seeing ghosts. He had no doubt the monster in the woods was real, yet somehow, what Sheriff Alberts had just told him still seemed impossible.

"You're telling me my family has protected that thing for hundreds of years?"

"That's my understanding," Alberts said.

Anger welled up inside Patrick.

"So you knew. The whole time, you knew the thing was real and you let the town think I was the monster."

"No, I didn't," Alberts countered. "I did everything I could to protect you. I officially cleared you both times. But the court of public opinion has a life of its own."

"How did they protect it?"

Alberts clutched the wheel, staring straight ahead at the road as they approached the turnoff to Swan Lake.

"The entrance to The Hollow is down past the cabin, in the opposite direction of Pilot's Point," he said, ignoring Patrick's question. "We'll have to go on foot once the road ends."

"Paul!" Patrick shouted, not dropping it. "How did my mother and her sister protect that thing?"

Alberts exhaled deeply, almost pained. "I don't know all the details . . ."

"No more lies!"

"Okay. They performed rituals they learned from an old journal that allegedly belonged to Mother Leeds."

"That's it?" Patrick asked.

"No." Alberts continued. "They kept it fed."

"With what?"

Alberts looked at him, telling him all he needed to know with his haunted expression.

"Jesus Christ!" Patrick blurted. In that moment, everything came together. His mother's late nights. Her strange bruises. The lockbox. The men's possessions within. It all painted the picture of the dark history of Leeds Point. And his mother's involvement with it. He had stopped seeking answers from Vivian for fear of knowing the truth. Now he knew, and he felt like he might vomit.

"I'm sorry, son," Alberts said. "You were never supposed to find out."

"Then why did she keep all that stuff? If it was evidence of crimes, why did you let her keep it?"

"I didn't," Alberts admitted. "She must have taken things here and there. Why? My guess: to use as leverage in case she ever got caught."

The word *leverage* triggered a thought. A missing piece that explained the sheriff's involvement.

"Eric Chase," he said. Alberts clutched the wheel,

his knuckles whitening as they had back in his office when he pressed them into the blotter. "That's why you've let this go this long."

"How much do you love my daughter?" the sheriff asked.

"What?"

"How much do you love my daughter?" Alberts repeated.

"More than anything," Patrick answered.

"What if she died at the hands of someone who was entrusted with her care? Someone who was high on fucking drugs?"

"I honestly don't know," Patrick admitted, thinking about it. He'd definitely want vengeance, but would he actually carry out murder? "But you're the sheriff. You could have put him in jail."

"I was going to," Alberts said. "But imagine my surprise when Robert Lumley showed up at my door one night and asked me to take a ride with him."

"Where?"

"To a roadside motel in Galloway. When I got there, I found Chase bound and gagged on the bed."

"How did he find him?"

"He never skipped town. The bastard went and got drunk at Parkhill's. That's where your mother came in. She drugged his drink. When he started slumping over at the bar, she called a cab to get him home. Only it was one of Robert's men who picked him up. They brought him to the motel in Galloway where I found him bound and gagged. I was going to bring him in, but his captor offered me something else. He told me that the man wouldn't do any jail time. They'd already revoked his medical license and they'd send him to rehab, but he'd be a free man within a year. He'd be free and Georgia would still be gone." He took a breath. "That just didn't feel right to me. When I asked what he was proposing, he took me to The Hollow."

"You actually saw their ritual?"

Alberts nodded. "Patrick, I wanted that man dead more than anyone, but when that thing came out of the pit in the center of that damned place and tore him apart, I had to look away."

"It didn't attack you?"

"No. Your mom and her sister were chanting something the whole damn time. They were wearing these weird robes. The thing stayed back, taking what was left of the doctor's body with it before disappearing into the trees beyond the pit. I regretted getting involved immediately, but I was too blinded by revenge. I had become a part of it whether I wanted to be or not. Starting that night, I've spent thirty-plus years covering for them. And I've regretted every fucking minute of it."

Patrick didn't know if he felt sorry for the sheriff or if he wanted to punch him in the face. As another question came to mind, the dilemma leaned heavily toward the latter.

"Why did they kill Brandon?"

"They didn't. At least as far as I know."

"What do you mean?"

"Your mother was very selective about who she would lure from the bar. She went with loners. Drunks. Wife beaters. She could never be one hundred percent sure, but she did her best to try to keep the innocent away. She would have never sacrificed a child, let alone your best friend. But more than that, Brandon's death brought attention from outside agencies. It shined a spotlight on Leeds Point that made it difficult for your mom to continue her work."

"What about Vivian?"

"She didn't like getting her hands dirty. She was happy to lord over Cindy from her estate on the edge of town. That's not to say she wouldn't ever bring a sacrifice of her own, but she was happy to let your mother take the risk."

"Why didn't Mom tell her to fuck off?"

"Isn't it obvious, Patrick? Because of you. If the current version of the Leeds Devil dies, the curse passes on to the next in line. Eventually, it would get to you."

"Why not just keep it trapped in The Hollow?"

"It's a no-win situation. If they let it loose, it would draw attention. The cops would get involved. Maybe even the military. That thing is powerful, but it won't survive against an army. Especially one with modern weapons. They'd kill it, then they'd kill the next one and the next until the bloodline was wiped out. If the legends are true, that's the end of everyone in Leeds Point.

"But to keep it trapped, they have to keep it fed or it will die anyway, with the same result.

"Like I said, no-win situation."

Alberts killed the engine and the lights as they reached the end of the road.

"We go on foot from here," he said.

The men exited the SUV and walked around to the rear, where Alberts popped the trunk. He unlocked a 12-gauge shotgun and loaded it with shells. With the weapon in hand, he pulled his Glock from his holster and handed it to Patrick.

"You can handle a gun?" he asked.

"I've been to the range. I can manage this," Patrick replied. Still, Alberts felt the need to give him further instruction.

"Keep your finger away from the trigger and the barrel away from anything breathing unless you want it to stop. Get me?"

"Got it."

The two men proceeded into the woods. Alberts took the lead. His shotgun was low, but he could position himself quickly if need be. Patrick did as he was told and kept the pistol in a similar ready position. The night was cool. Patrick had thrown on a hoodie and jeans, but he could still feel the chill. The deeper they got, the more the air seemed to thicken, taking on an acrid smell. It was smoky, transporting him back to that terrible prom night. As the path narrowed, that odor mixed with the aroma of rotting meat. It must have meant they were getting close.

There were so many questions still whirling around his mind. The Leeds Devil's existence was never one of them, but could that really be his fate to become like it? If his mother did the things Alberts said she did, she must have believed it. Maybe Vivian manipulated her. Maybe it was all bullshit and his aunt had turned her sister into an accessory on false pretenses. Still, Vivian had been hell-bent on getting him to stay in town. She must be a true believer.

Also, Alberts hadn't answered his question about Brandon. The sheriff said Patrick's best friend wasn't a planned sacrifice, but the devil still attacked him. And outside The Hollow. He didn't understand how that was the case since the whole point was to keep it contained. Maybe Alberts didn't know. But Vivian did. And once they made sure Megan was safe, he was going to get his answers.

Patrick became aware that the path had disappeared, making it so they had to step carefully through the thick brush. The stench in the air was becoming overpowering and the chill was penetrating further into his bones. Finally, when Alberts pushed aside an overgrown branch, revealing a line of trees pressed so close together that it was impossible to get through, he knew they were on the edge of The Hollow.

The ghost of Delphia Shourds, the woman Patrick long ago dubbed Helena, stood before him. On her right was the broken, tragic specter of Brandon Murphy, the boy whose death was the catalyst for the nightmare

Patrick's life had become. On her left stood the melancholic spirit of Patrick's mother, the late Cindy Shourds, a woman Patrick always knew had secrets but until tonight, he never knew how horrific they were.

"What?" Alberts asked, realizing Patrick had stopped. The sheriff looked back at him, then to the barrier as he continued to regard the phantoms of his past. "This is it. What are you looking at?"

Patrick realized Alberts wasn't seeing them. His eyes were still locked with his mother's as he answered, "Nothing."

With that, the ghosts faded into the night, leaving the path to the ominous structure unimpeded. The sheriff approached the barricade, running his fingers along a sigil carved into the pine. Patrick looked in every direction, but couldn't find anything resembling an entrance.

"How do we get in?" he asked.

"Stand next to me," the sheriff replied, raising his shotgun. "And be ready."

Patrick did as he was told, moving toward the wall of pines. As he got closer, he felt the ground rumble beneath him. When he took his place at Alberts's side, he asked, "What's going on?"

"Don't ask me why," Alberts responded, "but only someone with Leeds blood can open the pathway."

Before Patrick could even be skeptical, the trees parted like the Red Sea, ushering them into The Hollow.

Chapter 41

On their way over, Patrick thought about two things. The first was what The Hollow would be like. As expected, it was a nightmarish version of the Pine Barrens, lined by dead trees, the ground coated with a thick fog. In the center was a pit that must be the spot where Alberts said the Leeds Devil had taken Eric Chase's body. The few areas where the ground was visible were lined with bones of past sacrifices. A stench of burnt death suffocated the air, making it hard to breathe. Everything about the place dripped with malevolence.

The other thing Patrick worried about was how difficult it would be to find Megan once they were inside. Turns out, it wasn't very hard at all.

She was kneeling on the ground in front of the pit, her hands tied behind her back. Her clothes were dirty and there was a small bruise on her neck, but otherwise, she appeared unharmed. That could change in a heartbeat, however, because two robed figures stood behind her with hoods drawn over their heads.

One of them held a large knife to Megan's throat.

As deadly as the situation was for her, behind them was something even worse. The Leeds Devil towered over the figures, eyes glowing with demonic fury, wings unfurled and ready to strike. Neither of the cultists seemed concerned, however.

Behind him, the entrance remained open, Patrick being in close enough proximity to keep it that way. He thought he should take care how far he stepped so they could escape quickly. But how he would free her with a knife to her throat and a monster behind her was the more pressing issue.

"Megan!" Alberts shouted, aiming the shotgun at his daughter's kidnappers.

"Come no closer, Sheriff," a familiar woman's voice said.

"Enough, Vivian!" Alberts shouted.

"Yes," Vivian said as she lowered the hood, revealing herself to the men. "No need for such theatrics anymore." She looked at her companion and grabbed their hood as well. "Your hands are occupied, dear. Let me get that for you." She pulled it down to reveal Caterina, a malicious smile painted across her face.

"What the fuck is this about, Vivian?" Patrick asked, then ordered, "Let her go!"

"Oh, Patrick," his aunt said. "You foolish, stubborn boy, this is all on you."

"What the hell do you want from me?"

"I just want you to stay." She paused and thought about something. "Stay and have children with one of these lovely ladies. Or both. Is that so bad?"

"So the Leeds bloodline can continue?"

"Yes. As simple as that."

"And if I say no?"

"Then the curse finally wins. After three hundred years, this town will die." She reached over and stroked Megan's cheek. "And I assure you, sweet little Megan here will die first. Painfully."

"Why the hell am I so important? There's got to be others out there."

Vivian shook her head. "No, Patrick. There isn't." His aunt unzipped and shed the heavy robe, leaving her wearing one of her signature black housedresses. "The Leeds bloodline has been dying out for quite some time."

"Weren't you charged with keeping it alive? Sounds like you did a pretty shitty fucking job."

Vivian's face warped into a sneer. "It wasn't for lack of trying, you flippant little shit!" She took a calming breath. "When Daniel Leeds first formulated his plan to save the town, he took in a girl named Anna who was his brother Japhet's bastard child. He married her to a man named Thomas Shourds, a distant relative of the man who raised her, promising Thomas's father a handsome dowry that would multiply with every child she bore. He also wed Anna's half sister, Mary, to his son Jeremiah. That brilliant strategy yielded two new branches of the Leeds family tree. One keeping that very name. The other bearing the name Shourds."

"Then how did it come down to just me?"

"Oh, it's not just you, dear," Vivian said. "There is another, but he is not long for this world."

"Robert," Patrick said.

"Yes," Vivian confirmed. "Once my beloved husband passes away, all that will be left of the Leeds bloodline is his son."

Patrick knew it, but hearing it still hit like a sledgehammer to the gut. Robert Lumley was his father. He looked at Alberts to see if he knew. From the look on his face, he did.

"I'm sorry," the sheriff said.

Megan whimpered, not crying out for fear the movement would drive the blade into her jugular. Her father may have known, but she didn't. Behind her and the other women, the creature's chest heaved as a growl slowly rolled out from its throat. Patrick raised his gun in response, but the beast remained in place.

"Why Mom?" Patrick asked Vivian. "Why didn't you have your own fucking kids?"

She shook her head and looked to the ground momentarily, as if ashamed. "Do you think we didn't try? No matter what we did, we couldn't conceive. Your mother was always reluctant to do her duty, but things had gotten so dire, she had no choice."

"You mean you forced her to be with your husband, you sick bitch!"

"She did her duty to save this town!" Vivian spat back. "The descendants of both bloodlines increasingly could not have children over the years." She took a breath, becoming more reflective. "It was the curse. It was like a cancer. It kept trying to eat away at Leeds Point, while keeping the bloodline strong was like chemotherapy. But eventually, one or the other would win out, and the cancer has gotten very aggressive."

"So let it die!" Patrick said defiantly.

"That's so easy for you to say, isn't it, Patrick? After all, you walked away without a care in the world. You left your mother and this beautiful girl heartbroken. You ran away like a coward. But what do you think happens if the curse wins? A town dying does not just mean it falls into economic ruin. It means the people die too. Hundreds dead. Because you refuse to fulfill your obligation."

"What makes you think I'll be any different? Maybe I can't have kids either."

Megan whimpered at that. He didn't know if it was a reflexive response to the potential of not having a future family or a reaction to the knife at her throat.

"A lot can happen in three hundred years, Patrick," Vivian explained. "While the Shourds name carried on, sometime around the turn of the twentieth century, Leeds became Lumley. As our families died off during the fifties, sixties, and seventies, it became apparent that something needed to be done because children were not being conceived to replace those we lost. That's why the decision was made to remerge the Shourds and Leeds branches. Your mother shared your reticence to do what was required, so I offered myself to marry Robert. But after five years of trying, we found out that I was unable to have children. Your mother had no choice but to step in. She conceived almost immediately."

Patrick couldn't believe what he was hearing. This was insane. The whole fucking thing was batshit crazy.

Yet, somehow, it also made perfect sense. There was, after all, a seven-foot cryptid standing behind his aunt who was rattling off her plans like a goddamn Bond villain.

"If Mom was so fertile, why am I an only child?"

Vivian laughed, but it was humorless. A bitter utterance. "If the curse couldn't prevent her from conceiving, it would make sure it wouldn't happen again."

"I don't know what that means."

"Unsurprisingly, you were a difficult birth. Your mother suffered a uterine rupture delivering you. The doctors were forced to perform an emergency hysterectomy to save her life. You can't have children without a uterus."

He swallowed hard, guilt crushing him. Patrick never really cared that he didn't have a sibling. He remembered life being good until Brandon died. He and his mother were a dynamic duo, going to the movies, to the park, to the mall. Even though it was just the two of them, Patrick had all he needed. He never knew she had suffered such trauma during his birth.

"No smart-ass comment, Patrick?" Caterina asked.

"Of course not," Vivian said to her. "He's too shocked to learn the depths of his ignorance." She put her hand on the Italian woman's shoulder as she turned back to her nephew. "Once my sister was no longer an option, we started hosting exchange students. Some of them were more than happy to be with a man of my husband's wealth and stature, thinking they were getting one over on me, not knowing that I fully approved. Others rejected his advances. But they still served their purpose in satiating Abner."

The creature snorted at the mention of its former name. Patrick gritted his teeth, resisting the urge to squeeze the trigger and shut her up.

"You're fucking sick, Vivian."

"No!" she shouted angrily. "I am the only thing standing between this town and utter destruction!" She rubbed her temples, frustrated by her nephew. Caterina kept the knife at Megan's throat but moved her other hand to rub Vivian's back.

"It'll be okay," she said as if she were comforting someone who'd just lost their job.

"Thank you," Vivian said before shooting her glare back at Patrick. "Caterina was a blessing when she showed up at our door. Not only did she willingly try to be the vessel to continue our lineage, but when we learned Robert had become infertile, she took to my teaching. She learned the spells needed to keep Abner docile. Of course, she does not carry our blood, but as long as she is with me and performs the rituals appropriately, she is safe."

"And what about my mother? Did she keep working with you?"

"Ah, my stubborn little sister," Vivian lamented. "Once you left, she lost all taste for this work. I appealed to her. Pleaded with her. Tried to coerce her. Nothing worked. With you gone, she was defeated. Hell, there were times I think she *wanted* to get caught!"

That explains the lockbox full of evidence, Patrick thought while his aunt continued.

"Want to know a secret, Patrick?"

"I've had my fill."

She ignored the quip. "Your mother was *happy* that you left. Not that she didn't miss you. She did. Terribly. But she never wanted any of this for you. She hoped that if Abner died, the curse would pass to Robert. With any luck, you'd live a childless life and die alone along with the Leeds bloodline before you ever had the chance to inherit our family's legacy." She put her head down, almost as if in mourning, but when she raised it again, her lip was protruding in an exaggerated pout— part of the dramatics Patrick had come to expect from her. "It broke my heart to have to kill her."

Rage exploded through Patrick. How he didn't pull the trigger that time, he would never know. It was probably out of an overriding concern for Megan's safety, but through all his years of bullying and torment, this was the first time he ever considered killing another human being.

"You're a fucking monster," he told her.

"You have such a simplistic worldview, Patrick. I take no pleasure in this work. It's an obligation our family was born to fulfill. When your mother shirked that responsibility, she left me no choice. We had to get you back here. What better way than your mother's funeral? So, Caterina and I snuck into her home using the spare key and put her to sleep. It was quite peaceful, I assure you."

"Jesus Christ, Vivian," Alberts said. The sheriff had mainly been listening. Patrick put together that the man already knew much of this, but clearly there were things beyond even his awareness. "So, the disappearances? That was you too?"

"Just Mr. Savila. We fed him to Abner because we couldn't just let Patrick sell the house and leave. So we texted him with a prepaid phone, pretending to be Patrick. When he got to the bar, we knocked him out and sliced his head open to get some blood on the scene. Make it look like more than a simple man getting drunk and lost in the woods."

"You ever watch professional wrestling?" Caterina asked. "They use a razor to make it look like they got cut during a match. It's brilliant entertainment!"

"We thought that would be enough to have the police scare you into staying in town. But you, clever boy, knew they couldn't legally do that without filing charges. It was worth a shot."

"What about Zach Torres?" Alberts asked.

"Abner went rogue on that one," Vivian admitted. "You got into a fight with him at the bar that night, Patrick. Did you not?"

"We had words."

"Did he accost you?"

"He pushed me."

The creature blew a puff of steam from its nose. The snort echoed through the dead trees.

"Abner is very protective of his family," Vivian explained. "That man putting his hands on you earned him a death sentence."

"What?" Patrick asked, understanding practically smacking him in the face. That was what happened that day in the Pine Barrens, by the foundation of the devil's home. He and Brandon were play fighting. When Brandon accidentally knocked him over, the monster killed him. It was the same thing years later after prom. Tyler Murphy shoved him, was ready to attack. Only when the devil came for him, he wasn't alone. Twenty-seven classmates were there too. And they all died because of it. But that begged another question.

"I thought you kept it contained?"

Vivian sighed. "The spells aren't perfect, Patrick," she said. "Delphia was able to keep it satiated with small animals and even some herbs. But when Abner first turned, Daniel Leeds did make one mistake. He assumed larger game would keep it docile longer. As the head of the town, he controlled everything. Including the prisons. He would bring the dregs of society to The Hollow, accompanied by Anna, and feed them to Abner. Unfortunately, once our dear relative got a taste for human flesh, there was no going back." She turned and looked up at the creature, but its red eyes were locked on Patrick. "Cindy and I are descendants of those who practiced witchcraft, but none were trueborn witches like Jane Leeds. Over three centuries, things get lost. Mistranslated. They lose their efficacy. When Delphia Shourds first discovered the thirteenth child in The Hollow, she was only once removed from the witch who bore it. Her daughter Anna was reluctant and therefore, a subpar student. She even tried burning Jane's diary. Thankfully, a chambermaid discovered and extinguished the flames before the whole thing was lost. With less powerful spells and a taste for blood, it was hard to contain Abner at all times. Especially when he was angry and protective."

"So you failed."

She seemed like she was genuinely contemplating his words. "There is some truth there," she admitted. "I did the best I could, but it wasn't always as good as it could be. I relied too heavily on my sister at times—to all of our detriment—but that doesn't mean there isn't still time to correct our mistakes. She went to Caterina and Megan, putting a hand on each woman's shoulder. "Stay with us, Patrick."

She couldn't be serious. "If it's all the same, I'll just take Megan and leave."

"That's not an option, Patrick," Caterina sneered.

"It isn't," Vivian agreed. "But you can have a life here. Marry Megan, have all the children you can, and bring Leeds Point back from the brink of ruin! All you have to do is be with the woman you love. What could be the downside?"

"How about the murders, for one thing?"

"We'll make sure the people we sacrifice to Abner are the kind of people who deserve it!"

"No one deserves that!" Patrick shouted in response.

"Sure they do, Patrick. And when it comes to saving the lives of everyone in Leeds Point, isn't that a small price to pay? You and Megan can keep your hands clean. Caterina and I will take care of the rest. And after I die, Caterina is young enough to carry on for decades." A sly grin stretched Vivian's wrinkled face. "You can even have her too. Have a whole harem if you prefer! It's all for the greater good!"

Caterina gave him a seductive stare that told him she

was more than okay with that plan. Megan squirmed, risking getting cut in the process to show that she was not.

"Not happening, Vivian," Patrick said. "Let her go and we'll leave. Things will play out how they are supposed to."

His aunt shook her head in resignation. "You don't get it, Patrick," she said, jaw clenched. "This is our last chance. So, if you're rejecting my offer to stay here and be the savior we need, then it ends tonight. All of it."

Patrick and Alberts exchanged a side-eyed glance and readied their weapons. Caterina pushed the knife further into Megan's skin but did not yet break it. The Leeds Devil snarled, a pending roar building in the back of its throat. This was it.

Just as Patrick was ready to pull the trigger, a voice came from behind them.

"Everybody drop their weapons! Now!"

Chapter 42

The events that occurred next did so in rapid succession.

The new arrival was Cam Gideon, flanked by detectives Stermak and Masters as they rushed in through the still-open entryway. Alberts stepped behind Patrick and faced the police, his back to the monsters and the cultists.

"Cam!" the sheriff shouted. "What are you doing here?"

"We followed you, Paul. You haven't been acting right! What the fuck is going on? What the fuck is that thing?"

"Enough!" Vivian shouted, the sound as forceful as it was surprising coming from the old woman. "You all need to drop your weapons or everyone dies. Starting with Miss Alberts here."

To illustrate her leader's point, Caterina pushed the blade into Megan's neck just far enough to draw out a trickle of blood. The sheriff returned his focus to his daughter's captors, aiming his shotgun at Caterina's skull.

"Don't you fucking hurt her!" he threatened, but didn't need to follow through because what happened next surprised them all.

Caterina's chest exploded as a monstrous claw burst through, showering Megan's hair with a bucket of blood. Caterina's arms fell to her sides, and as the creature hoisted her from the ground, its arm still embedded in the cavity, she dropped the knife. Seizing the opportunity, Megan retrieved the blade and scrambled over to Patrick and her father, huddling behind them.

Vivian was enraged. "Abner! Kill them! Kill them now!" she ordered.

Patrick fired the first shot, clipping the beast in its shoulder. It reeled back with an ear-piercing howl as Alberts and the other lawmen opened fire. Many of the shots missed as the beast took flight, its arm still embedded in the dead woman's chest cavity. Two bullets pierced its wings and another ripped through Caterina's thigh on ascent. The monster didn't give them time to adjust their aim as it hurtled the corpse at them. Stermak and Cam dodged, but one hundred and twenty pounds crashed into Masters, knocking him to the ground.

"Masters!" Stermak shouted as he watched the Leeds Devil pounce on the downed man, biting a chunk out of his skull, killing him instantly. "You fuck!" the devastated detective screamed as he unloaded a barrage of bullets into the creature's back while advancing. Unfortunately for Stermak, he judged the creature's reach by its arms, but not its wings. By the time he realized it, the clawed finger of the monster's patagium had pierced his throat. Blood pooled around the gaping neck wound from both ends, spilling down the front and back of his suit. The dying cop continued pulling the trigger, the *click* of the empty gun sounding over his dying gurgles.

Cam's gun was empty too. He reached to grab a spare clip from his belt, but his hands were unsteady, resulting in the magazine falling in front of him. He scrambled to recover it as the Leeds Devil advanced on him, its massive frame riddled with bullet wounds, the coarse fur matted with dark blood.

Patrick and Alberts aimed, intending to fire on the beast, but a shrill scream from behind distracted them. They whirled around in time to see Vivian charging Alberts, a knife identical to Caterina's held high and ready to strike. The sheriff was caught off guard and unable to get a shot off. He braced himself for the knife to penetrate, but Vivian suddenly stopped in her tracks, a choked gasp escaping as she froze. Her mouth agape, a rivulet of blood spilled down her chin.

Looking down, Patrick saw Megan holding the hilt of Caterina's knife in her bloody hand, the blade buried entirely in Vivian's stomach. A crimson flower bloomed around the fabric and the old woman's weapon tumbled from her grip, falling behind her. Megan withdrew the knife with a squelching gout of bodily fluids as Vivian fell to her knees, clutching at her pierced gut, a river of blood seeping through her fingers.

While Alberts was saved for the moment, Cam was

not so lucky. The second time he failed to load the clip sealed his fate as the Leeds Devil thrust its claws into his abdomen and pulled it apart as if it were opening a book. Cam, like his friend Tyler, died knowing that Patrick was telling the truth.

Cam's involuntary sacrifice gave Patrick and the sheriff the opening they needed. Alberts used the distraction to get close enough to do real damage with his shotgun, shooting the monster where its left wing connected to its back. The membrane disintegrated under the blast and the wing flopped uselessly to the ground, barely hanging on.

But the monster still had fight in it. Stermak's mistake had been not accounting for its wings. Alberts risked it all to get as close as he could and ended up paying for it. The creature hit the sheriff with a backhand blow that sent him flying off his feet and crashing onto his back, dropping his shotgun on impact.

The sheriff was lucky it hit him with the back of its hand and not its claws because, although winded, he was alive. That was something the thing intended to rectify as it stomped toward the downed man. Its ability to fly was taken away, but it was still fast. For the second time in a matter of minutes, Alberts was inches from a killing blow. But he was saved again, this time by Patrick, who threw himself on top of the sheriff.

With a member of its bloodline blocking its path, the Leeds Devil came to a halt before it could strike.

"Megan! Get behind me!" Patrick ordered.

She didn't hesitate to run around and kneel beside her father, letting Patrick shield them from the monster.

It snarled, a mix of pain and rage as it took a step back, stumbling slightly as the severity of its injuries took its toll. Patrick held his arms out and reached for the shotgun, slowly picking it up.

When the thing took another step back, Patrick swung the weapon forward and fired without hesitation, hitting the creature center mass, sending it crashing onto its back. Behind him, Vivian, still supine and trying to hold her guts in, grunted out a pained scream as the thing she'd been charged with protecting her entire life fell in battle.

Patrick paid her no mind. The immediate concern was the beast. It was incapacitated but not dead. It writhed on the ground sluggishly, braying like the wounded animal it was.

Megan helped her father up. He'd gotten rocked, but otherwise, appeared unharmed. Still, he was shaky, so she slung his arm over her shoulder and put her hand on his abdomen, helping him along as the trio approached the Leeds Devil. Patrick pumped the shotgun and pointed the barrel at its chest.

"Wait!" Megan cried. "If you kill it, doesn't it just pass the curse to the next in line?"

"We don't know that for sure," Patrick said.

"He must live . . ." Vivian said weakly from their rear. "Abner must live . . ."

Patrick thought about it. As insane as everything he learned tonight was, there was nothing to make him think it wasn't the truth. But he had no choice. The monster had plagued his life for twenty years. It killed his best friend and classmates and drove his mother to commit horrible acts in the belief that they would protect her son.

He felt a presence in front of him. Looking up, he saw Cindy standing over the downed monster. Next to her was Brandon. Seeing them brought every ounce of anger and sadness rocketing to the forefront of Patrick's mind, and he felt their loss all over again.

Propelled by that grief, he pulled the trigger and blew a hole in the Leeds Devil's chest, killing it.

"No!" Vivian screamed as the creature's demonic eyes lost their evil glow, dimming to black.

Patrick dropped the shotgun and picked up Cam's discarded pistol. He then grabbed the clip and slid it in, chambering a round as he approached his dying aunt. He looked down, her skin a ghostly white, her hands coated in blood. Part of him wanted to just let her bleed out, to make her last moments replete with pain and suffering. But he chose mercy instead, aiming between her eyes.

"The Leeds Devil is dead," Vivian said, barely above a whisper. "Long . . . live . . . the Leeds Devil."

Those were her last words before Patrick shot her in the head.

The three survivors stood amid the carnage. The bodies of their allies and enemies scattered about the scarred landscape of The Hollow.

"What do we do now?" Megan asked.

Patrick knew the answer.

"Robert. I have to go see if what they said was true."

Alberts nodded in agreement. "I'll call in reinforcements. Megan, you come with me."

"No. I'm going with Patrick."

"Megan . . ." her father began, then stopped, realizing subsequent words would fall on deaf ears.

"It's okay, Dad. We know the monster won't attack him, so there's no one safer for me to be with than Patrick," she reasoned. "And I can help him if need be."

"Megan," Patrick said, "that's not a guarantee. It's too dangerous. You should go with your dad."

"No, goddamn it!" she snapped back. "You're not leaving me again. We're in this together."

Patrick and the sheriff exchanged glances, each knowing her mind was made up.

Resigned to the situation, Alberts echoed the directive he gave him on prom night sixteen years ago, "Keep her safe."

Chapter 43

Patrick killed the headlights of Cam's SUV as he pulled onto the access road leading to the Lumley estate. He didn't know what would be waiting for him inside the house. Putting aside the potential that his bedridden uncle had turned into a winged monster, he also didn't know if there were any other aides his aunt had converted to her cause. It didn't seem that way, but he couldn't be sure.

They parked in the same spot Alberts had when he'd first brought him here upon his return to Leeds Point. Moving quickly out of the car, Patrick grabbed a freshly loaded shotgun while Megan was armed with a pistol. Keeping to the shadows, they approached the house, rounding the back. The rear door was locked as expected, but there was no time to stand on ceremony. He used the butt of the shotgun to shatter the window pane, allowing him to reach in and unlock it.

Once inside, Patrick took point, leading with the shotgun as he scanned every corner of the room. He wasn't a trained cop or soldier, so he could only mirror what he'd seen in the movies, his heart pounding a mile a minute as he cleared each room.

"This way," he told Megan as they made their way to the staircase with Robert's lift sitting unused. They moved swiftly but silently up the steps, turning into the hallway at the top. "The one at the end," he said as he moved toward the double doors leading to the master bedroom. To confront his father.

They took positions on either side of the doorframe: Patrick on the left, Megan on the right. Patrick raised a hand with three fingers extended. He lowered each as he mouthed a countdown, "Three . . . two . . . one!"

With that, Patrick burst into the room, flanked by Megan. He knew the bed was in the center, so that was where he aimed.

Only it was empty.

The ventilator and IV drip were both disconnected, and the sheets were disheveled and tossed to the side. Patrick's stomach dropped. He had expected to find either a dying man unable to get out of bed or the reincarnation of the Leeds Devil. The thought that there'd be nothing more than a vacant bed never crossed his mind.

"Hello, son," an older man's voice said from behind the door. "Welcome home."

The words weren't even fully out of Robert Lumley's mouth as the once-bedridden man grabbed the barrel of Patrick's shotgun and swung it toward the side of the room so quickly that he didn't even have time to release it. He was in midair when he lost his grip, flying unarmed into the wall.

Megan pointed the Glock at his head, but Robert was too fast, slapping it away, sending the bullet crashing through the window instead of his cranium. He yanked the weapon free of her grip and tossed it across the room before swinging his fist back, then striking the girl and sending her crumpled to the ground.

Still holding Patrick's shotgun, he regarded the weapon for a moment before folding the barrel over onto the stock, rendering it useless. With the gun no longer a threat, he tossed it at his son's feet, demonstrating the danger he posed.

Patrick rolled onto his back and slid against the wall, propping himself up as he watched the approach of the man he'd just learned was his father. Robert's eyes glowed red and when he smiled, fangs protruded from his gums, displacing the teeth that spilled from his mouth and clattered to the floor in a puddle of bloody drool.

"It would appear Abner is dead," Robert said, his tone emotionless. "Imagine my surprise when I found I could sit up." The skin on either side of the man's forehead protruded, stretching the flesh, and his body performed a symphony of pain as his bones cracked and his limbs extended. "I spent years afraid this would happen to me!" he shouted, his voice deeper, bordering on inhuman. "But after years of being trapped in my own body, this isn't so bad."

As the transformation continued, Patrick scrambled to his feet, circling past Robert and over to Megan. He helped her up and pushed her into the corner, standing in front as a human shield.

The lumps on Robert's forehead extended to the breaking point before erupting in a geyser of blood as two horns burst through the skin and curled around the top of his skull, new features of this iteration of the Leeds Devil. The couple watched in horror as the transformation continued. With the shotgun ruined, Patrick thought about running for the Glock but didn't want to leave Megan exposed. Besides, he knew the pistol would damage the thing, but wouldn't be enough to kill it.

"What do we do?" Megan asked, clutching his shoulders.

"Just stay there," Patrick said. "If it's like the last one, it won't attack while I'm in front of you."

If, Patrick thought. Physically, this one was different with the horns. A long, snakelike tail also grew from its back, a sharp, jagged bone sticking out of the tip of the appendage. With the metamorphosis complete, Robert Lumley, the Leeds Devil, Patrick's father, roared.

As it regarded Patrick and Megan with a malevolent stare, those demon eyes burned with fresh intensity. The standoff went on for long enough that Patrick began to doubt that the thing wouldn't attack him. Trapped between the creature and the exit, the only thing he could think to do was to make a dash for the pistol, hoping he'd be fast enough to recover it and fire off enough shots to distract it so Megan could escape.

"Megan," he whispered. "I have to go for the gun. Stick behind me. When I fire, make a run for it."

"No fucking way!" she said, squeezing his shoulder so hard he thought she might break the skin. "Together, remember?"

"Damn it!" he exclaimed, frustrated. "We don't have any other choice!"

Patrick lurched forward, ready to sprint, but the creature did the same and roared, the hot stench of its rotten breath slapping him in the face. The sudden movement was enough to make Patrick rethink his plan, and he pressed back against Megan in the corner.

With one last growl, the monster turned and hurled itself out the window, shattering not only the glass but splintering the frame as it made its escape.

Out of immediate danger, Patrick ran to the window and watched as the winged monstrosity flew over the pines, headed for Leeds Point.

This time, with no one to contain it.

Chapter 44

Chris Boland sighed as he wiped down the bar. Only a handful of patrons had come through since lunch. The fraternity guys were the only ones still at Parkhill's, having stayed long past happy hour and were now hanging out for the evening baseball games. They were tipsy for sure, but not sloppy, and Chris wasn't at a point where he could afford to turn down paying customers.

With Megan gone, it was just him and Teddy manning the fort tonight, but with the sparse crowd, that was all they needed. Chris was really considering closing up shop for good. When it came to the town of Leeds Point, the writing was on the wall. That was a metaphor, of course, but suddenly the pictures on the actual wall—including the slashed sketch of the Jersey Devil—started rattling. Must have been a hell of a truck barreling down the road.

They'd have been better off if it were a truck, because what crashed through the paneling was so much worse. The creature he'd thought was a myth invaded his bar. He didn't even have time to scream before the thing slashed its claws from his forehead, down his midsection, and across his pelvis, tearing deep gashes into his flesh as easily as the drawing that had once been on the wall.

Chris slumped onto the linoleum as the monster upended the bar, tearing it from the floor and sending it smashing into the frat boys, their reactions slowed from hours of drinking, crushing them under the weight of the heavy counter. As he bled out, he watched the creature smash through the kitchen doors.

His cook's dying screams were the last thing Chris heard as his life slipped away.

"Oh my God!" Megan cried as she saw the gaping hole in the side of Parkhill's pub. "Chris! We have to check on him!"

Patrick ignored her as he drove past. "There's no time," he said apologetically, but firmly. "It's already been in there. He's dead." He watched Megan slump in the passenger seat of Cam's SUV. She knew he was right, but that didn't make her friend's death any less painful.

They'd been giving chase since they fled from Robert's house. Not long after they'd pulled onto the road, they'd seen a mangled car. Patrick had stopped and gotten out to check on the driver, only to find his jaw ripped off and stomach torn open. Another wrecked car half a mile down the road presented a similar grisly scene and told Patrick there was no need to check on anyone else.

Now they were following a trail of carnage as the thing that used to be Robert Lumley rampaged through Leeds Point, destroying everything in its path. Whatever Vivian and his mother had used to keep the last one at bay was no longer working. If they didn't stop it, the Leeds Devil would bring about the destruction of the town its ancestor had cursed three hundred years ago.

But to stop it, they needed to *catch* it. The thing was far ahead of them and each mangled car and destroyed home was a reminder of their failure to do so.

They both jumped when Megan's phone rang. It was her father. She put it on speaker.

"Megan! Are you okay?" the sheriff asked in a panic.

"We're not hurt, Dad," she told him. "But those psychos were right! Robert turned shortly after we got there. We're chasing it, but it's too fast! Oh my God, Dad, it's killing everyone in its path!"

"I have a plan," Alberts said. "Is Patrick with you?"

"I'm here, Paul."

"Good." He paused. "Meet me at the foundation of the old Leeds place. You remember how to get there, right?"

Patrick remembered. He couldn't forget if he tried.

"I remember," he told the sheriff. "We're on our way."

Patrick slammed his foot on the accelerator.

The nightmare was going to end in the place where it all began.

Chapter 45

Paul Alberts was standing in the center of what was left of the house where the Leeds Devil was born. Patrick saw him raise one arm to shield his eyes from the headlights and the other held his shotgun. Pulling in next to the sheriff's SUV, Patrick turned off the engine but left the lights on. The first thing he noticed as he exited the vehicle was a strong smell of gasoline. As he got closer to the foundation, he saw the red canister next to Alberts.

"What's going on, Paul?"

"We need to draw that thing away from town," he answered. "Maybe if we set fire to the foundation of its old house, that will do it."

"You think that will work?" Megan asked, looking at Patrick.

"I don't know," he replied, "but it's all we got." He turned to Alberts. "What do we need to do?"

"Help me spread the gas around the perimeter," the sheriff instructed. "I laid down some, but we need more. Megan, grab the flares from my trunk so we can light it."

"Okay," she said, running over to the SUV.

Patrick joined Alberts in the middle of the ruined home. The sheriff held out the can and pointed to the opposite end by the remnants of the chimney. "Start there."

"Got it," Patrick agreed, reaching for the can, but Alberts didn't let it go.

"I'm sorry for everything that's happened to you, son," he said. "And I'm sorry for the part I played in it. You were always a good kid, even after all you'd been through. Under any other circumstances, I'd be honored to have you marry my daughter."

Patrick felt a surge of emotion at the sheriff's words. Alberts released the grip on the gas can, letting him take it.

"Paul," Patrick said, putting his hands on his shoulder. "You know something funny?"

"What's that?"

"Despite everything, you're the closest thing to a father I've had in my life."

Alberts swallowed hard, and Patrick saw tears pool in the corners of his eyes. He'd delivered the message. There was nothing else to say on his part. But Alberts had one last apology to offer when Patrick turned around.

"I'm sorry, son."

Before he could respond, Patrick felt a sharp pain as something struck him in the back of the head. He collapsed to the ground as stars danced across his field of vision. He felt Alberts grab his collar and drag him to the center of the foundation as he heard Megan's voice.

"Dad, I can't find the fla— What the fuck are you doing?"

Alberts reached into the gap in the fireplace and retrieved a hidden flare. Before Megan could reach them, he ignited it and tossed it into a pool of gasoline, trapping him and Patrick in a ring of flames.

"No!" Megan screamed! "Don't do this!"

"I'm sorry, sweetheart," Alberts said as he picked up the gas can and started dousing Patrick. "This is the only way."

The first splash hit Patrick on the shoulder, the cold liquid soaking through his shirt instantly and running down his back in rivulets. He turned to fight back but was met with another splash to his chest. The fumes rose immediately, stinging his eyes and making his head spin even faster. The smell was so overwhelming he could taste it, like metallic poison on his tongue.

"Don't fight it, Patrick," Alberts said. "This thing has to end and you know what's going to happen if we kill Robert. It's just going to transfer to you. This is the only way to stop it for good!"

"Dad!" Megan screamed through sobs over the crackle of the fiery prison. "Please!" Alberts ignored her as he raised the can above his head, letting the rest of its contents spill over his own body. Patrick tried to see through the blaze and glimpsed Megan's horrified face, lit by the flickering flames. "Oh my God! What are you doing?" she screamed, continuing her fruitless pleas.

"Get up," Alberts said.

Patrick did as instructed, holding his hands up.

"Paul," he said, "this is crazy."

But was it? Patrick knew the sheriff was right. They'd killed Abner only for Robert to take its place as the new Leeds Devil. If Patrick truly was the next and last of the bloodline, the same thing would happen to him as soon as they killed Robert. But what if that wasn't the case? Robert had been with many women over the years, according to Vivian. Maybe one of them had gotten pregnant. It was a slight chance, but still a chance. He couldn't think straight as the thoughts bounced around his mind, worsened by the blow to his head and the overpowering gasoline fumes.

Alberts pumped the shotgun. "I'm sorry it has to end this way, son."

Patrick heard the flapping of heavy wings approaching as he braced himself to be shot. Just as Alberts pulled the trigger, a large rock bounced off his head, causing the shot to go wide and miss its target.

"Daddy!" Megan yelled, sounding farther away than she was. "I'm sorry!"

Alberts righted himself and prepared to fire again, but didn't have a chance as the Leeds Devil crashed into him from above, giving Patrick an instant feeling of déjà vu. The sheriff choked out a grunt as his collapsed lungs filled with blood.

Patrick was trapped. He couldn't rush through the fire because he was soaked in gasoline, clearly Albert's contingency if he failed to shoot him. He was also trapped with the creature inside the burning ring. Maybe he could climb the small section of chimney, but he'd have to leap over the fire and he wasn't sure he could clear it without immolating himself in the process.

Fear seized Patrick as the Leeds Devil turned its attention from the dying sheriff to him. The monster rushed him, and for a moment, Patrick thought his blood would no longer keep him safe from being torn apart. But instead of tearing into him, the creature reached out and picked him up off the ground. With a roar, it hurtled Patrick into the air, easily clearing the wall of flames.

He crashed to the ground and Megan rushed over to him, grabbing him under the arms and pulling him back farther from the fire. She helped him up as they watched the thing advance on her father.

"No!" she screamed again as she lunged forward with no apparent plan. Patrick grabbed her and pulled her back. There was nothing they could do but watch.

Inside the ring, the creature's distraction in protecting its lineage proved costly. Alberts, despite his grave injuries, inched toward the edge of the foundation, closer to the fire. The beast pounced and plunged its claws into the sheriff's chest. As Paul Alberts screamed in anguish, he reached as far as he could, his fingertips grazing the flames. That was enough.

The fire spread throughout the man's body almost instantly, and as his dying act, he reached up to the beast and wrapped his arms around it. With its coat of coarse fur and the residual gasoline, flames erupted across its body as it unleashed a demonic scream. Patrick held Megan tight as it threw itself into the air and flew away, a flying inferno in the night sky.

With the monster gone, Megan sobbed into Patrick's gas-soaked shirt as her father's body burned.

Chapter 46

The trees of The Hollow parted once again, granting Patrick and Megan access into the cursed realm.

Patrick had given her as much space as he could, but the mourning would have to wait. The creature had flown off into the night and they needed to go after it. They needed to find out if it survived. Patrick hadn't turned, which meant that either it wasn't dead or the curse would not pass on this time. Either way, they had to know for sure.

Megan held their only remaining pistol, but as the entrance to the damned place opened, Patrick gently took it from her and again led the way. Like the last time he'd entered this place, they didn't need to go far to find what they were looking for.

Stepping past the bodies that remained from the earlier confrontation, they made their way to the black pool where the Leeds Devil lay sprawled on the ground. What was left of its fur was soaked through, having used the dark liquid to douse the flames. But the fire had taken its toll. The creature's skin was melted in numerous places on its body, the charred flesh sloughing off its bones. Its wings were little more than a skeletal frame, the membrane burned almost completely away. The red in its eyes was fading and it exhaled heavy, laborious breaths, its scorched chest rising and falling with each rattling growl. It would be dead soon.

The ghosts of Patrick's past stood vigil over the mortally wounded monster. Helena, the woman he now knew as Delphia Shourds, stood by its head, her face stoic and purposeful. His mother stood by her left side, the sorrow palpable. And Brandon flanked her on the right. For the first time since his best friend died, the spirit showed emotion. It was a barely notable smile, anticipatory of a true reunion.

Patrick knew what he needed to do.

He aimed the gun at the monster's head and took a long look at Megan. He saw her face shift from confusion to realization to panic.

"Patrick!" she screamed. "What are you doing?"

"I'm sorry," he said, feeling the tear spill down his cheek.

"Wait!" she said. "You don't have to do this!"

"I do," he replied. "It's the only way to be sure."

"We can just leave it. Maybe it'll survive and be trapped here. Maybe it can live off whatever animals are here. If it's trapped and alive, the curse won't pass to you."

"You know that won't work."

"I can learn the rituals!" she offered. "We can do what needs to be done to keep it alive and fed."

"No," Patrick said emphatically. "I will not let you sacrifice your soul for me."

Tears spilled from her eyes. "I can't lose you again."

Patrick held up his arm so she could see the goose tattoo. "You never lost me. There's never been anyone in my heart but you. I love you, Megan. I always have and I always will. You're my goose."

With that, he put a bullet in the monster's head.

Megan screamed and covered her face with her hands. She held them there for several long moments before she dared to look. Patrick saw a glimmer of hope in her eyes when she did.

He was still himself. Looking down, the creature had stopped breathing and the crimson glow of its eyes was extinguished. It was dead, but he didn't feel any different.

"Patrick?" Megan asked tentatively. "Are you . . . okay?"

He looked down at himself, wondering the same thing.

"I don't know," he said. "I think—"

The pain ripped through him without warning, feeling as if the fires of hell raged through his body. It was so sudden, it caused him to drop the gun and sent him crashing to his knees.

"Patrick!" Megan screamed as she stepped forward, but he screamed at her, freezing her in place.

"Stay back!"

Every nerve ending seemed to be firing at once, and he felt a searing pain in his skull as something tried to push out from within. A similar pain radiated from his back and he felt the skin rip as two membraned wings expanded behind him.

Megan shrieked in terror as she watched the love of her life transforming into a monster.

Patrick felt himself slipping away. His internal monologue turned to gibberish before clearing back to something he understood. In one of those moments of clarity, he knew he had one last chance. Using all the willpower he could muster, he willed his hand forward to grab the pistol, wrapping his fingers around the grip and pulling it from the dirt. He pressed the barrel to his temple and he saw Megan scream through his reddening vision. He tried to say something else to her, but his ability to speak was lost. All he could do was manage one final thought.

The curse ends with me.

Patrick pulled the trigger.

Chapter 47

Megan watched helplessly as the love of her life died in front of her eyes. The bullet through his head stopped his transformation as his lifeless body fell to the ground next to the monster he'd just learned was his father.

She ran and kneeled beside him, cradling his head in her arms. His eyes had begun to glow red just before he shot himself, but now they were those beautiful brown eyes that used to look at her so lovingly. They were empty now, the light gone forever. She rocked back and forth, caring little that the blood from the exit wound seeped into her clothes.

Megan's time to mourn was cruelly short as the earth shook. She jumped to her feet and saw the mist above the pool dissipate as twin waterfalls formed in its center. Not understanding at first, she quickly realized the ground underneath was separating. Panicked, she reached under Patrick's body, hooking his arms as she tried to pull him away from the encroaching gap. He was too heavy. It was as if he had gained a hundred pounds in the last few minutes. She fought until the breach was right on top of them, giving her no choice but to let go.

She scrambled back and got to her feet, watching helplessly as the hole widened and swallowed Patrick along with the others.

Across the pool, the darkened trees crumbled and collapsed inward, kicking up a cloud of foul-smelling dust that suffocated the already thick air. The shaking intensified, and Megan found it difficult to maintain her balance. With no other choice, she ran.

Sprinting to the exit, she saw the trees closing, putting her escape in jeopardy. She pushed harder, fire building in her lungs, exacerbated by the oppressive environment. It looked like she wouldn't make it, but suddenly the trees caught on something, preventing them from moving. It was only a moment before they bore down again, but it was enough for Megan to slip through.

Once on the other side, she created some distance before daring to look back. The barrier was closed once again, but the rumbling chaos within was still audible. To her horror, the sound continued to rise as the pines sank into the ground. A massive sinkhole opened, swallowing The Hollow into the earth, sending the cursed place back to hell where it belonged.

Fate remained cruel to Megan. The hole continued to grow, stretching out beyond the place the Leeds Devil once lived. As it swallowed the surrounding woods, she was again forced to run.

Keeping her eyes forward, she ran as hard as she

could, feeling as if she might vomit but not allowing herself the time to do so. The sound of the ground collapsing behind her remained steady and she feared her body would fail her before she could escape.

Keep going! Don't stop!

It was Patrick's voice she heard in her head, spurring her on. She didn't know if it was his spirit or her subconscious, but it did what was needed and she pressed on. Finally, she reached the foundation of the Leeds house where the fire still burned, making it impossible to reach her father's body. The flames had now caught the surrounding brush and were spreading toward the trees, presenting another hazard.

She jumped into Cam's SUV, remembering that Patrick had left the keys in the ignition. She had it started within seconds and threw it into reverse, creating enough distance to spin it around and drive down the path, gunning it as fast as possible.

When Megan reached the highway, she skidded onto it. The hole continued to chase her, swallowing trees and asphalt as it expanded. She gripped the wheel tight, her foot pushed all the way down on the accelerator, taking the fastest route she knew to the town limits.

Every time she thought the sinkhole had reached its end, it continued. And it only seemed to grow faster, making it hard for even the car to outrun it. Her chest tightened and her clothes were clinging to her, soaked through with sweat.

Finally, she saw the sign up ahead. A bright blue marker with bold white letters that read *Leaving Leeds*

Point. The car was incapable of going any faster, but she still pushed her foot harder to the floor, feeling like she might actually stomp through it. A bump from behind rattled the vehicle, and her stomach lurched.

No! I'm so close!

But the SUV remained on a forward trajectory. The sound of collapsing ground grew to deafening levels and the vehicle shook so violently, she thought it might fall apart.

Finally, she passed the sign and the town limits. As soon as she was on the other side, the car stabilized and the chaos behind her diminished in volume. She kept her speed up and continued driving until it stopped completely. Even then, she went five more minutes before daring to take her foot off the gas.

When the car stopped, she put it in park and slumped over the steering wheel, exhaustion overtaking her body.

After a few minutes, she snapped awake, momentarily disoriented, then quickly remembered where she was and what had happened. She wanted to break down. To fall onto the highway and curl into a ball and cry at the fact that she had just lost everything. But she had to know just how bad it was, so she put the car in drive and made a U-turn, making her way back to see what was left of her town.

Megan saw the sign from the opposite side. From this direction, it read *Welcome to Leeds Point*. Only there was no more Leeds Point to welcome anyone. She parked a distance away to be safe, taking a moment to turn the car the other way in case she needed to make another rapid escape.

Every bone in her body ached as she approached the giant crater where her hometown had once stood. But none of that compared to the pain in her heart. The universe that she believed had brought her and Patrick together proved to be a cruel one.

Smoke and dust billowed from the fresh sinkhole. It went deep, but Megan could see the remnants of pine trees lining the bottom. Sirens sounded in the distance, no doubt the initial wave of first responders that would not be enough to sort through this disaster. After three hundred years, Jane Leeds finally had her revenge on the town that shunned her.

Megan stepped forward, her toes just past the edge of the gap. For a moment, she considered jumping. With all that she had lost, no one would blame her.

Don't.

The familiar voice came from behind. She whirled with a hope she knew was rooted in foolishness.

"Patrick?"

But there was no one there. Still, she knew what she heard. Patrick had been haunted by ghosts for years. She had no illusions that he would be the same for her. It was more likely her subconscious telling her that her love wouldn't want her to die too. He sacrificed himself so she could live. She couldn't betray that.

Megan turned back toward the devastation and kneeled on the ground as the sun began to break over the horizon. She rested back on her heels as she stayed in silence for several minutes. Then, the first tears fell, followed by stunted heaves as her breath hitched. She finally stopped fighting it. There was no reason to.

Megan Alberts sobbed before the wreckage of her hometown.

Chapter 48

November 2025

THE ATLANTIC COUNTY GAZETTE

Serving Southern New Jersey Since 1891

Leeds Point Cleanup Continues as Death Toll Climbs Past 800

Six weeks after sinkhole disaster, families still wait for answers

LEEDS POINT – The massive cleanup operation at the site where the town of Leeds Point once stood entered its seventh week on Monday, as state officials confirmed the death toll has risen to 847 people, making it the deadliest natural disaster in New Jersey history.

The entire community of over 1,200 residents vanished in a matter of minutes in the early morning hours of September 17th when a sinkhole estimated to be nearly 400 feet deep and spanning eight city blocks opened beneath the historic town. Emergency responders described the scene as "catastrophic" with homes, businesses, Daniel Leeds Elementary School, and portions of surrounding state highways and county roads swallowed by the earth.

"We've never seen geological activity of such massive scope in this region," said Dr. Allison Chen, the geologist leading the investigation. "The speed and scale of the collapse defies any conventional understanding of sinkhole formation. We're working with a large team of specialists to help us determine what caused this tragedy."

While teams have recovered 847 bodies from the debris at the bottom of the enormous crater, 384 residents remain missing and are presumed dead.

"Every day we don't have answers is another day these families are denied closure," said Atlantic County Executive Brian Morrison at a press conference on Friday. "We owe it to the victims and their loved ones to understand how this happened and to make sure it never happens again.

"We will not rest until we have answers," Morrison pledged. "The people of Leeds Point deserve nothing less than the full truth about what happened to their community."

The disaster has prompted calls for more comprehensive geological monitoring throughout South Jersey, particularly in areas with similar soil composition. State legislators are considering emergency funding for expanded geological surveys and early warning systems.

For now, the massive crater remains cordoned off by state police as recovery operations continue. The once-quiet Pine Barrens community that traced its roots back to colonial times exists now only in memory and in the hearts of those who lost everything on that September morning.

If you have any information that can assist with the investigation, please call the Atlantic County Emergency Services hotline at (609) 555-1184.

Megan shut the tab on her phone and slid it into her purse as she leaned back in the chair, resting her head against the wall.

The waiting room felt smaller than she imagined it would be. The decorative prints, mainly oil paintings of generic landscapes, were no doubt intended to create a soothing atmosphere, but somehow made the environment seem sterile. She clutched her purse tightly, nervously fiddling with the leather strap as she scanned the room. There were only two other people in there, sitting off to her left: a teenager and an older woman, probably her mother. They both had their eyes glued to their phones in deliberate silence.

Megan felt a chill. It was cold in there, the soft hum of the air conditioner echoing from somewhere overhead, the only sound in the room outside of shuffling papers and people shifting in their seats. In front of her was a table with scattered magazines, the typical generic doctor's office fare—*Better Homes & Gardens*, *People*, and *Women's Health*. Megan picked up the copy of

People, thinking some light celebrity gossip would be better than reliving the nightmare of the past month and a half.

The entire country was focused on their small town and it wasn't on the famous Jersey Devil for a change. How she longed for the days when that was just a silly urban legend that inspired a hockey team and a really bad episode of *The X-Files*. Now, everyone was talking about the Leeds Point sinkhole disaster and how terrible they all felt. Celebrities were taking to social media with all the typical performative earnestness as they urged their fans to "help in any way you can."

It was all bullshit. No one really cared. They would spend a few months talking about the environment and how their hearts go out to the families of the people who lost their lives. Then they'd go back to their mansions and their yachts and their fancy-ass parties while the people who actually lived here would never again go to work, or their kids' baseball games and dance recitals, or the dentist.

In a way, Megan supposed she was lucky. Only a handful of Leeds Point residents who were fortunate enough to be out of town that night survived. Megan supposed she was the only person actually *in* the town who made it out. But it wasn't just that. She *knew* her father was dead. She *knew* Patrick was dead. There were still hundreds of people who knew their loved ones were gone, yet still had the cruel sliver of hope that somehow they'd be granted a miracle.

At least she knew, with certainty, what happened to the people she loved.

She checked her watch and saw that she still had a little less than ten minutes before her appointment. Putting the magazine down and leaning back again, she focused on her breathing, taking slow breaths in and out, attempting to steady her nerves. Still, she jumped in her seat when she heard the door open.

A woman Megan had never seen before emerged from the hallway, moving slowly but steadily to the exit. Megan caught her eye just for the briefest of moments, sharing an understanding that didn't require words.

You're doing the right thing, Megan. You can't take the chance of this happening all over again.

She knew her inner voice was right, but she still struggled with what she was about to do.

Megan thought she'd never again cry as hard as she did while she watched Patrick die. That was, until she sat on the bathroom floor staring at the two lines on the pregnancy test. The crushing knowledge of what that could mean destroyed her.

Thinking back to when she and Patrick had ordered the DNA tests when they were teenagers, she remembered how nervous she'd been to tell him she wanted kids someday. Fun and fancy-free Megan Alberts diving into the serious topics. But Patrick was receptive and it made her fall in love with him even more, knowing they had common goals.

Then, when she found out she wasn't at risk for her mother's condition, she was elated, but also heartbroken because Patrick had left town and hadn't answered any of her calls. She didn't know if she'd ever see him again and—high school relationship or not—

she didn't want to be with anyone else.

The roller coaster ascended once more when Patrick came back into her life almost two months ago. But once it crossed the peak, it not only came crashing down, it flew off the rails entirely.

So when she found out she was pregnant with Patrick's child, she was devastated. Here she had a chance to have a part of the man she loved, the man who was taken from her twice. Megan so desperately wanted that piece of him they'd created together, but she knew what could happen. Patrick said the curse died with him. Maybe that was the case, but she wouldn't know unless the child was born. And the curse of the Leeds Devil had already killed far too many people. She couldn't take the chance, no matter how much she wanted to risk it.

Patrick was right. The curse dies with him.

I'm so sorry, Patrick. This is the only choice. I love you so much, goose.

"Megan Alberts?"

The voice came from a nurse in purple scrubs standing at the entrance to the hallway. Megan hadn't even heard the door open. The woman held a clipboard and offered a gentle, professional smile.

Megan stood on shaky legs and gathered her purse and jacket. She placed her hand on her stomach and fought back a tear. Taking a deep breath, she followed the nurse down the corridor.

Chapter 49

June 2009

Patrick grabbed his suitcase from under the bed. He and Megan had gotten their diplomas earlier that week and bought bus tickets right away. The first line took them south toward Tennessee. There, they'd switch over and make their way west until they reached Arizona. His body thrummed with excitement. He couldn't wait to pick her up.

Mom had left for work an hour ago, on for the night shift at Parkhill's. He waited ample time because it wasn't unusual for her to forget her purse or phone and have to come back. He didn't want to have to explain what he was doing with a suitcase and bus ticket. Patrick felt guilty, but a note and a clean break seemed the best way to tell her he was leaving. He placed the envelope on the breakfast nook before making his way to the door.

When he opened it, he was startled to find Paul Alberts on the other side.

"Going somewhere, Patrick?" the sheriff asked.

"Uh . . . taking a trip," he said, not sure what else to

say.

"Where?"

He blurted out the first state he could think of, "Vermont. Need to clear my head."

"The skiing up there sucks in June, Patrick," Alberts said. "Where are you really going?"

"I told you."

"You planning on taking Megan with you?"

Patrick stood silent for a moment, knowing there was no way around this.

"If she wants to come."

"I'm sure she does. And I know you want her to. My question is, do you think that's what's best for her?"

"If it's what she wants . . ."

"What we want isn't always the right thing. My daughter would follow you to the ends of the earth. And I'm in no position to stop her."

"So what are we saying, Mr. Alberts?" Patrick asked. "I'm confused."

The sheriff put his hand on Patrick's shoulder and gave it a gentle squeeze. "I'm saying that you know the things that have happened to you in your life. Brandon Murphy was one thing, but now twenty-seven of your classmates were killed. Can you say, for sure, that type of thing wouldn't follow you wherever it is you're going?"

"It's worth a shot," Patrick said, trying to sound confident.

"For you, maybe," Alberts replied. "But is that something you're willing to risk Megan's life for?"

A lump formed in Patrick's throat. He tried to

swallow but couldn't. Their plan was to escape. He didn't consider that the horrors of Leeds Point may follow them. Would he be putting Megan's life in danger if she stayed with him?

As if answering the question in his mind, he saw something move in the cul-de-sac behind the sheriff. Looking over his shoulder, he saw Brandon staring at him as he always did, reminding him of the reality of what his life had become. He looked back at Alberts as the tears welled in his eyes. To his credit, the sheriff looked sympathetic, but unwavering.

"Do the right thing, son."

Patrick boarded the bus bound for Illinois. Alberts had given him a ride, the two not speaking a word to each other, even as Patrick got out of the car and walked into the station without a look back. Once there, he exchanged his ticket for the next departing bus, which was the one to Chicago. Now, as it departed, he pressed his head against the glass that still felt warm despite the cooling night air. He thought about the second letter he wrote before he left.

Inside the envelope, he placed the silver goose pendant he had bought the other day at the mall, intending to give it to Megan to commemorate the start of their journey. Instead, he watched it slide to the bottom of the envelope before sealing it and placing it next to his mother's. He had written *Megan* on the front and dropped the pen like it was on fire, walking as fast as he could to the door, outrunning the temptation to look back.

Dear Megan,

I know I changed the plan last minute, and I'm sure you're royally pissed off at me. I am sorry. Please believe that.

Just know that I couldn't risk having you around me. I don't know why, but bad shit seems to follow me and it hurts the people I love. I don't care if it gets me. I really don't. But I couldn't live with myself if anything happened to you.

That's why I'm leaving. I'm not going to Arizona. If I tell you where, I know you'll come after me. So I'm not going to tell you. (God, you're going to hate this next part.) It's for your own good.

Sorry.

Just remember, after you're done cursing me and throwing things and generally being super pissed off, know this:

<u>I LOVE YOU</u>.

You'll always be my goose.

-Patrick

Epilogue

Wilmette, Illinois

November 2025

Nora Kaminski paced the length of the double vanity across from the walk-in shower of their sprawling master bathroom. If this one was nice, she could only dream of the one in the new house once it was finished.

Oh God. The new house.

Construction had been delayed again, but this time, not because of Aleks's ADHD, but because their contractor had died in that sinkhole disaster in New Jersey.

She felt her stomach lurch. Typically, it had been happening in the morning the past week or so, but this time it wasn't from what she suspected. It was from the thought of Patrick. Why the hell did she ever have to screw around with him? Sure, she felt sad that he was dead, but they just had a fling. There was no emotional connection.

She looked at her phone. Surely it had been five minutes.

Shit! Less than two!

She stared at the stick resting on the counter by the sink, resisting the urge to look before the time had passed.

Calm down, Nora, she told herself. *It's going to be fine.*

Of course it was going to be fine. Why wouldn't it? They'd used protection. For the most part. Still. There was no way.

No way.

She looked down at her phone. Two and a half minutes.

Ugh!

"You okay in there?" Aleks called from the other side of the door.

"Just a minute, babe!" she called back, trying to even out her voice.

Let's say there was even a snowball's chance in hell that it was Patrick's. Even so, he was dead. There wasn't anyone else who knew she was sleeping with him. She hadn't even told any of her friends. She guessed Patrick and Aleks looked kind of similar. If you squinted real hard. And had a few drinks. But the baby would probably look like her. Her genes were strong.

It's all going to be fine.

Back to her phone again. Four minutes.

Fuck it! I'm looking!

A minute later, she opened the door to find Aleks eagerly waiting for her, brimming with anticipation.

"So?" he asked.

Nora held up the positive pregnancy test.

"We're having a baby!"

Afterword

Hamilton, NJ

June 2025

I'm exhausted.

It's just after 11:30 a.m. on Friday, June 6, 2025, as I'm starting to write this afterword. It's a beautiful day in New Jersey (yes, we have those). I'm looking at the sun shining through my office window right now and I'm doing my best not to get distracted. But it's not just the weather that makes it beautiful. I finished the manuscript for the book you just read (and I sincerely hope you enjoyed) about eleven hours ago.

I was up against a deadline I didn't think I'd make, but thanks to some marathon writing sessions and a lot of coffee, I did! Not only is it finished, but I'm thrilled with how it came out. My original plan was to hold off on writing this afterword until I got it back from the editor, but I'm still buzzing about finishing it and wanted to put my thoughts on paper sooner rather than later.

Although this is going to be a bit stream of consciousness, so bear with me.

When I first got the idea to write my American Horrors series, focusing on a different urban legend from each state, there was never any doubt that the book set in my home state would be about our most famous fictional resident.

No, not Tony Soprano.

I'm talking, of course, about the Jersey Devil. A mythical cryptid said to haunt the Pine Barrens in the southern part of the state. The legendary creature has inspired countless businesses to adopt the moniker, has the state's hockey team named after it, and has been the subject of a bunch of film and TV adaptations that totally missed the mark. (Its hilarious cameo in *What We Do in the Shadows* notwithstanding.)

But the question was, did I want to tell a Jersey Devil story for the first book in the series?

I decided I didn't. My two prior novels both took place in New Jersey. I did write a novella set in Jacksonville, Florida, but that was a prequel and the setting wasn't necessarily important to the story. For the American Horrors series, however, the locations were the very keys to those stories. I wanted to challenge myself and write a book set outside of my home state. That book ended up being *The Dead Children's Playground*. I was ecstatic that my first book was a success because it allowed me to keep going and bring you *Devil of the Pines.*

I wanted to challenge myself again with this one, so that's what I did. This time, however, I was very familiar with the location, so I had to find other ways to put my storytelling to the test. I had two goals.

First, I wanted to tell this sweeping mystery across multiple timelines. All my books to this point have been linear, outside of some flashbacks. But for *Devil of the Pines*, I wanted the reader to spend enough time in one timeline to get them intrigued before switching to another to answer some questions while still posing new ones. I've always loved that model of storytelling.

The other was to write a no-doubt-about-it horror story where the Jersey Devil is very much real and very much a threat. That's been my issue with adaptations of the legend. They either are a low-budget mess, or they don't give you the version of the monster that lines up with the folklore (lookihe *Jersey Devil*. I was set to interview a group called "The Devil Hunters" who performed investigations in the Pine Barrens. Unfortunately, they were paranoid I was going to make them look foolish and they ghosted me three days before the shoot.

Fortunately, my good friend Chris Boland—a name you no doubt recognize by now— stepped in to recount some eerie experiences he had camping in the Pine Barrens back when he was a Boy Scout. He also told the story about a bar where there was a drawing of the Jersey Devil with claw marks across it. The owner told him the same story Chris told Patrick about the creature rushing in and slashing at the picture before rushing off into the night.

Chris really bailed me out on that one by driving with me and my cinematographer from South Orange to the Pine Barrens—a good ninety-minute drive—with each of us nursing wicked hangovers (it *was* college, after all)! So I repaid him by brutally murdering him in this very book!

Love ya, Boland!

Then another time, my friend Jeff and I decided we wanted to drive down to the Pine Barrens and "look for the Jersey Devil." All that really meant was we took Route 539 and somehow ended up in Atlantic City. In our defense, we did look at the trees on the way down in case we saw it, so *technically,* we did what we said we would do. Ah, the follies of youth.

All this is to say, I had all the backstory I needed to write this book. That said, if you are interested in learning more about the legend of the Jersey Devil than the summary I'm about to give you, check out these books coauthored by James F. McCloy and Ray Miller Jr., both of which I have on my shelf:

- *Phantom of the Pines*
- *The Jersey Devil*

They're both out of print, but you can get used copies online or check out your local library.

Okay, enough backstory on me. Let's talk about the origins of the Jersey Devil!

THE THIRTEENTH CHILD

For the *real* story of the Jersey Devil, go back and reread the prologue. See you all next time!

I'm kidding. Kind of. The truth is, what I wrote in the prologue is essentially the legend. A woman, most often referred to as "Mother Leeds," was pregnant with her thirteenth child. The birth was especially difficult, and in a moment of anguish, she cried out, "Let this child be a devil!" From this stage, there are several variations of what allegedly happened.

In the most popular version, the same one I recounted in the prologue, the baby is born normal, but soon changes into a monstrous mix of different animals with the head of a horse, wings of a bat, and horns and hooves of a goat. In other versions, the child is born as a monster from the start.

What happens next is where it varies. Some variations of the story say the creature killed everyone in the house before flying through the roof/out the window/up the chimney. Others say it escaped without injuring anyone. Yet another version says Mother Leeds cared for the child, keeping it hidden away in the woods until she died.

So, who were the members of the Leeds family?

Some have said Mother Leeds was a woman named Deborah Leeds. This is mainly due to Atlantic County records detailing that she was married to a man named Japhet Leeds, who named twelve children in his will written in 1736. I guess when kid number thirteen is a demonic monster, they don't get their cut of the inheritance.

While Deborah seems to be the accepted name for Mother Leeds, an article in the Asbury Park Press in 2021 ames the Jersey Devil's mother as *Jane Leeds,* which is the name I went with. Why? Because I have two books (*Black Friday* and the upcoming *Mischief Night*) and a short story (*Chuckles Wuz Here*) that all have characters with some variation of the name Deborah. I don't know why, so don't ask me, but I figured it was best to switch it up since there was another option available.

Side note: it didn't hit me until later that I referenced Breaking Benjamin as one of Patrick's favorite bands and Jane's journal aka her diary—you know, "The Diary of Jane"—plays a big part in the latter part of the story. I wish I could say that was intentional, but it's one of those happy coincidences that sometimes come together when you're writing.

Back to the story. (I did warn you this was going to be stream of consciousness.)

Some stories say Mother Leeds was a witch, explaining how she could curse the child. That's what I went with because I felt it added an extra layer to the narrative. Many of those same stories claim that the child's father, Mr. Leeds, was the Devil himself.

As to said father, while there are records of a man named Japhet with twelve heirs, many believe the Leeds of legend were an amalgamation of several historical figures, including Daniel Leeds. The real-life Daniel Leeds died in 1720, fifteen years before the story begins, but his inclusion was one of those creative liberties we authors take from time to time.

Daniel Leeds was an interesting figure in American history. In fact, there is good evidence that the moniker "The Leeds Devil" was not in reference to a legendary cryptid. Rather, it was an insult against a man.

Arriving in New Jersey in 1677 and settling in Burlington, Daniel Leeds published an almanac, but committed the grave sin of including astrological symbology within. This led to the Quaker community shunning and mocking Daniel as evil. Putting aside the fact that he himself was a Quaker.

After Daniel died, his son Titan took over the almanac. That put the Leeds family in the crosshairs of a historical figure you may have heard of—one Benjamin Franklin. Yup. That one.

Franklin published his own almanac under a pen name, "Poor Richard" Saunders. The eponymous *Poor Richard's Almanack* predicted Titan Leeds would die in 1733. Titan did not, and called Franklin a fool and a liar. Franklin countered by saying Titan actually did die, and it was his ghost making a fuss. Titan kept trying to defend himself, but Franklin kept insisting his prediction had been right and Titan was simply resurrected from the dead.

Kind of makes you think politics has always been an absurd shit show.

Titan died for real—or again, depending on who you ask—in 1738, but the damage to the Leeds family had been done. Their support of Lord Cornbury, a pro-British empire cross-dresser with a penchant for "being loose with the colony's taxes," didn't do them any favors either. The term "Leeds Devil" was more likely than not an early example of mudslinging.

But that's no fun for a horror book, right?

According to NJ.com, the talk of the Leeds Devil died down, fading into obscurity after the Revolutionary War.

It wasn't until the turn of the twentieth century that the legend became what we know today. Also, according to NJ.com—and a huge shout out to Brian Regal for writing such a fascinating, in-depth article—a public relations man out of Philadelphia plucked the term from the forgotten annals of colonial US history, and from that point forward, the "Leeds Devil" became the "Jersey Devil." As the idiom goes, *the rest is history*.

One interesting note before we move on. While Leeds is the generally accepted name for the Jersey Devil's family, in some variations of the story, the Jersey Devil was actually born of a family with the name *Shourds*. This has sometimes been mistranslated as *Shrouds*, with the cabin in the woods being referred to as the "Shrouds House." So, those of you who were more familiar with the history of the legend probably figured out Patrick's involvement early on.

And, yes, the foundation described where Brandon is killed and Alberts made his final stand is based on what is really left of the devil's alleged birthplace in the Pine Barrens. But it's on private property, so I don't recommend you go looking for it.

WHAT THE HELL WAS THAT??

The thing that really keeps the Jersey Devil legend going is the preponderance of sightings over not just years, but centuries! And we're not talking just tanked-up locals after one too many beers. Some relatively prominent figures in history have reported seeing the Leeds Devil! Here are some of the more notable sightings throughout the years:

Stephen Decatur

Commodore Stephen Decatur, an American naval hero, reportedly saw a flying creature while visiting a firing range. He fired a cannonball directly into it, but it didn't even faze the thing as it flew away.

Joseph Bonaparte

Joseph Bonaparte, whose brother Napoleon you may have heard of, was a former king of Spain who fled Europe after Napoleon's defeat at the Battle of Waterloo in 1815. He settled in Bordentown, New Jersey, on a large estate called Point Breeze. He chose to live there because (a) he wanted a more peaceful life, and (b) it was between New York and Philadelphia, so he could quickly receive the latest news from Europe.

While hunting one snowy afternoon, he spotted some strange tracks on the ground. He allegedly described them as resembling a "two-footed donkey," with one slightly larger than the other. They ended abruptly. As he was trying to figure out what he was looking at, he heard a hissing noise behind him. He turned and saw the creature with a horselike head and wings. He froze, too scared to even raise his rifle. They stared each other down for several moments until it hissed again and flew away.

One interesting note about this sighting is that Bordentown is well north of the Pine Barrens in the central part of New Jersey. (Yes, Central Jersey exists—if you're from the area, you know the debate.).

Phenomenal Week

As detailed in McCloy and Miller's book *The Jersey Devil*, there was one week when the Jersey Devil, after years of inactivity, was seen in thirty different towns during the third week of January in 1909.

Between January 16th and 23rd, *thousands* of people claimed to have seen the devil, or at least its footprints. Eyewitness accounts called it things like "jabberwock," "kangaroo," "flying death," "kingowing," "woozlebug," "flying horse," "cowbird," "monster," and even "prehistoric lizard." When it was determined that all these sightings were of the legendary Jersey Devil, it got so bad that schools and workplaces closed and the newspapers speculated on the reason behind the stunning events.

Sunday

It started in the late hours of Saturday, the 16th,

carrying over into Sunday, the 17th. There was one sighting in Woodbury, NJ, while several other people claimed encounters in Bristol, PA. Thack Cozzens of Woodbury was leaving the Woodbury Hotel when he said he heard a "hissing sound" and looked across the street, seeing "two spots of phosphorus—the eyes of the beast." He also said it moved "fast as an auto."

Later on Sunday, the Jersey Devil's tracks were spotted in the snow in areas both north and south of Burlington City. James Fleson, a Gloucester City liveryman, found prints in eight different yards that day. Mrs. Ed Shindle described the hoofprints found in her yard as belonging to a "two-legged cow with wings."

Monday

The Lowdens of Burlington found tracks in their backyard next to their garbage can, the contents of which had been devoured. Others claimed to have seen the monster, referring to it as "flying death." People vowed to track and kill the creature, gathering in hunting parties around the state. In Jacksonville, a hunt was organized, but dogs refused to follow the trail. The men went on their own, but four miles into the trail, the tracks vanished.

Tuesday

Tuesday, January 19th was the day the Jersey Devil made, according to McCloy and Miller, its "most vivid and lengthy appearance so far."

At 2:30 a.m., in Gloucester City, Mr. Nelson Evans, a paere multiple hoofprint sightings that day all over South Jersey, notably in Camden.

Wednesday

On Wednesday morning, a Burlington police officer claimed to have seen the Jersey Devil, saying it "had no teeth" and "its eyes were like blazing coals." The policeman identified it as a "Jabberwock" (see *Alice in Wonderland*). Later that morning, a reverend named John Pursell saw the creature in Pemberton. Another search party was formed in Haddonfield. (Fun fact: Haddonfield is the birthplace of Debra Hill, co-writer and producer of John Carpenter's *Halloween,* and yes, Haddonfield, New Jersey, was the inspiration for the fictional Haddonfield, Illinois. Fun Fact 2: the exit sign in Haddonfield off I-295 reads *Haddonfield* and *Voorhees*, or as I call it, "The most evil exit in New Jersey.")

Sorry. Stream of consciousness.

There were additional sightings that day in Moorestown and Maple Shade. In the latter, a man named John Smith saw it near Mount Carmel Cemetery. Smith, clearly having a brass set, chased the creature until it disappeared into a gravel pit.

Thursday

Thursday marked the most intense day of Phenomenal Week as, per McCloy and Miller, the devil "rampaged through the Delaware Valley."

At the Black Hawk Social Club in the seven-hundred block of Ferry Avenue in Camden, a meeting was interrupted by an "uncanny sound." Members found themselves face-to-face with the creature through the back window. The club members seized what weapons they could, and the Jersey Devil, sensing the threat, flew off emitting "bloodcurdling sounds."

As the Public Service Railway Trolley passed Haddon Heights, passengers watched as the thing flew outside the window. When the car had to stop for a passenger, the creature circled above, "hissing violently" before flying away.

It traveled north after that, to the birthplace of yours truly—Trenton. (I say that simply to note I was born there. Trenton is not known in historical context as the birthplace of James Kaine. At least not as of this writing.) William Cromley, a doorkeeper at the Trent Theater, was returning home when his horse got spooked. Jumping out of his buggy, Cromley saw the beast before him, which he described as ". . . about the size of an average dog, with the face of a German shepherd . . ." As was becoming a trend, the thing hissed and flew away.

Across town, Trenton City Councilman E.P. Weeden was jolted awake by the sound of something trying to break in through his door. His bedroom was upstairs, so he ran to the window. He didn't see the devil, but he did hear the flapping of wings and observed hoofprints on the snowy ground below.

By this point in the week, several poultry farmers

were dismayed to find scores of missing chickens. Attendance at local churches had picked up significantly as well. The tracks were so prevalent in Roebling that some said it "looked like a herd of Shetland ponies had stampeded there in the dark."

These are just a few of the prominent sightings. McCloy and Miller go on for at least five more pages describing various Thursday encounters. You should really check out their books to learn more!

Friday

By Friday, the panic was spread full bore throughout the state. In Mount Ephraim, people locked themselves in their houses and the school closed for the day. Absentee rates for many workers were high, with mills in Gloucester and Hainesport being forced to shut down. A performance set for a theater in Camden was canceled.

Despite the fearful atmosphere, the Jersey Devil was mostly quiet throughout the day. That was, until dusk, when two women returning home from Chester, PA, heard a strange noise from a nearby stopped train. They were terrified as the Jersey Devil flew out of a boxcar. There were further sightings from Trenton all the way down to Salem, where the final sighting of Phenomenal Week occurred when a Mrs. D. W. Brown's bulldog valiantly drove the creature from her backyard.

There has never been an explanation for why there were so many incidents with the Jersey Devil that particular week in 1909, but one thing is certain: a mass hysteria spread through a good part of the state and the witnesses couldn't all have been delusional.

Right?

BRINGING THE LEGEND TO LIFE

Now that you've learned a bit about the legend, let's talk about how I molded it into the story you just read.

The first thing I knew I wanted to do was to make the Jersey Devil very much a threat. We've gone through a good number of sightings throughout history and you can see one thing they all have in common: the creature never really attacks anyone. It usually just shows up, makes some noise, and then flies away when confronted. That may be unsettling should it happen to you in real life, but it doesn't make for a very compelling horror story.

That's also been my problem with a lot of the Jersey Devil's appearances in film and television. To illustrate my point, here are some examples (chock-full of spoilers, so consider this your warning to skip ahead if you don't want them).

Season 1, Episode 5 of *The X-Files*, titled "The Jersey Devil" aired October 8, 1993. Mulder and Scully go to New Jersey (filmed in a very non-Jersey-looking Vancouver) to investigate a partially eaten body. They find the Jersey Devil is actually a feral, bigfoot-type woman whose mate was killed or something. I don't remember; it was so bad. It certainly wasn't the Jersey Devil. It's a shame, because so much of that show was great.

In 1998, I was excited to watch the movie *The Last Broadcast*. It was a found footage film about a pair of cable-access hosts who go into the Pine Barrens to search for the Jersey Devil. They go into the woods, but only one comes out alive. Guess what? The other one killed him. There is no Jersey Devil. Humans are the real monsters. Yawn.

In 2002, there was another movie called *The Thirteenth Child*. My friend Jeff (the same one who went with me to look for the Jersey Devil before we ended up in Atlantic City) and I went to see it. It had some names in it: Cliff Robertson (Uncle Ben in Sam Raimi's *Spider-Man* trilogy) and Christopher Atkins (*The Blue Lagoon*) among them. This one had an actual Jersey Devil in it, but everything else about it was terrible. They completely did away with the legend in favor of a Native American curse, the creature design was lacking and barely used (understandable given the budget), and atrocious dialogue. Oh yeah, and the Jersey Devil is named Bruno. For no reason. At least I explained why Vivian called him Abner.

Jeff wanted to leave before it was over. I stubbornly insisted that I paid for the ticket and I was going to see it out. I should have listened to him.

The only decent movie I've seen about the Jersey Devil is 2012's *The Barrens* by Darren Lynn Bousman (director of the second and third *Saw* movies). The movie starred *True Blood*'s Stephen Moyer, ironically using his real accent despite living in New Jersey, and *24* and *Not Another Teen Movie*'s Mia Kirshner. While the Pine Barrens setting is cool and there is a good amount of tension, most of the plot follows Moyer's character slowly losing his mind from getting bitten by his family's rabid dog while secretly putting it down. Why he would go camping with his family instead of—you know—the hospital was a hard plot point to get past.

Granted, the devil's sparse appearances did create some tension, but the ambiguous ending is confusing and abrupt. Still, not a bad watch.

The best television appearance I've seen was in 2022 on *What We Do in the Shadows*. The Jersey Devil appears in Season 4, Episode 7. I'm not going to tell you about it. Just go watch it. It's hilarious.

There are some other appearances I know of, but haven't seen yet:

2006's *Satan's Playground* is a *Texas Chainsaw Massacre*-style "deranged family takes lost tourists captive" story, but does include an actual depiction of the monster. It then appeared in a 2007 episode of *Teenage Mutant Ninja Turtles*, fighting our "heroes in a half-shell." *Leeds Point* is a 2008 horror mystery and 2009's *Carny* presents an accurate depiction of the creature, but set in Nebraska for some reason. Weird. And, of course, Sam and Dean Winchester went hunting for the Jersey Devil in Season 7, Episode 9 of *Supernatural*, titled "How to Win Friends and Influence Monsters." Guess what? It ended up not being the Jersey Devil they were after. Seeing a trend?

For me, who grew up in New Jersey and had a home in Galloway, none of these stories ever did the legend justice. Disclaimer: art is subjective and even though I had issues with these adaptations doesn't mean others won't enjoy them. And the irony that I'm doing a whole series of adaptations of urban legends is not lost on me. That's why I write these detailed afterwords so people can see the research and thought process that went into the writing. Will I always get it right? Probably not, but I'll always try my best to stay true to the folklore while still writing an entertaining story.

That's the *why*. Let's talk about the *how*.

From the start, my concept of the story was about a man returning to his hometown of Leeds Point following the death of a parent. I knew that his family was going to be connected to the Leeds family somehow. I knew that Shourds was a potentially alternate name for the creature's family, so I thought that was a good starting point.

The original plot was going to start with Patrick living in the Midwest. He was being plagued by nightmares of a colonial woman and a cabin in the woods. Eventually they would compel him to return to his home of Leeds Point to seek answers. He would travel with his supportive girlfriend, and after a hike through the woods punctuated with disturbing supernatural occurrences, they would end up at a cabin that they would, in time, learn was the birthplace of the Jersey Devil.

While taking shelter from a storm, the couple would be interrupted by another pair. I didn't get so far as naming them, but the new arrivals would be a mobster out of Atlantic City and the boss's wife with whom he was having an affair. The mobster was injured, having been shot in the escape from the rest of his crew who had tracked him to the Pine Barrens. The four would find themselves under siege by both the hit squad *and* the very real Jersey Devil. My version would be large and mean, over seven feet tall and scary. I didn't think the three-foot version detailed in some of the sightings would cut it.

It was a fun concept, but ultimately, it didn't have that emotional resonance I was looking for. I love a good siege story and I have a few to tell, but this wasn't it. This is my state's most famous urban legend. It needed to be more than that.

Going back to the drawing board, I again started with Patrick, living in Chicago and having similar visions. They would become stronger until he received a call from his estranged father telling him his mother had died. Patrick would then travel home and be linked to a series of murders and disappearances, ultimately learning that he was cursed, much like he was in the final version.

In this earlier iteration, Patrick's dad started trying to take over his mother's work of kidnapping and sacrificing victims to keep the curse from claiming Patrick, but he could not properly perform the rituals, unleashing the creature on the unsuspecting town.

Another difference in this version was that Patrick was married, but his unraveling mental state hurt their relationship to the point where she was having an affair. She planned to leave him, but had to hold off once he learned his mother had died. She would reluctantly accompany him to Leeds Point for the funeral.

One thing at this point I wasn't sure of was how I was going to end the story. The answer came to me one day while driving—ironically, to Atlantic City. I asked my wife to grab the pad and pen I keep in my glove compartment and to jot down this line:

"The curse ends with me."

At that point, I knew Patrick was going to sacrifice himself to keep the curse from spreading. And, of course, me being me, I had to leave a little stinger of doubt at the end. It would turn out that Patrick's wife was pregnant, but she didn't know whether the child was his or her affair partner's. And that was where we were going to end it.

That second version was better, but still needed work. I'm a heavy plotter. I will write and rewrite detailed chapter-by-chapter outlines until I have every plot point in place, and it's just a matter of fleshing it out. This time I did a little something different.

I ended up wanting to tell a story that branched out over three different timelines. To keep everything straight, I put together a document I titled "Timeline of Events." Starting in 1735, I wrote out everything that happened to the characters that was relevant to the story in chronological order, including some things that didn't make it into the book. (Side note: you'll have an opportunity to check out this document, along with reading some additional material filling in the gaps in *Devil of the Pines: The Lost Chapters*, a free e-book for members of my VIP Readers Club. More on that soon.)

Once I had this detailed backstory, I had the book almost entirely plotted, except I was having trouble bridging some gaps.

One simple switch had everything fall into place. Initially, Robert Lumley's medical aide was a large, mute man named Lars. I replaced him with Caterina, which added a different dynamic in trying to seduce Patrick. I also created the characters of Cam and the two state police detectives, whom I gave names similar to two of my father's colleagues when he himself served in the NJSP. They were able to provide a foil for Alberts, who would have simply been fine with getting Patrick out of Leeds Point.

Once those changes were made, everything fell into place and I wrote the version you hold in your hands. It's definitely bloodier than *The Dead Children's Playground*, but that's the difference between a creature feature and a ghost story. I hope you enjoyed both in their own way.

I won't keep you *too* much longer, but I wanted to share a few other fun facts about the writing of this book:

- Pete Savila, Paul Alberts, and Chris Boland are all based on real-life friends of mine (although Chris is the only one where I used his real name). We were all in the Sigma Phi Epsilon fraternity, which makes a cameo in later chapters. Parkhill's was one of our favorite bars where we'd go to watch football every Sunday. It wasn't in South Jersey, though. It was down the shore. It's since shut down before reopening under new ownership with a new name.

- Originally, Alberts was going to survive, but I didn't think that was fair to Pete and Chris. Sorry, "Paul."

- The goose theme about mating for life is something my wife Jessica says. The first time she brought it up, I told her she was thinking about penguins. She insisted and it turns out she was right; so I thought it was unique to use geese as the symbol of "mating for life." I even bought her a silver goose necklace for her birthday a few months ago. Also, unlike Megan, she doesn't have any animosity toward penguins.

- Yes, I know Ewan McGregor is Scottish, but he uses a British accent in his portrayal of Obi-Wan Kenobi.

- The horseflies a.k.a. "greenheads" in Galloway were a real problem when we had our house down there. Especially by the pool. Their bites hurt like hell. And yes, we used Skin So Soft, which worked, but just barely.

- Alberts's receptionist, Carole, is based on my mother-in-law. She *loves* BTS.

- My wife is a fan of *Vanderpump Rules*, hence their inclusion as Megan's show of choice. In fact, there's a lot of her in Megan. For instance, as I was finishing the book, we had a mild disagreement and she cursed while making her point. Me being a smart-ass, I told her to watch her mouth, to which she responded "Fuck, fuck, fuck, fuck, fuck!" I then showed her the scene I wrote with Megan and her dad and we had a good laugh, and just like that, no more disagreement!

• DeLorenzo's is modeled after our favorite pizza place here in Hamilton. The one on Sloan Avenue, not the one in Robbinsville. That one's good, but ours is better.

• Alberts mentions "Lucille's" as a lunch destination with Megan. There is a Lucille's luncheonette on Route 539 in Warren Grove. We pass it all the time on the way to Atlantic City. There's a statue of the Jersey Devil right outside, so I felt it called for a small cameo! I confess, I haven't eaten there yet, but my mom has and said it was great food! I really have to stop there soon!

• There used to be a miniature golf course near our home in Galloway. It was thirteen holes and each one had a plaque telling another piece of the story of the Jersey Devil.

• There is evidence that Leeds became Lumley at some point, so I used that as Robert and Vivian's last name to hide the fact that they were part of the Leeds bloodline. The fact that it could also serve as a reference to Brian Lumley of *Necroscope* fame was a bonus!

- I really liked the concept that it didn't take any special weapons to kill the Jersey Devil. Sure, it could take a ton of damage, but it could be killed with guns or fire. But the concept that each time it died would bring the curse closer to taking Patrick and eventually destroying the whole town, I felt really created a compelling obstacle for our heroes!

- *Die Hard* **is** a Christmas movie.

THANK YOU!

That's about it for me. I hope you enjoyed this little behind-the-scenes look at the history of the Jersey Devil and how I wrote *Devil of the Pines*. This was truly the most challenging, yet rewarding book I've written so far!

Before I let you go, I'm going to ask you a small favor.

If you enjoyed this book, please consider leaving a review on Amazon, Goodreads, social media, or anywhere else you are willing and able to. Reader reviews are the best way for independent presses like Horror House Publishing to get our books in the hands of readers. The more positive word of mouth we can generate, the more we can grow and keep providing high-quality, entertaining horror stories like the one you just read.

REVIEW ON AMAZON:

REVIEW ON GOODREADS:

Thank you again and I'll see you soon with more American Horrors!

June 13, 2025

Sources

1. Phantom of the Pines (James F. McCloy & Ray Miller Jr.)
2. The Jersey Devil (James F. McCloy & Ray Miller Jr.)
3. App.com - "This is not a cartoon - it's a monster." The Jersey Devil's very real Pine Barrens Origin (Jerry Carino)
4. NJ.com - The forgotten political feud that spawned the Jersey devil (Brian Regal)
5. AtlanticCountyNJ.gov - Jersey Devil - Fact or Fiction (Carol Johnson & David Munn)
6. PhiladelphiaEncyclopedia.org - Point Breeze (Bonaparte Estate (Richard Veit)
7. AmericanFolklore.net - The Jersey Devil Legend (S.E. Schlosser)
8. CommunityNews.org - The Jersey Devil in TV and Film (Dan Aubrey)

JAMES KAINE

LIVING YOUR NIGHTMARES

A TRIO OF TWISTED TALES

What Scares You?

We all have nightmares, but when they truly take hold, they will chill you to the very bone.

You can live just some of these yourself with this exclusive FREE eBook available only to members of my **VIP READERS CLUB**!

In *Living Your Nightmares*, you will experience three terrifyingly twisted tales that are certain to make sleep hard to come by!

In *Another Day at the Office*, an ordinary day turns to paranoia when a man is followed by a mysterious SUV whose driver may have sinister intentions...

In *Chuckles Wuz Here*, a woman tries to put aside her fear of clowns for her son's birthday party, only to find that some things are smart to fear...

In *Merry Fucking Christmas*, a dying mob hitman is haunted by the ghosts of his past sending him on a rampage in the present that may ensure no one has a future...

The only way to get this book is to become a **VIP READERS CLUB** member!

There is never any cost to be a member and you'll get all kinds of exclusive perks, like:

- Exclusive stories!
- Access to Kaineiac Kove, a members-only area of my website were you can
- All bonus content on all my books!
- First news on new projects, cover reveals, upcoming appearances, and more!
- Monthly merch discounts for my web store!
- Indie author spotlights!
- Contests and giveaways!

Sign up today at **www.jameskaine.com** or by scanning the code below and become a card-carrying Kaineiac!

(No actual card will be provided.)

About the Author

James Kaine is a bestselling author, publisher and filmmaker born and raised in Trenton, NJ. An active pro member of the Horror Writer's Association, he brings readers visceral, haunting tales of terror via his *Horror House Publishing* imprint.

BookLife by Publisher's Weekly proclaimed his novel, *The Dead Children's Playground*, "will chill readers to the bone." The book, the first in his *American Horrors* anthology series, has been a #1 bestseller in U.S. Horror on Amazon, a reader selection for the 2025 Books of Horror Indie Brawl and is being translated into multiple languages, bringing James's cinematic style of scary storytelling to a global audience.

He resides in Hamilton, NJ with his wife, Jessica, their two children and an energetic Boston Terrier. When he isn't writing he loves to read, travel, cook, watch movies and learn new skills.

Become a Kaineiac and get exclusive stories, first-look news and discounts by joining James's free VIP Reader club at **www.jameskaine.com**.

For bookings, media inquiries and any other requests, send an email to **james@jameskaine.com**.

Books by James Kaine

AMERICAN HORRORS SERIES

The Dead Children's Playground

Devil of the Pines

MY PET WEREWOLF SERIES

My Pet Werewolf

Gunther

STANDALONE

Pursuit

Black Friday

Mischief Night

www.ingramcontent.com/pod-product-compliance
Lightning Source LLC
Chambersburg PA
CBHW022254310726
48973CB00001B/64